MORE PRAISE FOR JULIE KENNER!

APHRODITE'S KISS
Winner of the *Romantic Times* Reviewers' Choice Award
"Like a carnival fun house, full of surprises and just plain good old-fashioned entertainment."
> —*Romance Reviews Today*

"Adorable characters and hilarious story lines set Julie Kenner apart. . . . *Aphrodite's Kiss* is pure delight!"
> —Trish Jensen, author of *Stuck With You*

"A true original, filled with humor, adventure and fun!"
> —*Romantic Times*

THE CAT'S FANCY
"Funny, witty, and unbelievably erotic."
> —*Affaire de Coeur*

"*The Cat's Fancy* deserves a place on any reader's keeper shelf!"
> —*Romance Communications*

"Ms. Kenner's debut novel sets the stage for more glorious stories to come. I can't wait!"
> —*The Belles & Beaux of Romance*

THE HERO RETURNED

Lane licked her lips, her face contorting as if she'd just tasted his words and found them bitter. "You can't," she said. "It's done. Over. You left me. I've moved on with my life, and we can't go back. Not unless you can turn back time." For a brief moment, hope entered her eyes, and he saw just how much weight she gave Protector powers.

"Er, I don't think anyone can. Well, Zephron, maybe, but—"

"Not you."

"Not me."

"Oh." She nibbled on her thumb, then lifted her head to look him straight in the eyes. "So you can't make it up to me, and we can't go back. But you *are* going to rescue my son."

"Our son," he corrected.

"He's all I have," Lane said, tears spilling out of her eyes. "You can't let anything happen to him."

Despite the cuffs binding his wrists, Jason twisted and managed to grasp her hands, squeezing until she squeezed back. "I know," he said. And he did. Once upon a time, she'd had him, too. But no more. Now it was just Lane and Davy. And if Jason wanted back into their family, he was going to have to work his tail off. He was going to have to rescue Davy—and he was going to have to do a whole hell of a lot more, too.

Aphrodite's Secret

JULIE KENNER

LOVE SPELL NEW YORK CITY

For lo, ap, dp, and cek—it is, after all, AAT.

LOVE SPELL®

May 2003

Published by

Dorchester Publishing Co., Inc.
276 Fifth Avenue
New York, NY 10001

ISBN 0-505-52509-7

The name "Love Spell" and its logo are trademarks of Dorchester Publishing Co., Inc.

Printed in the United States of America.

Visit us on the web at www.dorchesterpub.com.

ACKNOWLEDGMENT

Thanks to the folks at the Sea World information line for answering my odd mishmash of questions. And thanks to Steve Carver for taking such great pictures and video to refresh my memory of the San Diego Sea World. Any errors, omissions, or changes to the park details (on purpose or in error) are strictly my own.

Aphrodite's Secret

VENERATE COUNCIL OF PROTECTORS
1-800-555-HERO
www.superherocentral.com

Protecting Mortals Is Our Business!

Official Business

Jason Murphy
Protector, Second Class
Marina del Rey, California

Greetings and Salutations:

A routine inspection of Protector Census Records reveals that you failed to file a Notice of Halfling Nascence contemporaneously with the birth of your halfling offspring. As you are aware, a Protector parent's failure to register a halfling birth is grounds for expulsion from the Council, resulting in said Protector parent being Outcast. Pursuant to Regulation 42(F)(2)(iii), you are hereby officially notified of the default. Please correct this oversight by the anniversary of the halfling's seventh birthday to avoid being Outcast and the requisite unpleasantries associated therewith.

Form 863(b)—Notice of Halfling Nascence—is enclosed for your convenience. Please note that the form must be signed by you and filed in triplicate. Alternatively, the form may be completed and submitted over the Council's secure server. In either case, the signature and/or electronic identification of the mortal parent is *not* required. In an effort to strengthen mortal-protector relations, however, the Council's new official position (see Circular 87A) is that Protector parents should reveal their status as such, and their offspring's status as halflings. While such disclosure is not required under the Mortal-Protector Treaty of 1970, it is encouraged. You are also encouraged to read Circular 87A and to visit the *So You've Sired A Halfling* page at the Council website, www.super herocentral.com, for more information on raising a healthy, happy halfling.

In furtherance of a recently implemented effort to foster bonds between halflings and their Protector parents, we are enclosing Council Publication Numbers 1758-A(3), 2987-Z(9), and 4589(D)(2)(a), respectively titled "So You're A Halfling," "The Venerate

Council: A Brief History in 1200 Pages," and "Favorite Protector Tales—an Illustrated Board Book."

As you are undoubtedly aware, halfling enrollment in Council-sponsored elementary school is both permitted and encouraged. Moreover, because of the genealogical issues and considerations surrounding your offspring—i.e., the unfortunate existence of an Outcast grandfather—the Inner Circle of Elders has determined that such Council-sponsored education would be in the best interest of the child, particularly in light of your lack of direct involvement in the upbringing of your offspring. Accordingly, please deliver said offspring to the Olympus Elementary Facility, Principal's office, prior to the seventh anniversary of the birth of the child. Your failure to deliver such offspring will result in the assignment of a Protector Retrieval Team to gather the child and deliver him safely to his new school. Of course, we highly recommend that you explain the necessity for removal of the offspring to the offspring's mortal parent prior to such removal. In our experience, mortals tend to react badly to the unannounced disappearance of their offspring.

You are entitled to a hearing on the Circle of Elders' decision regarding the education of your offspring. Please submit Form 234(D)(3), Request for Hearing, along with all necessary backup documentation, in triplicate, to the Office of Dispute Resolution. You will be notified of the assigned hearing date in due course. Considering the current backlog, please allow six to eight months before contacting the Council with inquiries as to the status of your request.

Julie Kenner

Thank you for your attention to this matter, and good luck in your continuing adventure in parenting.

Sincerely,
Phelonium Prigg
Phelonium Prigg,
Recording Secretary, Inner Circle of Elders

jbk:PP
enclosure

Chapter One

He was a dead man.

No question about it. Superpowers or not, the moment Jason told Lane that their son, Davy, was a halfling, she was going to have his head. And then, when he added the bit about how Davy needed to leave for boarding school halfway across the world in five days, she'd take his head, plunk it on a stake, and mount it in her front yard.

Not exactly the way he'd hoped to reunite with the mother of his child.

Scowling, he leaned up against the aquarium's glass wall. Doing so was against the rules, of course, but right now he wasn't in the mood to follow *any* rules—the Council's or Sea World's.

Throngs of kids poured through the Shark Encounter, whistling and pointing at the creatures that

5

glided through the clear water all around. Jason watched them, his stomach twisting as he thought about his own little boy. He needed to go introduce himself to his son; he needed to make up for years of being away. What he *didn't* need was to be cooling his heels here.

But Zephron himself had assigned Jason to this supposedly urgent mission at Sea World, and no one crossed the High Elder. Especially not a Second-Class Protector who'd screwed up big time almost seven years ago and let himself get trapped like a rat in a cage—or, more accurately, like a fish in an aquarium. And certainly not a Protector with a father who just happened to be a maniacal Outcast bent on enslaving the mortal population.

For the most part, Jason's identity as Hieronymous's son was a secret—Jason's mother had seen to that. But even though the general membership of the council didn't know, its Inner Circle was fully aware of Jason's parentage. It was a little fact they hadn't hesitated to point out when Jason escaped a year ago and asked the Council for re-assignment.

He drummed his fingers on the thick glass of the aquarium wall, irritated. Maybe other young Protectors got a hearty "welcome back" when they escaped an Outcast's clutches, but not him. Even though he'd flatly turned down Hieronymous's demand to join forces, still the Inner Circle had given him *that* look—the one that suggested they were just waiting for him to chuck it all and go over to the Dark Side. He snorted; every time he thought about his father,

Jason had an image of Darth Vader holding out his hand, imploring, *"Luke . . . Luke . . ."*

Really, the whole thing was ridiculous.

He wasn't anything like Hieronymous. Sure, he'd made mistakes. He'd been a little freaked out when he first learned the truth about his parentage, and, yes, the timing had been unfortunate. He'd learned that his father was the ultimate Outcast on the same day that he'd learned his girlfriend Lane was pregnant. He'd freaked; he could admit that now. He'd feared that his blood really *was* bad. He'd feared the stigma that would be placed on his child. And he'd rushed off in a fit of testosterone and misplaced fatherly duty to foil the bad guy and reclaim his familial pride. . . .

Which would have worked beautifully if Hieronymous hadn't captured him. As it was, he'd not only screwed up the mission; he'd left his son fatherless and deeply hurt the woman he loved—all things considered, not the outcome he'd been hoping for.

To add insult to injury, Hieronymous had somehow discovered their relation and invited Jason to join his merry band of Outcasts.

Jason hadn't hesitated. He'd flatly refused and been willing to suffer Hieronymous's wrath. But did the Elders believe him? Nope. They only saw a man who'd spent six years with the enemy. A man who shared Hieronymous's bloodline. A man who surely wasn't strong enough to have avoided corruption by his dynamic Outcast father.

They'd fidgeted and fussed in their bureaucratic way, none of them willing to come right out and say that his blood was bad. Instead, they'd called him a loose cannon. And then they'd backed up that assessment by pointing to some of Jason's earlier missions.

"Renegade," they'd said. "Failed to follow procedure." And they'd *tsk-tsk*'ed and shaken their heads while Jason had silently seethed. Those missions had all been successes. So what difference did it make if he bent a few rules?

He frowned. Apparently, it made all the difference if your father was a notorious Outcast who'd held you captive for six years.

Damn them all, and damn himself for getting caught in the first place!

With a sigh, Jason casually scoped out the entire room: darkish but open, with only a few nooks and crannies. He squinted. With any normal bad guy, he'd assume the room was clean. With the diabolical Hieronymous, he couldn't be so sure.

A metal trash can caught his eye, and he sneaked over, then yanked off the lid. Leaping backward, he ignored the curious glances from other Sea World patrons. Nothing happened.

Well, better safe than sorry. Not only were some Outcasts capable of shrinking to a quite diminutive size, Hieronymous's technical know-how meant that he could easily have placed a bomb or some other remote-controlled gizmo in the can.

He rummaged through the trash, nodding politely at a tall brunette who grabbed her son firmly by the shoulders and steered him away.

Nothing. Well, nothing except some empty cups, a

few plastic bags, and the leftover remains of a Pink Thing.

He groaned. This had hardly been a productive exercise, and now to top it off his hands were sticky. Great.

He moved back to the aquarium wall and banged his head against the glass. This was *so* not going well.

Bad day? Inside the tank, his buddy Lester glided forward. Jason had spent a lot of time here at Sea World and knew the shark well.

You could say that, he answered, speaking in a low frequency inaudible to human ears. Of course, his mouth moved a bit, but mortals never noticed—or if they did, they just assumed he was talking to himself and cut him a wide berth.

He gave the shark a quick rundown of the Council's edict about Davy. *Plus, I've spent the last eight hours primed to foil my father's supposed plot to wreak havoc here. So far, no plot, no evil deeds, no nothing.*

Major bummer, the shark said. Having lived the last ten years in a tank in San Diego, Lester had developed the speech patterns of a surfer dude. He eased in closer, his snaggle teeth gleaming as his snout tapped lightly against the glass. The nearby kids—and a couple of adults—shrieked and stumbled backward. *Oh, man,* the shark complained. *I hate it when they do that.*

Despite his mood, Jason stifled a laugh. *They're never going to believe you're friendly,* he said. *It's the teeth.*

Lester's black eyes turned sad, and Jason felt a twinge of sorrow at having to remind his friend of the inescapable truth: no one was going to believe that a sleek gray eating machine just wanted some-one to play with.

Have you seen anything? Jason asked, trying to get his mind back on his mission.

Lester rocked from side to side. *Nothing.*

Jason nodded. He'd expected that. In fact, he was beginning to think this whole assignment was a big waste of time. So far, the only nefarious deed he'd seen was a tough-looking nine-year-old giving a wed-gie to a pasty-faced little boy. Jason had put a stop to it right away, levitating the bully's shoes so he tripped over his own feet and then landed facedown in a tide pool. It might not be saving the world, but it was something.

You really think he's going to strike here?

Jason shrugged. *That's what the Council says.* Intel-ligence had warned that Hieronymous intended to attack this Southern California park. Apparently, the evil mastermind was after some sort of talisman and believed it could be found here.

Jason shook his head. Zephron had sworn that his assignment to the case was purely the luck of the draw, but Jason wasn't so sure. It *might* be coinci-dence . . . but Jason had a sneaking suspicion that the Inner Circle was testing him.

Hieronymous, Lester said, his teeth and powerful jaws making him look like something out of a horror movie. The shark turned away, nestling down behind a nearby rock. *Scary.*

Sissy, Jason teased.

Not at all, Lester argued. *I'm a pragmatist. Why do you think I'm here? I get all my meals prepared, humans in wetsuits to play with, and no one running and scream-ing if I swim up near a beach to try to make a friend.* His tail twitched. *But if Hieronymous really does want some-thing here, I'm probably better off in the ocean.*

Jason nodded. The shark was right. *I'm going to keep making the rounds,* he said, turning to leave. *Keep your eyes open.*

Outside, Jason made a quick pass by the manatee habitat, wishing he could ask the creatures if they'd seen anything suspicious. Manatees had excellent reputations as responsible observers, but Jason's powers were limited to communicating with fish and cetaceans. Manatees were just too far removed.

The dolphins weren't much better. While they were eager to help—he'd expected their coopera-tion, since much of his spare time at Sea World was spent hanging out with the sleek mammals—they didn't have much to say. And their habitat was open, so the crowd of kids tossing them dinner tended to distract them from Jason's purpose. When he finally did manage to communicate his question, all Jason learned was that the dolphins had seen nothing but had thoroughly enjoyed their somewhat slimy snack.

Not exactly useful information.

Jason checked his watch. Almost two o'clock. In a few minutes, Shamu's show would begin, but until then, Jason could get a decent view of the park from the roof of the staff building. He walked toward it and the orca's pool.

The whale might be helpful, too. At over thirty-five years old, the beast was the oldest orca in the park. Originally named Corky, he'd readily adopted the Shamu stage name, loving to entertain the children who came to see him. If Jason was lucky, the observant cetacean might have seen or heard something out of the ordinary. Shamu was as clever as they came; if there was trouble brewing at Sea World, he would likely know.

As he arrived at the whale's theater, kids were already grabbing seats in the stands. It wouldn't do for them to see him, so Jason reached into his Council-issued utility pack—craftily designed to look like nothing more than an ordinary day pack—and pulled out his Propulsion and Invisibility cloak. The cloak was a new model, not yet standard issue for Protectors, but one of the advantages of being stuck on Olympus for months had been being able to schmooze his way into access to some of the upgraded gizmos and gadgets the Council scientists were developing.

Jason looked at the staff building. As soon as he'd closed his cloak around himself, rendering himself invisible, he pressed off with his heels, letting the garment's propulsion carry him to the roof. Once there, he crouched on its edge, his muscles taut as he pulled out a pair of binocs and surveyed the park.

Still no sign of Hieronymous or any of his mischief-making Outcasts.

Absently, Jason tapped his holo-pager. He knew he shouldn't call the High Elder, but this was turning out to be a complete waste of time. In theory, he could handle such frustration. After all, a large part of the superhero gig involved watching and waiting. But today, the waiting was grating on his nerves. His personal life was in a shambles, and the last thing he needed was stress on the job. Save the world? Sure. Waste precious hours on a false lead? No, thank you.

Frustrated, he plucked the pager off his belt and started idly fiddling with the dial. He didn't transmit—not yet. He couldn't quite work up the nerve. He'd dedicated his life to being the good guy: watching over mortals, rescuing them from danger, and, whenever possible preventing the danger from striking in the first place. He hadn't abandoned that philosophy, not at all. If anything, his long interment and subsequent escape had solidified just how worthwhile his efforts to foil his father's band of Outcasts were. Hieronymous was a boil on the butt of humanity, dangerous to both Protectors and mortals, and Jason intended to stop him. Not only was that one of a Protector's sworn duties; for Jason, it was personal. Even more personal now than it had been before his capture.

He might have screwed up seven years ago, but this time he wouldn't fail. He'd best his father and, in doing so, prove himself to the Inner Circle. Then, finally, he'd get his promotion to Protector First Class.

Even more than that, though, he'd get revenge for the family Hieronymous had stolen from him. Revenge for the fact that he hadn't been able to be a father to his son.

Six years. Hieronymous had stolen more than six years, and Jason could never, *ever,* get them back. But where he couldn't have restitution, he damn well intended to extract payment. When Jason was through, Hieronymous would regret imprisoning him. Hell, when Jason was through, Hieronymous would regret *siring* him.

He took a deep breath, tamping down on the familiar anger that had dwelled so long in his breast, a strong current pulling him to action. He was free now. He'd done his time debriefing on Olympus, and now he was ready to meet his family.

Of course, when he'd finally gotten permission to leave Olympus a month ago, Jason had realized he didn't know the first thing about being a dad. Better to be prepared: he'd learned *that* well enough six years ago. Which was why he'd postponed his arrival on Lane's doorstep and instead gone out and purchased every book on the subject—from *What to Expect the First Year* (Davy was a little past that, true, but Jason thought he needed the background information) to the latest Terry Brazelton. He'd memorized *Goodnight Moon*, knew all the words to every song the Wiggles had ever belted out, and felt like he was close, personal friends with Bob the Builder. He hadn't watched an adult-oriented television show or read an adult-oriented book in four weeks, but, by Zeus, he'd made himself ready to have a conversation with his son. Loving, yet firm. Nurturing, yet with boundaries. *Oh yeah.* He'd nailed this parenting thing down.

Then the Council's letter had arrived and shot his plan all to hell. Forget smooth introductions. Forget lazy picnics in the park. Forget three times around the block with training wheels. Now he would be forced to just swoop in, drop the bomb, and haul Davy off to boarding school. But first he had to finish staking out Sea World. Duty over family and all that jazz.

With a sigh, Jason clipped his pager back onto his utility belt. He'd do his job, wait this out; then when the park closed, he'd report in that the day had been a bust. After that, he'd head over to Lane's house and deliver his news—*then* he'd really see some action.

Sighing, he once more raised the binoculars to his eyes and surveyed the park. A guy in a wetsuit far below was climbing into Shamu's retaining pool, getting the whale ready for the upcoming show. Across the way, a dozen or so kids were playing in the tide pools. A shrill scream ripped the air behind him, and Jason started to leap—then he realized it was just the kids on the roller coaster.

All in all, a typical day at the park.

The gate opened below, and Shamu eased into his pool. The whale made a quick lap around the perimeter then leapt out of the water, dousing his audience with a huge splash as he landed.

Show off, Jason called down.

The whale rolled onto his side, one flipper in the air as he waved to the giggling, clapping crowd. *Just giving the people what they want,* he replied, unperturbed by the voice coming out of nowhere. *Good to see you again, Jason. Too bad about the circumstances.*

Yup. What's the word around the pool?

Just that you're hot on the lookout for Hieronymous. The

whale went silent as he leapt from the water in a spray of foam.

Jason knew Shamu's routine by heart. One of the downsides of his particular superpower was that he had to spend every full moon as a dolphin. As a child, his mother had begun taking him to this park for each transformation. During his debriefing on Olympus, that tradition had been reinstated. Apparently the Council assumed he couldn't get into much trouble here.

Shamu circled the pool twice, then launched himself out and onto the shallow concrete "beach" for his prize of raw fish and a pat on the head by a cute brunette with braids. *It's not Broadway*, the whale called, *but it's a living.*

The kids screamed and applauded, clearly having a great time. Shamu's words didn't fool Jason. He knew the huge creature loved his life.

Let me know if you notice anything out of the ordinary, he yelled over the crowd's shouting.

The whale splashed his tail in assent, then dove back into the water, ready to start his next round of tricks.

Jason took off from the platform, leaving Shamu's theater and zipping over the crowd to perch on the top of the Sky Tower to continue his surveillance of the park. A shock of coppery-red hair caught his attention, and he leaned forward, adjusting the binoculars to zoom in. There was something familiar about the woman standing there. Something—

Zoë Smith.

He blinked, yanking the binoculars away, and sat

back frowning. Zoë Smith—now Zoë Taylor—was the most famous recent addition to the Council. She was also, as Hieronymous's niece, his cousin. But she didn't know that. She was famous in the Council because not only had she foiled her uncle, she was happily married to a mortal. Jason had seen her quite a bit recently, too. Zoë's husband was Lane's brother, and both times Jason had sneaked a peek at Lane and Davy, Zoë and Taylor had been there as well.

But what was Zoë doing at Sea World? Had Zephron sent her in as back-up? Or worse, had Zephron sent her in because he didn't think Jason could get the job done?

Until now, Jason had thought Zephron was in his corner. Maybe he'd misjudged the High Elder. Maybe Zephron, like the other elders in the Inner Circle, expected Jason to leap into the abyss and follow his daddy to the Dark Side. The possibility irritated Jason, and he lifted the binocs again, intent on figuring out what Zoë was up to.

He focused straight in on her face, expecting to see her scanning the park, looking for danger. Instead, she was licking a Fudgsicle with an intense expression, as if she wasn't quite sure if the chocolate was a good or a bad thing.

With one hand rubbing his temples, Jason watched a bit longer, sure there was some official purpose to Zoë presence. But no, after watching her consult a park map, toss out her half-eaten frozen treat, and call to someone beyond his field of vision, Jason was certain he knew the score: Zoë Smith was here as a civilian.

Odd, but possibly helpful. If Hieronymous did strike, Jason could use all the assistance he could get. In fact, he ought to head down and tell Zoë the situation right away.

He was just about to do so when a familiar figure stepped into view. Towheaded and energetic, the figure turned, looking up into the sky as if he could feel Jason watching him.

Davy. *His son.*

Then, before Jason could even process the development, Hieronymous struck—and all hell broke loose.

The little café in Westwood was hopping, unusually busy even for a Saturday afternoon. Writer types were hunched over scripts; actor types were busy emoting; banker types were catching up on past issues of *Kiplinger's* and *The Wall Street Journal,* and law school types were sitting, eyes glazed, staring at pages and pages of text, rambling on about *Erie, Pennoyer* and *Marbury v. Madison.*

Lane Kent sighed, fighting off a teeny-tiny wave of guilt. As a first-year law student and a mom, she *should* be either studying or spending time with her kid. She wasn't doing either. Instead, she was on a lunch date, and Davy was at Sea World with his aunt.

Out of habit, Lane dipped her hand into her cavernous purse to get her cell phone. Zoë's number was programmed in the #3 slot. The #2 slot was assigned to Lane's foster brother, George Bailey Taylor. The #1 slot was currently empty, having been assigned at various times to a series of men who—

truth be told—hadn't been worth the trouble of battling the phone's convoluted programming system.

Finally, though, Lane had wised up. No longer did she program in her boyfriend du jour. No, she and the #1 slot were staying open, waiting it out until Mr. Right arrived, proving he was slot-worthy by sweeping her off her feet.

She frowned, mentally correcting herself. She wasn't looking to be swept away. Not anymore. She'd been swept away once, and it had backfired utterly. She'd been hopelessly, painfully in love then. She'd been young, practically a kid, but she'd known deep in her heart that Jason was the man—her friend, her lover, her soul mate. Everything had been wine and roses.

She hadn't intended to get pregnant, but when the little pink line had appeared on the stick she'd celebrated, her joy ultimately overcoming her natural fear and insecurity. She was young, she was single, but she had a man who loved her and would take care of her and her son. A good man.

Or so she'd thought.

Apparently her instincts had needed some serious fine-tuning. Instead of embracing her as she'd hoped, Jason had seemed decidedly uncomfortable with her news. He'd said he was excited, but his eyes told a different story. They had seemed almost angry—which had really ticked her off, since she hadn't exactly been alone in making a baby.

The evening had disintegrated from there. And when she'd tried to smooth out the weird vibes by telling him how lucky she felt to have fallen in love with a man as good as him and what a wonderful father he'd make, he'd said a hasty good-bye, flat-out lying to her and telling her he had to go take care of something, but he'd be back in the morning.

Yeah, right.

They'd parted ways that night, and he hadn't come back. And when she went to the marina to confront him on his houseboat two days later, the slip was empty and the office said he'd left no forwarding address.

Bastard.

She'd smartened up. Now, seven years later, instead of a good romance she just wanted a good man. She didn't have to be madly in love with him; but he had to be madly in love with her son. Most important, he had to be a man she was certain would never, *ever*, leave.

Lane's own childhood had been fraught with upheaval. She'd been bounced from foster home to foster home, never staying in one place long enough to put down roots, never really forming a bond with any of the foster families she stayed with. She didn't want that for Davy. No, she wanted him to have everything, the whole Norman Rockwell package. And that meant Lane needed a man who'd put Davy first, her second, and everything else third. A stable man. One who'd always be there. Davy'd been without a daddy long enough. And when she found the right candidate for the job, Lane intended to recruit him heavily, sign him up, then have the guy start making up for lost time.

Automatically, her eyes drifted across the restaurant to where Aaron stood chatting with the owner. His constant schmoozing was one of the downsides of dating an attorney who was working his way up the ladder. But if Aaron was a shark, Lane had to admit that he was a nice one. In the short time they'd been dating, they'd gone out alone only a few times. On most outings, Aaron had insisted Lane bring Davy along—an insistence she appreciated, since her recent return to school left her with precious little time to spend with her son.

And Aaron was great with the boy. They'd done the Disney thing, of course, watching all the movies ad nauseum and making the trek to Disneyland twice, but Aaron didn't have to rely on cartoon characters to entertain the almost seven-year-old. No, he was more than happy to get down on the floor and play with Davy's trucks. Plus, he naturally *oohed* and *ahhed* over all of Davy's "inventions." Lane couldn't help but approve. The man had definite daddy potential.

She was pretty sure he had other potential as well—which, while not a requirement in her new set of priorities, was definitely a plus. So far, he hadn't done more than plant a sweet good-night kiss on her cheek, but she could sense interest on his part, and from what she could tell, all systems were go. They might not have started the countdown, but they were definitely inching toward the launch pad. So maybe—just maybe—Aaron would end up in the coveted #1 slot of her cell phone.

Inside her purse, her fingers slid over the phone's plastic casing, her finger itching to push its buttons.

Restraint battled with maternal concern. It would be so easy. Just one tap of her finger and she could check up on her sister-in-law and on her son.

Of course, if she called, Zoë would think Lane didn't trust her to keep watch over Davy. Which wasn't true. Not at all.

Really.

"Something on your mind?" Aaron slid into the chair next to her, a knowing grin on his face. "Or someone?"

She stifled a grimace. Already, the man knew her too well. "I'm not overprotective. I'm just . . . curious." She nodded, emphasizing the point. "I'm an involved mother. I like to know what my kid is up to all the time."

"Uh-huh." The side of his mouth twitched.

"Okay. *Fine.* Maybe I'm a little overprotective, but that just comes with the territory. I mean, I've been solely responsible for Davy since the day he was born." Heck, even before, considering that Jason had left at the negative seven-and-a-half month mark. "Davy means everything to me. If something happened to him, I'd—"

Aaron's mouth closed over hers, effectively shutting her up. His tongue, warm and possessive, sought entrance, and she relaxed, giving in to the pleasure of being held by a man. She closed her eyes, her body limp and ready for the sweet tingling sensation.

Nothing. Just a warm, gentle touch. Demanding, yes. Sensual, absolutely. But stirring? Sadly, no.

Well, damn.

With each kiss, she'd hoped . . . and with each kiss,

she'd been sorely disappointed. Stifling a sigh, she opened her eyes, peering at Aaron from under her lashes as she gently broke away. His eyes opened, soft and dreamy, and he smiled. She smiled back, flattered and sad at the same time. But still hopeful. She was distracted, that was all. He'd surprised her. And didn't the experts say that stuff about rockets and bells was just a fairy tale anyway?

Except she knew better. She'd had fireworks. Wonderful, explosive fireworks. Amazing pyrotechnics that had sizzled all the way down to her toes.

But the man who'd set off those rockets had left. Not exactly a testimonial for the lasting power of passion.

Aaron stroked her cheek, his smile full of promise, as the waiter delivered their drinks. "Davy's fine," he assured her. "You said yourself that Zoë would never let anything happen to him."

Lane nodded. True enough. That was one of the benefits of having a superhero for a sister-in-law: ultraresponsible child-care.

Of course Davy was fine. She was just being silly. With Zoë, there was no doubt. After all, her kid was with a superhero. Really, you couldn't get much safer than that.

Chapter Two

The storm whipped into a frenzy. Lightning crackled across the sky, thunder shook the buildings, and the wind blew cups, napkins, and plastic shopping bags around like so many leaves on an autumn afternoon.

Automatically, Jason's gaze went to Davy. Zoë was right beside him, talking to a blond mortal while she pulled a child-sized Windbreaker out of her backpack and urged Davy into it. Jason had seen the blonde before with Lane, and now he searched both women's faces. Neither looked concerned. Or, rather, they didn't look concerned about anything other than keeping dry. All of which confirmed Jason's assumption that Zoë wasn't on duty. She was simply here with his son.

Zephron must not have realized that the boy was going to be around. If he'd known, he would have sent a Protector other than Jason here. Council Directive 827B made perfectly clear that Protectors were not to be assigned to any mission in which their offspring or mate were in danger. Which made sense, Jason supposed. A distracted Protector could end up botching his mission. Or worse.

His jaw tightened. He'd screwed up once before; he didn't intend to do so again.

His cloak flapped around him, catching on the wild wind as he twisted, his eyes scouring the park for Hieronymous.

Nothing. No sign of the big, bad wolf anywhere. Yet he knew his father was involved in the storm.

A bolt of lightning cut the sky only inches from him, reaching down to split a tree with its finger of fire. The air hummed in its wake, Jason's skin tingling and his hair standing on end. Around him, his cloak seemed to sag and fizzle. Looking down, Jason realized its invisibility shield was short-circuiting, leaving him visible to anyone who might glance up to the top of this building. He banged the heel of his hand against his forehead in frustration: he should have known better than to take a cloak that was still in beta-testing.

At the moment, though, that was a small worry. He had more important things to be concerned about. He reached for his holo-pager, this time actually turning it on. He set the dial for Council Dispatch, and almost immediately the operator appeared.

"Go ahead."

"Jason, Protector Second Class. I have a level-two incident brewing. Backup requested."

"Backup informed and en route. Over," the dispatcher responded.

Jason clicked off, clinging tight to his perch with one hand as he used his binocs to search for any signs of Hieronymous, his band of Outcasts, or even the monstrous Henchmen that Hieronymous was prone to send out to do his mischief. Again, nothing. Just a freak storm that—according to Jason's gut, at least—wasn't freak at all. Surely he wasn't wrong?

You better get over here, Shamu called. Despite the urgency in the whale's voice, Jason smiled, happy to know his instincts weren't failing him. *Now,* the whale added.

Roger. He wrapped his cloak tight around himself, preparing to jump down. Beneath him, the Sky Tower shifted, and he heard a child cry out. The tower tilted precariously and a cacophony of screams filled the air. The tower was also a ride, and it was now swaying back and forth—the terrified cries of the people inside growing as the tower looked ready to crash into the ground.

Jason glanced around, his mind sorting through possible ways to steady the pitching tower even as he searched the skies for his backup. *No one.* He glanced down, prepared to recruit Zoë's aid. But what he saw made his heart almost stop beating. Or, rather, what he *didn't* see.

No Zoë.

No Davy.

Even the blonde was gone.

All that remained in the small enclosure was a child-sized yellow Windbreaker—torn, forlorn, and dejected on the the park's wet pavement.

"Zoë! Zoë, wake up!"

Deena's voice, high-pitched and bordering on hysterical, filtered through the haze in Zoë's brain. She groaned, the only sound she could manage.

"Zoë?" Deena peered into her face, forehead creased with concern.

Her muscles screamed in protest, but Zoë tried to push herself up to a sitting position—only to realize that her wrists were behind her back, rather inconveniently tied to her ankles. She blinked, then blinked again, willing the world to come back into focus. "Davy," she mumbled, her eyes opening wide as the import of her words struck her. *"Where's Davy?"*

Deena shook her head, her eyes reflecting the fear that was fast consuming Zoë. "I don't know. I came to just before you did."

"Davy!" Zoë shouted. "Davy! Are you out there? Davy!"

No answer. Zoë took deep, even breaths, trying to stay calm and rational, to let her training kick in, even though all she wanted to do was scream hysterically.

She took another five deep breaths. "What in Hades happened?" she asked, not expecting an answer.

"Thomone thnuck up on uth, I gueth," Deena said. The woman wasn't quite as trussed up as Zoë, and at the moment she was gnawing away at the ropes binding her wrists.

"Hieronymous," Zoë whispered, tugging at her own restraints. Every time Zoë blinked, Uncle H seemed to be doing something evil.

"We don't know that," Deena said, lifting her head. "Maybe we were just plain, old-fashioned mugged."

"And tied up like this?" Zoë asked, using all her strength to urge her hands and ankles apart, willing the rope to fray. No luck. She exhaled, exhausted from the effort. "I don't believe it. Too many coincidences. Davy missing. Us knocked out—"

"And some sort of magic rope, I guess," Deena said, nodding toward her. "I mean, if you can't get free . . ."

Zoë just nodded. Now probably wasn't the time to tell Deena that her powers had gone utterly wonky. "The storm, too," she said instead. "I don't think it's really a storm."

A burst of lightning illuminated their tiny prison, the glow seeping in through tiny cracks in the metal walls around them. A clap of thunder soon followed, and those walls shook angrily. Zoë cringed, hoping Davy had run inside somewhere, safe from the inclement weather.

"*This* isn't a storm?" Deena said. "Trust me, Zo. It is."

"I mean it's not a *natural* storm," she clarified.

"Hieronymous can control the weather?"

Zoë shook her head. "I didn't think so. That's what makes it all the more scary. Weather control's a pretty rare talent. And unless he hid it from the Council for years, it's not in Hieronymous's skill set."

Because of their past run-ins, Zoë considered herself well briefed on what Hieronymous could and couldn't do. He had an amazing power of invention and a natural affinity for all things technical. He also had the Midas touch in investments, and he'd amassed a substantial fortune by trading in companies run by the mortals he so despised. But his superpowers weren't up to this. Which meant . . .

"He made a weather machine," Zoë said, voicing her guess. "Either that or he's recruited a new Protector to do his dirty work. A powerful one."

"Either way," Deena said, "it sounds like he's back to being a bad guy."

Zoë nodded. Not that Hieronymous had ever stopped. Yet months had passed without a peep from the notorious Outcast leader.

It had been an interesting few months, with the Council focusing on other troublesome Outcasts. Hieronymous, it seemed, wasn't the only one with delusions of grandeur. He was, however, the most notorious—so Zoë had been surprised when Zephron told her that her uncle was vacationing on an island somewhere. Apparently, he'd done enough work on his tan; now he'd returned to wreak havoc once more on the world of mortals.

"But why?" she asked. "Every time he's popped up in the past, he's wanted something particular. What does he want now?"

"Davy?" Deena guessed.

Zoë shot her friend a nasty look. "That's not even funny." There was no reason on earth why the Outcast boss would want a mortal six-year-old. "Davy's probably right where we left him, wondering where the heck we went off to."

"Duh!" Deena said. "We are *so* stupid! I forgot about your X-ray vision. I'll just pull your glasses off and you can look outside. Maybe he's sitting right there."

Zoë swallowed. "Right," she said. "No problem." She held her breath, hoping it *wouldn't* be a problem but knowing it probably would.

Deena scooted toward Zoë on her rear end, digging in with her heels as she inched forward. When she reached Zoë, she lashed out with her still-bound hands, managing to knock Zoë's tortoiseshell glasses to the ground.

Zoë blinked, then opened her eyes wide and looked around. Considering her most honed superpower was her X-ray vision—usually negated by her Council-issued glasses—she hoped the walls would turn transparent and she'd get a view of Davy, bored out of his mind and wondering where she and Deena were hiding.

Nope. The walls stayed quite solid, thank you very much, and no matter how hard she concentrated, squinted, or silently cursed, the world beyond the wall simply refused to reveal itself.

Zoë licked her lips, not wanting to concern Deena, and not wanting to confess about this new and inconvenient loss of her powers. The *cause* might be reason to celebrate, but the *symptom* was definitely a problem. Especially if it meant she was going to have to face Hieronymous without any superpowers. She gulped. *That* didn't sound like a good time at all.

"Well?" Deena asked.

Zoë shook her head. "I don't see Davy," she said. Not *exactly* a lie . . .

Deena's brow furrowed. "Well, hopefully you're right and he's just headed off to the information center to wait for us like we told him." They'd given the little boy very clear instructions about what to do if they got separated. He was a brilliant kid, but still . . . Zoë's stomach twisted at the thought of him alone in a park with Hieronymous running around wreaking havoc. Hopefully some nice mommy type would take care of him until she could get back.

She banged her head against the wall in frustration. She hated not knowing what was going on. And right now, she didn't know anything about anything—where Davy was, or what Hieronymous was up to. No, instead of having a bead on the problem, she was sitting in the dark, as helpless as a mortal.

Her stomach clenched, its knots tightening as much as the ones around her wrists. "I didn't even hear anything coming," she said with a scowl. So much for her supposed super senses. "Damn hormones." They'd been affecting her moods as well as her powers to the point where she didn't trust her own judgment, much less her ability to manufacture an escape from this predicament.

Deena glanced up from her bindings long enough to offer a quizzical look. Then she tilted her head back down, gnawing at the ropes like a rat. Zoë sighed. That could take forever.

"Got it!" Deena yelled.

Or maybe not. Zoë cocked her head. "You got your wrists free?"

Deena nodded, scrambling forward on all fours. "It wasn't a very good knot," she admitted.

"Can you find my purse?" Zoë asked hopefully. "Find my cell phone?"

"You want to make a *call?*" Deena asked, her voice rising with incredulity. "You can leap tall buildings in a single bound, but you're going to call the *cops?* Puh-lease!"

"But—"

"Just roll over," Deena insisted.

Zoë did. It was easier than arguing, and as soon as she was free, she could look for her own phone. Deena started tugging and yanking on the ties that held her captive. After a few grunts and groans and a surprisingly minimal number of colorful curses, Deena managed to work the knots free. "Ta-da!"

Glancing around the room, Zoë stretched, happy to be free but not sure they were any better off than before. Especially since her purse seemed to be missing.

Deena leaned back on her heels, obviously pleased with herself. "Can you get us out of here?"

Zoë licked her lips. "I hope so." She looked Deena in the eye. "If I can't," she added, "Lane's never going to let me baby-sit again."

She purposely kept her tone light to ward off the fear that was fast threatening to consume her. Deep breaths, she told herself. Her powers might be wonky, but that was all the more reason to rely on her training. A superhero never freaked out. A superhero analyzed, then acted.

"Nothing's going to happen to Davy," Deena said, her voice firm. "And you're a wonderful aunt and Lane knows it."

Zoë frowned, not bothering to mention that a "wonderful aunt" didn't get tied up and lose track of her nephew. Instead, she examined her prison inch by inch, looking for a weak spot where—*maybe*—she'd be able to break out even sans her super strength.

As she meticulously searched, she compared herself to her sister-in-law. As moms went, Lane was as good as they came. As aunts went, Zoë had just a couple of years' experience under her belt. She'd only acquired a nephew after she married Lane's foster brother. It was only recently that she'd started to take stock of her child-care skills. Despite working as an elementary school librarian before becoming a full-time superhero, her mental assessment of herself had shown Zoë lacking. Apparently, checking out endless copies of *Ramona the Pest* wasn't the same thing as watching over a little boy 24-7.

That was why, in what she'd considered a burst of self-educatory brilliance, she'd offered to take Davy on the fun-filled trip to Sea World. A challenge? Sure. But she was always up for a challenge. She'd just expected something more along the lines of negotiating showtimes and exhausted-little-boy meltdowns. Getting separated from Davy, suspecting the meddling of her evil uncle, and being locked in a small room *definitely* had not been on her agenda.

"Any day now," Deena complained, her foot tapping.

Zoë gave her an irritated glance. "Do you mind? I can't just knock a wall down and end up in Hieronymous's lap or anything." Which, again, was literally true. Zoë just wasn't clarifying the little fact that, no matter how much she might want to, knocking down a wall wasn't in her current list of abilities.

"Fine. Sorry. Just hurry."

Zoë scowled, then sat back on her heels as she finished her reconnaissance. "Looks like we're in some sort of storage compartment," she said. She traced her hand down a seam in the wall. "It must open right here."

"Well, open it," Deena said, her patience clearly wearing thin. Zoë didn't blame her. She wanted to get the heck out of here, too.

Might as well give it a try. In a quick, practiced move, she twisted, bending at the waist as she sent her leg shooting toward the door with all the strength she could muster. Unfortunately, it wasn't enough. The rubber sole of her white Keds connected with metal plate, and a dull *thwang* echoed through the chamber. The door panel stayed firmly shut.

"I can't," she said, turning toward Deena.

Her friend looked at her like she'd just said the moon was made of green cheese. "Excuse me?" She cocked her head. "Is it made of lead or something? I thought that was just a myth."

"It is, but that's, uh, not the problem."

Deena cocked an eyebrow. "Care to elucidate?"

Zoë nibbled on her lower lip. "Let's just say I'm not exactly at my best right now." As a halfling, she'd had a more difficult time harnessing her powers than full-blooded Protectors like her half brother Hale. But she'd been working her tail off and, recently, she'd gotten her powers pretty much under control. Except right now all her hard work seemed for naught. She couldn't get her powers to cooperate in the slightest.

Deena looked concerned. "Are you okay? Have you seen a doctor? You have been acting tired lately. Does the Council have some Dr. Bombay type dude on retainer who can examine you?"

"I'm fine," Zoë reassured her. "Really. I've been thoroughly checked out. It's just a short-term thing. Should pass in a few more weeks." She mentally calculated. Yeah, about nine more weeks and she'd be past this phase. "But in the meantime, it's very disconcerting."

"Not to mention inconvenient," Deena complained. She aimed one more quizzical glance at Zoë but didn't press the subject, and for that Zoë was grateful. "So, what do we do? We need to find Davy. We need to stop your uncle." Then she shook her head and frowned. "No offense, but if you're . . . under the weather . . . *how* are we going to stop Hieronymous? For that matter, how the heck are we going to get out of here? Your cell phone?" she finished, hopefully.

"I already looked," Zoë said. "Gone."

"Then how?"

Zoë shook her head. "I wish I knew," she said. "I really wish I knew."

Mordichai stepped back from the whale's pool, certain Shamu was shooting him dirty looks. "I think he's on to us," he whispered, knowing the tiny microphone hidden in his molar would transmit his voice back to his father.

A burst of static, and then a rhythmic *tap, tap, tap* registered in his earpiece. The sound was crystal clear, and Mordi could imagine Hieronymous sitting behind his enormous desk, fingers drumming its surface in that damnably irritating manner he had.

"He?" Hieronymous asked. "If you are referring to that beast of a whale, then I don't understand the cause for concern. What is *he* going to do? Perform tricks so fascinating that all the Council will gather to watch?"

Mordi licked his lips, his mouth unbearably dry. He glanced toward little Davy, tied up nice and tight and dangling from a wire strung over the whale's pool. Before kidnapping the boy, Mordi had shifted, taking the form of a Sea World employee and then sneaking up behind Zoë and Deena to capture and stash them safely out of the way. Then he'd ushered the audience out of the stands, claiming Shamu was going to have to miss this performance.

Next, Hieronymous had kicked up the tempo of the storm, using the vile weather to keep the patrons in the rest of the park occupied while Mordi did his father's dirty work and trussed Davy up like a turkey.

Despite Davy's predicament, the boy wasn't crying.

Good for him. Mordi always had liked the kid, and now he felt even more affinity. After all, Davy was a halfling, just like Mordi himself—only Davy didn't know it yet. Being a halfling could be tough. Worse, the poor kid was about to be kidnapped, holed up in one of Hieronymous's sterile "guest" rooms, and scared out of his wits. He wouldn't enjoy that.

Lane, the boy's mother, wasn't going to be happy about the arrangement either. Too bad. Mordi rather liked her. They'd had their past little run-ins, but Mordi liked to think she'd forgiven him.

He sighed, then addressed his father once again. "I'm just not certain this is the best—"

"Not certain? Not *certain?*" Hieronymous's howl blasted Mordi's eardrum. "Did you hear that, Clyde? My son isn't *certain.*"

Mordi cringed as he imagined his father drawing himself up to his full height and stomping about his Manhattan penthouse apartment. Clyde, his father's Chief of Guards, would be stomping right along behind him.

"My offspring. Fruit of my loins. And he's not certain."

In the background, Mordi could hear Clyde snicker and add, "He *is* a halfling, sir."

"A fact I'm well aware of," Hieronymous answered. The derision in his voice was inescapable. "He is also, however, my offspring. And one must take what one can get."

Mordi straightened, telling himself that his father's cruel words didn't matter. Maybe once, a long time ago, Hieronymous's opinion could have hurt him, but not anymore. *Not anymore.*

He took a deep breath for courage. "I just meant that the timing might not be right. We haven't had a chance to plan, to consider all the variables." And he hadn't yet had the opportunity to check in with Zephron and update him.

Sometimes, being a mole was very, *very* complicated.

"This boy is the key to my plan," Hieronymous snapped. "I've been observing him, biding my time, for weeks now. And I consider it a stroke of supreme good fortune that I learned the boy would be here today. And, then, to learn this morning that the Council has ordered the boy's father to whisk the little tyke away to boarding school . . ." He trailed off, and Mordi imagined his father's icy smile, the evil twisting of his hands. "I couldn't have asked for a better situation."

"But if you only want Davy, why don't I just grab him and run? Why go to all this trouble?" He gestured toward the child dangling above the water, knowing Hieronymous could see him. The Outcast's penthouse apartment was lined with monitors. One was always devoted to some financial program, but the remaining eleven varied from surveillance to entertainment. Often Hieronymous indulged in a variety of films. *Superman II* was his favorite; he identified with Zod. And he had other films he would watch repeatedly. But today, of course, Mordi was certain at least one monitor displayed this scene at Sea World—courtesy of Hieronymous's skill at illegally tapping into Council-controlled satellites.

"Fool," Hieronymous hissed, and behind him Clyde snickered. "Why simply take the child when we have the opportunity to do so much more?"

"More?" Mordi inquired, almost afraid to ask.

Hieronymous hissed. "I am surrounded by unimaginative idiots." He shook his head. "I will explain only once. Do try to follow."

Mordi gritted his teeth but remained silent. After almost thirty years, he'd learned when to keep his mouth closed.

"All the pieces have come together. I will acquire the boy, of course, but in doing so, I will ensure that the Council—and the mortal world—believes it is his father who absconded with the little brat."

Mordi nodded. He understood. Jason had escaped from Hieronymous's clutches, and Daddy Dearest was definitely one to hold a grudge. "But the Council will never believe Jason took his own son," he said.

"Nonsense. Your shapeshifting abilities will ensure the success of my plan. At least in that regard you are good for something."

Mordi's jaw clenched against the all-too-familiar insult.

"The mortals cannot see the boy's current predicament. And with the evidence we leave, the MLO will put a spin on the incident so that most mortals will believe this was a child kidnapped by his father. This will be a simple child-custody abduction, a dispute so common among members of that inferior breed."

Mordi nodded. His father was right; no matter what actually went on at the park, the Mortal-Protector Liaison Office would put a spin on it for the mortal press. The press liaisons at the MLO were damn good at their job, too. They had to be. Heck, they'd been covering up Protector activity—and Outcast uprisings—for years. So far at least, the bulk of the mortal population was none the wiser—except, of course, for the readers of the *National Enquirer,* whom no one believed anyway.

"But," Hieronymous continued, "the Council will know the 'truth.' They will see a video replay, since I remotely reprogrammed the recording system on their North American satellite. They will see Jason taking his child. They will believe he did it so that he can thumb his nose at the Council. Thumb his nose at propriety itself."

"I understand," Mordi said. And he did. His father's plan was nefarious. As usual. When the man put one of his plots into motion, he always pulled out all the stops.

Of all the Outcasts in the world, Hieronymous was the most ambitious. He wasn't content to sit in exile; he wanted to crush both mortals and the Council. He wanted to be supreme ruler, and his enthusiasm was magnetic, drawing other Outcasts to him like flies to honey.

Mordi knew better than any just how compelling his father could be.

Hieronymous continued, "As I said, the plan is perfect. Not only will I get the boy; the Council will think our young Jason has defied them and pledged his allegiance to me." He chuckled, a low, ominous sound.

Mordi had no idea why his father was so intent on destroying Jason. True, the Protector had escaped from one of his father's infamous cells, but others had escaped Hieronymous's clutches before. And yet Mordichai had never seen Hieronymous pursue his quarry with such vengefulness. Something else was going on, something personal, and Mordi had no idea what it was.

Under the circumstances, though, it didn't matter. At the moment, he didn't have any choice but to go along with his father's plan. To do otherwise would blow his cover. And while Mordi didn't have any clue why Hieronymous wanted the boy, one thing was certain: whatever the reason, it couldn't possibly be good.

Jason frantically searched the park, but he couldn't find any sign of his son. He wanted to leap from the tower, to search, to turn over leaves and ransack buildings until he found the boy, but he couldn't. Right now, the lives of about fifteen people trapped in the Sky Tower were in danger.

Beneath him, the tower pitched and swayed with the raging storm, and the trapped mortals screamed again.

In one fluid motion, he dove from the Tower, hoping like heck that the propulsion properties of his cloak hadn't short-circuited when the invisibility feature had gone kablooey. They hadn't, and he gathered speed, zipping toward the lagoon, the closest body of water he could find.

If this were a movie, he'd simply hover beneath the Sky Tower, the bulk of the structure's weight resting in one hand while he fought off an army of bad guys with his other. *Not likely.* He was strong, but not *that* strong. Maybe a few Protectors could pull off a stunt like that, but not him. No, his powers were subtler. He liked to think of them as classier. But he could still get the job done.

He broke the surface of the lagoon in a perfectly executed dive, the familiar feel of the water boosting his confidence. Almost immediately he flipped, turning 180 degrees until he was aimed back toward the surface. Without even pausing, he pushed off from the lagoon's sandy bottom to spring up and out of the water, determining his plan of attack as he did.

When he surfaced, the tower was listing even more to the left, pressed down further by the weight of several wide-eyed mortals who'd shifted to watch his plunge into the water. A sharp, cracking noise ripped the air; this time not thunder but the sound of metal twisting and breaking. A cacophony of sounds followed, topped by the frightened screams of the mortals in the tower.

Jason tuned out the noise, hearing nothing except the sounds of the water in which he dipped his fingers, dragging his hand through the storm-roughened surface of the lagoon. He took a deep breath, knowing he couldn't hurry the process, his body tense nonetheless. Around his fingers, the water molecules shifted, spinning and humming as they conformed to his will.

Almost . . .

The structure groaned, the noise mimicking a cry of human pain.

Almost . . .

Jason held his breath.

Just a little more . . .

In front of him, the Sky Tower gave one last gasp of protest and lost its valiant fight. Down it went, plunging toward the solid earth below.

Now!

With lightning speed Jason drew up his hand, then splayed it sideways, sending a solid stream of water shooting out from the lagoon toward the falling tower. The timing was perfect and, with a few yards to spare, the stream slipped under the tower, cushioning its landing. Slowly the water melted away. Soon it would dissolve completely, leaving the tower to settle gently on the ground.

The mortals inside had grown surprisingly calm. Instead of screaming or fainting, most were simply goggle-eyed, staring and pointing at their salvation as if they'd never seen anything like it. Jason supposed that was true. Water rarely solidified and moved of its own accord. And even if the adults had watched James Cameron's *The Abyss*—Jason's all-time favorite movie—chances were they'd never actually seen a solid column of water up close and personal.

He suppressed a grin, pleased with his solution: subtle and classy, if a little bit wet.

Of course, the mortals were going to ask questions, but the MLO would put a good spin on his work. A freak miniature tidal wave, maybe? And that was their problem, not his. Right now he needed to go check out the rest of the park.

Jason frowned, suddenly realizing that the storm had ceased. The sky was perfectly blue, not a single cloud marring it.

Thank Zeus, he thought, then immediately cringed, realizing he had nothing to be thankful for. There was only one reason for the storm to have ended so abruptly, and it wasn't good: while Jason was occupied with the Tower, Hieronymous had gotten what he'd come for.

Damn. Where in Hades was his backup? If he'd had some support, maybe they could have saved the mortals *and* prevented Hieronymous from finding the mysterious talisman he'd sought. As it was, Sea World was eerily quiet, so Hieronymous had probably gotten what he'd come for.

Jason's stomach tightened as he remembered Davy. His boy was somewhere in the park. And even if squashing Davy wasn't on Hieronymous's agenda, Jason was certain that the Outcast leader would have no qualms whatsoever about doing so if the opportunity presented itself.

With his heart pounding in his chest, Jason leaped—in such a hurry to get to his son that he didn't even check to make sure his cloak was still functional. Fortunately, it was. He adjusted its controls, and power surged around him, shooting him forward, across the park toward Shamu's theater. As he soared over the building at the back of the enclosure, the pool came into full view—and so did Davy.

Jason shuddered. His father had outdone himself this time. Davy was strung up above the pool, tightly bound with sturdy white rope. The only thing missing from the horrifying picture was sharks swimming below—though that, considering Jason was on friendly terms with all the sharks in the park, could have come in handy.

But, no; the water was clear with the exception of the lovable orca Shamu pinioned to the bottom of his pool by some particularly strong-looking cables.

Jason exhaled, fighting to stay calm and professional. But it was hard. Hieronymous had both his son and his friend. Both were okay for the moment, but one of the first things they taught young Protectors was that when evil madmen string up children above a deep pool of water, it's rarely for a nice reason.

In this case, of course, Jason knew the reason: revenge. This was retribution against him for not joining forces with his father.

His gut tightened, his hand clenching in anticipation of his own revenge. One way or another, he would make Hieronymous pay. And the more Hieronymous fought back, the worse it would be for him in the end.

Jason took two steadying breaths, focusing on the immediate problem of rescuing his son and Shamu. *What happened?* he called to the whale.

No answer.

Jason swallowed, fearing the worst. Unlike some

species, orcas didn't stay down for long, usually max-
ing out at fifteen or so minutes. And orcas needed
to be conscious to breathe. If Shamu had been
knocked out . . .

I'm okay. The whale's voice was weak from under
the water but understandable. *But I'm trapped.*

What happened? Who did this? Is Hieronymous here?
Jason spewed out his questions machine-gun style,
one right after the other.

Someone else . . .

Who? Jason looked around wildly. *Where is he?*

Dunno. He was here, and then he was gone. Confusion
filled the whale's voice. *He said something about me
being on to him, and then he talked to himself about how
this wasn't the right time; then the next thing I knew, those
squid guys were strapping me to the bottom of the pool.*

Jason grimaced. *Henchmen.* He'd suspected that
they'd be here doing Hieronymous's bidding. The
slimy, slithery creatures were a pain, but he could
handle them.

Protectors knew the truth about what mortals
thought was only a bedtime story: creepy, crawly
creatures really did roam the earth, often disguised
as humans. For centuries, the Council had been
tasked with locking in ancient catacombs those
things that went bump in the night. When released,
though, these "Henchmen" were loyal to a fault. And
Hieronymous had used them on more than one oc-
casion.

I'll get you out of there, Jason promised, still not sure
exactly how to do so without endangering the whale
or his son. There was, after all, only one of him. And

this was probably a trap. From what Shamu said, there was at least one Outcast and two Henchmen. Probably more.

From his perch atop the staff dressing room, Jason cursed, his mind going a million miles a minute. How could he do this?

A bolt of lightning streaked across the perfectly clear sky, followed by a clap of thunder so close it shook the stands. Jason's eyes went to the stage at the front of the orca's pool. There, a man had appeared front and center, his back to Jason.

Jason noted the invisibility cloak now crumpled at the man's feet, and he tightened his jaw, desperate to attack—but not so desperate that he forgot his training. Until he either understood the situation or assessed that Davy or Shamu had to be saved immediately, he was going to wait and watch. Most likely, the Outcast would make a mistake he could use to his advantage. He ducked down, flattening himself on the rooftop. His lack of his own invisibility cloak was an irritation; hopefully, it wouldn't become a liability.

The masked man nodded toward Davy, his polite gesture to the boy contrasting his decidedly evil intentions. "Please forgive the pyrotechnics," he said, his voice polished and proper, with the hint of an accent. "They were necessary to serve my purpose."

Definitely not Hieronymous, but . . . the voice was somehow familiar. Clearly, Hieronymous had directed one of his Outcast flunkies to this task, while the big dog himself called the shots from somewhere else. Jason snorted; that was just like the H-man.

Never quite willing to get his own hands dirty. That was why he was still allowed to roam freely, because there was never enough evidence to imprison him.

"Not that you care about my motives, of course," the masked Outcast said. "But there are other ears listening and other eyes watching. I'm betting on it." As he spoke, his hand drifted to his ear, and he nodded ever so slightly.

Jason frowned, wondering what the Outcast was up to. The reference to other eyes and ears had to mean the Council; even if they weren't monitoring at the moment, this whole afternoon would be played back from the recordings the Council's satellites made on a daily basis.

He crouched lower, maneuvering to the edge of the roof as he pondered the best plan of attack. At the moment, he believed Hieronymous's flunky didn't know he was there. A good thing, too. He needed the element of surprise. It was his only advantage.

His fingers itched with the desire to grab his cloak and zoom down to Davy's rescue. But that would be foolhardy. He didn't know how many Outcasts or other Henchmen were lurking about. And while he relished the opportunity to thwart one of Hieronymous's schemes, he could never intentionally do anything that might put Davy further at risk.

He had to think of another approach. A subtler one.

Clenching his fists, Jason looked at the smaller holding pool behind Shamu's tank. Maybe if he freed Shamu, the whale could somehow help him free his son.

Armed with a plan, Jason dropped back behind the building and ran to the holding pool.

As he did, the masked man continued speaking. "So many secrets," the Outcast said. "About family. About alliances. Of course, it all boils down to politics—the bane of all adults' existences. But you, Davy, are the key. Such a lucky, lucky little boy."

Jason frowned, trying to process the words that sounded more like a rehearsed speech than a passionate diatribe. *Politics? Secrets?* What did this guy mean? Was Hieronymous's flunky referring to the ongoing treaty negotiations between Protectors and mortals? It was no secret that Hieronymous was opposed to amending and expanding the Treaty of 1970. To him, mortals were nothing more than bugs to be squashed, and it irritated him to no end that the Council was negotiating with several governments to make a legitimate, open place in the world for Protectors.

Jason didn't know exactly how Davy fit into Hieronymous's plan, but he didn't intend to waste time analyzing. Instead, he took a running leap, tossed his cloak aside, and soared through the air. He twisted, forming his body into a perfect dive. Slicing through the water with no splash, he sank to the bottom of Shamu's holding pool. He felt his body change, his very pores drawing in oxygen.

Even as a human, he could stay down here forever. Today, though, he needed a disguise. He wasn't a full shapeshifter—someone who could assume any form—but he did have cetacean morphability. It was a handy trait inherited from his ancestor Delphinos.

A metal gate separated the holding pool from the performance pool where Shamu was trapped. In human form, Jason could easily raise the gate, but he didn't want to risk being so obvious. So far, he hadn't been noticed or recognized, and Jason intended to hold on to that advantage for as long as possible. He sped through the water, transforming at the same time. Faster and faster he went and then—as he approached the impenetrable metal bars of the gate—he launched himself, fully transformed as a gleaming, spectacular dolphin. He cleared the gate easily, landing in the main pool, just one more happy cetacean hanging out at Sea World.

As he neared the bottom his friend twisted, big black eye aimed straight at him. *I can't move,* the whale said.

I can see that, Jason replied. *How are you doing on air?*

Starting to feel a little woozy.

I'll get you out of here, Jason promised. *Then I need your help.*

The situation? Shamu asked.

Bad, Jason answered. *And only going to get worse.* He gave the orca a friendly nudge, then swam down toward the creature's tail. *I'm going to scope out what's pinning you down. Stay calm.*

Fortunately, Jason was able to make quick work of the bindings. Using the huge whale as cover, he changed back into his human form and released the latches. Then he shifted back into a dolphin.

Freed, the whale wriggled in delight and headed for the surface. Jason moved quickly to block his friend's path. *Stay down as long as you can stand it. We need to buy some time before that Outcast realizes you're free and I've helped you.*

You got it, Shamu said. *But I can't hold out much longer.*

Jason didn't waste time answering. Instead, he headed for the surface, then circled the pool, hoping his disguise was working. He didn't want to be recognized as a Protector. Not yet. Not until he could figure out a way to get to his son.

The masked man took a little bow. "And now, dear Davy, you and I must run," he said. "But before we go . . ." Reaching up, he grasped the neck of the ski mask and pulled it over his head. "Anonymity is so cowardly, don't you agree?"

And then the Outcast lifted his head, his disguise abandoned, his features clear for all to see.

Jason trembled, almost transforming back into human form from shock. Standing there on the stage, holding the child hostage and ranting like a madman . . . was *himself.*

Chapter Three

Lane's friends who'd moved to Los Angeles to attend UCLA Law School always expressed surprise at how green the city was. It had gotten a bum rap, and out-of-towners expected nothing but a beach, concrete, and a few palm trees. Except for Beverly Hills. Apparently, everyone expected lush greenery in Beverly Hills, as if the tinge of money alone could somehow foliate that suburb.

Lane had always loved Westwood's vibrant flora—just as much as she loved the pulse of the freeways and the glitter of neon that completed Hollywood's mystique. And now, walking hand in hand with Aaron beneath the intertwining branches of the magnificent trees that lined the UCLA campus, she knew with absolute certainty that there was no place else in the world she ever wanted to live.

"Penny for your thoughts," Aaron said, squeezing her hand.

She turned to him and smiled, happy with how comfortable she felt. There had been a brief awkwardness when he'd kissed her at the restaurant, but that had faded. Surely it had just been nerves. "The trees," she said, lifting their intertwined hands to point at the canopy of leaves shading them from the afternoon sun. "And the flowers." With her free hand, she swept a circle in the air, a gesture encompassing the Birds of Paradise, bougainvillea and succulents that lined the cozy path that snaked through the campus.

"Oh."

"And Davy," she added, automatically glancing at her purse where her cell phone nestled. "I hope he's having fun."

"I'm sure he's having a blast," Aaron said. "I only met Zoë once, but she seemed totally responsible. And it's clear Davy adores her."

"Oh, he does," Lane agreed. An image of Davy's smiling face flashed through her mind.

"They're having a ball. I mean, come on—what's not to like about Sea World?"

Lane nodded. "He *was* pretty psyched about going," she admitted. "Of course, the alternative was to stay home with me while I studied." She glanced at her watch. "I really do need to get back. This was supposed to just be a lunch date. I've got over a hundred pages to read before tomorrow."

Aaron nodded, pointing down a side path. "I had

a feeling you'd say that. I've been aiming us toward my car."

"Really?" She couldn't help but grin. Not many men would keep track of the fact that she needed to be studying.

"So, is that it?"

She frowned, not understanding his question. "It?"

"All that you were thinking about," he explained.

"Oh. Well . . . yeah." Her forehead creased. "Am I forgetting something?"

"No, of course not," he answered. There was a hint of disappointment in his voice.

She glanced up, surprised. And then she realized: he'd expected her to be thinking about him. And why not? They'd had a lovely afternoon; they were walking hand-in-hand down a charming path. The man scored a perfect ten on the boyfriend scale. Heck, she *should* have been thinking about him. Instead, she'd been thinking about plants. What the heck was wrong with her?

"Sorry. I've been so distracted about Davy," she said. It wasn't as good as saying she'd been thinking about him, but maybe it would take a bit of the sting off his ego.

"Well, it makes sense." His smile reached his eyes. "Go on. Give her a call. What's the point in torturing yourself?"

"Really?" she asked. "You don't think Zoë will think I'm an obsessive mom who can't leave her sister-in-law alone with her kid for a trip without having a total meltdown?"

"Probably. But I wouldn't let that stop you."

They paused in front of his Lexus, and Lane started to rummage in her purse. Really, the man was perfect: great-looking, a wonderful job, a fabulous car—and he knew how to handle a neurotic mother. If she were smart, she'd drop right down on one knee and propose to *him*.

Since that seemed a little extreme this early in their relationship, she just rummaged for her cell phone. It must have fallen to the bottom of her purse, and in a fit of frustration, she squatted down and dumped everything out. Her keys, the latest Nora Roberts book, Davy's monthly mystery package, last month's electric bill, an empty powder compact, a single piece of Dentyne and—*finally*—a cell phone: it all crashed onto the pavement.

She picked up her phone and hit the speed dial; then she listened, tapping her foot impatiently, while it rang and rang until the voice mail picked up: *"Hi, this is Zoë. I can't take your call right now, but please leave a message."*

She hung up and licked her lips, looking at Aaron over the hood of his car. "She didn't answer."

Aaron was at her side immediately, his fingers intertwined with hers. "They're probably on a ride or in a show." He squeezed her hand. "They're fine."

Lane blinked, edgy and unsure. "I know," she lied.

Aaron flashed an understanding smile, then knelt down to pick up her possessions. "Let's get you put back together." One by one, he tossed her things back into her purse, pausing at the brown-paper-wrapped present labeled DAVY. "Did I miss his birthday? I don't want to disappoint him."

"Oh, no," she said. "You've still got five more days until the big number seven. This is just his monthly present."

"Monthly?"

She nodded. "He's been getting anonymous toy deliveries once a month for about the last year." She took the package from his hand. "He got this one yesterday, and I forgot to give it to him."

"Who are they from?"

She shrugged and grinned. "Don't know. That's what makes them anonymous."

"Smart aleck," Aaron retorted, but he didn't seem offended. "Seriously, what's the deal?"

"I'm really not sure. I think one of my friends must have decided that Davy needed something fun and decided to send him surprise presents on a regular basis." She shrugged. "It's sweet, but it's a mystery."

Not that she didn't have a theory—she did.

At first, she had been certain that Zoë had been sending the gifts, perhaps a sweet gesture from a relatively new aunt. But a few of the packages had a "guy" feel, and so Lane revised her theory, deciding her brother Taylor was sending the gifts. But he openly showered Davy with presents, so secret gifts didn't seem to make sense. At last she'd determined Davy's mysterious benefactor had to be Zoë's brother, Hale. It had taken forever—not to mention the right woman!—for the Protector to warm up to mortals, but he'd always seemed to have a soft spot for Davy. So it only made sense that he was the one, keeping his gift-giving secret.

Not that she could explain all of this to Aaron. Instead, she just said, "There are a few candidates, but no one has ever 'fessed up." She gave him an end-of-story smile, then rummaged once again through her purse, double-checking to make sure all her belongings had found their way back to its depths.

"Maybe it's Davy's father," he said.

Lane balked, fumbling and almost dropping her purse.

Aaron reached out to steady her, the pressure of his touch warm and insistent. "I'm guessing you don't think that's a likely possibility."

"Maybe in some parallel dimension," she snapped, more derision lining her voice than she'd intended. "But not in this world."

"I see," Aaron said. His fingers stroked hers, tracing in and out between them. "We've never really talked about him. I take it he's out of the picture?"

"He was never *in* the picture," she answered. "I *thought* he was, but apparently he had other plans. Good-bye and good riddance." She said it lightly, and she meant it. Of course, it had taken her years of practice to get to that point. And even now she had fantasies—when Davy was asleep and all the lights were off and she had only her thoughts to account to—that Jason would return and make up for all the lost years. . . .

How, though, she couldn't imagine; so the fantasy usually failed. Because unless he'd been kidnapped by aliens and spent the last seven years on their mother ship, she really couldn't forgive his absence.

With his free hand, Aaron stroked her cheek. "Well, I am sorry for what he put you through, but I'm not sorry he's gone."

"You're not?"

"I'm not," he echoed. He moved closer, until he loomed above her and she was leaning back, her hand still entwined with his and her back pressed against the passenger door of his Lexus. "Because if he weren't gone, you wouldn't be here with me."

He leaned closer, and she wanted to meet him halfway—really, she did—but somehow her brain sent the wrong message to her feet and head. She ducked, and his lips brushed gently over her ear.

"I'm sorry," she said. "It's not you. I'm distracted. It's just . . ." She trailed off with a shrug, knowing she was being stupid.

He hooked a finger under her chin and twisted her face up. The smile on his lips warmed her heart. "Let's go to Sea World."

"What?" She blinked, surprised both that he'd tolerated her rejection and that he'd suggest such a thing. "Drive down to San Diego?"

"Sure. We'll be there in plenty of time to catch your sister-in-law before she calls it a day."

"But you've got a brief due next week. I thought you had hours of research ahead of you."

His shoulder lifted. "True. But I'll make time for you."

Oh, man. Her heart was going to melt. "That's so sweet."

"So, let's get going."

She took a deep breath, then shook her head.

"No, that's okay. I'm just overreacting. I'm sure you're right—he's just watching a show or something."

"You're sure?"

She drew another deep breath to strengthen her resolve. "I'm sure." She licked her lips, then squeezed his hand. This was a truly sweet man. Maybe there weren't sparks, but would sparks offer to drive her to San Diego? Hell, sparks hadn't even hung around to meet his own child. She'd be a fool to let Aaron get away.

"Lane?"

She smiled, then lifted up on her tiptoes to kiss him lightly on the cheek. "Really," she said. "Just take me home. And if you can spare a few minutes, why don't you come in for coffee . . . or something?"

Zoë paced back and forth, desperate to figure out an escape from the small room. "Maybe we can pick the lock," she offered. "Like MacGyver would."

"Sure," Deena said, nodding. "Yeah. We can do that." She cocked her head. "With what?"

Zoë sighed. "I haven't got a clue. I don't suppose you're wearing a barrette?"

Deena shook her head, blond curls flying. "Nope. You?"

"No." As usual Zoë wore one long braid down her back, and it was fastened with a rubber band. And the band wasn't even big enough to make a good slingshot.

"You picked a really lousy time to get sick," Deena complained.

Zoë grimaced, feeling sheepish. Who knew that raging hormones would whack out her powers, making them come and go? Unfortunately, *go* was much more often than *come*. "Sorry," she said, shoving uselessly on the wall's metal door. "Apollo's apples! This is making me nuts!"

"Maybe if we both shove," Deena suggested. She pressed her hands against the door and pushed, the muscles in her arms tightening visibly with the effort.

"Hold on," Zoë said. "If we're going to do this, we need to do it right." She steadied herself against the door. "On three. One . . . two . . . *three*." They both pushed with all their might. The wall didn't budge.

"Well, damn," said Deena.

Zoë silently seconded the comment, but she didn't say a word, too distracted by the craving washing over her. "Pickles," she said. "In chocolate sauce." She twisted around to look at Deena, who looked ready to gag. "Doesn't that sound fabulous?"

"That is just disgusting," Deena replied, her nose wrinkling.

"True. But it may be good news." She rushed back to the door, needing to tackle it before the craving faded. She kicked, and this time when her foot contacted the solid metal, the door slammed outward, its hinges breaking free just as the craving—and her powers—faded once more.

Deena let out a victory whoop, slapping her hand over her own mouth to muffle the sound, then followed Zoë out of the room. Outside, they both dropped to the ground and looked around. Zoë tried to get her bearings.

"Oh . . . my . . . God," Deena said in a dramatic stage whisper behind her. Zoë's previous comment had clicked. "You're *pregnant!*"

"Shhh," Zoë whispered, a finger over her lips. They were in some sort of service tunnel. A patch of light shone in from one end, while cracks in the surrounding structure let in slivers of daylight all around. Even better than being free was the fact that she could now hear what was going on. That was the good news. The bad news was that what she was hearing didn't sound good at all.

"Why didn't you tell me?" Deena asked, following at Zoë's heels.

"Will you be quiet?" Zoë hissed. She stopped to peer through a crack. "We'll talk about it later."

"Right. Sure." Deena nodded, then leaned in close to Zoë's ear. "So, your powers are back?"

Zoë shook her head. "They're gone again. The craving's gone, and so are my powers."

Deena raised an eyebrow. "Well, that sucks."

So it did. But Zoë had to admit that she now understood why the High Elder had told her to take a full year off from her Council duties under the Halfling Maternity Leave policy. She still had to fill out all the paperwork, but basically she was off active duty until the baby was six months old.

She felt a little guilty about telling Zephron even before she'd told Taylor—but he'd gone to Geneva for a conference sponsored by the Mortal Counterparts to Protectors Coalition, and she'd only told Zephron because the disappearance of her powers had scared her.

Of course, now Deena knew, too. Hopefully, no one else would figure it out. Zoë didn't want Taylor to be the absolute last person to find out he was going to be a daddy.

"So where are we?" Deena asked in a whisper.

Zoë had stood up and pressed an eye to a small crack in the low ceiling. She saw nothing more than a view of the bright blue sky. "Under the stands, I think." She got down on her hands and knees. "Come on." She started to crawl forward, toward a patch of light several yards away.

Someone was speaking, and the voice echoed beneath the stands. "Anonymity is so cowardly," the man was saying. "Don't you agree?"

Deena and Zoë exchanged glances, then rushed forward to peer through the tiny cracks in the wood, eager to see the enemy reveal himself. "I don't think that's Hieronymous's voice," Zoë whispered. "I'm guessing he got one of his underlings to pull off this little prank."

Deena shook her head.

"I'm still hoping for regular, old-fashioned muggers. I kind of had my heart set on a quiet, laid-back summer."

Zoë nodded toward the stage, where the man was tugging at his mask. "We'll know soon enough."

Up the man's mask went, and he casually tossed it aside. Zoë gasped, her eyes widening in surprise. "That's not an Outcast," she said, rocking back on her heels. "He's a Protector."

Deena twisted around, her forehead creased with concern. "You *know* him?"

"Not personally. Jake or Jason or something. I saw him interviewed on *Protectors Tonight* after he escaped from Hieronymous about a year ago."

"A shark in sheep's clothing," Deena said. Zoë raised an eyebrow, and Deena shrugged. "Well, we *are* at Sea World," she added.

Zoë rolled her eyes.

"Stockholm syndrome, I bet," Deena said. "He rejoined the Council, but he was really working all along for Hieronymous."

Zoë licked her lips. "You must be right."

"So what do we do?"

Zoë didn't answer. Instead, her attention was focused on the dolphin swimming in circles in the pool. Faster and faster it went, building up momentum and tracing the water's perimeter. One last pass, and the heroic dolphin leapt from the water, soaring through the air to smash right into Jake-or-Jason's gut. The bad guy fell backward, knocked on his tush.

"Yes!" Zoë yelled, not caring if the kidnapper heard her. "Come on!" She started running.

Deena grabbed her wrist. "What is it? Do you have a plan?"

"Yup," Zoë said. She nodded across the pool. "I may not have my powers, but if a big fish can take out that Protector, I think you and I should be able to hold our own."

Deena just blinked, her mouth hanging slightly open.

"Come on," Zoë said, bursting from their hiding spot. "We're going to go help that dolphin."

*   *   *

If there was one thing every Protector learned during his rigorous training sessions, it was never to do anything without a plan. Jason had already ignored, mangled, and tossed aside *that* rule. Yet even without a plan he'd managed to knock down the shapeshifter.

He knew, of course, that the maniac calling the shots on stage had to be a shapeshifter. The man looked like him, but Jason had not gone mad and was not holding his son hostage at the moment. Ergo, the bad guy had the ability to assume his form. Of course, no one except Jason and Shamu knew that. Worse, Davy's introduction to the likeness of his father was as a first-class creep. That wasn't going to help in forging a father-son bond.

He'd deal with that little problem later, though. Right now, Jason needed to rescue his son. He focused on the water, shaping the molecules with his will. A column rose from the pool, up and up toward the boy, faster and faster as it got closer, building up speed so it could carry him to freedom. . . .

Except it didn't work. The water didn't touch Davy. Instead, it slapped against an invisible wall and then splattered down like raindrops in a summer storm. *A force field.* Sweet Hera, Hieronymous's minion had surrounded Davy with a protective force field.

On the concrete, the shapeshifter climbed to his feet, brushing off his pants as he glared at Jason. Then he held up his hands, as if imploring the sky.

"Now would be good," he shouted, his voice much less confident than it had been earlier, almost as if he'd run out of script and had moved to improvisation.

Even before the shifter's voice faded on the breeze, clouds formed in the sky, darkening so quickly that Jason had the illusion he was watching time-lapse photography. The wind kicked up again, violent and demanding, turning the pool into a whirl that tossed Jason about on its waves. Jason fought to stay at its surface, his eyes on Davy, as he looked for a solution: a break in the force field, a mistake, *anything*.

Jason? Shamu called. *What's going on?* The whale surfaced, breaking the water in a leap, then splashing down to shower the Outcast. The Outcast didn't even notice; he just stood, his arms raised as if he were conducting a symphony. The wind swirled around him.

Davy bounced and swung in the wind, fear reflected on his little face despite an obvious effort to remain stoic.

What's the plan? Shamu called.

Jason wished he knew. *I'm working on it.* He took a breath. *I won't let anything happen to Davy.*

Shamu moved his head, a slight nod, then looked at Jason. *I know, so what do we do?*

"Aunt Zoë!" Davy's scream pierced the air, and Jason looked up to find the boy caught in the wind. The ropes binding him had been ripped away, and the boy flailed, trying futilely to get some purchase on the air swirling around him. The cyclone lifted him higher and higher above the whale's pool—as if he was Dorothy and the wind was taking him straight to Oz.

Which was good and bad. Bad in that Hieronymous was trying to steal Jason's little boy. Good in that Hieronymous couldn't move the child while his force field was in place. Which meant he must have dropped it.

Immediately Jason concentrated on conjuring another column of water, but it was no use; the water bubbled and sputtered but wouldn't congeal. His powers were tapped out; he couldn't even return to human form. The massive effort to save the Sky Tower and then become a dolphin had exhausted his energy, and it would take time to recharge.

Time Davy didn't have.

"Aunt Zoë!" the boy shouted again. The fear on his small face shot straight to Jason's stomach. But what *really* wrenched Jason's insides was that he was calling for Zoë.

"Davy!" Zoë screamed.

Jason held his breath, waiting for her to use her telekinesis to grab hold of the boy. But she didn't do a damn thing except run toward the ladder leading up to the platform.

The wind picked up, twisting Jason's son in a cyclone. Soon, Jason knew, the storm would hurl his boy out of this stadium into the waiting arms of Hieronymous. He had to act now. Maybe he couldn't control the water, but he had to do something.

And he had to do it fast.

*　　*　　*

Zoë tilted her head back, the muscles straining in her arms as she balanced on top of the platform and threw a coil of rope into the air. She maintained the futile hope that—for just one throw—her powers would return and the line would reach Davy.

No luck.

"Zoë! Look!" Deena shouted.

Zoë shifted her gaze down and watched, wide-eyed, as Shamu rose to the surface of his pool, a dolphin straddling his tail. The orca thrashed out, sending the dolphin hurtling through the sky, straight toward Davy. The two collided, dolphin and boy, then tumbled together through the air as Davy clung to the dolphin's slick skin for dear life.

Zoë held her breath. They pair had pulled free from the cyclone, but for how long? Would the wind try again?

The storm swirled back, dark clouds above reaching down like fingers to grasp their prey. The dolphin twisted, evading capture, even as it and the boy plummeted toward the water. Then . . .

They'd made it! They two had escaped from Hieronymous! Deena let out a cheer, and Zoë breathed a sigh of relief. When this was over, she was buying that dolphin a truckload of raw fish.

Except it wasn't over.

The Protector who'd turned traitor materialized over the water, hovering there, his Propulsion and Invisibility Cloak snapping in the wind. The dolphin squeaked and barked, the anger in its voice clear. Angry or not, though, it was no match for the Protector, who grabbed Davy by the shoulders even as the dolphin bit down on the boy's shorts. The water made a *schlooping* sound as the Protector pulled them both out. Up they went: the boy stoically silent and the dolphin locked onto the back of his pants.

Up, up, up they went as Zoë concentrated, willing her damned hormones to calm down.

"Zoë . . ."

She ignored Deena.

"Zoë!"

Still concentrating.

"Aunt Zoë!" Davy called.

Now!

She lashed out with all her concentration, managing to levitate a nearby bucket of fish—presumably Shamu's dinner. Her aim was unsteady, but she heaved with all her might and it headed straight for the turncoat Protector's head.

Whap! Dead-on perfect.

Zoë cheered while Deena let out a little whoop. Their celebration was premature, however, because the Protector didn't let go of his quarry. *Apollo's Apples!* What could Zoë do now? She didn't know, and so she did the one thing left to do—upended the bucket on the Protector's head, sending a flood of dead fish raining down on him.

The man howled in protest, fire shooting from his fingertips in anger. The fish bath had startled him too, though, because he dropped Davy, and both the boy and the dolphin fell from the sky and landed with a splash in the holding pool.

* * *

Jason burst from the water, exuberant, his boy clinging to his back. Davy was safe. Thank Hera, his son was safe!

But even in his jubilation, a nasty little finger of jealousy poked him. It was foolish and egotistical maybe, but he'd wanted to be the one to save his son. Hell, he'd even thought he had. But his effort hadn't been good enough—Zoë'd had to come to the rescue.

Some superhero he was. How helpful was transforming into a fish when there was serious superheroing needed?

"Davy! Mr. Dolphin! Look out!"

Jason dove back down, Davy clinging tight to his back, but it was too late. The shapeshifter Outcast hadn't been thwarted. He was an expert with his Propulsion Cloak, and now he swooped down for the kill.

"Davy!" Jason heard Zoë yell, but she didn't *do* anything except bounce up and down in frustration. Why wasn't she helping him?

He swam as fast as he could. Where, where, *where* was his backup?

The shapeshifter caught up, grabbing on to Jason's tail and spinning him over. Davy broke free and started paddling, his little cheeks puffed out, as he headed for the pool's edge.

Jason heaved his bulk back toward the shapeshifter, who held his tail. Dolphins might be cute and friendly, but they weighed a lot and packed a punch. The shifter was knocked backwards into the water, his motions becoming clumsy as he was submerged.

The Outcast couldn't stay underwater long, but Jason could. If he could just get on top of his enemy. If he could just block his path . . .

Each time the shifter headed for the surface, Jason cut him off, a living barrier to keep the Outcast from air. And it was working, too. The Outcast was slowing down, losing steam—the lack of oxygen was taking its toll.

A flurry of movement at the surface caught Jason's attention, and he took his eyes off his opponent long enough to look. His son flailed about, clearly fighting exhaustion and trying to stay afloat. Jason shifted, ready to lunge for the boy and push him out of the water, but Zoë dove in, wrapping her arm around Davy and carrying him to the side of the pool. Jason's body sagged with relief. *Thank Zeus!*

But his thanks died on his lips. He'd only been distracted for a split second, yet that was enough. As he focused his full attention back to the shifter, Jason was engulfed in a ball of living, breathing flame.

He writhed, the flames licking at him as the shifter propelled himself toward the water's surface. And it was only when the shifter wrestled the boy from Zoë's arms and soared into the sky that Jason realized the fire surrounding him was an illusion. Underwater, of course, it had to be. But his brief hesitation had cost him everything.

It was over.

There was nothing he could do—nothing, except watch as his enemy lifted his son into the wild winds above and shot off across the sky, finally fading into nothing more than a distant black dot. And as the

Outcast disappeared from sight, Jason thought he heard the deep, low tones of a maniacal laugh.

A scream of protest died in Jason's throat, and he sank, defeated, to the bottom of the pool.

Once again, he'd failed. He'd failed in his mission, and he'd failed his son.

Hieronymous had won.

Well, Jason didn't care if he had to sidestep every rule the Council had ever issued. *He* was going after Davy. And he was going to make his father pay.

All those lost years when he should have been with his son, with Lane . . . He could have been playing on the beach with Davy, teaching his son to ride a bike, to read, to swim. Instead, he'd been stuck swimming in an endless loop, with no laughter, no chubby arms around his neck, no diapers, no sloppy kisses—just the water of his prison and his own dark thoughts.

He clenched his fists against the memories. Hieronymous had thought his punishment so clever, but the man had no imagination at all. Jason did. He'd retrieve his son. He'd defeat Hieronymous. And, in the end, he'd feast on a revenge sweeter than anything the Outcast leader had ever dreamed.

Chapter Four

Mordi sailed through the sky, a squirming bundle of boy in his arms.

"Let go of me!" Davy hollered, his little legs kicking.

"Come on, kid," Mordi said, continuing to keep his face and voice disguised. "Don't you know me? Didn't your mom show you pictures? I'm your daddy."

Davy shifted, his eyes going wide then narrowing with suspicion. "You're not my daddy!" he howled.

He gave a few more kicks, one right in Mordi's gut. Mordi coughed, the wind knocked out of him, and lost control of his Propulsion Cloak; he and Davy tumbled through the sky. The boy screamed, clutching Mordi's waist as if his little life depended on it.

"Don't drop me!" he wailed.

Mordi sighed and righted them in the air. "Even if I dropped you, I'd catch you. Okay? It'll be fine. Now, can we just have a little peace and quiet?"

The boy twisted, looking at him with terrified but determined eyes. "You're not my daddy. You're a stupid-head."

Mordi sighed. "Sometimes I think you're right, kid."

"Stupid-head, stupid-head, stupid stupid stupid-head." The boy's singsong insults surrounded them.

Static blasted in Mordi's ear. "Would you shut that child up?" Hieronymous asked. "He's giving me a headache."

"*You're* getting a headache?" Mordi snapped. "How in Hades do you think I feel?" Okay, so maybe snapping at his father wasn't the most brilliant move, but Mordi was at the end of his rope. He was supposed to be the good guy—the *good* guy—but was he getting a pat on the head? A "Thanks, kid, we appreciate the sacrifices you're making for the cause"? Nope. Heck, he hadn't even gotten a gift certificate to a nice restaurant. Instead, he was getting yelled at by his father and kicked in the gut by a small child.

He needed a vacation. Hell, he needed *two* vacations.

The kid in his arms squirmed some more, pushing Mordi off course. Mordi counted to ten and then glanced down at Davy, hoping he looked stern and paternal and not just frazzled. "Calm down, would you? We're almost there."

Davy's eyes narrowed. "Where?"

Mordi pointed toward the yacht anchored in the marina just south of La Jolla. "There. That looks fun, right? Lots of boats. Kids love boats. So just be quiet and be still, okay? We're almost there."

"My *real* daddy's an astronaut," Davy said.

Mordi squinted at the line of boats, trying to remember at which slip Hieronymous had said the yacht would be docked. "That's nice."

"He's on a mission, but he got stuck on a space station. That's why he's been gone for so long. But I know how to get him back. I'm going to talk to the people at NASA, and then my daddy will come home."

Mordi stared at the kid. "And you know this how?"

"My mommy says so. I heard her talking to Aunt Zoë, and she said she needed to find a guy who wouldn't disappear into the heavens like my daddy did."

"Oh." Mordi frowned feeling sorry for the boy. "What if he's *not* an astronaut?"

Davy shook his head. "He is. And it's the trajectory." He tripped over the word but kept right on going. "I know all about the atmosphere and reentry, and they've got to fix his ship so he can get back. And when he does," Davy added, "he'll come straight to me and we'll go buy a puppy."

Mordi sighed. "Sometimes daddies disappoint us, kid." He found the right yacht and started to descend. "There isn't a darn thing we can do about it." He gave Davy a squeeze, then just as quickly pushed the boy away. "Remember that, okay? It'll save you a lot of heartache in the future."

But Davy wasn't paying attention. Instead, he was staring down at the deck of the boat. Hieronymous appeared, his black cloak whipping behind him in the brisk ocean breeze.

Davy turned to look at Mordi, his eyes huge. "Is *that* where we're going?" he asked, his voice little more than a whisper.

" 'Fraid so, kid."

"Uh-oh," the boy said. Mordi silently seconded the sentiment.

There was no point in giving chase—of that, Jason was sure. By the time he got his Propulsion Cloak, the shifter would be long gone; and without any idea of his destination, Jason could only fly around in circles. Of course, that was a moot point since he still needed a few minutes to gather his strength to transform. He circled the pool slowly, considering where Hieronymous would take Davy. He was certain of only one thing: Hieronymous wouldn't have the boy brought to his residence in Manhattan. No, Hieronymous would use a different base, and Jason had to find it. To do that, he would need help.

After a few dozen laps that seemed to take just as many years, he was strong enough to transform and ascended in a rush to the pool's surface. He swam with swift, sure strokes to the edge of the pool. Glancing quickly around for Zoë, he didn't see her. He could use her help, but at the moment he didn't have time to search for her.

Frustrated, he climbed out, then raced toward the staff stairs. Along the way, he grabbed a towel and wrapped it around his waist. His own clothes had sunk to the bottom of the pool, and there wasn't time to retrieve them. He might be half-naked, but he needed to get this mission underway. He needed to find his son.

Directive 827B prohibited him from being part of the formal Council mission that would surely come of this kidnapping, but he'd argue about that later. All that mattered now was getting Davy back, and if he had to tattoo an SOS on his butt to get the Council's attention, to let them know what had transpired, then that's what he intended to do. First, though, he'd try the more direct approach of contacting Dispatch on his holo-pager.

He needed satellite surveillance. He needed intelligence. He needed whatever the heck anybody at headquarters could think of to ascertain where Hieronymous had taken his son. Once they figured that out, *then* Jason would figure out a way to worm himself into the mission.

When he reached the top of the platform, Jason slowed down long enough to look for his Propulsion Cloak and the holo-pager tucked into its pocket. It wasn't anywhere to be found. He remembered then that it was on the other side of the barrier, on the ground near the holding pool. *Well, hell.*

He backtracked, heading toward the stairs, when Zoë stepped out in front of him.

"Thank Zeus," he said, his arm outstretched. "Pass me your holo-pager."

In one swift motion, the other Protector snapped a pair of golden binder cuffs on his wrist, twisted him around, and hooked his other wrist behind his back. "Zoë, no. I—"

"You lousy, stinking traitor," she said, her voice low and ominous. She glared at him as Deena ran up behind her. "I don't know why you came back, but I'm glad you did." She sucked in a breath, anger burning in her eyes. "Where's Davy?"

Jason shook his head, his annoyance building. Yes, the shifter looked like him, but dammit, he hadn't taken his own son!

"He can't be too far," Deena said. "This one wasn't gone long before you caught him."

"Is Davy in the park?" Zoë asked. "Where?"

Jason blinked, struggling to push words out from behind his red-hot anger. "You don't understa—"

"Aw, we don't understand," she mocked.

"Davy's my so—"

"I said don't move!"

Jason took five deep breaths, trying to calm down. He couldn't blame Zoë for being angry and confused, but he also didn't have time to argue. He needed to convince her, and he opened his mouth, not sure what magic words would bring her over to his side but willing to jump right in and start pleading. He didn't get a word out, though, because the backup he'd requested arrived in the form of a lone Protector who swooped from the sky, his emerald-green Propulsion Cloak marking his status as newly trained and assigned to the field.

"Officer Boreas reporting as requested." The young protector turned awe-filled eyes upon Zoë— apparently, Jason saw, her bit of celebrity had some cachet among the younger Protectors on beat duty.

Jason grimaced. Officer Boring here didn't seem the type inclined to think for himself. Great. The last thing Jason needed was an overeager Protector fresh from the Olympus training facility looking to score points with the Council.

Zoë ran her fingers through her hair, the only crack in her cool facade. "Take charge of the suspect," she directed, nodding to the officer.

Boring did, first slapping binder cuffs on Jason so that his hands were captured in front of him, then tossing the lariat looped at his hip over him. The golden rope draped from Jason's shoulder on one side to his hip on the other.

For good measure, Jason jerked against the binding, testing the power of the restraint. Despite the physical looseness, the immobility rope did its job. The lariat temporarily drained the power of any Protector wearing binder cuffs. A handy tool to prevent an arrested Protector from hightailing it away from the scene, bound wrists and all.

"Tell me what you did with the boy," Zoë demanded again.

"Dammit," Jason said. "I didn't do it! Detain me all you want, but *start looking for Davy!*"

"Where?" Zoë yelled back, her composure gone. Her eyes narrowed, and she got right in his face. Jason saw her fear, and that eased his anger. She wanted Davy back, too, and she was only doing his job. He reminded himself of that.

"You took Davy," she continued. "You're here, and that means that Davy is, too. We'll find him eventually, so just tell us. Where . . . is . . . he?"

Jason took a deep breath and silently prayed Zoë would believe him. "That wasn't me. That was a shapeshifter." He gestured with his chin toward her Council-issued glasses, knowing she had X-ray vision. "You can see past a shifter's disguise, right? Didn't you see who it really was?"

For the briefest instant, hesitation flashed in her eyes.

"Zoë?" Deena asked.

"I saw *you*," Zoë whispered. "That's all I saw." But doubt laced her voice, and she turned to Boreas. "Call Olympus. I want every intelligence officer we've got analyzing possible locations for Hieronymous, and I want every possible theory about who might have taken the boy or why."

Jason exhaled in relief and held up his wrists. "Tell Officer Boreas to unlock me. We can search while the Council checks up on Hieronymous."

Zoë looked back at him, and her eyes flashed again. Yet she didn't say anything, and she didn't move to loosen the cuffs or remove the rope. Jason's hope that she believed him disintegrated.

"Ma'am?" Officer Boreas prompted.

Zoë ignored his implied question, instead glancing at his pager. "Don't you have some calls to make?" she asked. He nodded, then scurried to the far side of the pool to do so, apparently afraid Jason might overhear some top-secret information or something.

At the moment, Jason didn't care where Boreas made his calls, just so long as they got made. He wanted every active-duty Protector on this case. If anything happened to Davy, he'd never forgive himself. And Lane sure as Hades wouldn't either.

Lane.

He squinted, an idea forming. After a second, he realized Zoë and Deena were both staring at him, suspicion in their eyes. He kept his mouth shut. They thought he was the bad guy, so maybe playing up that role would prove useful.

"What?" Zoë asked.

He shrugged, spreading his hands as much as his binder cuffs would allow. "Not a thing. I'm just sitting here watching you and Officer Boring there chase your tails." He leaned back against the railing, hoping he looked smug.

Zoë and Deena exchanged looks.

"He's bluffing," Deena guessed.

"Maybe," Zoë said. She cast Jason another quick glance, then focused on her friend and changed the subject. "I don't want to worry Lane, but we've got to tell her."

Deena nodded, her lips pressed tight together. "She'll want to know. And she won't want to just sit and wait to hear from the Council about finding Davy. That's not her style."

"I know," Zoë agreed.

Annoyed, Jason conjured a fake snort, then concentrated on twitching the corner of his mouth.

Zoë squinted at him. "You have something you want to share with the class?"

He shrugged. "I just hope you can get in touch with her. She might have things to do today. People to see." He gave a thin smile, knowing he was digging himself in deeper and deeper. But he didn't care. If this plan worked, it would be worth it. "Or maybe there are other people who *want to see her.*"

Zoë's eyes went wide with fear, and Jason felt a twinge of guilt for playing on her concern for the well-being of a friend. But he quashed the emotion. They had him in chains, and if this one little lie could help buy his freedom, he was more than happy to utter it.

It worked: Zoë turned and called for Boreas. The neophyte Protector trotted back, as anxious and eager to please as a puppy.

"Go with Deena and bring back Davy's mom," Zoë ordered. "And if you get even the slightest whiff of an Outcast hanging around her, beat him to a bloody pulp."

Boreas nodded, looking much too pleased with himself. Then he looped his arm around Deena's waist and took off, the rich green of his Propulsion Cloak in stark contrast to the vivid blue of the sky. Jason watched, trying to maintain a bland expression, even though he wanted to laugh with relief. They were bringing Lane—the one person in all the world who would never, ever believe that Jason would hurt his own son. Even if she were mad at him for disappearing, she wouldn't think him a monster. She'd convince Zoë, Zoë would release him, and Jason would go kick some paternal Outcast butt.

That was the plan, anyway.

He hoped to Hades it would all fall into place.

*   *   *

Davy didn't want to be scared, but he couldn't help it. The man on the boat didn't look nice at all, and Davy didn't want to go there. But they were going down anyway, and the boat was getting closer and closer, and the scary man was getting bigger and bigger.

Davy closed his eyes. If he wished really, really hard, maybe his mommy would be there when he looked again. But when he took a peek, he was still in the air and the scary man was still staring up at him. Only this time he was smiling.

It didn't look like a nice smile.

Davy pressed his lips together and made a *bbbb-bbbb-bbbb* sound, thinking about the way his lips were tingling instead of about the pretend daddy or how high up he was in the sky. The big man might be *a* daddy, but Davy was pretty sure he wasn't *his* daddy—*his* daddy wouldn't be taking him to the scary man.

"Let's cease and desist with the weird noises, okay? I can't hear myself think."

Davy clamped his mouth shut and breathed noisily through his nose. After a second, the pretend daddy looked at him, his mouth set in a stern line like his mom's whenever Davy shoved all his toys under the bed instead of cleaning his room. Davy just stared back, the same way he did with his mom. After a moment, the serious mouth disappeared and the pretend daddy sighed. Davy almost smiled. That *never* worked at home.

"It'll be okay. I promise."

Davy gave another glance toward the scary man on the boat. "Really?"

"Cross my heart."

As they neared, the scary man smiled wide. Davy had a feeling that he was trying to look friendly, but all Davy wanted was to crawl into his mom's bed.

Davy looked back to the pretend daddy. "How do you know?"

"I can't tell you that." The man took his hand and squeezed, and this time Davy thought he heard something familiar in the man's voice. "But you're going to have to trust me. Okay?"

Davy looked from the boat to his captor and then back to the boat. His mommy and his Aunt Zoë would find him. He knew for sure they would. But until they showed up, he was alone. And he didn't like that at all. He nodded—just one quick jerk of his head. "Okay," he said. "But I know you're not really my daddy."

The man shook his head. "Smart kid. But for now, let's pretend you think I am."

Davy looked down at the scary man on the boat and didn't ask why; he just nodded. "Who is *he?*"

The pretend daddy's jaw twitched. "That's Hieronymous."

Davy shivered. He'd heard that name before, and he'd never liked the way the grown-ups' voices sounded when they said it.

"He's *my* daddy," the man added.

Davy's eyes widened as they descended to the deck of the yacht, making a perfectly soft landing on the shiny wood. He wanted to ask the pretend daddy if he was teasing, because Davy couldn't believe that the scary man was *any*body's father. But now they were there, and Hieronymous was walking right toward them, his teeth so white they sparkled.

As he got closer, the man's smile grew even broader. "Well, well, well," he said. "At last you've arrived at my little party. So very good to see you, young man."

He thrust out a hand toward Davy and held it there. Davy wasn't sure what he was supposed to do, so he glanced back over his shoulder at the pretend daddy. But the pretend daddy just stood there, his gaze shifting back and forth between Davy and Hieronymous.

Davy did the only thing he could think of: he opened his mouth and yelled.

The little brat's high-pitched squeal drilled straight into Hieronymous's brain like a stainless-steel bit. He cringed, his smile twisting on his face so tight he thought his skin would crack. Hard to believe the boy was his flesh and blood, his *grandson*.

Bile rose in his throat and Hieronymous swallowed, the foul taste lingering. He already had one halfling descendant; the existence of another made him sick. Of course, without the lad, his newest plan for world domination would fail. So in that regard, Hieronymous supposed the tiny halfling was worth something.

It was Jason, really, who fueled his ire—his other son, a full Protector, in whose hands Hieronymous could have placed his fortune. Jason could have been his true heir—and yet the boy's very existence had been kept a secret from him. He'd only discovered the truth after Jason had infiltrated his secret lair in a brash attempt to capture him and destroy the empire he sought to build.

He'd captured the upstart, of course. That was seven years ago. And during the boy's internment, when he'd sought to learn more about Jason by combing the Council's records, using both spies and his own technological skills to delve deep into files to which he had no official access, expecting to discover that the boy was an agent, sent by the Council to destroy him, he'd discovered he had a son.

Damn Ariel for keeping the boy's existence a secret!

His anger at that had soon faded, though, replaced by the realization that he had a true heir, a son more worthy than Mordichai, with his compromised bloodline. But when he'd approached Jason— when he'd suggested they join forces—Jason had flatly refused.

Bastard. No one crossed Hieronymous and lived to tell. *No one.* And that included his son.

Jason had escaped the very night of his refusal, the unfortunate result of an off-shore earthquake that shook the island and cracked his tank—all in all, a rather fortuitous event from Jason's perspective because, considering Hieronymous's frame of mind, he would have gladly lit a fire under that tank and boiled the brat alive.

But it turned out even more fortunately for Hieronymous. Now he had no qualms about using his grandson for his own purposes. Had Jason joined him, Hieronymous might have been inclined to ignore the boy's existence, to find another path to his goal. Now, though, Hieronymous would use Davy— and take great pleasure in doing so.

In front of him, the boy still stared, his eyes wide. "Come, come, young man," Hieronymous said, forcing a cheery note into his voice. "I'm not so very scary, am I?"

The boy nodded, then turned and pressed his face against Mordichai's leg.

Hieronymous made a fist, his fingernails cutting into his palm. Clearly, this was going to be more trying than he had anticipated. At least he had been correct that Mordichai should be involved. Apparently the brat had taken to him.

He caught Mordichai's eye, hoping to convey his displeasure. Just to be sure his son understood, he mouthed the words, slowly, clearly: *silence the brat, or pay the consequences.*

Mordi placed a hand on the boy's shoulder, a kind gesture designed to reassure. Hieronymous almost snorted in disgust.

"Two halflings, sire," Clyde said, appearing on deck behind him. His voice was meant only for Hieronymous's ears. "Of course they're going to get along."

"Come on, kid," Mordi said. "Let's go down into the boat. You can get to know Mr. H. later." As he guided the child to the stairs, he looked at Hieronymous, their eyes meeting for only an instant. Hieronymous blinked, sure his eyes were playing tricks on him. For a moment there, he'd thought he'd seen contempt. But when he looked again, Mordi's green eyes were cold and emotionless, as always.

Good, Hieronymous thought. Yet for the first time he felt a hint of unease. And, quite frankly, he didn't like the feeling at all.

The paper filter practically overflowed with coffee before Lane realized she'd lost count of scoops. She nibbled on her lower lip, took one good look at the mound of dry grounds, then fished out two tablespoons full and tossed them down the sink as if speedy recovery were a substitute for having her head on straight.

"Need a hand?" Aaron called from the living room.

"No, no," she said as she reached for a box of cookies from the La Brea Bakery. "Everything's under control." Everything, that was, except her nerves.

A clatter of toenails sounded against the battered wooden floor, and Elmer skidded around the corner. The ferret backpedaled, trying futilely to put on the brakes before crashing against Lane's leg. He picked himself up, took a step back, then raised himself on his hind legs and waved his forepaws. After doing his little ferret dance, he raced to the doorway and paused to look back over his shoulder.

Lane ignored him. She'd learned long ago that the theatrically inclined ferret was a tad overdramatic. Not that his bombastic behavior lessened her regard for him. As opinionated ferrets went, Elmer was right up there on her list. And there was no doubt that the little guy adored her son.

Aaron, however, he did not adore. And Lane was certain that Elmer's current antics were nothing more than a not-so-subtle attempt to distract her from him. She wasn't having any of it.

"Stop it," she whispered. "He's perfectly nice."

Elmer didn't appear convinced. Instead, he hopped back and forth on his little ferret feet, then scurried into the hall and back again, all the while keeping an eye on Lane as if he expected her to follow.

"No," she whispered, more firmly this time. "I'm on a date. Deal with it."

Elmer's usual companion, Zoë's half-brother Hale, was a Protector whom until recently had exhibited a healthy disdain for all things mortal. Lane knew well enough that Elmer had picked up on Hale's prejudices, and although she might be ferret-sitting she didn't intend to coddle the creature.

"Go play in Davy's room," she ordered. "He and Zoë will be back in a few hours, and you two can go as nutso as you want."

At that, the ferret hopped and bounced even more, so Lane could only assume the idea of going nutso with her kid appealed to him.

"Did you say something?" Aaron asked. He stepped around the corner, his former-football-player frame filling the doorway.

"No, no," Lane explained. "Just talking to the ferret."

"Oh. Right." Aaron glanced down, saw Elmer, and took a step back.

"Let's go in the other room," Lane said, picking up the platter of cookies she'd been arranging and heading into the living room.

They didn't have far to go. Her tiny apartment consisted of a so-called living room that had enough space for a foldout sofa, a coffee table, and a bookshelf. The kitchen connected through a little swinging door—though Lane was pretty sure it used to be a closet and not a kitchen at all. Next was the bedroom where Davy slept, which despite being about the size of a large walk-in closet, seemed to work well enough for the kid.

Elmer raced ahead, climbing up onto the coffee table. He stood on Davy's United States jigsaw puzzle, chittering his little head off, before accidentally knocking the entire Pacific Coast onto the floor. Lane sighed. She liked Elmer, really she did. But why couldn't he have stayed in the bedroom, occupied with climbing up and down Davy's stash of toys?

With some hesitation, Aaron parked himself on the couch. He eyed Elmer suspiciously. "Why is *he* here?"

"I thought I told you," Lane said. She settled next to him on the couch, ignoring Elmer's hyperactive chattering. If the overgrown rat wanted to foil her love life, he was going to have to do a better job than that.

"All you said was that he belonged to your brother-in-law."

At that, Elmer stopped, his beady little eyes going blacker. Lane stifled a laugh. The truth was, Elmer didn't *belong* to anyone. He was his own ferret, autonomous to the max, and woe to the mortal—or the Protector, for that matter—who suggested otherwise. "Elmer's staying with me while Hale is out of town," she said, carefully avoiding any hint that she was acknowledging Aaron's proprietary verb.

"Wouldn't Zoë make more sense? Isn't Hale *her* brother?"

Lane nodded. "Right. He's a romance cover model, only this time he's doing a commercial." He was also a superhero, but she didn't mention that part. "He's on a shoot in Greece with his wife Tracy and their other—uh, the other ferret that lives with them." Elmer's significant other, Penelope, was a seasoned animal actress, and she'd accompanied Hale and Tracy to Greece as part of the production team. Elmer had wanted to go, but as the lead ferret on the increasingly popular television show "Mrs. Dolittle," he hadn't been able to get the time off work.

"I'm still not clear on why he's here," Aaron said.

"He and Davy are buds," she explained. "Sometimes I think they speak the same language." That much was true; Davy and the ferret got along like gangbusters. If Lane didn't know better, she'd think they *were* communicating. But only Protectors could talk with animals, and only a few Protectors at that.

Lane had become acquainted with several members of the Protector Council in the short time since she'd met Zoë. At first it had made her head spin, learning of a race that descended from the mythological gods and goddesses of Greece. Of course, those gods weren't really deities at all; that had just been their cover story, designed to give a more or less reasonable explanation for all their wacky powers.

Zoë and Hale were both descended from Aphrodite—which made sense when you looked at them, considering that both were drop-dead gorgeous. And all Protectors had different powers, like supersenses, invisibility, or the ability to conjure fire. So far, Hale was the only animalinguist in her Rolodex.

She glanced from Elmer to Aaron, wondering how much the little beast would protest if she grabbed him up and tossed him into Davy's room. Quite a bit, probably—but the furry chaperon was cramping her style. She nibbled on her lower lip. "Uh, should I take him to Davy's room?"

Aaron shook his head and with visible effort turned his attention from the ferret to her. "Nope," he said, holding her hand firmly in his. "I don't want you going anywhere."

Elmer leaped about some more, and she could imagine well enough what he was saying. She tuned him out, not really wanting to hear his off-color comments.

Aaron leaned in, and Lane's heart picked up tempo. He really liked her. Heck, he liked her enough to brave an attack ferret, and that was more flattering than the usual compliments she received.

When his mouth closed over hers, she made her body go limp and tried to lose herself in the kiss. She tuned out Elmer's persistent squeaks, as well as the hum of traffic outside. She focused, her entire body concentrating on the moment, and tried to conjure the sparks that surely were hiding just below the surface.

Maybe this wasn't the man of her dreams, but he was definitely the man she was now looking for: a good father, a good provider, a man with a wonderful sense of humor who didn't kiss like a vacuum cleaner.

Oh, yeah. This guy was pretty near perfect, even if he didn't make her body tingle and thrum the way Jason had. Determined to feel a connection, she moved her lips, welcoming his kiss, her hand snaking around the back of his head to pull him closer. Aaron was the guy who could make her family whole. She was certain of—

The door burst open with a *bang,* and before Lane even had time to breathe Aaron had been ripped away from her. He made a *whoosh* as the wind was knocked out of him. Lane jumped to her feet, and Aaron lifted his arms to shield his face from the young, lanky guy crouched over him. Behind them, Deena jumped up and down, yelling encouragement, even as Lane's head spun from the sheer bizarreness of the situation.

The intruder thrust his fist toward Aaron's face, shifting the scenario from bizarre to dangerous, and Lane reacted immediately. Without thinking, she dove into the fray, sliding neatly between Aaron's face and the intruder's fist. She closed her eyes, waiting for a blow that didn't come, all the while hearing the high-pitched wails of someone yelling, "Stop! Stop! Stop! What on earth are you doing?"

It was only after she opened her eyes that she realized the yells were coming from her own mouth. She clamped it shut as the intruder hovered over her.

And that's when she noticed his skin-tight black shirt and the gold monogram of SHC—the familiar Protector logo of Superhero Central.

The Council, it seemed, thought her date was a bad guy. The question, of course, was why.

Elmer leaped and cheered, thrilled that the neophyte Protector had flattened the mortal. He scurried forward, then whipped out his little foot, managing to land a kick on Aaron's perfectly Stairmastered thigh. He reared back, ready to kick again, but Lane caught him by the scruff of his neck and pulled him back.

"Stop it!" she shouted. "What are you doing?" She twisted around to look at the Protector. "And who the devil are you?"

"Uh," said the Protector, glancing back toward Deena, "we're here because, well, he . . . uh . . ." He climbed off Aaron, clearly confused.

I've been trying to tell you! Elmer chittered, even though he knew no one could understand him. *Hopping Hera, won't anyone listen to me? Davy's been kidnapped—I saw it on the map in his room! On the tracking device the kid invented.*

"Calm down, Elmer," Lane said, shifting him. "Jeez, you're spastic."

I'm spastic? I'm the only reasonable one here. I saw it! The green light was over San Diego, and then—poof!—the light was out over the ocean. Either Zoë decided to play cruise director or the kid was kidnapped! And you're working on your social calendar and calling me spastic. Harumph!

He kicked and spat and squirmed until Lane finally dropped him. Then he ran to the piece of California that had fallen onto the floor. *Right here,* he said, bouncing up and down on the jigsaw puzzle. *He's right here.*

But no one was paying attention to him. As usual, he was underappreciated and ignored.

"Where's Davy?" Lane asked.

Elmer jumped up and down. *Here! Here!*

"When I, uh, last saw him, he was at Sea World watching Shamu," Deena said. She licked her lips and cast a quick glance toward Aaron. "The thing is, I kind of need to talk to you about that." Once again, the blonde's lips thinned. She gestured to the Protector. "I thought maybe we could take a little trip with Boreas, here, and I'll explain on the way."

The blood drained from Lane's face and she dropped to the couch, using one hand to steady herself. Elmer crawled off California and settled down next to her, one paw resting on her leg. Her fingers twined in his fur, and he could feel her tension.

"Right," she whispered. She glanced at Aaron. "You've got a lot of work to do. You should probably head on back to the office."

"I can stay," he said. "It's no problem . . ." He trailed off as Lane got up and silently moved to the kitchen, ignoring him and everyone else.

Aaron turned to Deena. "What's going on?"

"PMS?" Deena suggested, her smile weak.

Aaron's head tilted just slightly. "Huh? I don't think so."

Deena's chest rose and fell in a sigh. Then she swung an arm around Aaron's shoulder and aimed him toward the door. Elmer silently cheered her on. "Whatever the reason, Lane asked you to go."

"Yes, but—"

"You don't want to be one of those clingy men who don't give women space, do you?"

"No, but—"

"I didn't think so." The door was open, and Deena shoved him through. "She really likes you," she added, then closed the door on Aaron's confused face.

Elmer had to applaud her performance. He couldn't have done it better himself.

"Come on, sweetie," Deena called to Lane as she headed into the kitchen. "I'll explain on the way." Boreas followed.

It was a full minute before Elmer realized they weren't coming back. Apparently they'd decided to take the less conventional fly-out-the-bedroom-window route, perhaps in case Aaron was still hanging around the front yard. Elmer raced toward Davy's room, slipping and sliding along the way, but by the time he got there the trio was just a speck in the distance.

Gone.

He knew right where Hieronymous had taken

Davy, but he was stuck in an apartment with no one to tell.

No dinner, no remote control, and no way to save the day.

This was definitely not one of his better moments.

Chapter Five

Kidnapped!

Lane's chest tightened, the thought of Davy alone
and helpless with someone as vile as Hieronymous
bringing fresh tears to her eyes. Her body seemed
to cave in on itself, and she struggled, needing air,
needing to get down, *needing to find her son.*

"Calm down, ma'am," Boreas whispered in her
ear, even as his arm tightened around her waist.
"We're almost there."

Lane nodded, trying to blink back the tears. She
was Davy's only parent, and damned if she was going
to fall apart now. Deena reached over and took her
hand, giving it a little squeeze. Lane gratefully returned the gesture. She wanted to be strong and
composed and in control but, considering the way

her insides were quaking with fear, she wasn't doing a very good job.

She looked down, then drew in a startled breath as she realized how fast Sea World was rising up to greet them. Only moments before, Boreas had linked his arm around her waist and taken off from Davy's bedroom window. Now they and Deena were almost a hundred miles away in San Diego. And while that reality might be a tad weird, it was also encouraging. The simple fact was that her friends were superheroes—if anyone would be able to rescue her son it was Zoë and the Protectors of the Council.

Unfortunately, though, that didn't calm her nerves. Her son was missing, and even if every single superhero, FBI agent, and police officer on the planet was looking for him, she wouldn't feel better until Davy was back in her arms.

Damn Hieronymous! Deena seemed certain the Outcast leader was the kidnapper, though she hadn't yet explained why. What on earth did that big bully want with her son?

She didn't know and, at the moment, she didn't care. She just wanted Davy back. That, and the opportunity to give Hieronymous a swift kick in the nuts.

But until she met Zoë's Uncle H face to face, she intended to dole out that particular punishment to the creep Deena said they'd caught. The one who'd taken Davy. The one who, hopefully, had hidden the boy somewhere nearby.

Officer Boreas twisted in the air, the motion jarring Lane from her thoughts. Her fingers were numb, and she realized it was a good thing Boreas was a Protector; otherwise his arm would be in pain from how tightly she'd been clinging to it.

Suddenly the ground was beneath Lane's feet and she was standing. She gasped, her balance unsteady. They were in Shamu's theater, and Deena's arm was around her, steadying, as Boreas ran off to talk with a group of similarly dressed people.

"Zoë must have called in more backup," Deena said.

"Where *is* Zoë?" Lane asked. "And where's the bastard who took my son?"

"I don't know," Deena said. "She was right there." Deena pointed to the far corner near a little building. Several Protectors were fluttering around there, looking busy, but no Zoë.

Then one of the Protectors moved aside, and there *he* was: the man who'd taken her son. His head was down, so she couldn't see his face, but she knew he had to be the culprit. For one thing, he was flanked on either side by burly Protectors in bone-white, official-looking cloaks embroidered with gold. In addition, his wrists were bound by golden cuffs. All very prisoner cliché.

The rest of him, however, wasn't from central casting. Not at all. Shirtless, the man's broad chest glistened, beads of sweat reflecting the sunlight. A simple white towel was knotted at his waist, and his feet were bare. She couldn't see his thighs, but his calves were well-formed, with long, lean muscles. His hair was dark, almost black, but other than that, she could see nothing of him from the neck up.

She'd seen enough. From an empirical stand-point, she could tell the man was magnificent. Lane felt a sudden surge of anger that someone so phys-ically perfect could be so morally vile.

With her heart pounding in her chest, she approached, her blood practically boiling. The Protectors might not have been able to wrest from this creep the location of her son, but Lane was quite sure he wasn't going to be able to withstand the interrogation of an irate mother.

"Where is my son?" she called out as she stomped forward. "What did you do with Da—"

She snapped her mouth shut, her voice suddenly blocked by her heart, which had leapt up into her throat the second the man lifted his head.

Jason.

The one man she'd ever truly loved, the only man she'd ever truly hated, was standing right in front of her, accused of stealing her child.

Hieronymous stepped from his private yacht onto the dock of his secret island in the South Pacific. Unlike some of his property, he'd managed to keep this island unregistered. And, despite his son Jason's escape from this very island, Hieronymous believed the Council remained unaware of its existence.

He allowed himself a small, self-congratulatory smile. Thanks to yet another of his brilliant inventions, he'd hidden this place from prying eyes. It was unknown and uncharted, and he intended to keep it that way.

In fact, he usually arrived by Propulsion Cloak—the Council's ridiculous rule prohibiting Outcasts from using any powers or equipment be damned—but on this trip his boat served the necessary purpose of transporting both his equipment and the irritating little Davy. He only hoped his device jamming the Council's satellite had functioned properly. Now was certainly not the time to have his little secret discovered.

He'd been surprised but pleased that Mordichai had actually managed to pull off the stunt without any setbacks. He'd been leery of sending the boy on so important an assignment, but Mordi's shapeshifting abilities had proven beneficial.

The clatter of little feet sounded on wooden steps, then Davy emerged from the yacht and stopped short, his eyes once again widening with fear as he saw Hieronymous. Automatically, Hieronymous plastered on a smile, despite the hypocrisy of it. Why in Hades should he care if the child was afraid? Certainly the boy had much to fear—as much as Hieronymous had to gain.

Mordi stepped out from the cabin behind the kid, then guided Davy toward the ramp. The boy's face relaxed, and Hieronymous marveled at his son's ability to calm the tyke. It was not a skill he'd expected, and was certainly an added benefit. If the lad trusted Mordi, it would be that much easier to get Davy in place and prepped for Operation IQ.

As he watched Mordi and Davy move down the dock toward the entrance to the island complex, Hieronymous stifled the urge to rub his hands together. Operation IQ—which he fondly referred to as Project Dumb and Dumber—had been stuck in the planning stages for years. Despite his keen intellect and superior technological skills, Hieronymous had never been able to make the last piece fit. Not, that is, until he came at the problem from a different angle. He didn't need to *think* harder. He needed to *be smarter*.

Which was where the halfling child fit in. Hieronymous had methodically scoured all halfling performance records. Young Davy, unregistered as he was, had been a challenge, but Hieronymous had spent hours in the last year, watching and reviewing past reports from the boy's mortal elementary school, even stooping to interview the boy's mortal teachers. It had been an unseemly task, but one that had paid off. The boy was positively brilliant.

Of course, the boy's genius was to be expected. After all, blood would tell.

As it turned out, the little prodigy's brain power was the perfect complement to Hieronymous's already existing intelligence. Now all he had to do was steal it. Just a few more days and he'd be in a position to do just that.

No wonder he was in such a good mood.

Lane couldn't move. No matter how hard she tried, she simply couldn't. And so she just stood there like an idiot, staring at Jason, unable to do anything but blink.

He looked much like she remembered: dark and

tan and masculine, his silvery eyes burning just the way they had so many years before.

Back then, she'd thought that look was seductive. Now she knew better. Now she knew it was dangerous.

For years she'd imagined their reunion—as if that would be a good thing. She'd fantasized about how she'd be asleep, how he'd slide naked between her satin sheets. In her fantasies, she could always afford satin sheets.

He'd press close against her, peeling off her clothes and leaving a trail of kisses on her newly bared skin. He'd silence her questions with a finger over her lips and then, after they'd made love until dawn, he'd tell her the previous years had all been a bad dream. He'd been there all along, and they were already living happily ever after.

Never in her wildest fit of imagination had she imagined Jason in cuffs, restrained because he'd kidnapped her son. *Their* son.

Why?

She blinked, forcing herself to glance from Jason to Deena. "What's going on? Tell me what's going on or I swear I'll scream."

Jason took a step forward, but one of the burly Protectors surrounding him held him back. A flash of anger crossed his face, quickly replaced by pity. Pity? How dare he? Her anger erupted, and she rushed forward to pummel him with her fists.

"Lane!" Deena cried out, pulling her away. "Lane, stop it!"

She struggled against Deena's arms, wrapped tight around her chest.

"You have to believe me," Jason was saying, his voice low and earnest. He shook his arm free of the nearby Protector's grip. "They're wrong. I tried to save him. And now he's gone, and *we need to find him.*"

The intensity of his voice cut to Lane's core, and she relaxed despite herself. An invisible band tightened around her chest, one that had nothing to do with the vise grip in which Deena held her, and she struggled to breathe. Once upon a time, she and Jason had known each other so well she could practically read his thoughts. Now, she didn't know what to think. All she knew was that her instinct was to believe him. And that instinct terrified her.

He couldn't be trusted. She should know that better than anyone. And she hated herself for thinking, even for an instant, that she could trust him now, when Davy's safety was at issue.

"I—"

"Don't believe him," Zoë interrupted as she rushed over from the far side of the enclosure. Lane closed her mouth, grateful not to have to finish voicing her thought. She wasn't sure what she'd intended to say, and at the moment she didn't trust herself. With relief, she stepped back, happy to let Zoë handle the situation.

"I saw him," Zoë continued, taking a step toward Jason. Her hands clenched into fists. "He took Davy somewhere, and if it's the last thing I do, I'm going to find out where."

One of the white-cloaked Protectors sidled up to

Zoë and whipped off a neat little salute. She turned to face him. "Well?"

"The rest of the park is closed and the few patrons who remained after the storm have been evacuated," he reported.

"How—" Deena began.

"The MLO handled it," Zoë answered, then turned her attention back to the Protector.

"Our search is continuing," he said, answering her unspoken question. "But there's no sign yet of the boy. The Council is exploring every possible location where the boy could have been taken off-site, and everyone who might have reason to take him."

Zoë nodded, then motioned for the Protectors flanking Jason to leave. The one in white left as well, and Zoë's expression hardened as she faced Jason once more.

"Dammit," Jason said, speaking before she could open her mouth. "You're not listening to me. That wasn't me. I would never harm Davy," he added, his face turning a deep shade of red under its tan. *"Never."*

Lane rubbed her temples, completely confused and more than a little scared. With her free hand she grasped a handrail, grateful for the solid metal under her fingers. At the moment she needed everything solid she could get. Her world was tilting out of control. Her son was missing, her ex-boyfriend was being held by Protectors, and the stench of Hieronymous overlaid the whole scenario.

She squinted at Jason, not sure why he wasn't more weirded out about being detained by superheroes. She'd deal with that later, though. Right now, she needed two things: her son and some answers.

As far as she could tell, everything possible was being done to locate Davy. She intended to do more; she intended to get the truth out of Jason.

She pulled herself up straight, and he turned to face her, his eyes unreadable. Yet even so, she couldn't escape the impression that, despite so many years, those deep, unfathomable eyes still could see straight into her soul.

That feeling used to make her feel loved and special. Now it just unsettled her, and she grappled for a firmer grip on her handhold.

"Lane?" Zoë asked, concern evident in her voice.

Lane mopped her forehead with the back of her hand, realizing she'd broken out in a cold sweat. Despite starting out well, today had descended into a total nightmare. Her first instinct might be to believe Jason, but she'd trusted him once before and been burned. Now Zoë was here, saying he'd tried to take her son away.

Lane clutched the rail, a terrifying possibility hitting her. What if Zoë was wrong and Hieronymous wasn't involved at all? What if Zoë had only assumed that? What if Jason was here because he wanted complete custody of his son?

Never.

She'd fight him to the ends of the earth. Who the hell did he think he was? Did he think he could hide the boy somewhere and she'd ultimately give up? Fat chance. He'd blown his opportunity to be a daddy, and if he didn't like it, that was just too damn bad.

Spurred on by a renewed burst of adrenaline, she marched forward and poked Jason's bare chest. "You *aren't* taking my son," she said. "Not in a million years."

His jaw tightened, a muscle in his cheek twitching. "How many times do I have to say it? *I'm trying to protect him.*"

Zoë got right in his face. "Then why did you grab Davy and get the hell out of Dodge?"

Jason tried to throw up his hands, and twisted around to face Zoë. "Dammit, we're talking in circles, and we're wasting time. We need—"

"You cowardly son of a bitch," Lane said, her patience snapping.

"Cowardly?" Deena said.

"Heck, yeah," Lane said. Jason turned back toward her, and she poked him again. "After almost seven years, a judge would never award him custody of Davy if he went about it the legal way. But if he kidnapped Davy . . ." She trailed off, tears streaming down her face, too angry to voice the full thought. She poked him again for good measure.

His hand closed over her finger, and she tilted her head back to look at him, surprised by the fury she saw burning in his eyes. He said, "I'll say it just one more time, and then I'm not saying it again. I didn't take Davy. Hieronymous or one of his agents took him. I was trying to save him."

"Wait, wait, wait," Deena said, holding up a hand. Everyone turned to her, but she looked only at Lane, her expression serious. "What do you mean, a judge?"

"A custody suit." Lane aimed her glare back at Jason. "And believe me, after disappearing for so long, no judge would *ever* give you custody."

Deena and Zoë exchanged glances.

"This is Davy's father?" Zoë finally asked.

Lane nodded, then squinted at the pair's odd expressions. "What?"

"It's just that—" Deena began.

"We didn't know that—" Zoë started.

"*What?*" Lane asked. Her nerves were frayed enough; she didn't need her friends going loony on her.

"We're just surprised that you never told us," Zoë finally said. "That's all."

"He skipped out, remember? Kind of hard to introduce you if he's not around. And you've known forever that Davy's father"—she paused to shoot a scathing look Jason's way—"left about three seconds after he learned I was pregnant."

"Well, yeah," Zoë acknowledged. "*That* we knew." She looked at Deena again, and Lane twirled her hand, silently urging her to get on with it. "It's just . . ." Zoë twisted her hands together, looking decidedly uncomfortable. "It's just that after everything we've been through together, I'm surprised you didn't tell me the truth."

Lane opened her mouth, poised to ask Zoë exactly what truth she was talking about. But her friend continued, her words making Lane close her mouth tight. *"I'm just surprised you never told us that Davy's dad was a Protector."*

All things considered, Lane thought she was taking the news pretty well. True, she'd collapsed to her knees, but it was a controlled collapse, which, hopefully, gave the illusion that she hadn't been blown completely away by the realization that the father of her child was a Protector.

Under the circumstances, of course, she probably should have figured it out on her own. After all, Hieronymous was hardly the type to be in cahoots with a mortal. But Lane wasn't exactly thinking clearly, so she forgave herself for not being at the top of her game.

A Protector. She shivered, remembering an event from long ago, the old man's words when she'd purchased the stone from Aphrodite's girdle. The man had said it was tied into her destiny. She'd assumed he was a nut case. Now, she wasn't so sure. Had she somehow been destined to have her life filled with superheroes? Certainly she'd lived the last few years on the fringes of Council activity. Heck, watching her friends fight the bad guys was what had prompted her to go to law school: she'd wanted to do her part in putting away the bad guys, too, even if her part was tiny and the bad guys were mortal.

Now, to find out about Jason, which meant that Davy—

She blinked, her thoughts finally gelling. "Davy's a halfling?" she asked.

Jason nodded, taking a step forward. His gaze locked on hers. "I need to talk to you about that. You see—"

"You son of a bitch."

He took a step back.

"We dated for over a year. I thought I was going to spend the rest of my life with you. And you didn't think to mention this to me?"

"It's a secret identity, Lane. The whole point of a secret is that it's . . . well, a secret."

"That's a lousy excuse and you know it."

"Would it help if I told you that I'd *planned* to tell you? In fact, I wanted to tell you the day you found out you were pregnant."

She raised an eyebrow, not the least bit willing to concede any ground. "Oh, *there's* a convenient story."

"He probably didn't tell you because he's working with Hieronymous," Deena said, her eyes shooting daggers at him.

Jason rounded on her with such vehemence that Lane held her breath, her hand pressed over her mouth. "I am not, and never have been, in alliance with that bastard. And if you know what's good for you, you'll never, ever say that again."

Deena stepped back, her eyes wide, and Zoë took a protective stance in front of her. Lane moved forward and clutched Jason's arm, her fingers tightening against his muscles, as if he still belonged to her. As if she still had some influence on what he said or did.

"Calm down," she said, her body reacting in warm, familiar ways to his touch. She swallowed, knowing she should back away. She needed to get some space between her and this man—even when she was royally pissed off, she was still drawn to him. And his power over her, especially after so much time, terrified her. "Deena didn't mean anything by it," she added.

"The hell I didn't," Deena said, her hands on Zoë's shoulders. She peered at Jason from around the other woman's head. "I know what I saw."

Jason's eyes narrowed, but he didn't reiterate his innocence.

Lane backed off, held up her hands in surrender. "Okay, time out. We need to find Davy. Everything else we can sort out later." Even as she spoke, she felt removed from herself; detached from the part that wanted to curl up in a ball and just whimper until her son returned.

Zoë swung an arm around her shoulder. "Do you want to go sit down? We're doing everything we can, and—"

"No." Lane shrugged out of her friend's embrace. "I can't hang out on the sidelines. I need to know what's going on. I need to help look for Davy. I need answers, and you guys are going to give them to me."

"But—"

Lane held up a hand. "No buts. My kid. My rules." She pointed to Zoë. "Tell me what happened here today."

And Zoë did. Told all about how Jason or some Henchman—she wasn't positive, since she hadn't seen him—got her and Deena from behind and locked them up. And then how, when they escaped, they found that Jason had trapped Davy. They'd tried to get the child free, and almost had with the help of Shamu and some heroic dolphin, but in the end Hieronymous had won and Jason and Davy had soared off into the sky. Since she'd found Jason only moments later, Zoë had assumed the cyclone had been a diversion, and he'd stashed the boy close by.

"But I may be wrong about that," she admitted.

Jason snorted. "About that and everything else."

Zoë ignored him. "I have the Council searching for every possible location for Hieronymous." She took Lane's hand and squeezed it. Lane squeezed back, grateful for the support. "We'll find him. No matter what, I promise you that."

Lane nodded, then sucked in a breath for courage, turning to face Jason. "That's Zoë's side. What's yours?"

"A shapeshifter," he said simply. "A shapeshifter who took *my* form and took *our* son." His mouth twisted into something resembling a grin. "And as for the heroic dolphin, I appreciate the praise."

"You?" Zoë said. "Puh-lease."

Lane frowned. Davy's father was a dolphin?

He nodded. "My powers are piscatorial and cetacean related."

"Huh?" Deena said, voicing Lane's question.

"I can talk to fish. I can live underwater. And, as I already said, I can take a dolphin's form."

Deena crossed her arms. "Prove it."

He nudged with his chin the rope draped over his shoulder. "Happy to. Untie me."

Lane and Deena both turned to Zoë, who gnawed

on her lower lip. After a second, she looked up. "The lariat dulls his power. If he's going to prove it, I *have* to release him. But I can't do that."

"Why on earth not?" Lane asked.

"He might escape, and then we'd never find Davy," Zoë explained. She gnawed on her lip again, looking decidedly uncomfortable. "I'm sorry, but I have to follow protocol on this one. Don't ask me why; I just do. I've got to do this by the book, and Protector protocol mandates that the cuffs stay on."

"Hopping Hades," Jason snapped. "Can you drop the bureaucratic bullshit? Following the Council's rules isn't getting us anywhere."

Zoë licked her lips. "Yes, I remember the profile they did on you after you escaped from Hierony-mous." Lane noticed the way she stressed the word *escaped*, as if she were being sarcastic. "You've never been big on following the rules or sticking with pro-cedure, have you?"

"Not when the rules are wasting valuable time."

Zoë just stared at him, holding Jason's eyes until he finally spoke again, his eyes as cold as ice. "Dam-mit, what do I have to do to convince you? Hierony-mous has my son. He has *your* nephew. Set me free so I can help find him. The Council's Keystone Kops aren't making any progress."

He gestured across the enclosure, and Lane glanced that way, immediately noticing Boreas talk-ing with another Protector. Neither looked particu-larly encouraging. Lane swallowed, a tear escaping as she thought of her baby with that monster and no one able to find him.

Hieronymous. She'd first learned of Protectors and the Council when the big-shot Outcast lord had sent one of his flunkies to steal a stone she'd bought—that turned out to be an heirloom of Aphrodite. Not that Lane had known it was special; she just thought it was cool. In retrospect, the event hadn't turned out so bad; she'd survived the encounter relatively unscathed, and she'd met Zoë. But it had also been a little like losing her virginity—after that, she was one of the few mortals *who knew.*

Which meant she knew just how bad Hieronymous really was. Pretty damn bad. If Hieronymous had Davy—

"Why?" she asked, interrupting her own thoughts. "Why would Hieronymous want *my* kid?" She turned to Jason, her hands on her hips. "Well?"

He shook his head. "I wish I knew."

Zoë shifted on her feet, the looks she and Deena were trading making it absolutely clear that neither woman believed him. Lane wanted to; it had been hard enough believing that he'd left. Finding out now that not only had Jason ditched her and Davy but that he was a Protector *and* working for Hieronymous . . . She shivered. Definitely not something she wanted to hear.

Yet she trusted Zoë and Deena. They'd all been through a lot together and, even more, Zoë was pretty clued in to the whole evil-Hieronymous thing. If she said that Jason had joined ranks with the H-man, Lane should probably listen.

She licked her lips, unsure. "I'm sorry," she said,

her gaze darting between Jason and Zoë. "I just don't know who to bel—"

Jason reached out, silencing her with his touch. And then, with his eyes never leaving hers, he cupped her chin between his hands. The gesture was demanding yet gentle. "Lane, this is me. *Me.* Yes, I left. But I swear to you I didn't mean to stay away."

She opened her mouth, but he shook his head, continuing.

"Even if you don't believe that," he said. "Even if you think I stayed away on purpose for all this time . . . Even if you believe all of that, do you honestly believe I could ever—*ever*—hurt my own child?"

"I . . ." Tears pooled in her eyes as Lane closed her mouth, unable to form words. She wanted to hurt him. To punish him for leaving her. To torment him for making her little boy grow up without his father. But she couldn't lie. No matter what, she couldn't do that.

No," she finally said, her voice strong. She twisted to face Zoë and Deena. "Jason may be a lot of things, but he could never hurt his own son. I'm certain."

They weren't: that much was evident in their expressions. But to Zoë's credit, she put one hand on Deena's shoulder and then moved back two steps, taking Deena with her, to give Jason and Lane the illusion of a private conversation.

Lane tilted her head so she could look Jason dead-on, knowing her eyes were filled with fear. "I still don't know why. Why does Hieronymous want my little boy?"

He shook his head, then reached out for her.

Without thinking, she curled up against him. His skin burned against her, but she sought comfort in his familiar scent, that enveloping warmth. With one smooth motion, he lifted his arms over her head, then caught her in the circle, the binder cuff firm against her back.

"I don't know exactly, Lane," he whispered. "But I'll find him. And I'll make him pay. That much, I promise."

She nodded, her face still pressed against his chest. It had been a confusing afternoon, and she still hadn't gotten anything straight in her mind. But she knew one thing for certain: Jason had promised to find her son. *Their* son. And she believed him. So help her, she believed him.

After seven years, Jason was unprepared for the ache in his heart and the burning of his blood when he held Lane again. Hell, he'd been watching her and Davy from a distance for a year, utilizing the Council monitors while he'd been stuck in the Olympus debriefing facility. But video surveillance was nothing compared to holding this woman in his arms, feeling the soft press of her breasts against his chest, feeling the rhythm of her beating heart.

From a camera, he couldn't detect the hint of vanilla she'd dabbed on herself. Couldn't see the way the sunlight caught her plain brown hair, turning it into a fabulous crown. And he certainly couldn't see her eyes, at first cold, slate-gray, and angry, but now warm and wounded—though those two emotions he'd put there, and neither one was good.

After a moment she pushed away, leaning against his chest, then looked up at him with raw, red eyes.

"You left," she said simply, her pain evident. His gut twisted, and he realized he wanted her angry again. Anger, he could fight. But the hurt . . . Well, he'd caused that. And seeing it in her eyes only reminded him of his guilt.

"You left me," she repeated "You left Davy."

He shook his head. "I was trapped, imprisoned. By *him.* I didn't mean to stay away."

A flash of shock crossed her face. "By Hieronymous? All that time? Jason, that's horrible."

Hope built in his chest. "I went after him. I thought I could defeat him. I *needed* to do that." He exhaled, his body sagging with the memory. "But I failed, and he trapped me. *He* kept me away from you."

Jason closed his eyes, fighting the fury that inevitably came with the memory. "Around and around," he said. "In a glass bowl. Nothing to see, nothing to do. And so very far away from you. From Davy."

A hint of pain appeared in Lane's eyes. "Oh, God, Jason. That must have been horrible."

He flashed a wry smile. "Believe me," he said. "Captivity's bad reputation is well-deserved. I would have given anything to get out of there and back to you." That wasn't entirely true, of course. He wouldn't give himself to Hieronymous's evil.

Lane's eyes were warm, but she shook her head. His stomach twisted as hope evaporated. "I'm sorry, Jason. Truly, I am. But the truth is, Hieronymous kept you away, but he didn't make you leave. *You* did that."

He could only nod. What she said was true.

She looked him in the eye, and a single tear trickled down her cheek. "I needed you, but you left. You walked away when I needed you more than anything. You didn't even wait until morning. You didn't hold my hand and tell me everything would be okay. You just went away, and you didn't even tell me why!"

"I know." He inhaled, trying to draw in courage. "But I want to make it up to you."

She flinched, recoiling from his words. Her brow furrowed, and she stared at him as if he'd gone mad. "How?"

A simple question, but it hung heavy in the air between them.

He wanted to shout the answer—*by rescuing Davy*—but he knew that wasn't enough. He'd rescue the boy; of that much, he was certain. But he wasn't naïve enough to think that returning their son to Lane would mend what he'd broken so many years ago.

"I don't know exactly," he finally said. It was an honest answer, and the only one he could come up with. Before, he'd entertained the fantasy of seamlessly stepping back into her life. Now, he was living the harsh reality.

She licked her lips, her face contorting as if she'd just tasted his words and found them bitter. "You can't," she said. "It's done. Over. I've moved on with my life, and we can't go back. Not unless you can turn back time." For a brief moment, hope entered her eyes, and he saw just how much weight she gave Protector powers.

"Er, I don't think anyone can. Well, Zephron, maybe, but—"

"Not you."

"Not me."

"Oh." She nibbled on her thumb, then lifted her head to look him straight in the eye. "So you can't make it up to me, and we can't go back. But you *are* going to rescue my son."

"Our son," he corrected.

"He's all I have," Lane said, tears spilling out of her eyes. "You can't let anything happen to him."

Despite the cuffs binding his wrists, he twisted and managed to grasp her hands, squeezing until she squeezed back. "I know," he said. And he did. Once upon a time, she'd had him, too. But no more. Now it was just Lane and Davy. And if Jason wanted back into their family, he was going to have to work his tail off. He was going to have to rescue Davy—and he was going to have to do a whole hell of a lot more, too.

The cold steel elevator descended. And descended. And then descended some more.

Mordi's head began to pound from breathing the car's stale air. And from guilt. He closed his eyes, remembering the look of betrayal on Davy's face when he'd been forced onto the elevator with Clyde. Those two had descended first, and by now Davy was surely tucked tight into one of his father's notorious "guest rooms."

Mordi himself had shifted back into his own self, happy to shed Jason's image. Now he was following Clyde and Davy down, right into the belly of the beast. He shifted his weight, one foot to the other, and tried not to think about the danger he was again in. One little accident of birth and he was stuck with an Outcast for a father who wouldn't know affection if it walked up and punched him in the mouth.

The elevator slid smoothly to a stop, its doors opening to reveal a cavernous, steel-reinforced room. "Wow," Mordi said, stepping out. His voice echoed through the near-empty chamber: *WOW . . . Wow . . . wow . . . wo . . . w . . .*

"I'm glad you approve," Hieronymous said. The man brushed past, his cloak managing to flutter despite the still air. Or was it still?

Mordi sniffed, for the first time noticing his surrounding no longer smelled stale. He glanced around, his curiosity increasing as his headache faded.

The room was the size of a large warehouse, essentially empty except for a large table, a metal grid hanging from the ceiling, a clear pool of water in the floor with three arteries snaking off beneath the stone walls, and a large blob covered with a piece of black silk. Mordi stifled the urge to peek under the material. "So, where exactly are we?" he asked instead.

"Under the volcano," Hieronymous said. "Don't worry; it's dormant, I assure you." The corner of his mouth twitched. "At least, it is now."

Mordi frowned, not sure what his father meant. "Now?"

"Now that your father's stolen its *oomph*," Clyde said, stepping into the cavern from one of the many adjoining hallways. Mordi made a mental note of which one. Presumably, Davy was down it somewhere.

Clyde shoved past, heading for the steel table that stood in the center of the room. Mordi ignored him. Clyde didn't like Mordi, and the feeling was quite mutual.

At the moment, Clyde was a fugitive, wanted by the Council for questioning in connection with a charge of Power Exploitation. Under other circumstances, Mordi would happily have turned him in. For this assignment, however, he would be forced to put up with the buffoon's presence. He was on probation with the Council, jumping through all the necessary hoops to prove he was a good guy, loyal to the tenets of the Venerate Council, eager to protect mortals from all forms of evil, including his father.

He knew that he was paying the price for his past foolish decisions, but it still irritated him that the Council didn't trust him. And so he was being forced to prove his loyalty. Hieronymous had managed to avoid capture in the past by delegating his dirtywork. The Outcast was at the center of so many nefarious plots, and yet he often walked away without a blemish. The Council knew what he was up to; proving it was a different matter.

Mordi was supposed to find the proof. Find it

and—if necessary—step in and thwart his father's schemes.

A daunting task. And one that, by necessity, put him in close proximity to Outcasts like Clyde who were not, in Mordi's opinion, at the top of the food chain. He didn't enjoy the duty.

He turned, trying to discern more about his father's scheme. "You harnessed the volcano's energy? How? Why?"

Hieronymous seated himself at the table, pushed an inset button, and a bank of monitors slid gracefully from the ceiling, already tuned in to world financial programs. " 'How' requires far too technical an answer for you to understand," he said.

Mordi scowled but didn't argue. He'd just been insulted, yes; but he could hardly get bent out of shape about the truth.

"As for why," Hieronyomous continued, "my latest invention requires more power than simply plugging in to ConEd. This volcano suffices. Also, so long as I am siphoning off its energy, the risk of an eruption is significantly reduced."

"An eruption?" Mordi gulped, then glanced around for a neon sign designating an emergency exit. Of course there wasn't one.

"A minimal risk," his father assured with a quick wave of his hand. "And well worth it for the outcome."

"Which is . . . ?" Mordi prompted.

His father's eyes burned with black fire. "Why— me, of course," he said. "Becoming even more brilliant than I am now."

Mordi blinked, unsettled by the implications. "Uh, I don't suppose you'd care to elucidate?"

Hieronymous's laugh echoed through the chamber. "Difficult to comprehend, I know. How could I possibly be more intelligent than I already am? But it's possible. Astounding, but true." The animation in his face made him look almost gleeful. The expression didn't quite suit.

"I'll try to explain," Heironymous continued. "Hopefully you can follow, and visual aides won't be necessary."

Mordi bit the inside of his cheek, reminding himself to keep his mouth shut.

"As you of all people know, halflings present certain unique traits," the Outcast leader said. "Most are disagreeable, but some are potentially useful—as in the case of our young friend."

Mordi shifted, stifling the urge to tell his father to quit blowing smoke and get on with the story.

"As a halfling, Davy's brain waves will alter at midnight on his seventh birthday, just a few short days away. I intend to tap into the boy's conscious at precisely that moment, allowing me to drain his Protector-enhanced intellect right from his head."

His father must have seen the grimace that crossed Mordi's face, because he nodded. "Yes, it is a rather nasty business when one thinks about it closely." A thin smile graced his lips. "I, of course, never do."

Hieronymous stood up and strode across the room, his gait full of purpose, as always. "Instead, I focus on my goal. With this plan, I shall become the most brilliant person—Protector or mortal—on the planet. And with my enhanced intellectual ability, I will finally be able to invent a method of, once and for all, reducing all mortals to slaves and disbanding that silly Council." He turned. "At the moment, I'm partial to a particle beam, but once my already superior intellect joins forces with Davy's untapped potential, I will undoubtedly come up with an even more clever approach."

Mordi swallowed. Whatever method Hieronymous devised, the end result would be the same: The mortals would be enslaved, the Outcasts would rise up against the Council, and Hieronymous would proclaim himself the leader of all—and who would dare challenge him?

"All it took was finding the right child," Hieronymous admitted. "A halfling with an intellect right to complement mine."

Mordi took a deep breath and counted to ten before answering. "And Davy is that child?"

"He is. The boy's a regular little Einstein, and his family doesn't even realize it yet. His particular Protector skill is tied to his intellect, much like mine. As his skills develop, so will his inventiveness. Or, rather, those skills *would* develop were I not about to usurp them. Once I have tapped the boy's potential, he will be merely average. His mother needn't worry, though. I'm sure he'll still do okay on his SATs—though I certainly can't guarantee a Harvard education."

"If the Council catches you . . ." Mordi trailed off, his voice little more than a whisper, his stomach in knots. As much as he wanted to prove himself, there was still a tug, drawing him close to his father even when he wanted to run far, far away.

No matter how many times he told himself that Hieronymous deserved it, the thought of his father suffering the Council's direst punishments sent a shiver down his spine. Permanent interment in the catacombs. An eternity of darkness and solitude. And there were other unspoken punishments rumored to be . . . well, *unspeakable*.

How could he wish that on his father? And yet, considering who his father was and what he'd done, how could he not?

If Hieronymous succeeded, Mordi would have to betray him. To do otherwise would be a betrayal of the Council.

"Don't you love the serendipity of it?" his father asked, fingers twitching. "How appropriate that it should be *his* son who will bring me my ultimate glory."

The man paused, turning to glance at the monitors, his mouth drooping into a frown as he read the stock ticker running along the bottom of the center screen. After a moment, he spoke again, his words surprising Mordi. "I was pleased with your efforts today. My son."

"I . . . Thank you."

Hieronymous nodded. "I trust you will continue?"

"Sir?"

"You will not disappoint me as we conclude this venture—will you, Mordichai?"

Mordi shook his head, his chin lifted ever so

125

slightly. "No, sir," he said, pleased that his voice didn't quaver with the lie. The truth was that he *would* disappoint Hieronymous. If he did his job right, that outcome was inevitable.

Closing his eyes, Mordi stifled a sigh. He shouldn't care anymore. He knew that. But he did. Damn it all to Hades. Even after everything he'd been through, after all the lip he took from his father, he still didn't want to disappoint the man.

Pathetic.

And dangerous. In Mordi's line of work, a single moment of indecision could get a Protector in trouble. Deep, deep trouble.

Chapter Six

Zoë was missing something, something important. But a bone-deep exhaustion was pulling her down, and the swill of hormones in her blood had her head in a muddle. She couldn't think, and her only recourse was to play by the book. Her nephew's safety was on the line, and she didn't intend to compromise that—no matter how much the boy's mother believed in Jason.

Two hours had passed since Lane begged her to uncuff Jason and let him lead them all to his houseboat docked in Marina del Rey. He wanted to tap into the Council's database to scour it for possible locations where Hieronymous might have taken Davy. And although Lane thought that was a marvelous idea, Zoë had reasonably pointed out that a dozen Protectors were already doing that very thing.

What did Jason expect to find that others couldn't?

"Unless he already knows where Hieronymous has Davy," Zoë had said. "And he just wants to poke around for a while to strengthen his story."

But Lane hadn't bought that. For better or worse, she believed Jason was trying to help. So at last Zoë had succumbed to her friend's wishes—but only because she was there to monitor Jason's activities and Officer Boreas was around as backup.

They were all in the kitchen now, keeping an eye on Jason from the doorway. Zoë frowned, watching him tap at the computer keys. He'd been focusing intently on the task for an hour, and he was still going strong, determined. "I still think this is a mistake," she said, not really meaning to speak aloud.

Lane shook her head. "He'll find something the others won't. And even if he doesn't, I understand what he's going through. He needs to do something—*anything.*" She shrugged. "I'm going stir crazy myself. I'm absolutely useless . . . no help at all to my son."

Zoë's heart twisted, and she gave her stomach a protective pat before walking to Lane and putting her arms around her. "We'll find him," she said.

And she meant it. Her hormones be damned, they were going to find Davy and save him.

From the small window over the sink, Lane watched as the sun slid closer to the horizon: a symphony of colors reflected on the calm ocean, deceptively beautiful. Night was falling, and still they hadn't found any leads. There *were* monsters in the dark, and her son was with one of them.

Deena walked into the room and Lane tried to conjure a smile for her.

"I just came in to tell you that I called Hoop. I thought it might be helpful if he were here."

Lane smiled a silent thank-you. She wished Taylor were around, but her foster brother was still at his convention in Switzerland. Zoë had called him, of course, but he wasn't going to be able to get back until morning. Hoop was Taylor's best friend, and a private eye as well. She was glad he was on his way over.

Of course, she wasn't sure how much help Deena's fiancé would be. She'd take whatever warm bodies she could get helping in the search, though, and maybe Hoop would think of something the dozens of Protectors already looking for Davy had missed. At the very least, he'd give her a hug. At the moment she could really use one of Hoop's clumsy but sincere hugs.

She paused. In truth, it wasn't Hoop's hug she wanted but Jason's. Earlier, at Sea World, he'd held her tight in the circle of his arms. She'd felt safe. Secure. His embrace had provided a barrier between her and horrible reality, and she'd succumbed to the pleasure, drinking in the optimism engendered by his caress.

Now, the memory of his touch teased her. How her body had heated when she'd seen him. And how right they'd felt together so many years ago—even if his departure had proved they weren't right at all.

Then again, if what Jason said was true, he would have returned if he could have. Which meant . . . what? There was still something there? After all this time?

She frowned. *No.* No way. Not after what he'd done.

The day she'd found out she was pregnant with Davy had been the most emotional of her life. Wonderful, but terrifying. She'd needed him there, wanted him holding her hand and sharing her joy and her fears.

But he'd walked away. Maybe he'd meant to return, and maybe he hadn't. The bottom line was that he'd put himself before her and her child, and she couldn't trust that he wouldn't do the same thing all over again. That was even more true now that she knew he was a Protector. She would never come first. Even—especially—if he was the good guy he claimed; saving the world would always rank just a little bit higher than being with her. Than being with his son.

Honestly, she couldn't bear that. She'd spent her childhood being shuffled from home to home, never truly being important to anyone. She didn't want that for Davy. Her son was her priority, and he needed to be the same to whatever man she ended up with.

From what she knew of Jason, he wasn't that man.

She sighed. She'd work with him to find Davy, but that was all. Once she had her son back, she'd get on with her life.

She stifled a shiver, the truth crashing in on her

once again as it had all afternoon: *Her son was missing.* For brief moments she could remove herself from that reality, could think objectively and know that everything was being done to bring him back. But then she'd return to her own skin, and the horror of it would surround her.

Her skin was clammy and her head throbbed. Her chest ached, and her eyes burned from tears both released and forced back. She was living her worst nightmare, worse than any situation she'd expected or worked so hard to prevent. So much for all her efforts at safety. None of her planning or worrying had protected her boy, and now she had to rely on the help of the one man she'd never expected to see again.

As if reading her thoughts, Deena and Zoë reached out for her, each squeezing a hand. She smiled, wishing she had more to cling to than just their friendship.

But she *did* have more. She had Jason's promise. And even if she didn't entirely trust him, she did trust *that.*

She turned to Deena, squinting. "Zoë thinks I'm nuts for trusting him. What do you think?"

Color rushed to Deena's cheeks, and Lane almost laughed out loud. Deena was *so* not the blushing type, and to see her now looking decidedly uncomfortable was funny. Of course, considering her own state of near hysterics, she'd probably laugh at Davy's favorite Protector joke; *How many superheroes does it take to screw in a lightbulb? None. They just find Electroman and ask him to light up.*

She clenched her fists and fought a burst of giggles. Yup. She was definitely hysterical.

After a couple of deep breaths, she felt reasonably in control and repeated her question about Jason. Deena licked her lips, but this time the woman didn't fudge. She didn't look at Zoë, either.

"I don't know what to think. Jason said the kidnapper was a shapeshifter." She turned to Zoë. "Since I'm not entirely sure what you saw . . ." She trailed off, her words laced with some import Lane didn't understand.

Zoë did, though. She sucked in a sharp breath, then closed her eyes. "Fire," she whispered. "*That's* what's been bugging me. He used fire."

When Lane's sister-in-law opened her eyes again, she looked straight at Lane and uttered a name. It wasn't as bad as Hieronymous, but still it was enough to turn Lane's blood cold:

"*Mordichai.*"

Davy shoved his glasses into the front pocket of his T-shirt. When his pretend daddy had kidnapped him, those glasses had been in his jeans. Now the arm had broken off, and his mom was going to be really mad. He'd only had the glasses for a month, and she'd made him promise to always wear them and not put them in his pocket, because they cost a whole bunch and she didn't have the money to replace them every time he sat on them.

This probably meant no Pokemon for at least a week.

The thought of his Game Boy sitting on his desk

at home made him start sniffling again. He did so loudly, then ran the back of his hand under his nose and wiped it on his shorts, determined not to be a crybaby. His mom and Aunt Zoë would come soon. Elmer would tell them where to find him, and then he wouldn't be stuck in this big white room all alone.

When the big Outcast named Clyde had taken him and gotten on that elevator, he'd been really scared—even after Clyde claimed they were just going to a secret hideout. Davy had been so scared, in fact, he'd been happy to be left all alone in this locked room.

He'd scoped it out really good, testing every single part of the walls just like he was playing Super Mario Brothers. But no secret passages opened, which meant that the room made a lousy secret hideout. Of course, by then he knew it wasn't really a secret hideout. Even though the walls weren't stone and the floor was carpeted, it was still a dungeon and he was a prisoner, and unless he figured a way out, he was stuck.

Now his tummy was rumbling and he'd looked at every single inch of the room. A twin bed was in the middle, and the walls were all white, with posters of Teletubbies—like he was a baby or something. There was a mirror hanging over the sink, and Davy felt certain there was a camera behind it. The toilet was right next to the bed in the middle of the room, which was kinda gross, so Davy was gonna hold it for as long as he could.

The door locked from the outside, and he couldn't find a latch. The one window above the bed had bars behind its sheer blue curtains. Davy looked around for a light or a switch but didn't find one. He also didn't find any way out—and since he didn't have any of his tools, he couldn't make anything to cut away the bars. All he had were his clothes and his Walkman, and that wasn't much to work with.

It was starting to get late, and it was definitely past his bedtime. The sun had fallen below his window, and the room had already gotten darker. As the sun continued to sink, it would just get worse. And even though he knew there weren't *really* any worse things in the dark than there were in the light, he still didn't want to be all alone in the blackness.

The floor was cold, but the bed squeaked and smelled funny, so Davy plunked down on the floor and took off his sneakers. With his left shoe, his belt buckle, the broken arm of his glasses, and his Walkman, he could probably make some sort of light fixture out of the toilet. It wouldn't be as cool as his SpongeBob lamp back home, but it would keep him out of the dark. He went to work, happy to have something to do other than sit on the floor watching the shadows move on the wall and wondering if his mom would show up before morning.

A little while later, when the sunlight disappeared completely, it didn't matter. He'd used the wire from the broken glasses and the metal from his belt buckle and connected them to the back of his red light-up tennis shoe. He'd used the batteries from his Walkman as a power source, along with the water in the toilet bowl, since water was a conductor. He thought it was cool that the toilet now glowed red.

However, he only had one shoe left. He could've used both and made the toilet even brighter, but the right shoe had the tracking device he'd invented, and he was pretty sure Elmer would see where he was on they Lite-Brite map and tell someone. He didn't want to give that up.

His tummy growled some more, and he wondered if anybody was going to come to bring him food— or if there was even anybody around. Curious, he pulled what remained of his glasses from his pocket and balanced them on his nose. With only one arm they tilted sideways, and he had to cock his head so they didn't fall off.

As soon as he looked through the lenses, the walls started to go all fuzzy, and soon they disappeared altogether. The lenses were the ones his mom had bought, except Davy had added an X-ray coating. He hadn't told his mom, because he didn't figure she'd want him to be messing with them—especially since she'd had to use "plastic" to pay for them, and that always made her grumpy. But Davy had wanted to be like his Aunt Zoë. And since he couldn't see through walls on his own, he'd used the chemistry set at his best friend Eric's house.

The set belonged to Eric's brother, but according to Eric's mother, "Ricky was flunking out of tenth grade because he couldn't stop listening to that darned, infernal music." So Davy had figured Ricky wouldn't care too much if he used his chemistry set.

Now Davy was even more glad that he had. Without these glasses, he wouldn't be able to see outside this room. Not that there was much to see. Just more rooms like his, but with no one in them. And a long, empty hall with no one in it.

He squinted, turning his head even more sideways to try to get a better view down the hall. *A shadow.* And it was moving.

Holding his breath, he backed up, half hoping it would go away and half hoping the shadow belonged to someone who was bringing him dinner.

Still . . . what if the shadow belonged to a monster? Unlike his friends at school, Davy knew that there were real monsters, and they had to live somewhere. He was pretty sure that a dark, scary island dungeon would be the perfect place.

The shadow kept coming, looming bigger and bigger. An orange light flickered on the polished walls, both it and the shadow getting nearer. And then a man appeared, a black cape swirling around him. His face was made of orange fire and dark shadows.

Davy couldn't help it. He screamed.

"Hopping Hera," Mordi hissed, aiming the flashlight at the magnetic keypad on Davy's cell. "You'd think you'd seen a ghost."

He shifted back to Jason's form and opened the door. Lane's kid was huddled in the corner, half a pair of glasses hanging off his face and his eyes wide behind their lenses.

Damn. The kid was really scared.

Well, considering the circumstances, Mordi couldn't blame him. In fact, he felt a little guilty, adding to what had to already be the worst day in the kid's short life. "It's just me, okay? I didn't mean to scare you."

"I'm not scared of you," Davy said. He crawled out of the corner and tucked his broken glasses carefully into a pocket. "But I thought you were a monster."

"And you *are* scared of monsters?"

Davy nodded. "Aren't you?"

Mordi frowned, sure there was some pop-psychology way to answer that question, but nothing brilliant came to him. "Yeah, kid," he finally said, figuring he might as well go with the truth. "As a matter of fact, I am."

He'd be especially scared if he was stuck like this kid, in a dark room with—

He broke off the thought with a frown, then glanced down at his flashlight. Sure enough, he'd turned it off, just like he'd thought. So where was that odd red glow coming from?

Squinting into the cell, he noticed an otherworldly looking toilet. "Davy, did you . . . ?"

The boy nodded. "I don't like the dark," he said simply.

"*You* did that?"

Another nod.

Chalk one up for the kid. Hieronymous had said the boy was a genius. Maybe it was true.

"If it's dark, my mom and Aunt Zoë won't be able to find me," Davy added.

Mordi thought of Jason Murphy, out there somewhere and surely pissed. Especially if word had gotten to him about how Mordi was impersonating him. "What about your real dad?"

Davy shrugged, looking a little sad. "I told you, he's an astronaut. He'd come if he could, but he's stuck in space."

Not a bad rationalization for parental failure, Mordi thought. Too bad it wasn't true of his own father. Hieronymous had been right there during Mordi's formative years. But despite his physical presence, his father had been absent. The situation had sucked then, and it sucked now. Mordi couldn't help but hope Jason really did manage to find and rescue his kid. And then stayed with him.

The odds, though, weren't in his favor.

For one thing, this island was hidden by a cloaking device, making it invisible to both mortal and Protector eyes. For another, Hieronymous had rigged it with all sorts of traps designed to make sure no Protector could get through.

Yes, the island was quite Council-proof. Which was a pity, because Mordi really didn't want Hieronymous to steal Davy's brainpower. And at the same time, he wasn't at all sure that he was up for the job of preventing it. Foiling his father in secret was one thing. It would be quite another to openly oppose him, to see that usual faint glimmer of disappointment change to outright hatred.

All he'd ever wanted was approval from his dad. And if he did anything to help save Davy, he could pretty much toss that possibility right out the window.

He cocked his head, his eyes going back to the jerry-built toilet. "So, you're a smart kid, huh?"

Davy shrugged. "I guess so. My mom's making me

go to private school next year. If she can figure out how to pay for it."

"Don't you want to go to private school? I bet you'd get even smarter."

"Yeah, but Eric goes to my old school."

"I see. Is that your friend?" Mordi tapped a finger against his chin, thinking. "So maybe you'd rather not be quite so smart."

"I dunno," Davy said. "Maybe."

"Makes perfect sense to me." Mordi stepped farther into the room. "Be normal, hang out with your friends." He nodded, more to convince himself than Davy. "Yes, maybe that wouldn't be so bad after all."

"Mister?"

Mordi jerked his head up, realizing he'd lost himself in his thoughts. "No matter," he said, striding to the child. He carried a bag of food for the kid, and now he plunked it down on the little table, next to the remains of what had once been a Sony Walkman.

"I hope you like peanut butter and jelly," he said, pulling a sandwich out of the bag.

Davy nodded, then hobbled over, his right foot bare.

Mordi rolled his eyes. "What's with the shoes?"

"The other one's in the toilet," Davy said, as if that made perfect sense.

"And you're walking around wearing only one because . . . ?"

" 'Cause Elmer needs it to find me."

"O-kay," Mordi agreed. Whatever fantasy made the kid happy. He pointed at the sandwich. "Dig in."

Davy did, and Mordi leaned against the wall,

watching the kid scarf down the boring little meal. He half-snorted, the possibility of rescue by tennis shoe amusing him.

The glow of the toilet caught his attention, and he frowned. Then again . . . If the kid could turn a toilet bowl into some sort of art-deco light fixture, then Hera only knew what he could do with a tennis shoe. He was a genius, right?

A small smile played across Mordi's face, and he hoped the kid was as smart as Hieronymous thought. Maybe Jason or Zoë would find him after all. "Stay on your toes, Davy," he whispered. "Maybe your daddy will come through for you."

"Mordichai," Zoë repeated. Was she right? Was her cousin really the culprit? That seemed to be the only reasonable explanation, what with the fire the kidnapper had used. That was one of Mordi's skills.

But Mordi? She didn't want to believe it was true. Despite everything, Zoë had a soft spot for her cousin. And after Mordi's most recent adventure with Hale and Tracy, Zoë had hoped to Hera he'd turned over a new leaf. If this new hunch was right, though, Mordi had yet to extricate himself from his father's shadow.

Lane shook her head, a jumble of emotions playing across her face. "What fire? And what does Mordi have to do with this? If he has Davy . . ." She trailed off with a shiver.

Zoë couldn't blame her. Lane's past encounters with Mordi hadn't exactly been warm and fuzzy. For that matter, Mordi had put Davy in danger before.

She opened her mouth to explain, but Deena got there first.

"When Zoë launched a bucket of fish at the kidnapper," Deena said, "fire shot from his fingers. And then, in the water, when he was wrestling with the dolphin, this ball of fire appeared out of nowhere."

Lane scowled. "In the water?"

"Yup." Deena nodded. "Sound like anyone we know?"

Lane met Zoë's eyes. "Mordi," she agreed.

Zoë shook her head in annoyance. "I should have realized sooner," she said, once again realizing she simply wasn't at her best.

And if this was all true, Jason was innocent and Zoë had wasted valuable time detaining him.

Deena took her hand. "You couldn't have known. And the Council has been searching for Davy since he disappeared, so it's not like we could have done anything differently."

"Why couldn't Zoë have known?" Lane asked, her gaze darting between them. "I thought all your halfling weirdness had settled down, that all you had to do was take off your glasses to see a shapeshifter's true form. Didn't you see that it was really Mordi?"

"Well, yeah," Zoë said, not really sure how to explain. "But right now I've—"

"Got a cold," Deena said. "A nasty cold. Maybe allergies. We're not sure."

Lane's confused expression morphed into one of concern. "And it's messing with your powers? Like Hale?"

Zoë nodded, grateful both for Deena's fast think-

141

ing and for her brother setting the precedent: He had the unfortunate habit of sneezing himself invisible when his allergies got out of control.

"Do you want a Claritin?" Lane asked, starting to rummage in her purse.

"No, no," Zoë said. "But we probably ought to head back in and see what Jason's found out."

Lane licked her lips, obviously wanting reassurance. "So you trust him now? You think he's okay?"

"I'm not sure I—" Zoë cut herself off as she noticed a photograph taped to the refrigerator, partially hidden behind a pot holder. Something about the image seemed familiar, and she looked closer. Sure enough, the image permanently recorded in the candid snapshot was Lane and Davy playing at a park. The picture had been taken maybe a week ago. Zoë moved the pot holder. Beneath, previously hidden, was another photograph, this one several years older. There were three, actually—a strip of pictures taken in a carnival photo booth. Lane and Jason were there, happy and very obviously in love.

And yet Jason had left. Why?

"Zoë?" Lane called from the hallway.

"Sorry," she said. "I'm pretty sure he didn't kidnap Davy now."

Whether she trusted him in Lane's life was another question altogether.

Jason wasn't thrilled about having Officer Boring attached to his hip, but the baby-sitter had been Zoë and Lane's compromise. For the most part, Lane had won—after all, Jason was back on his houseboat, doing what he had to—but Zoë had insisted that Boreas be part of the deal. Which meant that, for the foreseeable future, Jason had a shadow.

Oh, joy.

"It would go a lot faster if you closed some of the other programs you have running," Boring said, his finger snaking over Jason's shoulder to point at the screen. "And why are you going to the official file on Hieronymous? You don't really expect him to have taken the kid to one of his registered locations, do you?"

Jason gritted his teeth and breathed slowly, hoping that by the time he finished, Boring would have accidentally stepped out the back door and into the Pacific.

No such luck.

"You want to search?" he said. "Then get your own computer. This is my party."

In truth, Boreas was right. But Jason's machine was busy compiling the results of the other searches he was running, and there wasn't a damn thing he could do to speed it up.

Rather than feel useless, Jason had resorted to obvious sources of information—and held fast to the hope that he might get lucky. Hours had passed, and so far neither he nor any of the Council had found even a hint as to Davy's location. Jason was working on adrenaline and coffee alone. And even though he knew he should take a break and get some food while the computer did its thing, somehow he couldn't seem to drag himself away.

So he sat here, plodding through entries, the vibrant white light of his monitor the only illumination in his small living room.

Behind him, Boring slurped coffee, then dragged over one of Jason's footstools and kicked his feet up.

"Make yourself at home," Jason said.

"Thanks." Boring reached onto the desk and grabbed a pencil and a pad of paper, then gave Jason a smile.

Apparently, the young officer had trouble grasping sarcasm. Jason sighed. But, unlike Zoë, at least Boring seemed willing to believe he was really looking for Davy. Jason knew he should probably cut the guy a break, but it irritated him that Zoë had assigned him this shadow. He was taking it out on Boring, and if that was unfair it was too damn bad. Jason wasn't exactly having the best of days himself.

Twisting around, he turned his attention back to the computer. He'd already entered his password at www.superherocentral.com and had navigated to the database containing all registered Outcast information. Protector law required Outcasts to file quarterly reports identifying all property held in their name, or by a corporate entity in which the Outcast held a substantial ownership. Jason didn't necessarily expect Hieronymous had followed the rules, but considering how stiff the penalty was for noncompliance, he was willing to give this a shot. Who knew? Maybe the Outcast played by *some* of the rules.

It turned out Hieronymous had registered 427 properties around the globe, the most promising of which included a hunting cabin in the Arctic, a mud hut in Borneo, an abandoned winery in the South of France, and a ghost town in Arizona.

Boring leaned forward, his eraser tapping the screen. "Arizona's close. Maybe he just whipped over a couple of states."

"Arizona?" Lane's voice filtered in from behind them and Jason turned, the very sound of her voice warming him more than the T-shirt and sweats he'd thrown on to replace the towel from Sea World. "You think Davy's in Arizona?"

Jason shook his head, hating to kill the hope he saw in her bloodshot eyes. "I'm sorry, Lane. We still don't know where he is."

Her lip trembled, steadying slightly when Zoë put a hand on her shoulder. Lane's already pale skin seemed translucent, and shadows lined her eyes. Since he'd last seen her she'd pulled her hair back into a ponytail, and now only loose tendrils framed her face. Despite the strength he knew was at her core, Lane looked small and wan, and he immediately got up and took her elbow.

He led her to the small sofa by the window, but there, instead of lying down like he wanted, she sat up, her legs together, her hands folded above her knees, as if keeping herself together was as much a physical act as a mental one.

"I've got a team of fifty Protectors checking out each of Hieronymous's official addresses," Zoë informed no one in particular. She nodded toward the computer screen where Jason had just been pulling up that information. "In a few hours, we should know *something*."

Jason nodded, glad this route had been handled. Then he headed back to the machine and clicked the mouse on the toolbar, pulling up the Council-devised search engine he'd had running in the background. The software filtered through the property records of every city in every state in every country. Considering the massive amount of information to be processed, the program was surprisingly fast.

"Bori—*Boreas* is probably right. I doubt the kidnapper took Davy to a registered location. I've had the computer searching property records. I'm hoping we can locate some likely unregistered properties."

"That'll take forever." This was a new, male voice, and Jason swiveled in his chair to face the door. A somewhat rumpled man appeared whom he recognized from his past months observing Lane.

"Hoop!" Deena squealed, and then ran to embrace her fiancé. "I'm so glad you're here."

He kissed her head, then immediately moved to the sofa and put his free arm around Lane. Holding her close, he planted a chaste kiss on her forehead. Jason liked him instantly. "You doing okay, kid?"

She nodded, then immediately shook her head. "No."

"We'll find him," Hoop said. He turned toward Jason. "You're the dad?"

Jason nodded, grateful the man hadn't repeated Zoë's accusations. "That's me."

"So let's see what you've got so far." Hoop

squeezed in between Jason and Boreas, managing to block Boreas's view in the process. Jason's affection for the P.I. rose another notch.

He shifted to the left, giving Hoop a better view. "I think you got the gist of it as you came in. I'm letting the computer do its thing to see if any matches come up." He pointed to a box in the corner of the screen. "So far it's found ninety-seven properties potentially owned by Hieronymous."

"That many?" Lane asked from across the room.

"Afraid so," he admitted. "And it's only completed fifteen percent of the search."

She got up and moved toward the computer, and Jason automatically scooted over, making room for her on his chair. She hesitated, her tongue darting out to lick her lips. He patted the cushion, then stood up, letting her have the chair to herself.

"No. You're working," she said.

"And you want to watch. You don't need to be standing." He squinted at her. "Have you eaten anything?" His gaze shifted to Deena. "She should eat something."

"I'm not hungry," Lane argued, but she sat on the edge of his chair. "We can share," she amended.

Jason nodded, pleased she wanted him close. Before he sat back down, he shot another look in Deena's direction. She headed off to the kitchen—technically a galley, but the houseboat was so like a fancy apartment that nothing about it really felt nautical.

"Can you see the results so far?" Lane asked, her breath tickling his neck.

"Sure." Jason clicked his mouse, pulling up each specific file. Behind him, he could hear Boreas squirming, maneuvering for a better view. He scrolled through each entry, but nothing screamed evil Outcast abode.

"Nothing," Lane said. She closed her eyes, her hands clutching the side of the desk so hard her knuckles turned white. "This is hopeless."

"Mordichai," Zoë reminded, her voice little more than a whisper.

Lane's eyes opened, and she turned to Jason. "Of course," she cried. "Maybe the property belongs to Mordi!"

"I'm already on it," he said. And he was. "The computer's looking for any property that belongs to any derivation of Hieronymous's name, Mordichai's, or that Clyde guy who does Hieronymous's dirty work." He shrugged. "Of course, it's probably a waste of resources to plug Mordi's name in," he said. "After all, he's already on probation with the Council, and I can't imagine he'd risk that by letting his father—"

"Mordi's a shapeshifter," Zoë said, interrupting. Her voice was flat, but the message wasn't. Surprised, Jason turned to face her, and she nodded. "Sorry I misjudged you," she added.

Her expression wasn't exactly warm and fuzzy, but an apology was an apology, and Jason didn't intend to look a gift Protector in the mouth. "Under the circumstances, it was a natural mistake," he said. If he'd expected her expression to soften once she realized he wasn't holding a grudge, he'd been wrong.

Her lips stayed in a thin line, her posture overly straight and her eyes fixed on the back of Lane's head.

Ah. Well, he couldn't fault her for worrying about her friend, either.

"So it wasn't this guy?" Boreas asked, indicating Jason. "I don't need to keep an eye on him anymore?"

A shadow crossed Zoë's face, and she started to speak, looking none too happy about it. Jason knew what she was going to say and got there first. "You're stuck with me, kid." He met Zoë's surprised gaze. "Council rules."

"Right," Boreas said. "Of course. Regulation nine-seven-four, subpart d." He thwapped his forehead with the heel of his hand. "I can't believe I forgot."

Jason rolled his eyes at the neophyte's enthusiasm for the rulebook, then looked at Lane. "Until another Protector is conclusively involved, I'm still a suspect," he said, answering the question in her eyes.

Well, for Jason, that was more or less the status quo—at least until he proved himself to the High Elders. A protector like him with Hieronymous for a father would always be a little bit suspect. In that, he supposed, he had a hell of a lot in common with his brother Mordi. Someday, maybe he'd even meet the man.

Lane poked at her plate of scrambled eggs. She'd been doing so for about an hour, ever since Deena had put it in front of her. So far, she hadn't taken a bite.

At first, Deena had shot her optimistic glances, but she'd finally given up and now dozed in one of Jason's leather chairs. Jason and Boreas were still hovering in front of the computer, its monitor casting an eerie glow on their faces. Zoë was on the patio, talking on her cell phone to some council big shot, and Hoop was in Jason's bedroom, calling to see if any of his mortal law-enforcement connections had turned up any information.

Only Lane was useless. Sucking in air, she willed herself to eat. What Deena had said earlier was right: If she wanted to help, she needed to keep up her strength. With a grand effort, she stabbed a tiny clump of egg with her fork and lifted it to her mouth.

Her taste buds had ceased to function, so the bite seemed bland and rubbery. She added a bit of toast, but her mouth was too dry, and she just kept chewing and chewing, unable to swallow. After a moment she gave up and spit the whole mess into a napkin. "I'm sorry," she said, to no one in particular.

Jason looked up. "How about a milkshake?"

She shook her head. "No, I'm fine. It's okay."

"It's not okay. When was the last time you ate?"

She blinked, trying to grasp the concept of time. Years seemed to have passed since she'd had anything but water, and she frowned with concentration. "Lunch. Today. I mean yesterday. I mean—"

"You mean it's been a long time," Jason interrupted. "It's almost four in the morning." He stood up and headed into the kitchen. "Something cold and liquid. Strength, energy, and ice cream." His smile was sympathetic. "Just the ticket for a weary woman."

She nodded, having to admit it did sound good. But when Jason came back around the corner, his smile had faded. "I'm out of ice cream." He glanced toward the computer and the Protector sitting there. Boreas had fallen asleep. "We'll send *him.*"

She shook her head. "No, that's okay. I'm fine." Her stomach rumbled, apparently having come awake at the thought of ice cream. Her hunger triggered a memory, that of a likely hungry ferret trapped in her living room. She stood up, glancing around for her purse. "I, uh, need to go home anyway."

Jason shook his head. "I don't think so."

She crossed her arms on her chest. She'd come close to falling apart today, but she'd managed to hold herself together. The last thing she needed was to be told what to do. She stood up, marched to the table near the front door, and swung her purse over her shoulder. "Yeah, I *do.* I need to go feed Elmer and I want . . . I want . . ." She trailed off, blinking back tears. What she wanted was just to see Davy's room again, but she felt like an idiot saying that out loud.

Jason moved toward her, his bare feet silent on the polished wood floor. He slipped an arm around her, and Lane leaned against him, wishing she didn't need his comfort but not about to turn it down from some false pride. Especially since being in his arms felt so very right.

"I only meant that you don't have a car. You came

here under Protector power, remember?" He paused, then added, "If you need to feed Elmer, I'll take you. And as long as we're using my place for command central, you should probably pick up a few things."

She sighed. He was right. Getting Zoë to agree took a bit more effort, but Lane's sister-in-law finally gave in, even going so far as to not wake Boreas to go with them. Ignoring Regulation 974, subpart d was a big deal; Lane wasn't certain if Zoë now fully trusted Jason, if she was simply being accommodating, or if she was just too tired to fight. Whatever the reason, Lane didn't care. She just wanted to go home.

She soon found herself above Santa Monica, with nothing surrounding her but air and Jason's arm. Below, stop lights blinked red and yellow as traffic moved in a city that thrummed with activity even in the middle of the night. The night air chilled her, and she shivered.

"Scared?" he asked.

She shook her head. "I've done this before," she explained with false bravado. In truth, this particular Protector trick got her every time. Usually, she could focus on something else and keep the fear at bay. This time, though, the *something else* was even more terrifying. "Maybe a little scared," she admitted.

His arm tightened around her waist and he shifted her, pulling her below him so that he was essentially lying on her. Her back was pressed against his chest, her rear nestled against his crotch. Their ankles intertwined, keeping their legs together.

The heat from his body poured through her, staving off her chill. But his heat was so much more than just 98.6. No, the friction between their bodies was making things much hotter. It was doing things to her it shouldn't, making her body remember things it shouldn't. Making her want things she shouldn't.

She shifted, twisting against his arm, trying to struggle free. But he held fast. "No," she whispered. "Put me back the way I was before."

"Shhh." His mouth brushed the back of her ear. "We're almost there. And this is the safest way to fly. I'm tired, too. I don't want to accidentally drop you."

She doubted he would, but she appreciated his excuse. She didn't have the energy to argue. And, truthfully, she craved his touch—wanted it even as she wanted to be free of him.

The journey ended all too soon, and Jason put them down on the lawn in front of her apartment. Lane frowned, wondering how he knew her address, but she didn't ask. Under the circumstances, it was probably best not to know.

She slid her key into the lock and pushed open her front door. Immediately, Elmer scampered forward and started chittering.

"Hale's ferret?" Jason asked.

Lane nodded.

"Any idea what he's saying?"

"Not a clue," she said. "I'm guessing he's starving to death. He's used to hotels with room service. Staying up with me is really lowering his standards."

Reaching down, she rubbed his little head, thinking that would calm him down. Instead, it only seemed to excite him more. "I guess I better make with the food." She headed toward the kitchen, gesturing to the interior of the room. "It's not much, but it's home. Sit anywhere," she offered, clicking a button on the remote to turn on the television. "I'll only be a second."

Instead of sitting like she'd expected, he headed for the bookshelf. There he pulled down the carved wooden dolphin Davy had received a few months ago from his anonymous benefactor. Lane licked her lips, ignoring the hungry, hopping Elmer as she watched Jason stroke the polished wood. For the first time, she wondered if Aaron was right. Had *Jason* been sending these presents? But how could that be? He'd been locked up. Imprisoned. He'd told her that himself.

Surely he hadn't lied to her again?

A commercial ended, and the twenty-four-hour news channel came back on. As Lane pulled open the refrigerator, she heard the broadcast: *"A freak storm at the San Diego Sea World on Sunday resulted in an overload on that park's sewage system. All patrons were evacuated while environmental officials tested the facilities to ensure there was no contamination."*

Lane twisted, and her eyes met Jason's, a chill settling over her as the newscaster assured viewers that the park checked out fine and would reopen in the morning. She took a deep breath, and then another. When she felt composed, she popped the tops on two Diet Cokes and turned.

"Tell me about Davy," Jason said, still holding the

carving and standing in the living room. "Tell me about my son."

Lane opened her mouth, not to comply but to ask her own questions. But when she saw his eyes, she stopped, the sadness there making her want to cry.

The realization that she wasn't the only one who'd lost Davy washed over her. Jason had missed out on so much. And no matter what he did, there were some things Jason could never have. And despite what had come between them in the past, and no matter what might lie ahead in the future, Lane wanted Jason to know his son.

"He's wonderful," she said, not knowing where to start. "He's the best little boy in the world."

Despite his melancholy, Jason had to grin. Leave it to Lane to state the obvious.

He stroked the driftwood dolphin, the warm wood alive under his fingertips. He wondered if Davy had ever played with the thing, or if it just sat, cold and unloved, on a shelf, some curio given by an unknown benefactor.

Although he'd spent hours watching Davy and Lane, he hadn't looked into their apartment. He'd seen Davy chasing friends, he'd seen his son and Lane wrestling on the grass, he'd seen Davy and Lane eating hotdogs at the slightly rusty table in the courtyard—but the intimacies of their lives had remained a mystery.

"I was hoping for something a little more specific," he said.

Putting the dolphin back on the shelf, he headed into the kitchen, joining Lane in the cramped room. She handed him a Diet Coke and took a sip of her own. When she pulled a container out of the refrigerator, he grappled for some question that would provide loads of insight into his son. "What's his favorite food?" he finally asked. Not exactly insightful, but he was just getting warmed up.

Lane looked up from the glop she'd begun spooning onto a plate for Elmer—the ferret continuing to dance about her feet—the corner of her mouth curving into a smile. "Macaroni and cheese," she admitted. "Kraft."

He nodded. "The kid has good taste."

"I take it that's still in your cooking repertoire?"

Jason laughed. "That *is* my repertoire. That and microwave popcorn. You should remember."

"Slacker," she said.

"Yeah, well, I haven't exactly had access to a kitchen to learn anything new." He nodded down at the plate of glop she held, not wanting to talk about his absence. "Purina ferret chow?"

"Beef bourguignonne." She nudged the ferret with her toe. "Hale has a service deliver Elmer's meals. The little guy's spoiled rotten."

And, apparently, hyperactive. The ferret was bouncing around on the floor even more frantically, clawing at the hem of Lane's jeans and running in circles.

"He's a spaz," Lane said. "But I can't blame him for being hungry." She headed toward the door and squeezed past, her shoulder brushing Jason as she stepped into the tiny hallway. "Come on. I'll show you Davy's room."

In two short steps he was at the door, which, in case anyone might be confused, announced on a miniature license plate that it was "Davy's Place."

Jason wasn't sure what he expected inside, but he was pretty sure it wasn't the tornado-destroyed disaster area that confronted him. Stuffed animals were strewn all about, their apparent mode of transportation the collection of multicolored plastic trucks scattered across the floor. A variety of wooden blocks and Tinkertoys filled the rest of the space, ensuring that entering would be hazardous to one's health. He did so, anyway.

At the foot of the bed, the kid had mounted a map of the United States on a plastic board. Dozens of tiny lightbulbs made up its coordinates, creating a colorful display. Davy must not have changed the bulbs recently, though, because at the moment all were burned out except for one light humming in the Pacific.

"Cool, huh?" Lane said, nodding toward the map. "He spent days making it. And he begged me for one of those Lite-Brite kits. I said he could have it on his birthday, but he conned it out of me a few months early." She half-smiled. "I'm such a sucker."

Jason grinned. Imagining Davy's enthusiasm, he understood her weakness.

He and Lane moved around the map to the side of the bed, and her fingers absently stroked the walls. Jason noticed the movie posters that decorated every inch: *Star Wars, Monsters, Inc.,*—

"He likes Mike," Lane said, gesturing toward one of the posters. She put Elmer's plate on the floor in the corner next to a water dish, then plucked a green goblin-looking guy off the bed. The plush one-eyed creature matched the character on the *Monsters, Inc.* poster, and Lane hugged him close, her lips pressed together so tight they disappeared into a thin line.

"Why don't you bring Mike back to my house-boat?" Jason suggested. "That way you can give him to Davy when you see him again."

Lane nodded, her throat moving a bit, but she didn't say anything. After a moment she gave the monster's head a little kiss and looked up. "Green's his favorite color," she said, her voice hoarse. A tear trickled down her cheek. "And never leave anything electronic near him unless you don't mind it being taken apart."

Jason reached for her hand, and she let go of Mike to take it. He squeezed her fingers. "He's ruined some of your stuff."

She shook her head. "No. Actually, that's the funny part. He puts it back together—just not always when I need it. Of course, when I complain, he very seriously tells me: 'Mommy, sometimes you have to be patient while a genius is working.' " She laughed. "How am I supposed to argue with that?"

It sounded like something a son of his would say. "I'm pretty sure you can't."

Jason glanced around the room, noting the small gadgets and gizmos tucked away everywhere. And, he noticed, the presents he'd sent were all here, most looking like they'd been well played with. "So, what has his genius created?"

Lane sat on the edge of the bed, Mike secure in her lap. "Oh, let's see. A transporter beam so that I can go off into space and bring back his daddy." She met his eyes. "Apparently you're an astronaut," she added.

He nodded, trying to keep his face impassive despite his pain. "Good to know."

"And X-ray glasses. And a magic plate that eats your vegetables for you." She tapped a finger against her chin. "There's lots more. Every night he tells me what he invented that day. It's a game we started playing about a year ago. At first he just took his trucks apart and put them back together. Then he moved on to my clock radio, the toaster, and the VCR. After that, his imagination kicked in—we've got boogeyman repellant, tracking devices, animal translators, and mind-reading hats."

"A new one every day, huh?"

Lane nodded. "Yup. Well, usually. Sometimes he says a project's in development but needs funding. I don't know where he picks this stuff up. Other times he says the prototype's in production." A genuine smile lit her face, almost bright enough to hide the sadness in her eyes. "I swear, the kid thinks he's Thomas Edison or something." She shook her head. "Actually, if his science ever ends up as good as his imagination, he just might show Edison up."

Jason's stomach twisted. His son, the inventor. His son, accepting the Nobel Prize in physics. His son, *Time*'s Man of the Year.

Yeah, that would be cool.

"He's such a clever, special little boy," Lane went on. Her voice cracked, and Jason sat beside her on the bed, taking her hand in his. She aimed a weak smile in his direction. "Maybe he can invent himself a way to get free of Hieronymous."

He squeezed her fingers. "We'll get him back, sweetheart. I promise."

His pager hadn't vibrated, but he checked it anyway. No messages. He keyed in an entry, directing it to the others at his houseboat: *Progress report?*

No news, came the answer.

Damn.

Lane's bloodshot eyes darted down to the pager and then back up to him. "Nothing?"

"I'm sorry. But we will fi—"

"No." She whispered the word, her head shaking. "Don't keep telling me that." She got to her feet and then, with an icy calm, hurled Mike across the room. "Damn it all to hell!" Tears spilled from her eyes. "I don't want any more platitudes. I've had enough. I've reached my limit. I'm done, Jason. I want this to be over. I want my son. I want Davy back."

Her anguish came in a flood. Tears streamed down her face, and Lane pressed her hand over her mouth as she stumbled back onto the bed. On the way, she almost tripped over Elmer, who hadn't eaten and was still practically bouncing off the walls near the foot of the bed. Lane ignored the ferret, throwing herself down on Davy's mattress and curling up with his bedspread, her knees at her chest.

Jason was immediately at her side, leaning over

her, stroking her arm. He had no idea what comfort he could bring, but he had to try. His heart wrenched and he reached out, wanting to make Lane's tears stop.

Gently he brushed the palm of his hand over her hair, smoothing it back from her forehead. Her shoulders shook with silent sorrow, and he placed a soft kiss on her cheek.

"Lane," he whispered.

That was all it took. With a guttural sob that almost ripped out his heart, she rolled over and clung to him. Her hands clutched his sleeves and her cheek pressed against his chest. Her sobs were no longer silent, and he held her close, rocking from side to side, wishing he could do more to soothe her, wishing he'd never left, wishing he'd been just another dad at Sea World with his boy so that maybe this would never have happened in the first place.

If wishes were fishes . . .

With one hand, Jason stroked Lane's back, murmuring soft words, saying nothing but trying to communicate everything: hope, strength, most of all, the certainty that all would end well.

As her sobs slowed, Lane pressed closer against him, her arms tight around his waist. Even in the face of the surrounding horror, the moment felt right. *She* felt right. And Jason knew without a doubt that he would do anything—*anything*—to make sure Lane wasn't hurt again. By him, by Hieronymous, by anyone.

He stroked the small of her back. Her little T-shirt had come untucked from her jeans, and his palm skimmed her soft, warm skin. His own body felt hot, but whether from the warm room or the woman he loved, he wasn't sure. It didn't matter. Right now, nothing mattered but letting Lane know Davy would be safe.

"It will be okay," he whispered.

"How?" The word came out strangled, Lane's voice so raw it caused him physical pain.

This was all his father's fault, and Jason clenched his fist, pressing it against the belt loop of Lane's jeans, fighting the urge to smash his fist through the wall as a substitute for his father's head.

"Because I'll make sure it's okay," he said.

"But what if—"

He pressed a finger against her lips, unwilling to let her complete the thought. Hell, unable to think it himself. "Failure is not an option," he said, gratified when she grinned at the cliché. "I'm serious, though," he added. And he was. Deadly serious.

With the side of his hand he stroked Lane's cheek. She turned, and his palm slid over her warm, soft lips. The sensation rocked him, sending tremors through his body. He ignored them. This wasn't about him. Wasn't even about Lane. Not yet. This was about Davy. "I'll get him back," he promised. "Or I'll die trying."

When she'd first seen him hours ago, her eyes had been accusing. Now, she looked at him like a hero. A wave of fear rose in his gut—fear that he wasn't up to the task. His father had bested him before; what was to stop him from doing so again?

He shoved the thought aside. He *would* win. He

had to. For Davy, and because he couldn't bear the thought of this shadow crossing Lane's eyes again. Yes, he'd win. And, in the end, he'd make Hieronymous no longer a threat to anyone.

"Thank you," Lane whispered. "I'm sorry I . . ." She trailed off with a shrug. "I don't like breaking down like that."

"No one does," he said. "But I'd say you have a pretty good excuse."

"It's like he took me, too," she explained. "Like I'm being held prisoner with Davy. Only I don't know where, and if only I could see through the darkness we could run free." She looked up at him. A watery smile graced her lips, in sharp contrast to the sadness in her eyes. "Does that make any sense at all?"

He met her smile. "More than you know. Believe me, I know all about prisons. And I know all about Hieronymous."

She licked her lips. "Do you want to tell me?"

He shook his head, fighting the memories he'd worked so hard to block out, those years trapped all alone in a suspended crystal fishbowl, that prison within a prison, hidden on some desolate island in the Pacific. "Some other time," he said. "Right now we should get back to the houseboat."

She nodded, then scooted to the edge of the bed.

Poor lady. Poor Davy. And no one's paying attention to the ferret.

Jason frowned, cocking his head as he tried to locate the voice that seemed to come out of nowhere.

He stood and turned in a circle, his eyes scanning the room. Nothing.

Hello? he called.

Lane stared at him. "What are you doing?"

He ignored her, addressing the voice. *Is anyone here?*

You can hear *me? Oh, that's wonderful! I had no idea. Ask the ferret! You need to ask the ferret where Davy is!*

Jason turned to Lane. "Does Davy have a fish?"

Her eyes widened. "Oh, my gosh. I completely forgot to feed Dorothy." She reached to the headboard and pushed Davy's pillow aside. There, on the built-in bookshelf, was a simple goldfish bowl housing a tiny plastic castle and one small fish.

Thank Hera he wasn't losing his mind.

Immediately, Jason climbed back onto the bed and crawled to the headboard, coming nose to bowl with the fish.

"Uh, Jason?"

He ignored Lane, focusing on Dorothy. *What do you mean, talk to the ferret?*

The goldfish swam back and forth, building up speed with each turn. *The ferret's been rambling like mad. And the boy used to talk to him about a tracking device.*

You can understand the boy?

I understand him, but he doesn't understand me. He can talk to the ferret, though—he invented a translator.

His brilliant son . . .

Jason shook his head. Time for that later. *Can you ask the ferret?*

I don't speak ferret. Do you?

No, Jason certainly didn't. Which had never bothered him before, but now it caused him no end of grief. Yet there were other ways to communicate besides words, and he intended to get answers.

With a quick thank-you to Dorothy, Jason dove for Elmer, plucking him off the map and the brightly lit bulb plugged into the South Pacific. He wracked his brain for a way to interact with the beast.

"Jason?" Lane asked, her voice switching from slightly amused to slightly concerned. "What's going on?"

As Jason opened his mouth to answer, realization struck. He stared at the ferret now dangling from his hands, tiny ferret feet kicking in the air.

Jason swallowed as he glanced from the bulb to the ferret and back.

Surely it wasn't so simple . . .

The ferret twisted to follow Jason's gaze and then started to spaz out again, his little head bobbing up and down affirmatively.

"Dammit, Jason, tell me what's going on." Lane clutched his wrist so tightly he opened his hand, dropping Elmer.

"I know where he is," he answered, meeting her widening eyes. "I know where Hieronymous took Davy."

Chapter Seven

Jason stalked in front of his large Council-issued speedboat, which was docked near his houseboat. He was trying his damnedest to hold his tongue, and so far he'd managed for one entire length of the pier. Apparently, though, that was his limit. "I don't care about any damn directives," he said, stomping back in the opposite direction. "I'm going after my son."

Zoë ran a hand through her hair—or tried to, anyway. She wore it pulled back from her face in a tight braid. The hairdo had started out neatly that morning, but it was now a frazzled mess. "I'm not trying to be difficult," she began.

"Then don't," Jason snarled.

". . . but there's a reason for the rule," she continued, not missing a beat.

Lane stopped her own pacing, halting in front of Zoë. "I don't understand why we're waiting. Jason's right," she said.

Jason nodded, appreciating the way she had parked herself solidly in his corner.

"Or even if he's not right," Lane continued, apparently pulling out of *that* parking space. "His lead is the best we've got. We should be headed to the South Pacific right now, not arguing about directives."

Jason couldn't agree more. On the way back to his houseboat he'd radioed ahead, instructing Boreas to use the Council database to locate any islands owned by Hieronymous, Mordichai, or Hieronymous's flunky Clyde. The search came back negative, just as he'd suspected. Yet he knew such an island was out there somewhere. He'd escaped from it. He'd even given the coordinates to the Council during his debriefing; but when they'd sent a Protector to check it out, the agent had returned with bad news: no island, just miles and miles of ocean.

At the time, Jason had assumed he'd been mistaken on the coordinates. After all, his years of imprisonment there had been a pretty traumatic time. The High Elders had agreed he'd gotten the coordinates wrong. Now, though they hadn't said it out loud, Jason even wondered if they thought his mistake was on purpose, a way to protect his father's secret hideaway. After a few more attempts to locate the island failed, the Council had given up.

Well, even if the Council believed he'd been mistaken about his location, Jason was willing to take up the search again. Elmer seemed to think there was an island out there, and at the moment the word of a spastic ferret was better than nothing. He'd find the island. And he'd bet good money that Hieronymous had the boy stashed there.

To hell with them. He stepped onto his speedboat, jerking away when Zoë placed a warning hand on his arm.

"Dammit, Jason," she said. "I'll send Protectors. I'll send an entire team. Even if we consider you free and clear of any suspicion, you're too involved, too emotional—"

"Damn right I'm emotional," he snapped.

"That's the whole point of Directive eight-two-seven-b. You're going to react instead of think, and you're going to put Davy in more danger than he's in already. Don't you see? You're doing that right now."

"I will *never* endanger Davy," he said. "I want to make Hieronymous pay—I promise you that—but not at the risk of hurting my son."

He rubbed his temples, tired of having to jump through the Council's hoops: first proving himself to the High Elders, now proving himself to Zoë. "Look," he continued, "The only safe way in is under the island. And it's not exactly marked on a map. All we've got to work on is my memory and a ferret pointing to a light on a map. So I have to go, because I have the best chance. Another team will fumble around and Hieronymous will detect them. He's got sensors everywhere, and each is sensitive to Protector biorhythms. If a Protector enters from the surface, or spends too long stumbling around in one of those tunnels, the gig is up."

"Call the Z-man," Hoop suggested, appearing and ambling down the pier. "He's cool, right? I bet he'd let Jason go. What Jason says is reasonable."

"Good idea," Jason agreed. "Call Zephron." It was a gamble, but he was almost positive the High Elder would allow him to proceed.

"I tried," Zoë admitted. "But I haven't had any luck contacting him."

"Oh, just let the man go then," Hoop said. "That Council of yours is too bureaucratic by half."

Zoë licked her lips, and Jason could tell she was bending. He stepped all the way into his speedboat.

"Plus," Deena added from where she'd appeared, "if Jason fails—not that he will," she added quickly. "But if he does, he can always call in the cavalry. Right?"

Hoop pointed to Zoë. "Why don't you go along, too? You two can do a dynamic duo thing."

"No!" Jason said, remembering how erratic Zoë had been at Sea World. He didn't know the reason, but he wasn't about to partner up with a Protector whose powers were on the fritz. He looked her in the eye. "She can't come with me."

Zoë swallowed, her cheeks turning slightly red. "He's right. I shouldn't go."

"But—" Hoop began.

"No," Deena cut him off. "Jason's right. Zoë should stay here."

"Her cold?" Lane asked.

Jason frowned. He'd never once heard of a cold

mucking up a Protector's powers like had happened at Sea World, but whatever the cause, he didn't need to be worrying about his partner's abilities.

"Exactly," Zoë agreed. "And in case Zephron calls."

"That's fine," Jason said. He moved across the boat and was seated behind its wheel. "I work better alone."

"A pity," Zoë said. "Because the only way I'm letting you go is if Boreas goes with you."

As soon as the neophyte Protector was settled on the boat, Lane breathed a sigh of relief. She'd expected Jason to protest, but he'd surprised her by holding his tongue. Good. Time to get underway. In reality, of course, only a few minutes had passed since Jason's revelation. In her mind, though, it seemed like an eternity.

She grabbed her purse from where she'd dropped it on the pier, then carefully stepped from the wooden planks onto the boat's fiberglass hull. Her heart picked up tempo, her pulse echoing her anticipation.

Lane still wasn't entirely certain how Jason knew where Davy was. He'd told her that Dorothy had told him about the LiteBrite map, and that Elmer had confirmed on a tracking device that Davy was somewhere in the South Pacific. Since that's where Jason had been held hostage, he was certain Davy must be on Hieronymous's island. Lane had no idea how Elmer knew that, or, for that matter how Elmer had gotten his hands on a tracking device. But things had been moving so fast, she hadn't had time to ask. For that matter, she didn't care about the *how* of it. The point was, they had a solid lead and they were finally doing something. They were going to get her son.

She took another step onto the boat, then looked around for a place to sit down.

From the cockpit, Jason frowned. "What the hell do you think you're doing?"

She blinked, surprised at his tone, then reached for one of the life vests sitting in a pile on the floor. "Um, getting ready?" She slipped it over her head and started securing its Velcro straps across her chest. Despite growing up in Los Angeles near the ocean, she was a lousy swimmer—an unfortunate by-product of having spent her childhood bouncing among foster homes. Swimming lessons required some modicum of stability.

As soon as she could afford it, Davy was taking swimming lessons. Guppy, goldfish, whale, and beyond. No doubt about it, her child was taking lessons.

The boat shimmied, its engine coming to a stop. Lane looked up to see Jason stalking toward her. Boreas, apparently sensing trouble, slipped down the stairs and into the small cabin belowdeck.

"Getting ready for what, exactly?" Jason asked. His voice held a no-nonsense tone she remembered well.

Oh, no. She knew what he was thinking, and there was no way in Hell—or in Hades, as he would say— that she was getting off this boat. She tilted her chin

171

up, drawing courage from the defiant gesture. "Getting ready to go look for my son."

"Sorry, sweetheart, but I can only look out for one amateur today, and your friend already elected Officer Boring."

"No problem," she answered.

He nodded, looking smug, then stepped aside, presumably clearing her exit path off the boat.

"I can take care of myself," she said instead. She leaned back, trying to look collected.

"Lane . . ." Exasperation laced his voice.

"Don't even," she said. She almost stood straight, wanting to get in his face, but decided against it. For one, being in close proximity to Jason messed profoundly with her ability to think coherently. Mostly, though, she didn't want to give him the opportunity to push her overboard and then speed away.

Not that he'd do such a thing, but . . . she wasn't certain. And that tiny bit of uncertainty kept her butt firmly planted on the rail.

"We're wasting time," she said. "Which do you want to do? Argue with me, or go rescue Davy?"

The muscle in his cheek twitched, and Jason aimed a finger at her. "You do what I say, or I swear I'll tie you to the hull just to keep you out of trouble."

She nodded, not actually willing to make an out-loud promise, but willing to seem to agree if it would get him to start the boat up again. She couldn't hear what he muttered under his breath as he walked away, but she could tell it wasn't nice.

He cranked the engine and started to maneuver

them out of the slip. From the dock, Hoop untied the rope, then tossed it onto the deck. "Be safe," he called. "All of you."

Lane nodded, and her eyes met Zoë's. She saw the fear reflected there, and a quick stab of guilt cut through her heart. By going, she was giving her friend one more person to worry about.

About that, though, there was nothing Lane could do. She *had* to go with Jason; she had to go to Davy. He was all alone, and he was surely scared. For years they'd only had each other; she'd be damned if she was going to fail him now.

Soon they were out of the marina and zipping across the wide-open ocean. Lane stood up and unsteadily made her way from her perch to Jason's captain's chair. He was focused on the controls, just as he had been for the last ten minutes. Not once had he turned to look at her, and he didn't now.

Her temper flared. "Dammit, Jason. He's my son. I'm sorry if you think it's inconvenient to have me along, or if you want to play the hero all by yourself or something, but I'm here. Deal with it. You just can't run off on your own again."

Mentally, she patted herself on the back for standing up to him. But when he turned and she saw his face, all of her self-congratulations faded. "Jason?"

As quickly as it had appeared, the pain in his eyes vanished, replaced by a stoicism she found unnerving. "I'm fine," he said.

"I don't think so." She put her hand on his shoulder and squeezed. "Tell me what you're thinking."

At first she thought he was going to refuse, but

then he swiveled in his vinyl seat to face her while keeping one hand on the boat's controls.

"I lost Davy," he said. "And I don't mean this morning, but years ago. Now I have the chance to get him back." He reached for her hand, squeezed it so hard she grimaced. "I *will* get him back."

Her brow furrowed. They'd been over this ground before. "I told you, I believe you."

He released a tortured sigh. "But there's more. I can get him back from Hieronymous—I know I can. I'll fight the man to the death if that's what it takes. But who do I fight for the rest?"

She licked her lips, not sure she was ready to hear what he meant. "The rest?"

"I want my *family* back, Lane."

She grasped the edge of the control panel, its sun-baked chrome hot against her palm. Her knees weren't quite up to the task of keeping her vertical, but she didn't want Jason to know that. No matter how many bells and whistles he set off in her insides, she wasn't going down *that* road again. Best to nip this little fantasy in the bud.

She opened her mouth to tell him that, but nothing came out.

Now, she urged herself.

This time when she tried, words actually emerged. *Good.* Always nice to have control over one's mouth. "Listen, Jason," she began, then cleared her throat. She sucked in a deep breath, hating to hurt him but needing the record to be clear. "The thing is, you never had a family. There's nothing to get back."

"I know," he said simply.

Lane blinked. That wasn't the response she'd been expecting. "Oh." She licked her lips, trying to decide where to go next. In her trial seminar, the professor had said to never let the jury know when a witness's answer ruffled you.

But Lane had a feeling Jason already knew she was ruffled. So much for a verdict being returned in her favor.

"I didn't mean to be blasé," Jason explained. He took her hand, his fingers sliding between hers. "It's just that I've spent a lot of time thinking about the situation. A lot more time than you, I mean. As much as I wish it weren't true, it would be both arrogant and stupid of me to think I could just pop back into your life and pick up where we left off." He shrugged. "I mean, you're a beautiful, bright woman. Hell, I'm surprised you aren't already married."

"Oh." She wasn't entirely sure what to say to that.

"We used to be wonderful friends," he went on. "I hope we still can be." He bit his lip, then reached out to take both her hands. "And I meant what I said. You need to do what I say. I want you safe, and losing you to Hieronymous—whether you're my friend or lover—would kill me. You're my *son's mother*. No matter what else is between us, that's forever."

His words brought tears to her eyes. She told herself they were tears of relief. "Really?"

He nodded. "Absolutely."

He was saying all the right things, and still she frowned. "I do have a boyfriend." The words just

175

popped out, and she cringed at the non sequitur. But Jason needed to know, needed to understand that she had another life now, that she'd found a man who fit that life—a man who wouldn't leave her or her son to run off and battle boogeymen. "He's fabulous with Davy."

"That's great," Jason said. But Lane noticed the hint of a shadow cross his face.

She cleared her throat. "So, uh . . . we're on the same wavelength, then? I mean, I just want to be clear."

The corner of his mouth twitched, and she frowned.

"What?" she asked.

"Just that you already sound like a lawyer, and you've been in law school less than a year."

"Yeah, well, I'm a quick study," she said. She was so happy to share a light moment with him that she didn't pause to wonder how he knew she was in law school. "But are we . . . ?"

He nodded, then took her hand, his skin rough against her palm. "Absolutely," he said. "Friends. Good, old friends. I want in Davy's life, but I won't push. We'll figure something out."

"Okay, then. Great." She took a deep breath and stood up. Certainly, she couldn't argue with that. And everything he was saying was what she wanted to hear. "Well. Right. Okay." She headed for the stairs leading belowdeck. "I'm glad we got that straightened out," she said.

But in truth, she wasn't glad. As much as she

wished she were, she wasn't glad at all. And that, frankly, had her more than a little worried.

Jason vowed to take up playing poker. If he could convince Lane he didn't want her anymore—that he hadn't spent years yearning for her, fantasizing about her, remembering the feel of her flesh under his fingers—then he could sure as Cerberus make five or six guys think he had a royal flush when all he really held was a pair of threes.

So Lane just wanted to be friends—no rekindling of their romance, no going back to where they'd left off. Well, if that's what the lady wanted, that's what he'd give her. He had made a career of starting over. And if her wishes meant starting over as friends—and working his way up the ladder from there—then that's what he was going to do. Lane might have another man in her life, but Jason had the advantage of being Davy's father. No matter what, that kept him in the game.

He did one more quick check of the control panel to confirm they were still on course, then set the boat to autopilot. He would have preferred to simply take a couple of propulsion cloaks and head to the island that way. But Hieronymous's island was well guarded against Protectors and, as he'd told Zoë, any approach from the air would surely be detected. A sea approach was still risky, but Jason intended to come from under the water, not on it, and he hoped that they could find a chink in Hieronymous's armor.

He'd already plugged the latitude and longitude

177

from Davy's map into the boat's computer—it was very similar to what he'd suggested upon his escape from Hieronymous's imprisonment—but he wanted to do some double-checking as only he could. After all, the Council had already looked and found nothing.

He killed the engine and let the boat float on the ocean's gentle waves. Pulling off all his clothes, he tossed them on the deck and slipped into the water. Under its surface he looked around, trying to find a sea creature who not only looked adventurous but had an impeccable sense of direction.

A flounder appeared and flashed him a quizzical look, but Jason let it swim on by. Flounder had a reputation for being patently unreliable. About twenty feet below, he caught sight of a great white shark. Jason almost called out, then decided to let it pass. For the most part the beasts were reliable, but lately they'd developed a grudge against mortals. Jason would hate to hang his hopes on a pissed-off psycho shark deciding to send him on a wild-goose chase.

Finally, a Girabaldi appeared, swimming slowly, talking to itself about its plans for the day. Jason caught the fish's attention, and it floated over. After more time than he intended—as a general rule, Girabaldi tended to be very chatty and needed a firm conversational hand—Jason got down to the nitty-gritty. Yes, there was an island where Jason suggested: the Girabaldi had swum past it the other week. It was just past the kelp bed and then there was a right turn at the sunken pirate ship—exactly as Jason remembered.

Apparently, the Council had sent an incompetent to check out his story.

Jason offered the fish a hearty thank-you and then propelled himself back to the surface. He hoisted himself out of the ocean and gave his head a good shake. Straightening, he turned around—and found himself staring right into Lane's intent gaze.

"Forgot my sweatshirt," she said, clutching the dark green garment she'd laid over the back of his captain's chair. She swallowed, her gaze darting up and down his naked body. When her cheeks flushed red, he did his best not to smile.

"I was just asking directions," he explained.

A pile of towels rested nearby. He made a point not to take one.

"Right," she said. She stood up straighter and kept her eyes on his face. "I always knew you were different."

He sucked in air, feeling a wash of shame. "I already apologized for not telling you I was a Protector."

The corner of her mouth twitched. "That's old news," she said. Flipping her sweatshirt over her shoulder, she headed back to the stairs. "I just meant that most men won't ask for directions." She flashed him an innocent little smile, then disappeared, returning to the galley below.

He grinned, more amused than he cared to admit. Damn, but he adored that woman.

He wanted to follow, but he supposed that he

should wear clothes. Boring was down there. And there were adjustments to the boat's controls to be made, too. Once he was back in his shorts and the dials and knobs of the autopilot were set, Jason left the boat to its own devices and headed belowdeck. Officer Boring was asleep on one of the small bunks, apparently storing up energy for the adventure ahead.

Jason frowned, realizing he still didn't know what special Protector skills Boring held. To the best of Jason's knowledge, being a super sycophant wasn't a recognized Protector trait.

Lane looked over from where she was standing, and her smile whisked from Jason's head all thoughts except of her.

"Are you hungry?" she asked. For a small boat with an owner who couldn't cook, the *Whirling Dervish* had a surprisingly well-equipped galley. Lane was hovering behind its counter, the heat turned up under a saucepan.

Something smelled better than ambrosia, and Jason pointed in the general direction of the stove. "Whatever you're making would be great."

Color immediately rushed to her cheeks. Jason had no idea what he'd said to induce such a reaction but, considering she looked positively adorable, he didn't regret saying it.

"I'm, uh, making omelets," she said, not quite meeting his eyes.

Understanding dawned as a memory returned, and a low chuckle rose in his throat. "One of your omelets sounds wonderful," he said, careful to keep his voice level. "Especially if it's mushroom and cheese."

She shot him a suspicious glance, but he kept his face blank.

"And a little burnt around the edges," he added.

Her suspicion changed to a glare, but there was a hint of amusement underneath. "I *can* cook," she said. "You just weren't helping."

"There was no incentive." He slipped onto one of the stools in front of the counter. "It was more fun distracting you."

"*Distracting,*" she said. "Is that what you were doing? And all this time I thought you were just being a pain in the butt."

"Is that what you thought?" He slipped off the stool, then circled the counter to stand behind her. He leaned in close to peer over her shoulder. Sure enough, she'd added mushrooms and cheese.

The curve of her rear brushed him, firing his senses. The last time she'd cooked for him they'd started out pretty much this same way, but . . .

"Jason," she said, her voice low and breathy. Her tone held both unasked questions and untapped possibility. He wanted to answer each, slowly, methodically, until she didn't have to ask any more because her every desire had been fulfilled.

"What?" he whispered.

He saw the faint movement of her throat as she swallowed, then felt more than heard her answer— "Don't."

The word had no meaning to him. "Don't what?" He leaned in closer, breathing her scent: vanilla, mixed with the subtle smell of the sea. It was intoxicating. Hera help him, his body was reacting like this from nothing but the scent of her?

She twisted, wriggling away from him. "Don't *that*," she said.

He blinked, getting his mind around the situation. Not only had his body been pressed against hers; he'd curled one arm around her waist.

He took a step back. "Sorry," he said, even though the only thing he was sorry for was stopping. "These little trips down memory lane aren't exactly conducive to remaining platonic."

She licked her lips. "I can't censor everything I say or cook," she said. "We were together for a long time. Just about anything either of us does will strike some memory, and I can't have you—"

"I said I was sorry." The words came out colder than he intended.

Lane's face lost some of its intensity as she exhaled. "It's just that I thought we were on the same wavelength. We can be friends—I *want* to be friends, especially if you want to be in Davy's life. But I can't . . ." She trailed off, her eyes wide and unblinking. "There can't be anything more than that."

Then she blinked and, before she turned her head, Jason thought he saw the glint of a tear. That tear kept him from saying the words that begged to be released—*What about me? Imprisoned for years with nothing but the memory of the woman I loved? The child I didn't know?* He couldn't get the words out. Why? Because he knew the answer; hell, that single tear practically screamed it. He'd gone off to fight his

GET UP TO 4 FREE BOOKS!

You can have the best romance delivered to your door for less than what you'd pay in a bookstore or online. Sign up for one of our book clubs today, and we'll send you **FREE* BOOKS** just for trying it out...**with no obligation to buy, ever!**

HISTORICAL ROMANCE BOOK CLUB

Travel from the Scottish Highlands to the American West, the decadent ballrooms of Regency England to Viking ships. Your shipments will include authors such as CONNIE MASON, SANDRA HILL, CASSIE EDWARDS, JENNIFER ASHLEY, LEIGH GREENWOOD, and many, many more.

LOVE SPELL BOOK CLUB

Bring a little magic into your life with the romances of Love Spell—fun contemporaries, paranormals, time-travels, futuristics, and more. Your shipments will include authors such as LYNSAY SANDS, CJ BARRY, COLLEEN THOMPSON, NINA BANGS, MARJORIE LIU and more.

As a book club member you also receive the following special benefits:

- **30% OFF all orders through our website & telecenter!**
- **Exclusive access to special discounts!**
- **Convenient home delivery and 10 day examination period to return any books you don't want to keep.**

There is no minimum number of books to buy, and you may cancel membership at any time. See back to sign up!

*Please include $2.00 for shipping and handling.

YES! ☐

Sign me up for the **Historical Romance Book Club** and send my TWO FREE BOOKS! If I choose to stay in the club, I will pay only $8.50* each month, a savings of $5.48!

YES! ☐

Sign me up for the **Love Spell Book Club** and send my TWO FREE BOOKS! If I choose to stay in the club, I will pay only $8.50* each month, a savings of $5.48!

NAME: _____

ADDRESS: _____

_____

TELEPHONE: _____

E-MAIL: _____

☐ **I WANT TO PAY BY CREDIT CARD.**

☐ VISA   ☐ MasterCard.   ☐ DISCOVER

ACCOUNT #: _____

EXPIRATION DATE: _____

SIGNATURE: _____

Send this card along with $2.00 shipping & handling for each club you wish to join, to:

**Romance Book Clubs
20 Academy Street
Norwalk, CT 06850-4032**

Or fax (must include credit card information!) to: 610.995.9274. You can also sign up online at www.dorchesterpub.com.

*Plus $2.00 for shipping. Offer open to residents of the U.S. and Canada only. Canadian residents please call 1.800.481.9191 for pricing information.

If under 18, a parent or guardian must sign. Terms, prices and conditions subject to change. Subscription subject to acceptance. Dorchester Publishing reserves the right to reject any order or cancel any subscription.

JOIN NOW!

own battles, and she was terrified he'd do it again. She was sure he would leave at the drop of a hat, go off to fight the bad guys—to battle Hieronymous. And the truth was, he probably would.

She slid the omelet onto a plate and put it between them. He looked, a little disappointed to see the egg not even slightly burnt. Not only had she grown up in the last seven years, she'd also learned how to cook.

Who the hell was he kidding? Of course she'd changed. She'd been out living her life; raising a son, trying to make a better way for herself.

He took a bite, thinking about the life he knew she now lived. "Why law school?" he asked.

A genuine smile lit her face as she took some toast out of a toaster. "Your sort," she said. She cut a piece of the omelet with her fork and popped it into her mouth, her eyes dancing with mystery.

"My sort?" he echoed, smiling back.

"Protectors. Superheroes." She shrugged. "The good guys."

"I see you're a fan," he said, "but I'm still not sure how law school fits in."

"Zoë's become one of my closest friends. So has her brother Hale, for that matter."

Jason raised an eyebrow. Hale's reputation for being less than friendly toward mortals was widespread.

"Oh, he's not going to start manufacturing I-Love-Mortal buttons or anything," Lane explained. "But there's a few of us he genuinely cares about. Some he even loves."

Jason hadn't ever met Hale, so he didn't argue. "But I still don't see the connection."

"Those two are always fighting bad guys," she said, stabbing the omelet aggressively with her fork. "I started to feel extraneous. My friends were doing all this amazing stuff, but if I tried to flip a mugger over my shoulder, I'd end up in traction. The mugger would be proud owner of all my belongings." She shrugged. "I took a kickboxing course. I lost three pounds, but I'm still a klutz."

"A cute klutz," he proposed.

When she frowned, he held up his hands in self-defense. "It's an empirical fact. You're cute. Can't a guy tell his friend she's cute?"

She rolled her eyes. "Okay. We'll say that one was on the line."

"And on the line counts in tennis. Fifteen-love."

She tried to glare but didn't much succeed. "Just watch it, okay?"

His eyes didn't leave hers. "Happy to."

She didn't scold him again, just cleared her throat. Her cheeks turned pink. "At any rate," she continued, her tone no-nonsense, "I wanted to do something useful. Something that would make an impact. I guess I wanted to be a good guy, too."

"So, I'm betting you don't plan on representing the accounting departments of major corporations?" One of the benefits of being stuck on Olympus for almost a year—he'd had plenty of time to watch the news.

She shot him a wry glance. "A district attorney. You guys catch them, and I'll prosecute them. Just like Batman and the police commissioner."

"Yeah. Except the commissioner never knew who Batman was. You know all our secrets."

Instead of answering, she carefully placed a bite-sized hunk of omelet on the corner of a piece of toast, then bit down, chewing thoughtfully. Jason frowned, wondering what she was thinking.

"Why didn't you tell me?" she finally asked.

So much for *that* mystery. Despite what she'd said on deck, the fact that he hadn't disclosed his secrets so many years ago was going to be a point of contention. He cleared his throat. "If I'd known you were going to become a prosecutor," he said, "I would have told you the day we met."

Her raised eyebrow suggested that she wasn't amused by his response, so he tried to change the subject.

"How did you get hooked up with Zoë and Hale, anyway?"

This time her eyebrow rose in surprise, not annoyance. "I assumed you knew," Lane said. "The story was all over the Protector newspaper and website at the time."

He shook his head. "It's amazing what news you miss living your life in a fishbowl." He immediately regretted the words. He didn't want to talk about that now; the topic was too dark, and it rekindled his anger. All he wanted at the moment was to share a few nice moments with Lane—sweet moments, before they reached the island and the hellish reality of their situation crashed down around them again.

For a second he thought she *was* going to ask what

he meant, but then she simply answered his question, describing how she'd purchased the stone from Aphrodite's Girdle, and how Zoë had rescued her from Mordichai, who'd been out to retrieve it for his father. "Zoë saved Davy that day, too," Lane added, and Jason's heart twisted with her utterance of the boy's name.

Her head cocked to one side. "Wait a second," she said. "You're Davy's father . . ." She trailed off.

He frowned, not understanding where her thoughts were headed. "What?"

"I just don't get it. I mean, Davy was all over the Council's news—we both were. But no one bothered to tell me he was a halfling."

"Ah," Jason said, knowing that he was included in the *no one*. "That would be my fault."

A wry smile touched her lips. "Why am I not surprised?"

"A halfling has to be registered. Since I wasn't available—"

"You never filed the paperwork."

"Exactly."

She shook her head. "I swear, the Council has more paperwork than the I.R.S."

"Eventually they do get around to discovering all the halflings—and quarterlings and whatnot—out there. Apparently at the time Zoë was being tested, they hadn't found Davy yet."

"So you probably still have to file that paperwork, huh?"

He swallowed. This wasn't exactly the way he'd

planned to raise the Council's edict about boarding school. "Yeah. Something like that."

She squinted at him. "What's that supposed to mean?"

"Right before we, uh, met again, I got a letter from Olympus. From the Council."

She crossed her arms. "A letter?"

He nodded. "Notifying me that I hadn't filed the proper papers when Davy was born, and also, uh, putting me on notice about Davy's schooling."

Lane's arms stayed crossed and her eyebrow went up. "His schooling?"

"Yeah." Jason got up, taking the dishes to the sink. "The Council wants Davy to attend boarding school." He spoke quickly and kept his back to her.

"*What?*" she shrieked.

He whirled to face her. "Careful," he whispered, his finger to his lips. He gestured to Boreas, still asleep on the bunk.

"I don't care who I wake up," she snapped, but this time she was quieter. "My son is *not* going away to boarding school."

"Actually, I have an idea about—"

"Who the hell do they think they are?" Lane got up and started pacing the small area. "He's *my* son."

"They just want to be sure he's properly trained. His skills honed. That kind of thing." Jason had a feeling that it wouldn't be the best time to mention who Davy's grandfather was—or that Davy was starting with a black mark against him in the High Elder's minds, one that would require more of him than other halflings.

"Zoë didn't have to go to boarding school," she protested. "She told me her mom raised her. Tessa didn't have any idea Zoë was a halfling."

"Yeah," Jason agreed. "That's kind of my idea. You see, if—"

"I mean, how *dare* they." Lane paced past him one more time, and he caught her arm on the return journey, tugging her close. She tilted her head back, her eyes wide with surprise.

"Would you just listen to me?" he asked. "I've been thinking about this for days. I think I've come up with a solution."

From the look on her face, she trusted him about as far as she could throw him. And though her son might be a Protector, Lane wasn't. He didn't expect she could throw him very far.

Even so, she nodded, silently inviting him to continue.

"Me," he said.

She made a whooshing motion over her head.

He tugged her toward the stools and urged her to sit. She hesitated but complied.

"The Council's concerned that Davy's skills won't develop right," Jason began. "That he'll be . . . uh, vulnerable to nefarious influences if someone from the Council isn't around to watch over him."

"But Zoë—"

"—had her father and Hale when she was growing up. From the Council's perspective, Davy doesn't have anybody."

"Glad to know my contribution counts for so much," Lane muttered.

"You know what I mean," Jason said. "And your contribution does count. I know it, and you know it." He sucked in a breath for courage. "And *my* contribution can count, too. I think it can count a lot, actually."

Her head tilted to one side. "Your contribution?"

"If I worked with Davy every day, helped him to hone his skills. Basically I'd give him the kind of Protector guidance he'd get in boarding school."

He'd been constructing the plan ever since he'd received Prigg's letter. Considering his own iffy status with the Council, it wasn't definite. But by proving his loyalty wasn't with Hieronymous, surely he'd also prove he was competent to educate his son. Which was one more reason to see his father destroyed.

Lane still hadn't answered; instead, she was perched on her stool, leaning forward, her elbows on the counter. Jason moved to the far side so that he could see her face, and when he did so she looked up, a question in her eyes. "Have you been sending Davy gifts?"

He blinked. This wasn't the question he'd expected. But he nodded.

"Why?"

"After I escaped, I spent months in debriefing under surveillance." He shrugged. "I guess I just wanted Davy to know I was out there." He shoved a hand into his pocket. "Did he, uh, like them?"

Lane's quick smile lifted his heart. "Oh, yeah. All of them were a big hit." Her head cocked slightly, and he saw different questions behind her eyes.

"How did you know?" she asked. "About law school. And where we lived. About everything?"

He swallowed. He'd been wondering when they'd get to that. "The Council monitors," he admitted. "I used to watch you while I was on Olympus. It gave me . . . something to hope for."

She licked her lips, her eyes narrowing. "You said the letter was from Olympus," she said. "About Davy's boarding school."

"Yeah," he answered, with some hesitation. "That's right."

"But if you just left Olympus, why'd they have to send you a letter?"

Busted.

"Jason?" she prompted.

He took a deep breath. "I've been finished with debriefing for about a month. I moved into the houseboat, brought this boat back from Greece. I also took care of some other stuff."

"And didn't come to see us." Her chin lifted along with her eyebrow.

"No," he admitted. "I'm sorry. I—"

"Why not?" The words weren't harsh. Instead they were genuinely curious—and a little bit hurt. "You say you wanted us back. And yet . . ."

"I know," he agreed. He closed his eyes, searching for the right words. "I wanted to figure out what I was doing first."

Her brow furrowed. "I'm not following."

"I've never had a kid." He paused, grimacing. "I mean, of course I *have* a kid, but—"

"I know what you mean."

"I didn't know what to do with him. I didn't know how to be a daddy." He sighed. "Hell, I still don't. But I know every Bob the Builder cartoon backward and forward, and, if you want, I can sing the entire *Lion King* soundtrack."

Her mouth twitched and Lane's eyes softened. She reached for his hands. When she gave his fingers a quick tug, he resisted the urge to hold tight and pull her close.

"You'll do fine," she said. "Trust me."

His heart twisted, her vote of confidence meaning more to him than he could ever have imagined. "And the training?" he asked.

Slowly, she nodded. "That's fine, too. It's a good plan, if they allow it." She breathed in, and he heard the hitch in her throat. A teardrop appeared in her eye and clung to her lower lashes. "But—"

"Don't even think that," he interrupted, realizing the direction her thoughts had taken. "He's fine. *He's fine,*" he repeated, to convince himself as much as her. "And you'll be hugging him and embarrassing him with kisses very soon."

She gnawed on her lower lip, and when she looked up at him, the fat tear in Lane's eye plopped to the counter. "How do you know?"

"I just do," he said. And her rules be damned; he moved back around the counter and urged her from the stool and into his arms. For just a moment he held her like that, sharing his strength and drawing courage from her warmth. He was scared, too. But for Lane—and for Davy—he had to be strong. "You

191

said you trusted me about this," he whispered. "Did you stop?"

She shook her head, pressed her face into his chest. "I do trust you," she said, her voice muffled. "I'm just anxious. And worried. And—"

"I know," he said. "Me, too."

They held each other for a while, the boat's engine surging beneath them, moving them closer and closer to their son and to danger.

"How much longer?" Lane asked after a moment.

"Soon," he said. "This boat is faster than mortal craft, and I've programmed it to take us right to the vicinity. The console will signal when we're—"

A chime rang, and he nodded. "That's it. We're here." He checked a display on the wall, confirming they'd in fact reached the programmed latitude and longitude.

"Do you really think he'll be here?"

He shrugged as they walked toward the stairwell. "Yes. I've . . . been here before. When I escaped, I paid attention. And, uh, just to make sure, I asked a fish."

"To think," she muttered, "I almost married a dolphin. Well, I'm probably the only woman in my trial advocacy class who can say *that*."

He shot her a grin and climbed the stairs. He knew she was still afraid, but if she was cracking jokes, at least she was coping. "The island should be coming up on the port side," he said as he reached the deck. He leaned down, giving her a hand up the narrow stairs.

As they both stood up, a slight shiver wracked his

body. He turned to see his former prison.

Except it wasn't there.

Here they were at the coordinates Davy's map had given and Jason remembered, yet just like the Council had reported, there was no island.

Chapter Eight

"It should be right here," Jason said, a knot of fear tightening in his chest. Was the Council right that the island wasn't in this location? Had he arrogantly run off to follow a red herring?

He pounded his fist on the side of the boat. "Right *here*. Heck, we should be only yards from one of the beaches."

"Maybe you read Davy's map wrong." Lane's teeth worried at her lower lip.

"No." He couldn't believe that. They had to be in the right place. He'd confirmed the location with a fish, for Hera's sake!

Damn it all to Hades. His son was in trouble. They didn't have time to be chasing ghosts. "No," he said, gripping the side of the boat. "This has to be the right place. Dammit, where's the island?"

"Maybe it's right in front of us." Boreas's voice startled him, and Jason twisted around. The neophyte Protector was in the stairwell, but he stepped all the way onto the deck, moving to join them at the rail of the boat.

"Are you delusional?" Jason snapped. Trying to keep his temper in check, he swept his arm at the miles of water spread out before them. "*There's no island.*"

Boreas's eyes widened, and Jason felt a quick twinge of guilt for being obnoxious. But it faded as fast as it came. He had other things to worry about than whether his Council-sent shadow thought he was being mean.

Besides, Officer Boring seemed to recover fast enough. The young man straightened his shoulders, lifted his chin, and pointed toward the water. "It's supposed to be right there?" he asked.

"Yes." Jason gave Lane's hand a gentle squeeze, letting her know he was still thinking about the real problem even while he entertained Boreas's useless questions.

"Maybe we just can't see it. Maybe it's cloaked."

"A whole island? That's the stu—" Jason snapped his mouth shut. As much as he hated to admit it, Boring just might have a point.

"Jason?" Lane asked.

"Stunningly insightful," he said, hooking an arm around Boreas's shoulder. "That's the most stunningly insightful idea I've heard all day." He aimed the kid toward the captain's chair and got him seated. "Go on."

The cadet shifted, looking none too happy about being steered. "It's, uh, just that Hieronymous is so good at inventing things. That's his skill, right? I mean, we studied him in Psychology of Outcasts during my last year at the Olympus Academy."

"Okay," Jason prompted.

Boreas looked from him to Lane, then back to Jason again. "Well, yeah. It's not like I've got a scientific explanation or anything. But you said the island was here. Now we can't see it. So, either you're wrong, or . . ."

"Hieronymous built something that can cloak a whole island," Lane finished.

It was sure as hell a good possibility. "Good thinking, Boring," Jason said.

"Boreas," the kid said.

"That's what I said." He turned to Lane. "We should check it out. If Boreas is right, Hieronymous will see us sniffing around. He might already know we're here, but it's a risk we have to take. If he *doesn't* know, I want to work fast before he clues in."

She nodded. "Great. I'm not a very good swimmer, but—"

"No, no, no," he said. Was she nuts? "I didn't mean you and me. *We* meant me and Boreas."

"But—"

"No buts, Lane. That was our deal. Remember? You'd listen to me? I'm already going to have to keep an eye out for him. I can't be worrying about you, too. Stay here. Sit tight. And in just a little bit we'll be getting the hell out of here with Davy."

Once again she opened her mouth to protest. He

couldn't resist; he silenced her with a kiss.

She startled him by kissing him back, hard and demanding, before pulling away and meeting his eyes. "For luck," she said simply. "Bring back our son."

Jason nodded, then gestured to Boreas. The young Protector trotted over, happy as a puppy to be included, and Jason plucked his holo-pager off his belt. Before handing it to Lane, he set the frequency to his own assigned channel.

"Ever used one of these before?" he asked.

She shook her head, turning the small metal device over in her hand.

"It's easy." He leaned over her and punched the controls, turning off the hologram feature so that only its voice capabilities remained. "Works just like a walkie-talkie. You push here, and it signals on my end with a silent vibration." He gestured to the pager at his waist. "If it's safe, I'll take it off vibrate-mode and we can talk. That way, if you get antsy, you can check up on us."

She still didn't look too crazy about waiting on the boat, but she did nod. When she punched the button, the pager at Jason's waist vibrated. "Like that?" she asked.

"Just like that."

"So, what? Does the Council buy their equipment at Office Depot?"

It was a bad joke, a testament to her nerves. He just stroked the side of her face, then went into the boat's head. Inside, he stripped off his sweatpants and donned a thin wetsuit. He didn't need it, of course, but considering he was going to be wandering around inside Hieronymous's island labyrinth, he thought it best to be somewhat clothed. His pager, a small flashlight, a serrated knife, and a few other gadgets clung to his utility belt.

Exiting, he looked Lane up and down. "Are you wearing a bathing suit?"

She gave him a *duh* look and gestured to her shorts.

"Just put one on under your clothes, okay? There's one in the cabin, first drawer on the left." He'd bought suits for both her and Davy two weeks ago and had tucked them away, hoping for a more laidback outing. Now the purchase was coming in handy.

She raised an eyebrow but nodded.

He moved to the edge of the boat and then, with a quick salute, fell backward into the water. *Heaven.* The water surrounded him, buoyed him, gave him courage and strength. If he could just get Hieronymous into the ocean, it would be all over.

He shook his head, focusing on the task at hand. *Revenge, later. Davy, now.*

He did a quick flip underwater to get his bearings . . . and saw the base of an island due east. Just as Boreas had suspected: Above the water, the island was invisible, but it was there!

He frowned, looking around for the other Protector, then realized he was all alone. Exasperated, he kicked to the surface. Popping up beside the boat he saw Lane and Boreas were both still on deck, watching the water with curious glances.

"Are you coming?" he asked Boreas.

"Oh." The young Protector looked down at his clothes, to Lane, and then to Jason in the water. "Right. Yes. Sure. Uh."

Jason sighed. "Under the life vests."

Boreas looked and found a wetsuit. Lane turned her back, and Boreas scrambled into it.

"You'll need air," Jason said, rethinking bringing Officer Boring along. But backup might come in handy. He pointed Boreas to the air canisters he kept on board, just in case. The neophyte donned the tank.

Finally ready, Boreas dove into the water, not nearly as clumsily as Jason expected.

"I'll be back," Jason promised Lane before he descended. "And I'll have Davy with me."

"So, this is command central?" Mordi said, pacing behind his father.

"It is," his father agreed. "I'm pleased you are taking an interest."

They were no longer in the main cavern. They'd relocated to a smaller room that overlooked that hanger-sized space, much as a press box overlooked a football field. Three sides of this rectangular room were cut from stone; the fourth side—made of glass—provided a stunning view of the goings-on below.

Hieronymous sat behind a solid steel desk, his back to the window, and drummed his fingers on its polished top. In front of him, the usual row of computer monitors was mounted in the rock. Yet, in this room, there was no screen displaying a stock ticker. Every image was some part of the island: its silent corridors, its iron gates, Davy's small room.

On the far monitor, and out of the corner of his eye, Mordi saw figures near the gates leading into the water-flooded tunnels beneath the island. He sucked in a deep breath and held it.

His father turned to him, questioning.

Casually, Mordi moved to the left, blocking his father's view of the monitor.

"Is there something you wish to say?" Hieronymous asked.

"No, sir. I mean, yes, sir. I mean, uh, it's all just so awe-inspiring."

Hieronymous stared at him, and for a moment, Mordi feared the jig was up. Then his father nodded coldly, a tiny hint of a smile touching his lips. "Yes. It is. Much of what I do inspires awe—particularly in those less technologically-inclined."

"It is a lot to take in," Mordi agreed, moving toward the bank of controls. He started fiddling with the knobs, managing in the process to switch Davy's monitor to one that showed the mess hall, and all of Hieronymous's Outcast groupies sitting around chowing down on some disgusting-looking slop. He turned back to Hieronymous. "Maybe you could teach me the basics? I mean, if you think I could handle it."

An unfamiliar light flared in Hieronymous's eyes. "I think much of it should be within your grasp," he said. He laid a light hand upon Mordi's shoulder, even as he gestured at the full set of controls with the other. "We'll start with the basics."

One by one, he started taking Mordi through each dial's purpose. An odd feeling swelled in Mordi's gut. His father was actually working with him. Not patronizing—well, not much—but just working.

And, if all went well, Mordi would be asked to use everything his father taught him to foil the man's plan.

He told himself he shouldn't feel guilty, that right was right and wrong was wrong. And he knew that was true. But it didn't fill the hole in his gut. It didn't fill that same hole Hieronymous had started to fill, simply by placing a hand on Mordi's shoulder and a grudging but sincere vote of confidence.

Little by little the world shifted under Mordi's feet. And damned if he wasn't sorely afraid he'd lose either his balance or himself.

Davy sat cross-legged in front of the door, staring at its lock. His toilet lamp was turned off. The sun had climbed high enough to light the room, so Davy had put his shoe back on. It was a little squishy, but he figured he might need it.

It was hard to run in one shoe, and Davy was going to run away.

He'd waited all night for his mom or his aunt to rescue him, but they hadn't come. He knew they would have if they could, so they were either lost or Mr. Hieronymous had caught them. And Uncle Taylor couldn't rescue him or his mom or Aunt Zoë, because he was all the way in Switzerland. Davy had looked that up on his globe and it was really far away.

His tummy ached when he thought about the bad man keeping his mommy locked up, so he hoped she just didn't know where to find him. He didn't want her in danger.

Of course, Davy didn't know where he was, either. Or how to get home. He knew they'd taken a boat. He'd made a boat last month and cruised it around his bathtub, so maybe if he could get out of this room and find Mr. H's boat, he could at least make it go away from this island. The boat would have some sort of radio, so he could call his mom for help from there.

All he had to do was get out.

After the pretend daddy had brought him food last night, the man had held something flat, about the size of his mom's plastic money, up to the door. There'd been a clicking sound, and then the door had swung open. Since there wasn't a regular keyhole, Davy figured the lock must be electronic. Or magnetic. Or something. He just needed to find out which.

Easy squeezy. Well . . .

He sucked on his lower lip, wishing he had his tools. It wasn't actually going to be easy making a key from the stuff in this room.

He crawled around on his hands and knees, checking under the bed and looking behind the toilet, gathering up everything that might help. A few minutes later he climbed onto the bed and rested his chin on his fist. He stared at the pile of goodies he'd gathered.

His Walkman, one bedspring, the metal stopper for the sink, and four thumbtacks from the Teletubbies poster on the wall.

Cool. Now he just had to put it all together.

He looked out the window, trying to figure out the time. If he worked really fast, chances were he could be out by lunch.

Maybe he'd even be home by dinner.

A series of caverns wound beneath Hieronymous's island, opening back out into the sea at various points along its perimeter. The island was only about five miles in circumference, but Jason wasn't inclined to waste time examining each and every portal to find the one from which he'd escaped. Instead, he approached the first entrance he saw, with Boreas right at his heels.

The cavern's opening was gated: a wrought-iron contraption that looked like it had been untouched for years. But its padlock was brand-new and shiny.

Jason pointed to the lock and flashed Boreas a thumbs-up. If Hieronymous had bothered to place a lock on this door, odds were good it led into the complex.

Now all they had to do was get in.

He gave the lock a quick tug, hoping his superstrength would snap it. No luck. He turned to Boring and gave a shrug, then tried again. And again. And again.

So much for superstrength. Apparently it was no

match for Hieronymous's metallurgic skills.

He gave it one last shot, this time balancing his feet against the rock exterior of the cavern, his hand clamped firmly around the padlock. He tugged with all his might, using his foothold on the stone for leverage.

Again, he got nothing for his trouble except a sore shoulder and the subtle imprint of the lock in his palm.

Well, hell.

Boreas swam closer, gesturing to the bars. Jason shrugged, unable to make any sense out of his motions. Again Boreas pointed, and Jason shot him a scathing glance, irritated. He needed to figure a way out of this problem, not an overeager Protector bouncing around and distracting him.

Okay. One last try. He positioned himself once more, his hands on the lock, ready to tug. But as he did, Boreas bumped him. Jason grimaced, wanting to yell at the guy to stay out of the way—but yelling would only get him a mouth full of water.

Reaching over, he planned to bodily pick Boreas up and relocate him to the rock ledge above the gate. Surely he'd be out of the way there. But just as Jason reached, so did Boring. And reached. And reached.

Jason blinked, his mind coming to grips with what he was seeing: Boreas's arm stretching all the way through the bars to a bare rock wall inside . . . to where a single silver key hung on an ornate hook.

Guess that answered the what-power-does-Boreas-have question. Apparently, the man was made of rubber.

With a smug grin, Boreas drew his arm back and handed Jason the key. Jason took it, slid the key into the lock, and turned it. The tumblers fell into place. Boreas gave a little bow, and Jason shook his head and rolled his eyes. The gate creaked open, and they swam inside.

They'd made it into Hieronymous's complex. Now they just had to find Davy.

"I've done my rounds, sire," Clyde reported from the doorway. "All is well."

"Excellent." Hieronymous stood up and walked toward the window wall, gazing down at the cavern below. "Only four more days. The anticipation . . ." He shivered. "It's intoxicating."

For Mordi, it wasn't intoxicating; it was unnerving. He'd managed to switch the monitors showing Davy's cell and several underground corridors to different views, but Hieronymous might notice at any moment. And Mordi was antsy to see what was happening, too. He shouldn't risk it, but . . .

He couldn't stand it anymore. With one quick glance to make sure his father was occupied, he flipped to the monitor showing the corridors beneath the island. Two dark figures clad in wetsuits padded through the dark, their backs to the walls.

Mordi sucked in a deep breath, relief flooding him. *Jason.* If Jason could free Davy, the ball would no longer be in Mordi's court. There'd be one less dilemma he'd have to deal with.

Another quick glance over his shoulder confirmed that Hieronymous was still talking to Clyde. Mordi switched the monitor's view again, this time flipping to an empty corridor. He moved down the console to the monitor tied in to Davy's room. He'd just take a quick peek to make sure the boy was doing okay—

"Are you comfortable with the controls?"

Mordi dropped his hand, turning to look at his father even as he schooled his face in a bland expression.

"Yes, sir," he said. "As a matter of fact, I think I've finally got the hang of this."

"There is an island, there is an island, there is an island."

Lane repeated the words over and over, hoping that mere repetition would convince her that it was true—because, frankly, it didn't *look* like there was an island. To her eye, she was stranded in a small boat in the middle of the ocean with nothing but water as far as she could see.

She tugged her life vest tighter and shifted her rear end from the edge of the boat to the captain's chair—just in case.

Gnawing on her lower lip, she peered out into the water, looking in the direction in which Jason and Boreas had disappeared. Shouldn't there be bubbles rising to the surface or something? How could they stay down there so long? And Jason hadn't even taken any air.

Surely hours had passed, and she was hot and scared and alone.

Her fingers closed around the pager Jason had given her. All Lane wanted to do was check in, see how they were progressing. But then she caught sight of her watch. *Six minutes.* They'd been gone for six minutes, and she was already freaking out.

She took three deep breaths, clipped the pager back on the waist of her shorts, and reclined, trying to be calm.

Fat chance. If she survived this afternoon without going crazy, it would be a miracle.

"My sentry has detected intruders, sir." Clyde stood in the doorway and gave Mordi a disdainful glance.

Mordi licked his lips, sure that he was a dead man for having "missed" seeing the intruders on the monitors.

"What?" His father's voice cut a cold path down his spine.

"In the east corridor, sir. If they continue forward, they will surely seal their own doom. Nevertheless, I wanted to report them to you."

"As well you should," Hieronymous agreed. He walked toward Clyde. "Come, let us see these brave but foolish visitors."

He paused at the door, and Mordi held his breath, fearing his father would want to sneak a peek at these security monitors, which, at the moment, held no image of the east corridor.

But, "Keep an eye on the boy," was all he said. Then Hieronymous turned on his heel and followed Clyde out.

Mordi sighed in relief. He didn't envy Jason's upcoming confrontation, but at the moment he was simply happy to have dodged his own bullet.

As soon as he could see Hieronymous and Clyde through the window in the cavern below, Mordi locked the door and switched all the monitors back. He pressed the button to feed sound directly into the room, and then he settled back to watch the east corridor, hoping that, no matter who won, he would be on the right side of the eight ball.

Oh, crap.

Jason remembered this corridor. He'd almost gotten killed here during his escape. It was littered with booby traps, and he hoped that after a year he could remember how to get past the dang things.

Back then, it had taken him seven solid hours to work his way slowly and methodically down the craggy hallway. Today, he didn't have that kind of time.

"Hurry up," Boreas whispered. "Someone's going to see us." The young man brushed past, sending a swirl of sparkling dust through the shaft of light that cut through the darkness before him.

Light? Jason frowned.

Boreas moved forward, the light hitting his shoulder.

Hopping Hera! Jason dove, throwing himself on the other Protector and slamming him to the ground.

"What the—?" Boreas struggled to get up. Jason held him down. Dozens of razor-sharp spears whizzed by, barely missing their flattened bodies and smashing into the solid rock wall behind them.

When Jason let Boreas roll over, the man's eyes were wide. "Wow. I wasn't expecting that."

Jason exhaled, irritated with the cadet but glad they'd both survived. "Directive four-three-seven-b. Never rush into an unknown situation." He aimed a stern glance at Boreas. "Next time do what I say, okay?"

"No problem," the other Protector said, looking more than a little sheepish. He squinted at the wall from which the spears had spewed forth. "But how'd you—"

"Instinct," Jason lied, crawling on elbows and knees past the trap.

Boreas followed, scooting on his belly. "Really?"

Footsteps sounded in the distance, and Jason edged against the wall, pushing Boreas back. The shadows were deep enough to hide in, and they barely breathed, waiting for the sound to pass.

"A guard?" Boreas whispered when it had. They started forward again.

"Probably," Jason replied. He wasn't entirely sure. The footsteps had been erratic, not the usual measured steps of a sentry walking a post. Whoever it was, Jason wasn't inclined to meet him.

He crooked a finger, urging Boreas to follow. Maneuvering past a few more traps, they negotiated the hallway, slipped around a corner, and walked into a cell block.

It wasn't hard to figure out which cell would be Davy's: the only one with a closed door. Jason crept over. The door was locked, of course.

Boreas just smiled. "Leave this to me."

He rushed off before Jason could stop him—back toward the possible sentry. Jason fumed, and was just about to follow when the neophyte returned.

"Don't ever . . ." Jason trailed off when he saw the plastic card dangling from Boreas's finger. "How?" he asked.

"Easy," the kid said. He stretched his arm out a good five feet, made his fingers ultra-thin. "If I don't make it as a superhero, I can always support myself through the fine art of pickpocketing."

Jason grinned. Taking the key, he opened the cell door and stepped inside, his heart pounding. "Davy?"

No boy ran to him. In fact, the cell was quite empty. A half-eaten sandwich was the only sign that someone had been there at all.

Chapter Nine

He wasn't answering her page.

Lane sucked in four deep breaths and told herself to be calm. He was probably just occupied. Busy. Right in the middle of rescuing her son. Surely he wasn't flat on some concrete slab with a buzz saw about to slice and dice him.

She glanced at her watch. Thirteen minutes since they'd left.

Dammit, he should be answering!

She tried again. Waited. Still no answer.

Visions of snarling, drooling hellhounds filled her thoughts. Mad scientists, performing experiments on the captured Jason and Boreas. Davy, kicking and screaming as Hieronymous burst through a glass ceiling à la *The Poseidon Adventure*, and then flew away, his maniacal cackle echoing over the waves.

Sharp pain shot through her hands and she realized she'd dug her fingernails into her palms, drawing blood.

This time she took five deep breaths. They didn't help. She tried another page. Still no answer.

Okay, then. Apparently it was up to her to rescue her son, her former lover, and a freshman Protector. No problem. Except for the swimming-to-shore part, no problem at all.

With one more deep breath for courage, she slipped off her shorts, revealing the bathing suit Jason had provided her, and peered over the edge of the boat. The water looked deep and black. If there were sharks down there, were they going to think she was lunch?

And what if the boat had drifted? She thought the invisible island had been to the left, but maybe it was now to the right. Should she jump in and just start paddling? She might reach Australia before she reached Davy.

Not that that would happen, of course. She'd be fish food long before she made it to Australia.

Still, what choice did she have? Her son was in danger, and so was Jason. By God, she was going to help!

Carefully, Lane stood and placed one foot on the edge of the boat, then the other, until she was balanced on the side. Quickly, before she had time to think about it, she held her nose and jumped.

Warm water enveloped her, but her head didn't go under thanks to her life jacket. She started paddling, hoping like heck she was headed in the right direction.

After a bit, the air shimmered in front of her. She blinked, wondering if her serious lack of food was going to her head. The air shimmered again, only this time, Lane thought she saw the faint outline of rocks and palm trees. Wishful thinking? Or the island?

She paddled faster, this time adding a kick for good measure. Her toes hit something solid and she recoiled, fearing she'd just smacked a hungry shark in the head. But when she looked down, she didn't see a shark, but sand.

She'd made it! And the island was closer than she'd realized. Looking up, she saw its wide expanse: a sandy beach ending in dense foliage.

Something moved in the foliage, and Lane twisted, futilely searching for a hiding place. She tried to duck under the water, but her life vest kept her up, so she just held her breath, staying very, very still, and hoped that whoever was coming wouldn't look in her direction.

More movement, more rustling of leaves. Just past the beach the branches shook, something emerging from the shadows. There was a flash of skin, and then—

"Davy!" With her heart about to explode, Lane sloshed forward. Her life jacket was wet and heavy, so she yanked it off, tossing it over her head.

"Mommy!" Her son's eyes widened and he ran to her, his little legs splashing through the surf.

They met at the top of the beach, and Lane

scooped Davy into her arms, dropping to her knees and smothering him with kisses. "Oh, my sweet baby!" she gasped. She gripped his shoulders and pushed him back to look him over. "Are you okay? Did Hieronymous hurt you?" She lifted his shirt and started to look for bruises.

"Mommy," he protested, smoothing the shirt back down. "I'm okay." He pressed closer, his arms tight around her neck.

Lane's legs turned to rubber and she sank down, sitting fully on the sand with Davy in her lap. She didn't want him to see her crying, so she pulled him close, pressing his head against her chest as she fought tears. They were inevitable, she knew that; but maybe if she tried hard enough she could hold off until she was home, curled up on the sofa, with a pillow pressed tight to her face.

With effort, she pulled herself together, then leaned back, needing to look at him one more time. She stroked her boy's hair, laughing with delight at the way he squirmed, his protests of "Mo-mmy," falling on deaf ears.

Thank God he was safe. She just kept repeating that over and over in her mind, like a mantra. *Thank God, and thank Jason.*

She frowned, looking around, but there was no sign of him. Had he stayed behind? Had he been caught by Hieronymous? Did he need her help?

"Where's Jason?" she asked, tilting Davy's head up. She held her breath, half-expecting to hear that he was trussed like a turkey above a vat of boiling oil. She didn't expect the answer she got.

"Who?" Davy asked.

"Jason," she repeated. "Your . . . uh . . . the man who rescued you."

He shook his head, his eyes wide. "Nobody rescued me, Mommy. I rescued myself."

Jason's stomach twisted as he and Boreas crept through the tunnels searching for Davy. The boy's cell was empty, which meant Hieronymous must have taken him somewhere else. Jason didn't know where, but he damn sure would find out.

His pager vibrated, and Jason cupped his hand over it, just about to answer when they reached the end of the corridor. A cavern loomed ahead, huge and foreboding. Inside, Hieronymous stood before a massive structure covered with midnight-black cloth.

Davy was under that cloth; somehow, Jason just knew. He had to get his son free.

In a flash, Jason pressed his back against the wall, slamming Boreas back as well. His heart pounded in his chest, so loud he feared his Outcast father could hear. His pager vibrated again, but Jason couldn't do anything but stand stock still. He wanted to answer, to tell Lane that he was all right and that he'd find Davy, but Hieronymous was too close. He couldn't risk the man overhearing him.

"Well, well, well." His father's deep voice echoed through the chamber.

Jason cringed. *Too late.* Hieronymous was walking toward them.

Passing Boreas the vibrating pager, Jason signaled

for him to get back. Then he took a deep breath, drew himself to his full height, and stepped into the center of the corridor—and into Hieronymous's clutches.

"Look, Clyde," Hieronymous said to the Outcast standing beside him. "The prodigal son returns." He lifted his hand, revealing a silver orb resting in his palm. Returning his full attention to Jason, he asked, "Are you coming to accept my invitation at last? Or to meet your doom?"

"Neither," Jason answered. He clenched his fists, fighting the urge to once and for all go *mano a mano* with his father. Time enough for that later. Right now, he had to help Davy. He met Hieronymous's icy gaze. "I'm here to rescue my son."

"Pity," Hieronymous said. "I had so hoped to have a son—*an heir*—who was worthy of inheriting my empire."

"You don't have an empire," Jason snapped. "You have a delusion."

A dangerous smile touched Hieronymous's lips. "Ah, but I will have one." He extended his hand, the silver orb balanced on his palm. "And you can be part of it. Or you can die."

"I'm gonna go with none of the above," Jason said. He moved with lightning speed, retrieving the knife from his utility belt and taking deadly aim. But just before the blade left his hand, Hieronymous's orb hummed with power and emitted a flash of light.

Jason howled, recoiling, as pain seared his arm. He glanced down to see an angry red welt where his wetsuit was sliced below the shoulder.

"Bastard," he snarled.

"Next time, the beam will find your heart." Hieronymous took another step forward. "Perhaps you would like to reconsider my most generous offer?"

Jason gave him the finger.

"How very eloquent," Hieronymous replied. He looked sideways toward Clyde.

Jason took advantage of the moment to rush forward. It was foolhardy, maybe, but dammit, he wanted to get his hands around his father's neck. As he moved, Clyde called out.

Hieronymous turned back, and immediately hurled his orb at the ground in front of Jason. The impact released a burst of white fog, sickly sweet, like apples simmering in brown sugar.

Jason tried to continue on, tried to get to Hieronymous, but his muscles wouldn't work. His legs couldn't support him; he fell backward against the cavern wall, hanging on to a rocky outcropping for dear life.

"Dear boy," Hieronymous asked, striding toward him over Clyde's crumpled form. "Did you really think you could defeat me? With my intellect? With my resources?" He shook his head. "How silly."

He bent over to retrieve Jason's knife. "It pains me to do this, of course. I get no pleasure in disposing of one of my own blood."

"Davy," Jason said, forcing out the word as his fingers dug into the wall behind him in an attempt to stay upright.

"The boy will survive my procedure, I assure you." Hieronymous's shoulder lifted just slightly. "He will,

217

of course, have a somewhat altered brain, but that simply can't be helped. You, however . . ." He trailed off, hatred kindling in his eyes. "You could have been everything to me, and yet you chose to slap me in the face. You, *son*, will not survive."

Jason tried to will his muscles to move, but they would not. Hieronymous threw the knife. As the deadly blade headed straight for Jason's heart, a dozen regrets danced through his head. He closed his eyes, thoughts of Lane and Davy filling his last moments. And then—

Nothing.

He opened his eyes, his brow furrowed.

The knife clattered to the floor across the room, and Boreas's arm—long and elastic—was snapping back. The young Protector had shot his arm out, slingshot style, and knocked the blade clear. Now, on his hand's return journey, Boreas grabbed the back of Jason's wetsuit and pulled him back into the tunnel.

As Hieronymous looked on, dumbfounded, Boreas took Jason in his arms and bounced both of them across the chamber toward the water in its center.

"Davy," Jason said, his voice a weak protest.

"Lane has him!" Boreas whispered. "I answered her page."

Relief flooded Jason. Davy was safe.

No thanks to him, of course.

With the bitter taste of failure still clinging to Jason's tongue, Boreas dove them into the water. The last thing Jason saw before the current took him, was

Hieronymous's dumbstruck face—and the vow of vengeance burning in his eyes.

Mordichai stared at the monitor, his mouth slightly agape. *Son?* Hieronymous had called Jason son?

All these years, he'd thought he was the only one, the heir-apparent to Hieronymous's definite fortune and dubious fame. Now, to find out that he had a brother, and a full Protector at that . . .

A twinge of jealousy prickled him, tempered by an odd sense of melancholy. Mordi stared, transfixed, at the monitor. Only moments before it had revealed his sibling, the man Hieronymous wanted for his heir. Not Mordi. Never Mordi.

Or maybe . . .

Now that Jason was so clearly out of the picture, perhaps Mordi's stock had gone up. In Hieronymous's eyes, maybe a loyal halfling son was better than a traitorous pureblood. *Interesting.*

He tapped his lip, wondering. What had he lost by not knowing of Jason's existence? More important, what might he gain in the future?

Lane couldn't stop hugging Davy. Couldn't stop looking in his eyes. Couldn't stop running her fingers through his baby-fine hair.

He was back. She'd gotten her baby back!

She was so wrapped up in Davy that she didn't notice the tripwire she'd scooted backward against and managed to pull taut. Davy's shriek alerted her, but by then, of course, it was too late; she and he were dangling upside down from a palm tree, caught in an old-fashioned hunter's net.

Not a great situation, to say the least. Even worse, from her new vantage point she could clearly see a camera mounted among the palm tree's coconuts.

Hieronymous was watching. Which meant he'd be coming soon.

"Mommy!"

"I know, sweetie. We need to get out of here." Lane tugged at the ropes with her hands, but they held fast. She needed something to cut them with, but she didn't have anything. She'd jumped into the water wearing only her bathing suit, a T-shirt, and a tiny waist pack with her keys, driver's license, a tube of Blistex, a pair of fingernail clippers, and some Coppertone. The pager had been clipped to the waist pack's strap, but now she could see it on the ground below her, half buried in the soft sand.

Great. This didn't leave her a whole lot of options.

She cocked her head, running the inventory through her mind one more time. Was there anything to cut with? Yes. "Davy, honey, can you reach my pack?"

She was half-sitting on him, probably squashing him, but she could feel him nod, then felt his little hands searching her. After a second, she heard her pack's zipper. "You want the clippers, Mommy?"

"That's right." She reached down blindly. "Can you hand them to me?"

He couldn't. His arms were too short. And he certainly couldn't throw them. Lane couldn't catch on her best days, and she wasn't about to try while hanging upside down and backward.

"Want me to start clipping, Mom?"

"You better believe it," she said. Then, while her son clipped, Lane did the only thing she could do. She waited.

By the time Jason emerged in the shallow water of an island lagoon, Hieronymous's drug had worn off, and Jason's body was his own again. He was half-tempted to turn right back around, to take his father on again, but then he caught sight of the beach. Upon it, Lane and Davy were suspended from a coconut tree.

"Jason!" she called. "There's a camera! Hieronymous! Is he coming? Do you see him?"

Jason didn't, but that didn't mean the man wasn't right behind him. Under the circumstances, Hieronymous was probably starting to comb the whole island for him—and now probably his son.

Familiar fear rose in his throat. They were all in danger now. And though he'd wanted his family back, he sure as hell hadn't wanted them all trapped together in a fishbowl.

With Boreas at his heels he raced forward, thrilling at the way his muscles again responded to his commands. His mind sorted through the fastest way to get his family down.

As it turned out, that wasn't a problem. Right as he approached the net split, and Lane and Davy tumbled to the ground. Davy immediately broke out in peals of laughter, but Lane just lay there. Jason was pretty sure his heart stopped the second she hit the ground.

"Lane?" he asked.

She groaned, rolling onto her side. "Ouch," she said.

He was next to her in an instant. "Are you okay?"

She nodded. "I'm fine. Soft sand."

Davy watched Jason through narrowed eyes for a moment, then scooted closer to his mother. It didn't trouble Jason. There'd be time enough for father-son bonding later. Right now, he was too relieved that everyone was safe to think about anything else.

Clutching her arm, he pulled Lane to her feet. The urge to throttle her was almost as strong as the urge to kiss her, to hold her tight—to never, *ever*, let her out of his sight again.

He pushed back, still holding her, but needing to see Lane's eyes. What would he have done if Hieronymous had captured her? Or worse? "What the hell are you doing here? Do you know how stupid—" The words were out of his mouth before he had time to think.

The expression on her face shifted from one of relief to one of irritation, even anger. Automatically he stepped back, increasing the space between them even as he continued to hold her arms.

No use. She jerked free, then took Davy's arm and led the boy to Boreas. "Get him to the boat," she said. The young Protector nodded, led Davy to the edge of the water.

The kid didn't look too happy. He kept looking back at Jason and Lane. "Mommy? Are you coming?"

"I'm right behind you, sweetie."

Davy aimed a glare at Jason. "With *him?*"

"That's right. It's okay. Trust me." She turned to Jason. "But as for you, where the hell do you get off? Did you really expect me to just twiddle my thumbs while you rushed off to rescue my son?"

He urged her toward the water. "I expected you to *follow the plan,*" he explained, his voice less harsh. She was safe, and his initial wave of fear had crested.

"The plan where you answered my pages and told me what was going on?" she asked. She looked ready to explode; then she sighed. "Okay, maybe it was stupid of me to come . . . but I was all alone, Jason. I thought Davy needed help. Hell, I thought *you* needed help."

They were in the water now. He cut through the waves with ease, one arm on Lane's elbow as he towed her forward. She glared at him, but didn't resist.

"You swam to shore?" he asked, surprised.

She nodded.

"That was brave," he said. It wasn't exactly an apology, but it was the best he could manage under the circumstances.

"Damn straight it was."

There was a pause; then he grinned, and she grinned back.

"I *am* sorry," she said. "I had to get Davy. I didn't know what had happened to you. I never meant to get caught."

"No one ever does," he agreed, thinking about his

past. And then there was this time. Boreas had done good.

"Yes, but he's *my* son, and I wasn't going to stand by when I could do something to help. He needed his mother."

Jason tugged her closer. "He's my son, too."

"By blood, maybe, but you didn't raise him. You didn't change his diapers. You didn't watch 'Barney' over and over until you swore you were going to take out a contract on that dinosaur's life."

"Don't you think I wanted to? Don't you think I spent every day that I was trapped in that aquarium dying inside?"

Tears began to stream down her face, mingling with the water of the ocean, and Jason's insides crumpled. He didn't want to see Lane cry. He hated feeling helpless, but he didn't have any idea how to stop the flood.

"I'm sorry I got Davy and me trapped," she said between sniffles. "But I had to come. I had to get Davy."

Jason sighed, her words cutting a hole in his heart. He understood. "No, it's my fault. I shouldn't have expected you to stay put. And, all things considered, I definitely shouldn't have expected you to trust *me* to find him."

She tilted her head back as he pulled her through the water, her eyes wide with surprise. "Don't say that. I *did* trust you."

He shook his head. "Well, it's a moot point, since the boy rescued himself."

"He's a smart kid," Lane agreed. She licked her

lips. "A lot smarter than me. I guess I didn't do much of anything except almost get us caught."

She twisted around in his arms to point back at the tree with the camera. "Why *didn't* we get caught?" she continued. "Not that I'm complaining, but Davy and I were in that net for a while." She frowned, floating alongside Jason as he continued to tug her toward the boat.

He shook his head. "I don't know. Maybe that camera was turned off. Maybe Hieronymous was too busy licking his wounds after he tangled with me and Boreas. Maybe Jupiter is aligned with Mars."

At that, Lane actually laughed. "That must be it."

Jason found himself pondering her earlier words, how she'd been hard on herself. "You've done a great job, you know." He nodded toward his boat, where Davy was climbing up the ladder. "Of being a mom, I mean."

A new tear slid down her cheek, and Lane stopped him from swimming. She pulled close to kiss him on the cheek.

The gesture was simple, but the effect on him was not. Heat spread through his body, and he was overwhelmed with a desire to kiss away her worries and her fears. Hell, he wanted her to kiss away his own.

"Thank you for that," she said. "And thank you for bringing me here."

He brushed his lips across her hair. "You're welcome," he said; then he pulled her close. And as they hung there, suspended in the warm water, their legs rubbing as he slowly treaded water, he realized that he couldn't live the lie she wanted.

He loved this woman. Dammit all, he always would. Whether she wanted him to or not. He didn't want to pretend to be her friend—not if it meant he could never be her lover again. He didn't want to be a part-time daddy, and he didn't want to work his way slowly back up the ladder into her good graces. He wanted his family back. He wanted Lane.

And one way or another, he was going to get her.

Chapter Ten

"Davy, there's something I want to tell you. And there's someone I want you to meet." Lane's voice filtered up the stairwell of the boat, and Jason's stomach descended to somewhere in the vicinity of his knees.

He and Davy had already met, of course. Sort of. On the beach, his son had aimed those distrustful stares his way. And when Lane and Jason reached the boat, Davy had squirmed and squealed and basically said that Jason was the spawn of the Devil. He'd gone on to say that, even though Jason had been nice, Mommy shouldn't be cavorting with such spawn. The kid had actually said "cavorting." What a clever little guy.

Fortunately, Lane had run interference. "Jason's not the man who took you from Sea World," she'd said. "That was a shapeshifter who looked like him."

"Oh." The boy had frowned. "A shapeshifter. You mean like how Mr. Mordichai can change into a dog?"

Jason and Lane had exchanged looks. "A *lot* like that, actually," Jason had finally said.

Davy had turned interrogative for a few minutes until at last he was convinced Jason hadn't kidnapped him. Only then had they moved on to Lane's fear that Hieronymous was going to follow.

Boreas had actually helped with that. "Regulations," he said, clearing his throat. "Hieronymous will assume we're following them. Which means he'll assume we've got backup."

Jason nodded in agreement. "He'll focus on securing his island and removing all evidence. By the time he realizes we came on our own and there's no arrest to be made, we'll be safe."

It had satisfied Lane, for the time being, so she'd taken Davy belowdeck, insisting that he needed a meal and a nap. That had been three hours ago. Now, apparently, naptime was over. It was time for "introductions."

Automatically, Jason smoothed out his shorts, then peeled off his sunglasses and wiped their lenses on his T-shirt. Footsteps sounded on the steps, and Jason's mouth went dry. He tried to swallow but couldn't manage.

Lane appeared first, and then Davy trudged up the stairs, his eyes still sleepy behind his glasses and his hair going every which direction. He gave his glasses a shove at their bridge, and Jason noticed that one earpiece had been meticulously reattached with tape.

His son glanced around the deck, eyes settling on the only other person up there—Jason.

"But I've already met him, Mommy," Davy said. "He's Jason, and he didn't kidnap me."

"Right," Lane agreed. She took the boy's hand and tugged him over. Then she met Jason's eyes and jerked her head, silently urging him to meet them halfway. She settled Davy at the deck's one little table.

Jason meandered over, in no particular hurry. True, he wanted Davy to know who he was. He wanted his family. He just didn't want this awkward, Humpty-Dumpty moment: putting the pieces back together, hoping like heck the king's men would finally get the job done right.

His son turned to him. "It's very nice to meet you again," he said. The boy shifted slightly, his gaze falling on his mother. "Can I go now? I want to watch the ocean as it gets dark."

The sun was fast setting in the sky. Jason had set the autopilot's speed so the boat would return to California early in the morning. At the very least, he'd figured Davy could use a good night's sleep under the protection of his father.

"Not quite yet, sweetie," Lane said. "I, uh . . ." She trailed off, looking at Jason for help.

He shrugged. None of the books he'd bought covered this particular scenario.

"Right," Lane said. "Okay. Here's the thing."

Davy's forehead crinkled, his face a mass of confusion. "Is something wrong, Mommy?"

"No, sweetie. Just the opposite. You see, Jason's your daddy."

Jason exhaled. The whole afternoon creeping around his evil father's island hadn't tired him out, but this one conversational exchange with his son would exhaust him.

"No, he's not," Davy said simply. "Can I go play *now*?"

Lane and Jason exchanged glances. From her expression, Jason could tell this wasn't the response she'd expected. Good. He didn't want to be the only one knocked on his fanny by an almost-seven-year-old's denial.

"Um, yes he is," Lane argued. "Trust me. Moms know these things."

Davy shook his head, then looked down, concentrating intently on the toes of his shoes. "He's not," he said. "I know he's not." He looked up, staring right at Jason, his eyes clear and intent. "What space station were you on?"

Jason wondered what the Brazelton book would say about that, because he sure as heck didn't have a good answer. "The *Poseidon*," he finally said. It was either that or tell the truth. And, at the moment, a lie seemed much more comfortable.

Lane crossed her arms over her chest, a bemused expression on her face. Jason shrugged—the tiniest of motions meant only for her.

Davy squinted up at him. "Really? How'd you get back down? You were stuck."

"A good question," Jason agreed. He got up and crossed to the cooler, partly because he needed something to soothe his parched throat, partly because he needed to buy some time to think of an answer. "Do you know why I was stuck?"

Davy nodded. "The heat shields," he said. He climbed up onto the table and sat cross-legged, his chin propped on his clasped hands. "They were bad."

Jason nodded. That sounded reasonable. It was a story he could work with. "They *were* bad," he agreed. "But I fixed them."

Davy's eyes narrowed. "Really?"

"Absolutely." Reaching onto the table, he grabbed one of several Orange Crushes he'd stocked on the boat. Popping its top, he took a long gulp, confident he'd passed the test.

"How?"

Jason coughed, trying not to spit out the soda. So much for his moment of triumph.

Beside Davy, Lane laughed. "Yes, Jason. How? I was wondering that very thing."

He flashed her an overly sweet smile. "Apparently not with *your* help," he said.

She laughed again, then mumbled something about being sorry. "I'll just sit here quietly," she added, a grin tugging at her mouth.

He rolled his eyes. "You do that."

"Mr. Jason," Davy prompted, *"how?"*

"Right. Yes. Well, you see, it turns out it was pretty simple."

Davy cocked his head but didn't speak. Which was

too bad, because Jason was hoping for a little prompting. Apparently, though, he was on his own.

"You see, most of the tiles were good—heat shields are made out of tiles, you know." Jason gave himself a mental pat on the back, happy he'd remembered that little tidbit from repeated viewings of *Apollo 13*.

"I know," his son said, but still didn't help out.

"Yeah, well, the problem was that the bad tiles were on the front. So I put on my space suit and went outside and removed those front tiles and replaced them with some good ones from the back." He glanced down at Davy, who seemed to be buying into the whole thing. *So far, so good.*

"And, uh, then I had to make sure that the brunt of the reentry heat hit the front." Unfortunately, Jason's knowledge of physics was pretty much exhausted, so he was just making everything up as he went along. "It's all about angles," he added. Hadn't someone in mission control said that? "And, uh, trajectories."

"Right," Lane said. "Trajectories are very important."

Davy nodded, his little face quite serious.

"So, uh, then I just aimed the space ship and took my best shot—and it worked."

"Wow," Davy said. "That's really cool."

"So . . . you believe me?" Jason asked. "That I'm your daddy, I mean." Mentally he rolled his eyes, knowing he sounded absolutely pathetic.

Davy twisted to look at his mother.

"It's true, honey," Lane assured the child.

"Okay," Davy said. He shrugged and picked at a

scab on his knee. "Do I have to *call* you daddy?"

Jason felt his heart break just a little. "No." He shook his head and tried to manufacture a smile. "You can call me Jason."

Davy nodded, as if that settled everything. Then he slid off the table and brushed his hands on the back of his pants. For a second he looked up at Jason as if he wanted to say something else, but then he didn't. Instead, he turned to Lane. "Can I have a candy bar?"

She met Jason's eyes, and he saw the apology in them before she smiled at her son. "Sure thing. I saw some in the little refrigerator downstairs. But only one."

"Okay," the boy said with a nod, then headed toward the steps. He stopped on the first, turning full-circle to face Jason. "If you're really my daddy," he asked, "can you get me a puppy?"

Jason looked to Lane, who looked about ready to choke on her laughter. Apparently, this fatherhood gig was going to be harder than he thought.

"*Empty?* What do you mean the cell is empty?" Hieronymous stalked around the chamber, his glare fixed on his chief of guards. Mordi sank back into the corner, happy for the moment to be out of the line of fire.

"Just what I said, sire." Clyde ran a thin, lizardlike tongue over his lips. "I went to deliver his meal, and no boy."

Hieronymous slammed his hand down on his

desk, his palm open. The resulting noise echoed through the room, and Mordi cringed.

"Fools!" Hieronymous hissed. "Can this day get any worse?" He glared venemously at Clyde. "Heads will roll over this. I am not feeling particularly forgiving today."

Clyde stood straighter, his eyes narrowing as he turned to face Mordi. "My sentries made their rounds, sire. They alerted us to the intruders. It was my understanding that these monitors were the security for the boy's cell."

There was a beat, then Hieronymous and Clyde both turned to stare at Mordichai. Mordi licked his lips, wondering if he should run, wondering if he'd make it.

Clyde marched forward to the console, his long, powerful strides bringing him quickly across the room. He pointed at the monitors, still tuned to alternate channels. "As I suspected," he crowed. "He wasn't even monitoring the boy's cell."

Mordi swallowed, trying not to let his eyes show fear. "I . . . I don't know what happened. I was adjusting the controls, practicing. I didn't mean to—"

"Did you observe our confrontation with the intruders?" Hieronymous asked, his eyes narrowing.

Mordi shook his head, the lie coming easily. "No, sir. I . . ." He swallowed, the gesture buying him precious seconds. "I wanted to. I wanted to see you overpower whoever it was. But the controls . . ." He trailed off, shooting an irritated glance at the console. "I couldn't get the east corridor to display on the screen." He hung his head. "I'm sorry, Father. I know I said I was competent at operating these controls."

"We should have left him in Manhattan," Clyde snapped, casting a derisive glance at him. "Useless half-breed."

Hieronymous towered over Clyde. "I would encourage you to watch your tongue. Whatever else he may be, Mordichai is still my son."

"Yes, sir," Clyde said, looking as shocked as Mordi felt. His Adam's apple bobbed as he gulped. "Of course, sir."

Mordi kept his feet firmly in one place, determined not to back away as Hieronymous approached.

"Did you reset the monitor on the boy's chamber?"

"Not on purpose, sir," Mordi lied. "But when I was trying to adjust the controls, I might have accidentally switched channels."

"I see." Hieronymous stared at him for a long moment, during which Mordi's entire life flashed before his eyes. But then his father finally said, "Very well," and walked away to settle himself behind his desk. The Outcast's fingers immediately began their *tap-tapping*, but except for the irritating noise of his pensiveness, Mordi's father seemed quite unfazed.

Clyde's brow furrowed. Clearly, the guard captain was as confused as Mordichai. "Uh, sir? What should we do?"

"Do?" Hieronymous shot a narrow glance Clyde's way, and Mordi felt a surge of relief that the father he knew had returned. "Why, reacquire the boy, of course. We are fortunate that there is still time. The moment of his hormonal shift will not occur until midnight on Thursday."

"Reacquire him? How, sir?"

Hieronymous's chest rose as he drew in a deep breath. "I find it irritating that I have to hold your hand through these matters. I would think the answer to this question is clear." He turned to Mordi. "Answer Clyde's question, son. How do you intend to reacquire the boy?"

Mordi's chest tightened. Despite his hope, his "miserable failure" with the monitors hadn't earned him a pass on this new assignment. "Uh, when the boy goes to school . . ."

"Excellent," Hieronymous agreed. He looked at Clyde again. "You will assist my son in this endeavor. The boy goes to and from school. He plays in his yard. He does those things mortal boys do. It should not be too difficult to secure him once again."

"No, sir," Clyde said. "I mean—yes, sir. I mean, I will do what it takes to bring the child back here."

Hieronymous shook his head. "You will do nothing but assist my son as he requires." His eyes turned to Mordi, deep and unfathomable.

Mordi swallowed, wondering if his father knew the truth.

"My son will return the boy to me," the man said. He faced Mordichai and raised his hands. "You *are* with me on this, are you not?"

"Of course, sir," Mordi answered.

A smile touched Hieronymous's lips—a rare gesture meant for Mordichai, his new favored son?

Mordi's heart twisted just a little, and he wondered if Jason's betrayal hadn't just sealed his doom.

"Davy!" Zoë jumped up and down on the dock, both she and Deena screaming at the top of their lungs even as they laughed and cried.

It was quite a sight, and Lane's own tears joined her friends'. There was just something about a homecoming. Even Boreas seemed moved.

Davy, bless his heart, launched himself right at his Aunt Zoë. "I was really brave," he bragged.

She kissed his forehead. "You sure were. The bravest." She smiled at Lane, the simple gesture speaking volumes: congratulations, fear, hope, relief. Every emotion Lane had experienced over the last twenty-four hours was reflected right back at her.

"Hey," Deena said, moving in to get a hug from the boy. "Who's ready for breakfast? I bet we could do pancakes."

"Oh, cool. Can we, Mom?"

Lane gnawed on her lower lip. "In a little bit, sweetie. We need to go home and get Dorothy and Elmer." She and Jason had already decided they'd stay together at Jason's houseboat—at least until they figured out why Hieronymous wanted their boy.

Her son yawned, clearly still zonked. "But, Mommy . . ."

"No buts," she said. "You don't want Elmer to starve, do you? And you can have your pancakes when we get back."

Davy didn't answer, but he didn't look happy either. Jason stepped from the boat and put a hand on Lane's arm. "Let him stay and eat. I'll take you home to get the ferret and the fish. We'll come straight back."

"No. I'm the mommy," Lane answered, not sure she liked the idea of leaving Davy's side, even for only a little bit. "And the mommy says he's coming with us."

"Okay," Davy said in a bit of a whine. "But I can bring back my Game Boy, right? And my other toys, too?"

"Of course," Lane said. "You can bring back whatever you want."

She glanced at Jason then, for the first time realizing he might not want a billion toys scattered all over his house. "Can't he?"

Jason smiled. "Of course."

"Okay, then. It's settled." She licked her lips. "But we're taking a car," she added.

Jason raised an eyebrow, and Lane shrugged. "It's not that far," she explained. "And, believe me, you don't want to lug back all the toys he's going to want." She sighed. "Besides, I've had it. By air, by sea—all under Protector-power. Right now, I want the ground under my feet and no possibility of spilling poor Dorothy into the middle of Wilshire Boulevard." She exhaled slowly. "I just want to get from point A to point B the old-fashioned way."

Jason laughed. "*That* I can handle."

As it turned out, he certainly could. Less than five minutes later, they were in Jason's marina's parking structure, and Lane was staring at his car, her mouth slightly open. "This is great," she said. "It's yours? You turned down the Ferrari?"

Jason nodded. "I turned down a Porsche, actually. Second-class Protectors are assigned a Porsche. First-class Protectors get the Ferrari." He shrugged. "But I like older cars. I rebuilt it while I was on Olympus. I had my buddies bring me the parts. You like?" It was a 1950-something Bentley.

"Are you kidding?" Lane ran her hand over the hood. "It's wonderful."

"It's totally cool," Davy agreed. "Can I drive it?"

Jason raised an eyebrow. "You're smart, kid, but I think you're a little young."

Lane laughed. "I let him sit in my car and pretend to drive. So far we've been to New York, Chicago, and Boise."

"Boise?"

She shrugged. "Ask your son. I don't pick the destinations."

Davy blinked. "I liked the name," he said simply. "We're gonna go to Paris one day, but I gotta figure a way to turn a car into a boat first."

"Right," said Jason. He opened the passenger doors. "Everybody in."

Davy scrambled into the roomy backseat, and Lane settled in the front, the car's leather seats warm and inviting. When Jason slid behind the wheel, Lane couldn't quite meet his eye, so she ran her hand over the dashboard, enjoying the way her fingers slid along the fine leather.

Her emotions were all in a muddle; she knew that. She'd been broadsided by emotion. Pent-up and bubbling, she'd been on the verge of boiling over when Davy had suddenly appeared. But the fire under her hadn't been completely extinguished. Instead, her emotional state was on simmer, and heat continued to come from the man sitting next to her.

She licked her lips, willing herself to get her thoughts back on track. She, Davy, and Jason were just going to pick up a ferret, for crying out loud. Her six-year-old son was in the backseat. This wasn't a date. And she didn't want it to be.

Jason pulled out the throttle, cranked the engine, and soon Lane was surrounded by a subtle thrum of power. She licked her lips, her thoughts drifting once again from his car to the man beside her.

"Ready?" he asked.

Her eyes widened in surprise, and then she shook her head, realizing what he meant. "Oh. Yes. Let's get going."

And fast. She wanted to get to her apartment, gather up the pets and the toys, and come right back to Jason's houseboat. Then she wanted to make certain that Zoë and Taylor and Boreas planned to stay for the night. Or several nights. Because considering the way her thoughts kept going, the more distractions she had—the less time she had to think about Jason—the better.

He almost laughed out loud when he saw the expression on the ferret's face. And then, when he saw Lane's expression, Jason *did* laugh out loud.

"Oh, great. Thank you," she said. "You're a big

help." She tapped the plate with her toe. "Now he's never going to eat."

"I don't know why not," Jason said, barely able to keep a straight face. "It looks so yummy."

The look she shot him was scathing on the surface, but he could see amusement underneath. "Can I help it if I'm not as culinarily inclined as his caterer? What's a ferret need with special-delivery food anyway?" She bent down and plucked the ferret up, then plonked him back down in front of his plate. "It's perfectly good lasagna," she said.

"From a box," Jason added.

"If it's good enough for me and Davy, it's good enough for Elmer."

The ferret, apparently, didn't agree. He took one last sniff, turned on his paw, and headed back to Davy's room.

"Great," Lane said.

"Want me to go retrieve him?"

She shook her head. "No. You'll just wake Davy." The boy had fallen asleep in the car about the time they hit the highway. Lane hadn't acted too surprised. Davy'd had a rather stressful couple of days, and she'd suggested they let him nap for a bit before they returned to Jason's boat.

"Let the ferret fret," she said now. "I've had a hell of a night, and he's being a grump about frozen lasagna."

"Well, you know the ferret has specific tastes."

With a not-so-subtle roll of her eyes, Lane twisted her hair around her finger, then fastened the pile in place with a chopstick that was lying on the kitchen counter. "Well, we have to hang out here while Davy sleeps, and we can let Dorothy enjoy the food I sprinkled in her water. As soon as Davy wakes up, we'll pack up both the pets and head back. Maybe if Elmer's really lucky we'll pick him up some to-go from Spago's."

"Haute ferret cuisine," Jason joked.

"Something like that." Lane picked up a towel and started wiping down the countertop.

"What about *our* cuisine?" Jason asked, moving closer, his voice low. With his finger, he brushed a loose strand of hair that hadn't been captured in Lane's makeshift 'do. "Shall we have lunch at Spago as well?"

She turned to face him, her eyes wide. "On my budget? I don't think so."

He caressed her cheek, his heart picking up tempo when he realized she hadn't turned away. "I wasn't suggesting we go dutch," he said. "My treat. A celebration's in order, don't you think?"

"I . . ." Then she turned, and Jason silently mourned his defeat. "Definitely a celebration," she said, from her new vantage point farther down the counter. "But I don't want to stay out with Davy very long."

"Or with me," he added.

"No, no," she said quickly. "It's not that. It's—"

"What?"

She sighed. "Okay, it *is* that."

He took her admission as an invitation and moved closer. "We were good together, Lane. We could be good together again. I—"

242

She shook her head, and he could see the battle raging in her mind. "I can't do this right now. I can't think."

"Then *don't* think." He brushed a kiss across her forehead, gratified by the little sigh that elicited. "Just trust your instincts."

She pushed away from him, and he kicked himself for saying the wrong thing. "I trusted my instincts before and got burned. By you." She licked her lips. "I don't suppose you want to explain further why you left that day, what was so important that you couldn't stay with the woman you supposedly loved the night she told you you were going to be a daddy."

It was his turn to move away, and he clutched the edge of the counter as he gathered his thoughts. He wanted to tell her. But her trust was so fragile now, and even though she was backing away from his caresses, still, her eyes held desire. If she knew who he was, would that light dim?

He had to tell her, he knew that. She had a right to know who her child's grandfather was. But for just a little bit longer he wanted Lane to see only him. Wanted her to *want* him. And she did right now; he knew she did. Even if she refused to say so out loud.

He faced her, sure she could see the desire burning in his eyes. "Don't turn me away, Lane. Not now. Not after what we've just been through."

In one long step he was at her side, could smell the salt that lingered on her skin from the sea. "For almost seven years I've been yearning." He reached out, removing the chopstick and letting her hair fall, caressing his hand.

She drew a ragged breath, her eyes reflecting his passion.

"Please," he whispered.

For one wonderful moment she moved toward him. But then a shadow touched her eyes, and she fisted her hands at her sides as she froze. "I'm sorry," she whispered.

He pressed his lips together, disappointment settling on his shoulders like a yoke. "So, too bad for me, right?"

"Please don't make this more difficult than it already is. I told you. I just—"

"Want to be friends. I know." He ran his fingers through his hair. "But I'm going to keep trying to convince you otherwise."

She laughed, the sound delightful. "I'm flattered. And I do want you in our lives. You're Davy's father. You have a right to know him, and he needs to get to know you." She licked her lips and added, "Neither one of us really knows you. Not anymore."

Jason's heart twisted with the truth of her words, as well as from what she didn't say: She'd moved on. She had another man now. Jason wasn't part of her big picture anymore. While his life had been on hold because of his bastard father, she'd moved forward.

"You know me," he argued, wishing he could make the words true just by speaking them.

The corner of her mouth curved up. "Part of you, yes," she agreed. "And I know I need to thank you."

"For what?"

"For getting Davy back."

He almost laughed. "Me? What the hell did I do?

244

Davy rescued himself, remember?" He'd been totally extraneous. Just like it seemed he'd been his whole life. Just like he was now. Lane didn't need him, and Davy didn't need a father. The boy already had a family—Lane, Zoë, Taylor . . . His life was full. Certainly the kid hadn't been sitting around bemoaning Jason's absence. Instead he'd just plunked him on a space station and that was that.

Lane shook her head, almost as if she could see the pity party Jason had going on in his mind. "He doesn't need grand gestures," she said. "He just needs a dad who's there for him."

"Oh—well, that's me, then." He couldn't help the self-derision in his voice.

She moved closer. "I don't know why you went away, but I do know that you didn't *stay* away on purpose." She took his hand and squeezed. "And without you, I wouldn't have gotten Davy back. You found him." She pulled herself up on her tiptoes and kissed him on the cheek. "Thank you," she said.

Her nearness intoxicated him. Hell, he'd never thought clearly where Lane was concerned, and that hadn't changed. He knew he shouldn't—knew he was crossing a boundary that he shouldn't breach—but he couldn't help himself. Instinct and desire and pure, primal lust took over: He held Lane's face gently in his palms, then closed his mouth over hers.

She made a little moan of surprise, then settled against him, her mouth seeking his, her hunger as potent as his own. She wanted him. Of that much he was certain. But she didn't want to want him.

He had to change her mind.

Pulling her closer, Jason moved his hands to stroke Lane's back. Her arm slipped around his neck, and she deepened their kiss, her tongue exploring his mouth, tasting and teasing.

She tasted like chocolate and honey—rich and exotic, delicious and addictive. He craved her, couldn't get enough. His body hardened, wanting more. Wanting all of her, body and soul.

With a low groan, Jason pulled her shirt free of her shorts, his hand slipping under it to caress her bare skin. With his other he cupped her rear, urging her nearer until her hips were pressed against his, her soft thigh rubbing his erection. Then—

"No," she said, her voice husky as she pulled away. She said the word, but her tone meant something completely different. Her tone meant *yes*.

It was her tone he answered. With a low moan, he slipped his hand under the waist of her jeans, skimming down her back until his fingertips brushed her tiny bikini panties. She gasped, but he didn't hesitate; still his hand moved lower until his palm caressed the bare flesh of her firm little rear. He tightened his fingers there and urged her closer, his erection straining against his jeans.

Lane squirmed under his touch, but her body melded to his, her desire more evident with each motion. With his free hand, Jason cupped her chin, tilting her head back so that she had no choice but to look at him.

She opened her mouth, but no words came out—just a low moan, a sound of pure, feminine pleasure. Jason brushed a kiss over her lips, his body pulsing with unstoppable desire. Lane's hands grasped his neck, pulled him closer, urged him to make the kiss longer, harder, deeper.

"Jason," she murmured, breaking away. "We shouldn't."

His tongue teased the edge of her ear. "Oh, yes," he said. "We *should.*"

"I . . ." She trailed off; then she leaned back in the circle of his arms, her eyes dark with passion. "I don't—"

"Shhh," he said, pressing a finger to her lips. "Unless you're going to tell me to stop, and then I'll stop. But tell me now," he said. "Because I swear to you that if another minute goes by with you in my arms, I'm not going to be able to."

For one horrifying second he waited, unsure of her answer. But then she looked at him, and he knew—knew from the dark passion in her eyes and the rose of her cheeks.

"Kiss me," she said. "Kiss me now, before I change my mind."

Chapter Eleven

Jason didn't even hesitate, and Lane gasped as his lips closed over hers.

He'd wanted her, she'd known that. But she hadn't anticipated the force of his desire. His mouth was hot and demanding, and she welcomed it eagerly, her passion as strong as his. He deepened the kiss, alternately forceful and gentle. His touch evoked erotic memories; and she melted in his arms, the echo of their past encounters heating her skin and making her anticipate the next stroke of his fingers, the next thrust of his tongue.

His hand cupped the back of her head; his fingers twined in her hair. His touch was possessive, and though she wasn't his—hadn't been for a long time—the power with which he claimed her was masterful.

His other hand stroked her back, each movement loosening her shirt until it pulled entirely free of the waistband of her shorts. His fingers stroked her bare skin. His heated touch enticed her, sent a firestorm of desire rocketing through her veins. She moaned and pressed closer until she felt the hard bulge of his desire firm against the apex of her thighs.

Her moan turned into a low mewl, a desperate cry of desire. She moved her hips without thinking, wanting to make him harder, wanting to be sure that he was just as desperate as she. Most of all, she wanted to make sure that there was no turning back.

Lane didn't know if she was being supremely foolish or refreshingly honest; all she knew was that being in Jason's arms was intoxicating. Her body sizzled and sang, crackling like a forest fire. And she wanted Jason to stoke that fire.

This wasn't real—dammit, she *knew* that. This was just a reaction to what had happened combined with a vivid memory of what they'd once had together. But Lane wanted the memory, wanted the touch, wanted it all—and if that was a foolish mistake, then so be it.

She would pick up the pieces later.

"Lane," Jason whispered, drawing away long enough to murmur her name.

She recaptured his lips with her mouth. She didn't want to talk, didn't want to analyze. She just wanted to make love to this man.

"Touch me," she whispered.

His physical response gratified her as much as his low, masculine groan, his primal sound of longing and need. The hand splayed on her back stroked upward, taking her shirt with it.

"Lift your arms," he commanded.

She complied without hesitation. The shirt's soft cotton grazed her skin, its light stroke almost over-whelmingly sensual against her already primed senses. Even the brush of the air against her breasts was torture. Boldly, Lane took Jason's hands, cupped them over her breasts. She hadn't worn a bra, and right then she was grateful for that decision—one less barrier between them.

"Sweet Hera," Jason whispered, his voice stran-gled. He took Lane's nipple between his thumb and forefinger, stroking and teasing, the pleasure so in-tense it bordered on pain. Then he kissed her nip-ples.

The touch scattered sparks throughout Lane's body, starting in her breasts and shooting straight past her belly to ignite the flesh between her thighs. Jason moved to pepper her neck with kisses, his lips dancing up her soft skin, the stubble of his beard tickling and turning Lane on more than she'd ever imagined possible.

His exploration paused at her ear, and he nipped at its lobe. His breath grazed Lane's cheek, even as his tongue explored the curve of her ear. A tremor wracked her body, and Lane clutched Jason's shirt, her hands balled into fists as she fought for control.

His hands abandoned her breasts, and she moaned in protest as he moved to grab her waist. His mouth had left her nipples damp, and she felt them tighten and peak in response to the room's cool air.

She arched her back, a silent demand that his lips find her breasts again, that he stroke and kiss her there, but he didn't respond. At least not as she suggested. His tongue worked another type of magic, dancing on her ear, the sensation unbelievably erotic, the thrusts timed with the gentle gyrations of his hips against her body.

Lane's blood heated, and she felt itchy with the need to feel his skin against her. She drew her hands down until she found the hem of his shirt, then slipped her fingers underneath, spreading her hands flat across his abdomen.

A slight tremor of the rock-hard flesh under her fingers and a little nip on her earlobe was all the encouragement she needed. Boldly, Lane pushed his shirt farther up, her fingers exploring Jason's smattering of chest hair. Her fingers tingled from the contact with his skin, and she felt light-headed and weak-kneed. Pushing his shirt even higher, she clutched his shoulders, seeking his nearness and needing his stability to keep her from sinking to the floor in a boneless heap.

In one bold move, he finished the job for her, tugging his shirt over his head and tossing it aside. He had to break contact to do that, and she mourned the absence of his touch.

He filled the void soon enough. No sooner had his shirt touched the floor than he scooped her up in his arms. She gasped, the sudden sensation of being airborne surprising. For a moment her eyes opened wide, she looked around, wondering if she really was flying—but no, Jason's feet were still firmly planted on the floor, and he was carrying her to the couch.

"Does it fold out?" he asked.

She nodded, unable to form words, as Jason gently lowered her to her feet. She stood there, hugging herself, as he tossed the sofa cushions on the floor and tugged out the bed. With one hand, he urged her onto it, and she went without hesitation.

He gave her a strange look. "Are you su—"

She silenced his question with one finger. "I'm sure," she said. Not about forever. Hell, maybe not even about tomorrow. But right then she wanted him. Right then she needed human contact, human connection. And, more than anything, she needed that connection to be with Jason.

He smiled in understanding, his hands pressing on her shoulders and easing her back against the bed. "In that case, I only have one other question."

She licked her lips and nodded, her heart pounding, fearful that he would back away, leaving her unfulfilled.

"Is Davy a sound sleeper?"

Laughing, Lane hooked her arm around his neck and pulled him down. "*Very,*" she whispered.

"Good," he said. Rolling onto his side, he traced his finger down her bare arm. "Because—I want you, you know."

"You've got me," she said.

"I want you . . . naked," he added, looking pointedly down at the shorts she still wore.

"Yeah?" she asked. "Well, what are you going to do about that?"

"Maybe I'll just show you." The grin he flashed was playful and full of promise. Lane remembered it vividly, and she stifled another little sigh.

He urged her onto her back, then moved to straddle her, cupping her waist with his hands. Little by little, he urged her shorts down. When he reached the elastic band of her underwear, he snagged those as well.

He knelt over her, lowering his mouth to her belly. He traced a trail of wet kisses down, lower and lower, until Lane realized she was holding her breath. He'd urged her shorts and panties down to mid-thigh, and now he pulled them off, taking his lips from her skin just long enough to complete the task of getting her completely naked.

The window was slightly open, and the breeze from the beach brought a chill into the room, but Lane hardly noticed. Her skin was on fire, burning under Jason's touch, and when he touched his lips to her inner thigh, the heat of her passion consumed her.

Desire overwhelmed her like hunger, and she spread her legs, giving him better access and begging with her body to be touched where she most longed.

He responded, understanding her unspoken pleas. He kissed her intimately, his tongue laving her, and she squirmed with almost maddening pleasure. Pure heat spread through Lane's body, and she moaned, wanting Jason to touch her—*there*—

needing him to find that one secret place that would bring her sweet release. He cupped her behind with his hands, holding her steady as he focused his assault.

Lane's body tingled, little tremors shooting straight to her toes. A steady pressure built in her belly and she held completely still, fearful that if she moved—if she breathed—she'd be on this wonderful precipice of pleasure and tormented anticipation for eternity.

He knew her fear, and he knew exactly what she needed. He stroked her, a flood of warmth building and building, his fingers teasing her, slipping inside her warm folds just enough to drive her absolutely over the edge.

The force of her fulfillment hit her, and Lane twisted, moving away from Jason's delicious onslaught. He held her steady, though, forcing her to ride the crest of heat and color until she was certain her body couldn't take it. She reached over her head, clutching the back of the sofa, her fingers gripping the upholstery as wave after wave of pleasure washed over her.

At last the tremors stopped, and she breathed deep, her body limp and languid. Jason moved up the bed toward her, trailing kisses up her body, his heat radiating everywhere.

Lane murmured his name, rolled into his embrace. Hooking her leg over his waist, she pressed close, her body seeking some sort of stability. *Sparks. Oh, yeah.* With Jason, there were definitely *sparks.* "That was wonderful," she said, her voice breathy.

He pressed a gentle kiss against her neck, the innocent gesture setting off another reaction in Lane's body that was anything but innocent. "I'm glad you think so, sweetheart. Because we've only just got started."

Heaven.

For years he'd fantasized about holding Lane in his arms again, about losing himself in her sweetness. He'd almost feared the reality of her touch wouldn't live up to the power of his memories. He'd been wrong. The responsive, sensual woman now in his arms put his memories to shame.

She'd been young and inexperienced when they'd been together. Her innocence and genuine pleasure from his touch had delighted him. Now, though, she was sure and experienced, taking pleasure as much as she gave. Her honest responses were still delightful, but there was a confidence about Lane that excited Jason even more.

Of course, he tried not to think about the source—or sources—of that confidence. About where she'd gained the sensual experience of which he was now reaping the benefit. He stroked her arm, trying not to think; wanting only to lose himself in the pleasure reflected in her eyes.

"Surely you're not tired already," she said, a tease in her voice. "From what I understand, superheroes have amazing stamina."

He grinned. "Well, sweetheart, you've heard right."

Slowly he rolled her over, sent his fingers dancing

across her bare skin. She was naked and utterly beautiful; he still wore his shorts—an oversight he intended to correct momentarily.

"Good," she said. He glanced up, noting the twitch at the corner of her mouth. "Because superheroes are supposed to be powerful, too." She licked her lips and shot a coy glance at his shorts. "Care to try to prove it to me?"

He laughed. "Careful there, unless you want to induce performance anxiety."

Her laugh joined his. "Well, I wouldn't want that. I'll keep my expectations silent . . . until later, when I flash my Olympic score card."

"Mmmm." He took her breast in his mouth, teasing her nipple with his tongue. Then, pulling away, he blew cool air on her now-wet skin, watched as the light-brown flesh puckered.

Lane moaned, her hand snaking down his back, fingers hard and insistent.

"I assume I'll get straight tens," he said.

"I don't know," she hedged, her voice a bit breathless. She arched her back, pressing her breasts closer to his mouth, need reflected on her face. At the same time, she slid her hand around to his belly, her fingers sliding under the waistband of his shorts and underwear. "The judging criteria is very strict. You'll have to work very, very hard."

It was his turn to groan, and he released a low moan of pure, desperate need as her fingers caressed the base of him. "Off," he said, forcing out the only word he could manage.

She understood, shifting her body so that she

could grasp his shorts and pull them off, down over his rock-hard shaft. But she didn't move fast enough to suit, and he struggled the rest of the way out of his clothes and positioned himself between her legs. The tip of him pressed against her soft, sweet folds, but with supreme effort he held back.

"I don't have a condom," he said.

"It's okay," she said. "We're fine."

Thank Hera. If she'd told him to stop, he wasn't confident that he could. He longed to sink himself into her, but he didn't want to move too fast. He wanted this as perfect for her as it was for him.

"*Now*," she whispered. "Jason, please. Why the hell are you stopping?"

He would have kissed her for that if her words hadn't robbed his brain of every rational thought. He heard only her words, though, reacted only to her command. In one clean, powerful thrust, he entered her.

Her velvety heat enveloped him, and he thrust deeper, silently obeying the commands of her body. Her legs tightened around him, and she thrust upward as well. With each inch he drove deeper, moved that much closer to the satisfaction that waited for him just a hairbreadth away.

He withdrew and entered her again. And then again. They rocked together, a union of both body and soul, until the world split and release contorted his body with an intensity that was almost painful. When the tremors passed, he collapsed onto her, bearing the brunt of his weight on his elbows. He stroked Lane's cheek and smiled into her satisfied eyes.

"As nice as before?" he asked.

"Nicer," she said, a charming pink blush tinging her cheeks.

He brushed her mouth with his lips, a light kiss that conveyed all the passion he felt. She was right. This time with Lane *had* been nicer. In the past, she'd blown him away, this woman with whom he'd expected to spend the rest of his life. Now, there was even more to her. He wanted to explore every facet, to learn every idiosyncrasy. He longed to be as close to her now as they'd been before. If only . . .

He shook his head, a wave of regret and anger crashing over him. Damn Hieronymous. Damn him to Hades for stealing Jason's life, both the time and his reputation.

"Jason?" Concern flashed in Lane's eyes.

He conjured a smile. "Just woolgathering." He shifted away to lie on his side, pulling her close beside him and capturing her in his embrace. "So?" he asked, making sure to keep his voice light.

She turned her head, twisting a bit to see him. Confusion colored her face. "So?" she repeated.

"The final score," he clarified.

She laughed. "Oh, right. If I tell you, it'll just go to your head."

"That good, huh?"

"Perfect," she answered. She twisted completely, turning in his arms to face him. In a quick motion, she planted a sweet kiss on the tip of his nose. "Every other man in competition is quaking in his itty-bitty briefs."

He raised an eyebrow. "Quaking?"

She snuggled up close. "Definitely quaking," she said. "And don't worry," she added in a whisper, her face pressed to his chest. "You're guaranteed the gold." Then, with a satisfied sigh, Lane closed her eyes. Her breathing evened, and Jason watched, mesmerized by the gentle rise and fall of her chest as she drifted off to sleep.

Jason didn't sleep. He didn't even doze. Instead, he kept his eyes wide open, memorizing every curve, every freckle, the position of every tiny hair on her body. Like a movie, he ran each touch, each caress, over and over in his mind, committing his and Lane's lovemaking to memory, needing to make sure he would never, ever forget.

At the moment, Lane was his. Of that, he was certain. It was the future he feared.

Phelonium Prigg's image sputtered and shifted, so Zoë gave her holo-pager one solid whack. A bit more static appeared, and then the Council bureaucrat came into sharp focus. He pulled himself up to his full height, all five feet four inches. Under the circumstances—as a projection on top of Jason's desk calendar—the Protector seemed even tinier.

Zoë exhaled, then propped her hands on her hips. "I was trying to reach Zephron," she said.

Prigg sniffed in that insufferable way he had. "Zephron is indisposed," he said. He held up his hand when Zoë tried to interrupt. "Certain matters have come to my attention, however, and I would be remiss not to raise them promptly with you."

Zoë drummed her fingers on her thigh. She'd never been terribly fond of Prigg. When she'd joined the Council, she'd spent almost a solid week filling out all the required forms and documents. Prigg had been no help whatsoever. Each time she asked a question, he managed to answer only by requiring her to fill out another form. She was absolutely certain that he had ink in his veins instead of blood, and that his epitaph would read: PHELONIUM PRIGG. FILED IN TRIPLICATE.

On the desktop, Prigg's hologram turned in a complete circle, clearly trying to see beyond the hazy image Zoë's pager projected back to him. From his frustrated expression, Zoë gathered he didn't see whatever he was looking for.

"What is it?" she asked, a bit too sharply.

Another sniff. "Where is *he?*"

Zoë scowled, turning to Deena and then to Boreas. "If you're referring to Jason, *he* and Lane went back to her apartment to get some things. They'll be back soon."

With the tip of his finger, Prigg slid his reading glasses down his nose and peered at Zoë. "You permitted him to leave? To accompany the boy and his mother without an escort?"

Zoë stifled a sigh. It had been a hell of a day already, and she really didn't feel like dealing with this twit. Thank goodness Hoop had gone to her apartment to fetch Taylor. Rather than give her husband directions to this out-of-the-way and difficult-to-find houseboat, sending Deena's fiancé had seemed the easiest plan. Taylor had just got back in the country, and Zoë expected him at the houseboat any minute. The sooner the better. If she had to deal with Prigg, she wanted her husband's arms tight around her.

On his dais, Prigg muttered something unintelligible. With her superhearing on the fritz, Zoë couldn't make out all his words, though *irresponsible* and *utterly improper* were discernible.

"Okay, okay," she said. "I give up. What's the big deal?"

"The man is a suspected traitor, Ms. Taylor." He tapped his foot, his arms crossed over his chest. "You yourself reported him to the council. And now you simply let him loose with his son's mother? What in Hera's name were you thinking?"

Zoë bristled. "I guess I was thinking that he'd just rescued his son from Hieronymous's island. Call me crazy, but in my mind that takes him off our most-wanted list." She planted a hand on her hip, daring him to argue with her reasoning.

He took the dare. "Normally, I would agree with you."

"Normally?" she repeated. "What? Are there *normal* circumstances where halfling children are kidnapped from Sea World by an Outcast arch-villain?"

Prigg paused. "Perhaps if those were the only facts, we could treat this case"—he cleared his throat—"*normally*. But the extenuating circumstances involved in this matter—"

"What extenuating circumstances?" Zoë snapped.

"Look," Boreas spoke up from behind her. "I think I should probably say I think that guy's great. Jason, I mean. He's a little—"

"His parentage, of course," Prigg said, ignoring the young Protector's speech.

Boreas clamped his mouth shut, his brow knitting in confusion even as Zoë gave a blank look. "What about his parentage?" she asked.

"His father is Hieronymous."

"*What?*" The word came out a screech, and Zoë almost didn't recognize her own voice. She cleared her throat and tried again. "What are you talking about?"

"Oh, didn't you know?" Prigg asked, but his voice was a little too innocent. Zoë narrowed her eyes as he continued. "The Inner Circle has always known. I am the Recording Secretary for the Inner Circle. So I am privy to these matters." He paused, buffing his fingernails against his chest.

"So?" Zoë prompted, trying not to let the fact that she liked Jason and disliked Prigg color her judgment. She needed to be objective, because at the moment all she really wanted to do was flip the holopager off.

"He has, of course, been monitored over the years. For six years, however . . ."

Zoë rolled her eyes, then twirled her hand, once again urging the old bureaucrat to continue.

"We don't know what happened during the six years Jason was imprisoned by Hieronymous. But we do know that Hieronymous is—shall we say—

persuasive. You've seen as much illustrated by your cousin Mordichai."

Zoë pressed her lips together. That much was true enough. It seemed that every time she thought Mordi had turned his back on Hieronymous for good, he did something that put him back in his father's good graces. A pity, actually, because she genuinely liked her cousin, despite all the grief he'd caused over the years.

She sifted through what Prigg had just told her. "Basically, you're saying that you don't believe Jason is strong enough to have stuck to his guns while he was imprisoned. That he must now be working for Hieronymous."

Prigg inclined his head, a hint of a nod.

"But you don't have proof."

"Proof is not always necessary where instinct is involved."

"Uh-huh," Zoë snapped. "Like I said, you don't have proof."

Prigg sniffed, a noise of righteous indignation. "Perhaps not. Unless you consider the fact that he confronted Hieronymous, had the opportunity to rid us of the Outcast leader once and for all, with evidence of wrongdoing aplenty . . . and yet Hieronymous still lives."

A chill settled over Zoë.

"Ah, yes," Prigg said. "Now you're understanding. A ruse. A ploy. Your new friend must have joined forces with Hieronymous."

"No," Zoë said, not willing to believe. "If that's true, why would Hieronymous let Davy go?"

"To gain our trust perhaps?" He waved a hand. "It doesn't matter. The situation is what it is. Jason Murphy is not yet trustworthy."

Zoë swallowed, a sick feeling settling in her gut. She didn't believe this. She trusted Jason.

And yet . . .

Could it be true? Had she been duped? Had her raging hormones allowed a traitor to pull one over on her? Had he only saved his son as a ploy? Was Jason planning to do something even more despicable?

She took a deep breath, steeling herself. "What do you know?" she asked, forcing the words out.

Prigg looked surprised. "Why, ask Officer Boreas, of course. His report was quite—"

"What?" She spun on her heel, her anger building. "His *report?"*

"Certainly," Prigg said, even as Boreas took a step backward, his eyes wide with fear. "As a cadet, Boreas must submit regularly sched—"

"Wait," Zoë said, and to her surprise Prigg actually shut up. The blood in her veins was ice cold, a result of both her fear and her anger.

"Is this true?" she asked Boreas, barely able to force the words past clenched teeth.

The young Protector took another step back and opened his mouth, but no words came out. He licked his lips and tried again. "Well . . . sort of, yes."

Then he backpedaled. "No! I mean, I did submit a report, but I told exactly what happened. Jason went after Hieronymous, but he got hurt—it all happened so fast—and I got him out of there by—"

"Foolish boy," Prigg said. "*Jason* was hurt, and you, a neophyte, remained unscathed? You gullible, gullible child."

Boreas scowled, but didn't say anything.

Zoë licked her lips, wishing her superpowers included lie detection. Something was going on. Prigg thought Jason had gone bad and the administrator had access to Jason's entire file. Boreas disagreed and had seen Jason in action.

"It wasn't like that," Boreas protested.

"However 'it was like,' " Prigg said with a little sniff, "you should not have permitted him to leave. The man's activities are suspicious. This will go on your permanent record, Officer Boreas. See that you don't make such foolish decisions again."

Boreas's jaw clenched. "Yes sir," he said.

"Very well." Prigg nodded curtly and signed off.

Boreas turned to Zoë, his arms tight over his chest. "He's not a traitor. I don't care who his father is."

Zoë tended to agree with Boreas, but she couldn't trust her own judgment. Which meant that, when she boiled it all down, she still didn't know what side Jason was on. Her gut believed him in his innocence—but she couldn't afford to be wrong.

Reaching a decision, she pointed at Deena. "Leave a message for Hoop," she said, shifting her gaze to Boreas. "We're going to go find Jason."

Rubbing her belly, Zoë thought about her husband, in transit, and the news she had for him. But that news was going to have to wait. Right now, she had to go interrogate her nephew's father. A man

who she hoped was a friend . . . but who might just
be a traitor.

Lane shivered, a chill settling over her body. She
groaned in protest and groped for the sheet, wanting just a few more minutes of sleep before she had
to get up, get Davy dressed, and head to school. But
her fingers closed around nothing but air.

No sheet.

She groped some more, her hand patting the bed,
her mind trying to focus despite its haze of sleep.
She was so tired, her body so stiff and sore. It was
like she'd run a marathon or something, except she
didn't run. Heck, she barely exercised at all.

Rolling over, she pressed her face into her pillow,
the vague scent of coffee enticing her. Thank goodness she'd remembered to set the coffeemaker. . . .

She sat up, reality thwapping her on the head. It
wasn't morning; it was late afternoon. And she *hadn't*
set the coffeemaker any more than she'd run a marathon. Instead, she'd—

Oh, my.

She twisted in bed, searching for Jason. But he
wasn't there, just a slight indentation and a pile of
covers on his side of the flimsy, sofa-bed mattress.

She bit back a smile. He always had hogged the
covers.

"Good morning, sleepyhead." Jason, following his
voice, slid around the corner with a steaming mug
of coffee in his hand. "Or should I say good evening?"

Lane grabbed her shirt off the floor, then sat up

and shrugged into it, a goofy smile on her face. This wasn't exactly breakfast in bed, but it was close. And she hadn't had breakfast in bed since she'd been sick in fourth grade and stuck under the covers for three solid days.

She accepted the mug from him and took a careful sip, its elixir working magic on her mind. "I'm so confused right now, I don't even know what day it is," she admitted.

"Still Tuesday," he informed her. "Only now it's nightfall."

"Davy," Lane said, sitting up straighter.

"He's playing in his room. I let him put in a video—*Spy Kids*. He looked pretty happy."

Considering Lane never let him watch videos during the week, she was sure Davy was probably thrilled. "And Zoë. They'll be worried."

"I sent a text message to Zoë's pager. I told her we were talking and to give us a call if she needed anything." He nodded toward the phone. "But, as you know, that contraption's been completely silent."

He moved to sit next to her on the bed, his arm propped behind her so that she could lean against him. With his other hand, he stroked her face, his finger tracing the line of her lips. She gasped, the power of his touch unsettling her.

That feeling of unease settled in, and she scooted backward, away from his touch. So it wouldn't seem too obvious, she got off the bed entirely and pulled on her shorts, feeling a little silly in so doing.

She'd wanted him in her bed; she could admit

that. She was a big girl, and she'd wanted sex. Wanted sex with *him*. Wanted to be held and loved and taken care of after the most horrible day of her entire life.

But now . . .

Now she was in her living room with a man who'd walked away from her. One who hadn't explained why. And her heart really didn't know what to make of that.

As if reading her thoughts, Jason took her hand and tugged her back to the sofa bed. The warmth of his touch seemed to steady and ground her. Clenching her fists, Lane shook her head: *No.* She had to be smart. Jason wasn't grounding her—far from it. If anything, he sent her off into the clouds. On a wonderful, sensual adventure, yes, but she wasn't looking for adventure. She was looking for steadiness. Security. She wanted Davy to have the life she'd never had: steadfast devotion with a permanent home and a permanent family.

And no matter how good the sex might be, permanence wasn't something she could expect from Jason. She ran her teeth over her lower lip. At least, she hadn't been able to expect it from the Jason of the past. This Jason . . .

Well, she really didn't know this Jason. Except to know that he was a superhero. Which brought up the question: Could she and Davy ever really be his priority?

She nibbled on her lower lip, wondering. Taylor and Zoë were getting along just fine. And so were Hale and Tracy. So maybe . . .

No. She was scared, so very scared of getting hurt again. She'd survived his leaving once. She didn't think she could survive it again.

With a gentle touch, Jason brushed away a strand of hair that had fallen over her eye. "I know that look," he whispered.

She felt her cheeks warm, and she shook her head, ever so slightly. "I don't have a look," she said. "No looks here."

"Regret." He punctuated the word with a smile, but she could see the sadness in it. A twinge of guilt settled in her stomach—guilt that she'd succumbed to desire but now, inevitably she was going to hurt this man. She didn't want to hurt him, but even more she didn't want to hurt Davy. And she certainly didn't want to be hurt herself.

"I . . ." She trailed off, licking her lips, her fingers clenched tight around her mug of warm coffee.

"I don't want to push you, Lane," he said, pressing his palm against her knee. "I just want to try again."

His words, though expected, hit her with the force of a sledgehammer. In her heart, she wanted to try, too. In her head, she kept screaming, *Be smart! Be smart!* She already had a nice man waiting in the wings, a man who didn't make her wonder if he'd be there the next day, a man Davy already adored who didn't have secrets.

But Aaron wasn't Jason. And despite everything that told her to run far and fast, that one little fact kept eating at her. She connected with Jason; she always had.

Lane shook her head, clearing her thoughts. Was

she doing nothing more than trying to justify what would surely turn out to be a bad decision?

Jason's fingers stroked her knee and Lane shifted, pulling her leg away so that she was sitting primly on the side of the sofa bed. She couldn't think with him touching her—not if she wanted to be rational.

She sat up straighter, still not really sure what she was going to say, and started talking. "I don't know, Jason. I really don't. I mean, I need to know you've changed."

"I have."

"No secrets. No finding out six years from now that you're a superhero or something."

He grinned. "Not a problem. We've already done that one."

Despite herself, she smiled. "And Davy comes first. Davy and me," she said.

"You always did," he argued.

She pressed her lips together, wondering whether to debate the point. "This isn't about the past," she decided, taking the middle ground. "I already told you, we can't change the past. What's done is done."

A shadow crossed his face, so she reached out to take his hand.

"I'm not making any promises," she said. She drew a deep breath, hoping she wasn't making a mistake. "But I'm not saying no, either."

His head cocked ever so slightly. "What *are* you saying?"

"I'm saying we'll see."

"That's it?"

Moment of truth time. "No." She shook her head.

"We'll move in with you, too. At least for a while."

"That wasn't even an issue," he complained.

She raised an eyebrow. "Excuse me?"

"We already agreed—until we're sure you won't have any more problems with Hieronymous, you two are staying right next to me."

He had a point, so she nodded. "Well, yeah. But this is about us. I want you to get to know Davy better, anyway. Plus, I want you to teach him everything you can. If that's the easiest way to avoid some ridiculous Council-mandated boarding school, then we'll try that."

"It'll work," he assured her. "And if the Council still insists, we'll think of something else. I promise no one will take Davy from you. No matter what I have to do."

"Thank you," she whispered.

Jason's face reflected something more than just concern for Davy—a passion, possessiveness. Lane swallowed, suddenly fearing she was making a huge mistake.

Desire, hot and needy, flashed in Jason's eyes. "And since we'll be living together, you and I should have plenty of opportunities to get reacquainted."

Lane licked her lips, liking the idea more than was reasonable. She twisted her hands in her lap, reminding herself why she wasn't just jumping into his arms and pulling him back into her life. "So, we're clear, though—right? No more secrets, no more—"

A sharp knock interrupted.

"It's probably pizza," Jason said, getting up. "I

thought you and Davy might want a bite before we head back to my houseboat."

Her stomach rumbled, and Lane realized she was famished. "Sounds great."

Jason pulled the door open, and she gasped. It wasn't a pizza delivery guy at all.

Aaron.

Well, damn.

Chapter Twelve

Automatically, Lane took two deep breaths and re-minded herself what she'd just suffered with Davy: a horrible, terrible, awful day. This—her current boyfriend staring at the man she'd just slept with, who happened to be the father of her child—was nothing compared to that.

Really.

Aaron, trial lawyer that he was, recovered quickly. He held out his hand for Jason to shake. "I'm Aaron," he said, his polite countenance covering his initial expression of confusion and hurt. "And you are . . . ?"

"Very pleased to meet you," Jason answered. "I've heard a lot about you."

"I'd say the same," Aaron suggested, "except I don't know who *you* are."

"Ah," Lane spoke up, leaning forward to interrupt. "About that. Um . . ." She squinted at Jason. "Go check on Davy, okay?"

"But—"

"Go," she insisted, pointing toward their son's room.

Thank goodness he went, though he didn't look happy. She wasn't in much of a position to argue; certainly she wasn't going to drag him bodily to the other room.

Aaron watched Jason go, his jaw firmly set.

"Can you step back outside for a second?" Lane asked.

"Lane . . ." His voice held a hint of warning.

"*Please?*" She needed a moment to get the room, and her head, in order.

"Maybe I should just shut the door behind me and leave," he said, his curt words like a slap.

She shook her head, blinking back tears and a wave of guilt-induced nausea. "No, please. We need to talk. But I need a moment." She met his eyes, sure hers were as full of guilt as his were of ice. "Aaron, please."

His shoulders sagged just slightly and he nodded. Stepping onto the walkway outside, he pulled the door shut.

Lane moved quickly, tossing the bedsheets into the middle of the couch. She grabbed the sofa bed and shoved it back together, then replaced its cushions.

Stepping back, she gave the living room an appraising glance. Jason's T-shirt hung over a chair, and she grabbed it, ran to Davy's room, opened the door, and tossed it in.

Inside, she caught a glimpse of Jason, with Elmer on his lap and Davy on the floor.

She held up a finger in response to his open mouth. "Not yet," she said. "Just stay." She blew Davy a quick kiss, then scurried backward, pulling the door closed.

She headed for the door, a little mantra—*I don't need this; I really, really don't need this*—echoing in her head.

Pausing at the threshold, she clutched the front door's knob and took three deep breaths. Finally feeling ready to confront the reality that was her life, she tugged open the door.

Taylor.

No Aaron? Instead, her brother—George Bailey Taylor—filled the doorway. Lane blinked, wondering when she'd stepped out of the real world and into Bizarroland.

He grabbed and tugged her into a bear hug. He gave her one long squeeze, then another—and then one more for good measure before he finally stopped and held her by her shoulders, looking her over.

His face was lined with fear and exhaustion. The exhaustion probably had something to do with the time change. The fear she attributed to the escapades of herself and her son.

"What the hell is going on?" he asked. "And where's Davy?"

"Davy's fine," she said. Squinting, she peered over

his shoulder, but she couldn't find any sign of Aaron. She wasn't sure whether to be thankful or not. She owed the man an explanation, that much was certain. But his timing wasn't exactly great, so maybe she should just thank Fate or whoever that he'd decided to skip out on her. She could, after all, track him down later.

"Lane?" Taylor prompted. "Where's my nephew?"

"Uncle Taylor!" Davy's door flew open, and then the boy himself raced from the room. "Uncle Taylor! I got kidnapped, but I got away, and I'm fine now, and the tennis shoes you bought me helped."

Taylor caught the boy on the fly and swung him around. "Hey there, sport. I heard you had an adventure. Pretty impressive for a little squirt." His eye caught Lane's, and she knew he still didn't have—but desperately wanted—the whole story.

Jason headed into the room, looking slightly frazzled. Lane stifled a smile. Less than ten minutes in a room with Davy and the boy's father was already experiencing overload. "I'm sorry, Lane. He heard George's voice and boom." He nodded toward Taylor. "It's good to see you again, George."

"I'm going by Taylor these days," her brother said, his face impassive.

The knot in Lane's stomach tightened.

Taylor deposited Davy back onto the floor. "Can you go back in your room for a sec, Squirt? I want to talk to Jason and your mother," he said. "When I'm done in here, I'll join you and you can show me those shoes."

Davy nodded, then scampered off. The very second the boy's door clicked into place, Taylor's formerly blank face erupted with anger. His shoulder shifted, and then—before Lane could even yelp—his fist shot out and connected with Jason's jaw.

Jason was knocked back, but he didn't go down.

Taylor, on the other hand, grabbed his hand and howled. "What the hell? Do you have some special superhero jaw?"

"You know about that?" Lane asked, surprised.

Taylor rubbed his hand. "Zoë told me," he said.

"She told you to hit me?" Jason asked, incredulous.

"Even after he got Davy off that island?" Lane added.

Taylor shook his head. "No." He looked Jason in the eye. "You get a thank-you for rescuing Davy," he said. "The punch was an old debt."

Lane stepped forward, positioning herself between the men, just in case Jason decided to respond in kind.

"It's okay," he said, reading her movement. "Taylor's got his reasons."

She shook her head. "No, he doesn't. You didn't mean to stay away. And hitting doesn't solve anything," she added, aiming a glare at her brother.

"Made me feel better," Taylor said. "That punch has been almost seven years coming."

"I'm okay with it," Jason added sheepishly. "Like you said, I may not have meant to stay away, but I did leave in the first place."

Lane blinked, still firmly grounded in the land of

the bizarre, and looked from one to the other. "Are you guys serious?"

Taylor shrugged. "Hell, yes." He stepped past her and clapped Jason on the shoulder. "And I was serious about the thank-you, too. I was worried sick when Zoë first called me. I'm glad you got Davy away."

"You and me both," Jason agreed. "But Davy is the one to applaud. A real trooper. You should go in and let him tell you about it. He'll make you proud."

Lane just stood there, staring from one man to the other. Less than a minute ago, her brother had punched Jason in the face; now they were deep into the guy-talk thing. *Men.* She'd never understand them. Not in a million years.

"Lane?" Taylor asked, taking a step toward the door.

"Go ahead." She waved toward Davy's room. "He'll be thrilled to tell you."

Taylor didn't quite make it, though. The clatter of footsteps came from the front porch; then Zoë and Deena, both breathless, burst through the door. They were followed in short order by Boreas, who hadn't even worked up a sweat.

"Taylor!" Zoë cried, flinging herself into her husband's arms.

He gave her a quick kiss, then pushed her gently away, his intense gaze looking her up and down. "You look winded," he said, surprise lacing his voice. "Are you okay?" He pressed a hand against her forehead, but she just ducked away.

"A little breathless," she admitted, "but only because I'm excited to see you."

"Zo—"

She put a finger to his lips to quiet him. "I'm fine." She turned to Lane, and real fear flashed across her face. "Is *Davy* okay?"

Lane's heart picked up tempo. "Of course. He's in his room. What's wrong?" She held up a finger, cutting off Zoë's answer. "Wait," she said. And even though she knew it was silly, she raced to Davy's room and poked her head in. Her son looked up, a ripped tennis shoe on the floor before him.

"I'm, uh, playing neurosurgeon," he said.

"Right," she said, ducking her head back out and closing the door. She trotted back to Zoë. "He's fine. What's wrong?"

"Hopefully nothing," Zoë admitted. "But Prigg swears that *he's* a bad guy." She aimed an accusing finger at Jason.

"Oh, come *on*," he said. "We've already been through this. I . . . did . . . not . . . kidnap . . . Davy. I'm the one who saved him."

"Look," Zoë explained. "I want to go with you on this one. I really do. But give me more to work with."

"More than rescuing my son?"

Zoë half-shrugged. "Prigg's convinced it's all part of an act, that you're just trying to get in good with us. That everything that's happened is somehow part of your father's plan." She raised an eyebrow. "I'm sorry, Jason," she said. "But you did neglect to mention that little bit about your parentage. It doesn't look good."

"Wait," Lane said. "Back up." She turned to Jason. "Father?" she asked, a sick feeling rising in the pit of her stomach.

"Tell her," Zoë said to Jason. "Tell her who your father is."

Jason frowned as Lane and Taylor exchanged a glance. Apparently, Taylor was as out of the loop as she.

"For Hera's sake, Jason," Zoë said, exasperation lacing her voice. "You owe us an explanation."

"Please!" Lane said, holding up her hand. "Somebody tell me what's going on."

"Hieronymous," Zoë explained, the single word quieting the room. "Jason's father is Hieronymous."

Lane balked, certain she must have heard wrong. She was about to ask, but she never got the chance.

"Hierony-who?" Aaron said, pushing the door open and stepping inside.

Zoë spun around. "Oh. Aaron. Hi. I, uh, didn't see you there."

The lawyer paused in the threshold, five pairs of eyes glued on him. His throat moved as he swallowed, and he gestured toward the door. "It was slightly open," he said. His eyes met Lane's. "And you said to give you a minute. If you really want to talk, then I'll listen."

"Talk," she repeated dizzily, fighting the cotton that was taking over her brain. "Yeah. Suddenly, I've got lots to talk about." A doozy of a headache had begun, and she moved to sit on the couch. What had started out as a pretty good morning was fast disintegrating into the second worst day of her life.

"I planned on just leaving," Aaron explained. "I even got to my car. But you mean too much to me to do that. You said you wanted to talk to me. If you still do, I want to listen." He looked around at the others self-consciously.

Lane held up a finger, her head spinning. "Yes. Okay. Good. Hold that thought." She turned to Jason. "Is she right?" She pointed at Zoë.

He stepped forward, his hand held out, imploring. "I was going to tell you. I just—"

"So it is true." She took a deep breath. "Hieronymous is your *father.*"

"Who the hell is Hieronymous?" Behind her, Aaron had whispered the question, aiming it Zoë's direction.

"So what?" Jason explained. "That doesn't mean I'm like him. I don't even know him. He didn't raise me. He didn't even know I existed for most of my life."

"Yes, but . . ." Lane trailed off. Even if everything he said was true, it didn't make the situation any better. They were talking about Hieronymous, after all. *Hieronymous.* Head evil bad guy. And now to find out he was Davy's grandfather? She stifled a shiver, anger and fear and general loathing overwhelming her.

But Jason was right. It shouldn't matter. It *didn't* matter. After all, Hieronymous was Zoë's uncle, and that didn't make her evil and weird. So, why should Jason be persecuted for it?

He shouldn't. Jason was who Jason was. He wasn't his father any more than Lane was the mother she'd never met, the woman who'd abandoned her at a day-care center and never looked back.

But somehow that didn't make her feel better.

Her gaze shifted from Jason to Aaron, and she nibbled on her lower lip, her insides all twisted up.

"Lane," Jason said, "listen to me. Hieronymous is the one who kept me away. Hell, he's the one who blocked every path in my life, even before I knew he was my father." He met her eyes, and his gaze was cold. "And I will get retribution. You can't hold who he is against me."

Lane licked her lips, tears pooling in her eyes. Jason had promised to keep no more secrets, and he'd made that promise knowing he still hadn't shared the biggest one of all. Who his father was didn't matter. That he had kept it from her? Frankly, that mattered a lot.

Worse, any illusion she might have been clutching that she and Davy would be first on Jason's priority list slipped through her fingers and smashed into a million pieces on the floor. She could see it in his eyes—they weren't his priority. They never would be.

Jason's priority was revenge.

Part of Jason wanted to scream, part of him wanted to hold Lane close until she trusted him again, and part of him just wanted to head back to Sea World and spend a day or two eating raw fish and frolicking with his *true* friends.

A big part of him, too, wanted to slug Boreas.

The door pushed open farther and Hoop walked in. Jason groaned. He liked the guy just fine, but he was getting further and further away from his fantasy of having Lane alone in a room where she would listen to him.

"Damn," Hoop said. He pulled a package of Twinkies from a plastic sack and started to tear apart the cellophane wrapper. "I leave for five minutes to go to the corner store and you guys decide to throw a party." He held out the confection. "Twinkie, anyone?"

Only Deena answered, moving forward and closing her hand around his wrist. "It's not exactly a party," she said. "You see, it turns out that Jason is Hieronymous's son."

"No kidding?" Hoop gestured toward Aaron. "So whose son is this? Zephron's?"

"No. He's here because I need to talk to him," Lane spoke up. "But I really don't think now is a good time."

"Who's Zephron?" Aaron asked.

"Zephron is who we all need to talk to," Jason said, turning his back on Aaron and getting to the point. "I'm not working for Hieronymous," he added, aiming his words at Zoë. "So quit looking at me like I'm the spawn of Satan."

"Who is Hieronymous?" Aaron asked again, stressing each word, though speaking to no one in particular.

Zoë got right in Jason's face. He sighed. Apparently she felt the need to overcompensate for her wonky powers. "Then why didn't you tell us Hieronymous is your father? Come on, Jason. Even if you're innocent, you must know where we're coming from.

It looks like you were covering for him. And Prigg thinks you're working with him."

"With him? Are you nuts? I would have killed him if I had the chance. Instead, he almost killed me."

"That's what I said," Boring piped up. "Prigg doesn't believe it."

"Whoa." Jason turned to scowl at the young Protector. "You *talked* to Prigg? You told him what happened on the island?"

Boreas backed up, looking as sheepish as Aaron looked confused. "I had to turn in a report. It's required. Regulation nine-three-four-C, subpart j."

Jason ran a hand through his hair, trying to make sense of everything. "But if you reported what happened, why does Prigg think I let Hieronymous go?"

"He thinks you staged it," Zoe said.

"And you believe him?"

Zoë nibbled on her lower lip, then leaned against Taylor. "Honestly? I don't know what to believe. I want to believe you. I really do. But . . ."

"So, why hasn't anyone called Zephron?" Taylor asked. "I know the man's busy, but I think he might be able to get some of this straight."

"I've tried," Zoë said. "I haven't been able to catch him. His assistant mentioned another Outcast uprising. I guess he's got more than just Hieronymous keeping him busy." She went for the pager at her belt. "I'll try again."

"Wait!" Hoop said, galloping across the room to grab the pager. "This guy's not—"

"What?" Aaron said.

"Interested in Zoë's personal calls?" Hoop finished. He shrugged and mouthed to the others, "Sorry. The best I could do."

"A relative," Deena explained, jumping in. "Jason's, uh, relatives are planning a party for Davy for his seventh birthday. And, uh, they're only inviting family."

Jason winced, certain he'd never heard a more ridiculous story.

"Uh-huh," Aaron said, probably thinking the same thing.

Lane blinked but didn't say a word, looking more than a little clueless.

"It's been this whole big argument," Deena continued. "Because, uh, Davy wants me and Hoop to come. But we're not related. And, um, Lane wanted you to come, too, Aaron. But you're not related either."

"You did?" the man asked, smiling at Lane. Jason stifled the urge to slug him.

"Absolutely," Lane agreed, nodding a bit more energetically than the situation called for.

"Oh," Aaron said.

"Make sense?" Hoop asked.

"I'm not s—"

"Good," Lane said. She swung an arm around his shoulder. "Maybe we can talk about it later?"

They were at the door. "I'd like that," Aaron said. "Breakfast tomorrow?"

Lane pulled open the door even as Jason opened his mouth to say no. "Sure, that would be great," she said. She urged the man out over the threshold.

Before she could close the door, though, he managed to take her hand and kiss her fingertips. "I don't know what's going on here," he said, "but we'll talk tomorrow."

"Oh, absolutely," Lane agreed.

The door closed, and she pressed her back against it, her shoulders sagging in relief. "Let's call Zephron," she said.

Jason agreed, even though at the moment Jason couldn't care less about the High Elder. All he wanted to do was run after Aaron and inform the man, in no uncertain terms, that Lane was his and she wouldn't be going out on dates with anyone else.

Except she was. She was having breakfast with Aaron.

And there wasn't a damn thing he could do about it.

Lane had heard all about the secret Ops Center deep below the Washington Monument. Every time Zoë and Hale had an encounter with Zephron, that's where they met him, and since the first time she'd heard about it, Lane had wanted to someday see the installation.

Today, unfortunately, wasn't going to be that day.

"He's going to think I'm a slob," she said, pushing past Hoop to get into the closet next to the door. She shoved aside an ankle-length, black wool coat that was wholly unnecessary in Los Angeles and grabbed the handle of her Hoover vacuum. "This place is a mess."

With a yank, she managed to free the vacuum,

then dragged the cord to the nearest socket. From her half-upside-down position plugging it in, she shot glares at the others in the room. Deena and Hoop, Zoë, Taylor, and Jason all stared back at her, their faces either blank or confused.

"Well?" she prompted.

Deena's tongue traced the edge of her mouth, cleaning up a tiny bit of filling from the Twinkie she'd snagged from Hoop. "Well, what?"

"Don't just stand there," Lane said. "Start picking up some of this clutter." She swept her arm to indicate the room and all the textbooks, study outlines, and Harry Potter books that covered its every horizontal surface.

Zoë had managed to get through to Zephron, and instead of the High Elder ordering them all to Washington, the grandfatherly old man was coming here. To her apartment. And he would surely arrive any minute.

Here her friends and Jason were, standing around doing nothing.

"Move," she snapped. She shoved the handle of her vacuum into Jason's hands. "Clean." She wiped the palms of her hands on her shorts, her gaze taking in everything of her tiny apartment. This was not the lap of luxury, but it would do. "Okay. I'm going to go make cookies or something." She had slice-and-bake. Nine minutes for soft and chewy. No problem.

In truth, as much as she wanted to see the Ops Center, she was secretly grateful that Zephron was coming here. And focusing on cleaning for her friends' head honcho's arrival meant she didn't have to think about Jason, his recent revelation, or the rather surprising update to Davy's family tree.

Jason's hand closed over her wrist, and she started, looking up at him with surprise. "Uh, Lane," he said. "Zephron's not coming here. Just his hologram." He glanced around the room. "Trust me. He won't be able to see a thing. Or have any cookies."

"Oh." She blinked, reaching out to clutch the vacuum, then hung on to it like a life vest. "Well. Hmmm."

"We should talk." His low voice, meant only for her ears, was caressing. She shivered, despite herself.

"Zephron," she said. "There's no time. He'll hologramize or something here any minute."

"Lane . . ." Jason's voice held a hint of reproach, and she scowled.

"*I'm* not the one keeping secrets," she snapped. "You've had your entire life to get used to the idea of who your father is. At the very least, you owe me twenty minutes to get my thoughts together."

She never heard his response, because Zoë's pager beeped, signaling Zephron's call. Zoë placed the device on the floor, and it emitted a swirl of light that ultimately solidified, forming a shape. The soft edges of that light faded, leaving only Zephron, glowing like some ethereal creature right in the middle of Lane's still-unvacuumed seventies-style shag carpeting.

Lane had always thought the Internet was cool, but this hologram was downright amazing.

"I understand Hieronymous has been up to his old

tricks," the High Elder said without preamble. Zephron looked just as Lane had imagined: a kindly grandfather with a hint of Merlin mixed in.

"I had nothing to do with it," Jason piped up.

Zephron's eyes softened. "I would never believe that you did."

Zoë sighed. "I'm sorry about calling you here, but Prigg . . . and Jason's father . . . and, well, everything—"

Zephron interrupted. "Would you have the Council judge you by the fact that you're a halfling? That your uncle is an Outcast? That you are married to a mortal?"

Zoë shook her head, silent.

"And well you should not." The High Elder straightened, seeming to tower over everyone in the room despite taking up a mere eight inches of space from the floor to the top of his projection. "There are those in the Inner Circle who question Jason's loyalty. I, myself, do not. Character will prevail."

Jason sighed. "So, why are you here? Can't you set Prigg and the Inner Circle straight?"

"The boy," Zephron said. His hologram turned to Jason. "You are a man and capable of taking care of yourself, of making your own decisions. But the boy needs our protection. Under the circumstances, Hieronymous will surely double his efforts to reacquire the child."

"Circumstances?" Lane asked, barely able to force the word past the dryness in her throat. She stumbled forward, intent on heading for Davy's room, just to take a peek, just to make sure he was all right.

Deena's hand closed over her shoulder. "Stay," the woman whispered. "I'll go."

Lane nodded, grateful to have friends who knew her so well.

"Why?" Jason asked. "What does he want with Davy?"

"His mind," Zephron explained.

Lane blinked. "Excuse me?"

"The child is brilliant. And he will become more so—perhaps one of the smartest of our kind."

"It's true," Jason said. "Dorothy told me he made a tracking device. That's how Elmer could help tell me where I could find him."

Lane shook her head, shocked. None of that made any sense. "Davy made it?" She shook her head, amazed that she'd completely misunderstood what Jason had told her about the Lite-Brite map. "I thought his inventions were just toys," she said. "I never even suspected—"

"Nor would most mortals," Zephron said. "But I assure you it is true. And soon his mental prowess will reach the first moment of . . . adjustment."

"What's that?"

"A halfling's seventh birthday," Zephron explained.

"I remember that," Zoë said. "My powers went nuts then."

"Indeed," Zephron agreed, smiling at her like a prize pupil. "And so will Davy's. Unlimited potential. Shifting in his mind. Sorting through the corridors of his brain. Loose energy looking for an anchor."

"This makes no sense at all," Lane muttered,

harsher than she intended. But, damn them all, this was her son they were talking about. She didn't need riddles. She needed answers.

As if reading her mind, Zephron aimed his calming smile her way. "Hieronymous seeks to usurp the boy's power. At midnight on his seventh birthday, that power is, in fact, in flux. With the right equipment, Hieronymous could, shall we say, bottle Davy's intellect."

Lane swallowed. "And what happens to my son?" Her voice came out only a whisper, and she reached for Jason's hands, reassured by his fingers, which closed tight around hers.

Zephron shrugged. "The child would live, but he would lose that part of himself forever."

A tear trickled down Lane's face, and she brushed it away, hating herself for being emotional. Still, nothing would happen to Davy. *Nothing.* Hieronymous wouldn't get past her.

"But it has to be on his seventh birthday," Zoë spoke up, all business. "On the midnight leading into his birthday. So . . . between Thursday and Friday?"

Zephron nodded. "Correct." His image shifted, and he turned, taking in each one of them. "Remember: midnight. Protect the boy until then, and the boy will be safe forever." He smiled. "Safe, that is, from this danger at least."

The High Elder's image sputtered and sparked, and then it disappeared, leaving them all alone in the living room. Lane hugged herself, feeling both hopeful and terrified. She leaned against Jason, drawing strength from the arm he wrapped around her.

"We'll just keep him inside until then," Taylor suggested. "It's that simple. Me and Zoë and Boreas, too. We'll all stay here."

"What about me and Deena?" Hoop asked. "I'm tracking a deadbeat dad, but I can put that on hold if you need me."

Jason shook his head. "I appreciate the offer, but I think we've got it covered."

"He's right," Taylor said. "Go earn a paycheck."

"Besides," Jason added, "the houseboat's pretty small. One bedroom, and not too many places to sleep in the rest of the place."

"The houseboat?" Taylor asked.

"Absolutely," Jason said. "I know the boat better, it's already secure, and I feel safer on the water."

Taylor and Zoë exchanged glances.

"Lane and I have already talked about it," Jason added.

Lane nodded. He was right; she'd agreed. But now . . . She licked her lips, unsure. Being in such close quarters with Jason—she wasn't certain it would be smart. But if his houseboat was the best place to keep Davy safe, she really didn't have a choice. "I agreed we'd stay until Davy's safe," she said, needing to make sure the boundaries were clear.

Jason nodded. "Then we're settled." He grinned. "Looks like Hotel Jason is open for business."

* * *

Dinner at Hotel Jason would never earn a four-star ranking, but Davy had a great time, which counted big in Lane's book.

"You're sure he liked it?" Jason asked from behind her. The houseboat had two stories, and Jason's bedroom was on top. A balcony opened off that room, separated by a sliding glass door. Lane stood on the balcony, her arms wrapped around her to fight the chill of the ocean breeze.

"Are you kidding?" she asked. "Mac and cheese and hot dogs? That's a six-year-old's idea of heaven."

"Taylor looked pretty grossed out," Jason said.

"True," Lane admitted. She took his hand, squeezing his fingers. "Don't worry about it, though. They're here to help, not to critique your cooking."

"I . . ." He shook his head. "Never mind."

"What?"

"They're your family. Your friends. I'm already starting at a disadvantage. I'm the guy who walked away."

She didn't know what to say. The truth was, he was right. For years she'd complained about the jerk who'd left her. Here he was.

Rather than tackle the topic head-on, she sidestepped it. "So . . . Why didn't you tell me?"

He sat down on a wrought-iron settee, pulling her down next to him. "I wanted to," he said. "You don't know how many times I started to." He squeezed her hand. "About being a Protector, I mean. The other— Hieronymous being my dad—that, I didn't find out myself until . . . well, the timing wasn't good."

She cocked her head, not understanding. "You

didn't know who your father was?" Of course, she'd never known her father either. Her mother was a shadowy, irresponsible figure; her father was a complete mystery.

"My mother figured it was best I didn't know. She didn't tell Hieronymous either. He had no idea he had a son. I found out later from the Inner Circle. Apparently some of the elders did a bit of genealogical research—they were convinced I had bad blood." He snorted. "Hell, when they first told me, I thought the same thing."

Lane was silent a moment, then asked, "What did you mean by bad timing?"

Jason took a deep breath, then kissed her fingertips. The simple gesture sent shock waves through her body, and Lane struggled to maintain her composure. She and Jason were just talking. *Talking.* Nothing more.

"One of the elders told me about my father the same day you told me you were pregnant."

"Oh, my," Lane whispered.

"Yeah," he agreed. "So off I went to capture my big, bad dad."

"Except he captured you."

Jason smiled, the expression slightly sick. "Got it in one," he said. "And Hieronymous kept me locked up for years. I lost track of time—that happens when I'm transformed—but at some point Hieronymous figured out who I was. He offered me money, power, whatever I wanted. All I had to do was join him."

"But you said no."

"And he didn't take that particularly well."

"What happened?"

Jason squeezed her fingers. "I finally escaped. A good thing, too. I'm not certain Hieronymous would have let me live. He's not the type to take rejection lightly."

"Then it should be over," she said. "The elders must know you're on the Council's side, and—"

He pressed a finger to her lips.

"No?" she murmured.

"No." He drew in a deep breath, his face taking on an intensity she'd never seen before. "But they'll know soon enough. Hieronymous stole my life from me. He stole years, he stole you, he stole my son. And he stole my honor. Soon enough, I'll have my revenge. And once and for all the elders will know just where my loyalty lies."

The icy fury in his voice scared Lane, and she pulled her hand away. The ocean's chill once again touched her, and she felt anger of her own. "You'll do what you have to do," she said. "I know that better than anyone." She turned back, faced him. "But don't do anything until Davy's safe. I don't care about your 'honor,' I don't care about your 'stolen years.' I don't care about revenge. I want my son safe."

He took her hand. "I know."

"Do you? Let me be perfectly clear. You ran off once before when I needed you. I need you again now, and so does Davy. Dammit, you better come through. I don't care what you do on Friday, but until then, you stick to your son like glue. After that, you can go off and do whatever you like."

He took her face in his hands, pressing a kiss to her forehead. She felt the tears trickling down her face, and she tilted her head back, blinking. He caught her mouth, and she returned his kiss hungrily, angry at herself for wanting him so much.

"I promised you," he said, breaking away. "Nothing else will happen to Davy."

She nodded, then lifted her head for another kiss. She wanted to lose herself in his lips before she lost him entirely. She'd seen the intensity in his eyes. Once Davy was safe, Jason would be gone. He had a debt he wanted paid, and she saw now he put that debt above her. Above his son.

She told herself she wasn't hurt. But she was. She didn't want him to leave. Jason had come back into her life such a short time ago, but there was no question it still felt right.

She pulled away, breaking their kiss. She'd already screwed up once this time around; she didn't intend to make the same mistake twice. She'd had her life under control before Jason had come back into it. Best she stayed centered on the path she'd plotted.

"Lane?"

"I'm okay," she said with a watery smile. And it was even sort of true.

Because, with or without Jason, Lane would make sure she and Davy were fine. And that would be true no matter what.

Chapter Thirteen

"There," Hieronymous said, pointing at the center monitor. "The fools. They took the boy to the most obvious place."

Mordi squinted at the screen, trying to make out the fuzzy images: a marina, a houseboat, and—moving about just past the glass door—a little boy. *Davy.*

"It's probably safer than any other place they could take him," Mordi said. "His father's surely got the thing rigged up with tons of security devices."

From the corner, Clyde snorted. "Your father can penetrate any security device."

Hieronymous ignored his Chief of Guards, instead staring down his son. Mordi swallowed, wondering what the hell he'd done wrong this time.

"Safer?" Hieronymous asked. "Is that a question in

your voice? A passive-aggressive suggestion that you do not approve of my methods?"

Mordi licked his lips. The last time he blinked, he'd been in his father's good graces. Now, apparently, he was scum. So, what else was new? "No, sir. I'm only saying that Jason intends to protect his boy."

Hieronymous didn't answer, just tapped his fingers on his desktop.

Clyde stepped forward, his shoulders pulled back and his chest sticking out. "Shall I go retrieve the boy, sir?" He looked down his nose at Mordi. "Or are you still sending *him?*"

His father regarded Mordi, then shook his head ever so slightly. "No. It is already Wednesday. Success is crucial." He met Clyde's eyes. "We shall send one of my little pets."

Mordi cringed, wondering if Hieronymous would have found Jason lacking. He told himself it didn't matter; Jason had turned his back on his father, and Mordi was still right here. One simple twist of fate, and despite his perceived failings, Mordi had become the favored child. The son who stood by his father. The loyal son. The true heir.

It was a new perspective on the world, and it was one Mordi wasn't certain he wanted to give up.

He had to decide soon, though. The plots and schemes and plans of attack were all centered on him. His father was pulling one way, the Council the other.

Here he was; caught in the middle, just one more pawn in someone else's game.

* * *

"I used the circuit board from my Game Boy, and then I used some parts from the clock radio, and then I just put it all together." Davy shrugged. "It was easy."

Jason settled down on the ground in front of his son, looking at the automatic coffee timer the boy had created and been in the process of installing when he had stepped into the kitchen.

He'd about had a heart attack when he saw the kid balancing precariously on a stack of pillows atop a three-legged stool. And then he'd come near to suffering an aneurysm when he realized Davy had taken apart the machine's wiring and was splicing some sort of gizmo into its center.

"Mommy likes coffee right when she wakes up," the boy had said.

"Uh-huh," Jason responded. He'd grabbed Davy around the waist and, over his howls of protest, schlepped the kid to the patio that opened off the dining area. One nice thing about his boat: it had lots of patios.

Now he was outside, with his almost-seven-year-old, and had absolutely no idea what to talk about. Part of him wanted to go back indoors and start breakfast, but Lane and the rest of the gang were still sleeping, scattered across the boat in all its nooks and crannies. If he and Davy went in, they'd surely wake someone. Besides, his son looked perfectly content. It was Jason who hadn't a clue what to say.

"So . . . uh, what else have you invented?" The question wasn't exactly worthy of Dr. Spock, but Jason gave himself a pat on the back nonetheless.

Davy pursed his lips, his small brow furrowing in concentration. "Lots of stuff," he said.

"Like what?"

"Um, I made X-ray glasses."

Jason cocked a brow, not sure he believed that. "No way," he finally said.

"Did, too." Davy reached into his pocket and pulled out his glasses. "I don't think Mommy was happy when she saw the broken part."

"Your mom was just happy you were safe," Jason assured him.

"So, it's okay that I broke the glasses?"

Jason sighed. So much for his try at daddy-hood; he had no idea what to say. "You can talk about that with your mother."

Davy rolled his eyes. "Well, duh."

Jason sat forward, trying to regroup. "So, they're really X-ray?"

"Uh-huh. I wanted to be like Aunt Zoë." He pressed them into his father's hand. "Want to try?"

With metal Harry Potter–style frames, the spectacles looked like ones any second grader might wear. There was a slight sheen on the lenses, but for all Jason knew, that was UV protection.

They didn't fit, of course. Still, with the missing earpiece, the glasses actually balanced pretty well on his nose. At first he didn't see any difference. However, as his eyes focused through the convex glass, molecules started to buzz and shift until the walls, furniture, and everything else solid turned transparent.

Jason half-smiled. *Pretty damn cool.*

He tilted his head back, his line of sight an angle into the bedroom above their heads. Sure enough, the floor disappeared. Then the bed faded, until all he saw was the woman asleep atop it. The mattress started to haze out, then the oversized T-shirt Lane wore as a nightgown. . . .

She stretched, rolling over in her sleep, facing down on the bed—right toward Jason.

He swallowed, the view enticing. His palms started to sweat and his stomach twisted into knots. Looking away, Jason took off the glasses and gave them back to Davy before he totally abandoned his pride and took another peek.

He'd see her naked again. That much he was sure of. But when he did, she was going to know it. If he had his way, she'd even beg for it.

"Mr. Jason?"

At the sound of Davy's voice, Jason wiped the smile off his face. "Sorry."

"Did they work for you, too?"

Oh, yeah.

Jason cocked his head, something Lane had said gnawing at his memory. "Your mom thought all your inventions were make-believe," he said. "How come you never showed her?"

"Dunno," Davy answered, eyeing the floor and suddenly acting shy. "I told her about everything, but Mommy's always busy. She's got school so she can get a good job and move us to a better apartment and buy a car that smells new and doesn't have duck tape on the seats."

Jason grinned. "Right." For years, Lane had been working her tail off trying to make a home for their son. Jason had only managed to entertain the child for twenty minutes. One tick in the Jason column; eight billion ticks for Lane.

He scowled, another thought occurring to him. "Did you tell Mr. Aaron?"

Davy shook his head, his eyes wide.

"Why not?" Jason asked, more thrilled than he cared to admit.

"I dunno. Elmer said most mortal boys can't make things like animal translators. I figured he'd think I was weird."

"You told me," Jason said.

"You already knew," Davy explained reasonably. "Besides, you're weird, too."

True enough.

"Can you invent stuff, too?" Davy asked.

Jason shook his head. "I can barely work my coffeemaker, much less make one from scratch."

"Oh." Davy looked slightly disappointed, and Jason wondered if he was already losing points on the daddy-front. Then the boy said, "I can't see through walls like Aunt Zoë can. Not without my glasses."

Jason nodded, slowly realizing what was going on in his son's little head. "We all have different powers," he said. He tapped Davy on the noggin. "Most of yours are up here."

"That's boring," Davy complained. "I want to be able to shoot fire like Mr. Mordi."

Jason grimaced. "Let's go easy on the emulating Mr. Mordi thing, okay?"

"I didn't used to be able to make things. And then it got easier."

Jason blinked, not really sure about his son's segue, but willing to follow the boy's lead. "That's because you're getting older. When you turn seven, you'll be even better."

"Will I be able to whack someone?" Davy asked. He got up and karate-chopped the railing. "Aunt Zoë's good at whacking."

"You sure will," Jason said. "Most Protectors are super strong. Halflings, too. And you'll likely be able to levitate stuff."

"Really?" Davy put his glasses carefully on the ground, then stared at them, his brow furrowed, his eyes squinting, and his lips pooched out. He made a little snorting noise.

"Uh, Davy?"

"I'm trying to lebitate them. But nothing's happening."

Jason laughed. "We'll work on that. You'll be surprised. Friday you'll start getting your powers more and more. And your mom and I talked about it—I'm going to hang around. Teach you how to use those powers." He cocked his head, trying to read Davy's face for a reaction.

"Can I have an Eggo?"

Jason sighed. So much for a burst of excitement from the boy that he would be a permanent fixture.

"Please?" Davy begged.

Jason looked through the door. Zoë was still asleep on the sofa, and Taylor was sacked out on the floor just below her. "Everyone's still asleep," he said.

"And the sun's barely even up. Can't you wait just a little while longer?"

Davy shrugged. "I guess. . . . Can you whack?"

"Oh, yeah," Jason said. "I'm great at whacking."

The boy was silent for a moment.

"You weren't really in space, were you?"

Jason took a deep breath, not sure what to say. In the end, he decided on the truth. "Nope."

"Oh." Davy filled his cheeks with air and then popped them. "What can *you* do? What are your powers?"

"Other than whacking?" Jason asked, relieved when the boy laughed. "I mostly hang out in the water."

"Really? Why?"

"Remember the dolphin at Sea World?"

Davy nodded.

"That was me."

Davy's eyes widened. "Cool."

Jason's chest swelled a little. His son thought he was cool.

"What else can you do?"

Jason tapped his jaw, thinking. "Well, I had a conversation with Dorothy, and I can hold my breath underwater for a really, really long time." Actually, he didn't hold his breath at all, but explaining the transfer of oxygen from the water through his skin to his bloodstream seemed a little much for a six-year-old. Then again, this *was* Davy.

"Is Dorothy nice?"

"The best," Jason said.

The boy hugged his knees to his chest. "I'm glad

she's here," he said. "And Elmer, too. I can talk to Elmer, but I haven't made a translator yet for Dorothy." He shrugged. "I'm gonna, though." He played with the Velcro strap on his sandal for a while before looking back up at his father. "Why does Hieronymous want me?"

Jason sighed, then glanced up at the bedroom above. Too bad he didn't have the glasses anymore. He'd like to know if Lane was awake. This was one of those parenting moments he wasn't entirely sure he was ready for.

Unfortunately for him, no one seemed to be stirring in the house.

"Mr. Jason?" Davy prompted. "How come?"

"He wants what's in here," Jason explained, tapping Davy's head with the tip of his finger. "He wants your smarts."

"Can he get them?" Davy asked, real awe in his voice.

"I guess so," Jason admitted. "Do you think you could? Invent something like that, I mean."

"A smarts-stealer?" Davy's face puckered up in concentration. "Yeah. Maybe. I guess so." He shook his head. "But I wouldn't. That's a bad thing."

"Yup."

"So, are we going to live here with you forever?"

Jason's breath hitched. He certainly hoped so. But not for the reason Davy meant. "Just until Friday," he said. "After your birthday, you can go back home."

"That's good," Davy said. "I like my stuff." He got up and walked to the edge of the patio, looking down at the water lapping against the side of the boat. "But I like the ocean, too."

Jason moved to stand behind him, thrilled to find a bit of common ground other than Lane. "Why don't we take a quick swim?"

Davy shook his head, stepping back from the rail. "I don't know how."

That surprised Jason even more than the X-ray glasses. *His* son, unable to swim? "Haven't you ever had lessons?"

Davy shook his head. "Mommy wants me to, but she can't afford them. And she doesn't swim very good, so she didn't want to teach me. Uncle Taylor said he'd teach me this summer."

Jason clenched his fists. If he'd been there, Davy would be swimming like a fish. A knot of anger rose in Jason's gut. *Damn Hieronymous.*

He took a deep breath, determined to enjoy this moment with his child. "Why don't I teach you now?" he asked.

Davy licked his lips but didn't jump at the offer.

"Or, better yet, why don't we just play a little?"

At that, Davy's eyes widened. "Really?"

"Sure." His houseboat was moored at the end of the dock, which meant there was a small, enclosed swimming area that Jason often hung out in. When he was feeling adventurous, he'd dive down and swim under the boat docked next to him—a huge yacht owned by some celebrity who used it about once a year. Now, with Davy, he'd just do a couple of quick circles around the enclosure—just to whet the kid's appetite.

He stood up, eager to have some activity with his son that belonged solely to them. "What do you say? Shall we give it a shot?"

Davy's head bobbed, stopping abruptly to scowl up at Jason. "But I don't have a bathing suit."

"Right. Hmmm." He peered at the boy. "What are you wearing under those shorts?"

"Underwear."

"That'll work," Jason said.

"Wear my underwear?" Davy's voice rose a few octaves.

"Sure. Why not? I'll wear mine, too."

"Really?"

"Absolutely," Jason said. And to prove the point, he stripped off his T-shirt and shorts and stood there in his navy blue Hanes briefs. A little father-son bonding in the morning.

Davy giggled, then did the same. Soon he was standing in nothing but a pair of Scooby-Doo skivvies.

"This is gonna be cool," he said. And then he marched over, held out his hand, and waited for Jason to take it.

A lump rose in Jason's throat and he sighed. Baby steps, maybe. But they were stepping in the right direction.

"I'm sorry about the weird arrangements," Lane said as Zoë led Aaron onto Jason's balcony. It truly was awkward, but when he'd called on her cell phone, she'd had to explain where she was staying. "But I really want to stick close to Davy."

"Where is he?" Aaron asked.

"With Jason," Zoë answered. "When I woke up, they were having an earnest conversation on the back patio."

Lane nodded, pleased that father and son were getting along. For a second she considered having Davy join her and Aaron, but then she decided against it. He'd had precious little time to simply hang out with Jason one-on-one; she didn't want to interrupt them now when they were having a good time.

"I think they're playing in the water now," Zoë added.

"The water?"

"Yup," Zoë said. She pointed over the balcony. "See?"

Sure enough, Davy was hanging on to Jason's back as his father splashed and spun in the water. The little boy kicked and squealed and seemed to be having a great time. Goodness knew he deserved a great time after all he'd been through recently, but . . .

Lane nibbled on her lower lip. "Do you think it's safe?"

Zoë raised an eyebrow. "What, the water? He's with *Jason*."

Good point. If anyone could keep Davy safe in the water, it was Jason.

Zoë licked her lips, bit her tongue.

"What?" Lane asked, immediately concerned.

"Nothing," Zoë said in a rush. "Really. I was just thinking about, uh . . . stuff. There's something I've been trying to tell Taylor and we keep getting interrupted." She glanced at her watch. "I think I'll go see if he's up yet." And she did.

After Zoë was gone, Aaron moved up beside Lane and put a hand on her shoulder. "So, what's going on?" he asked. "Can I help?"

Lane shook her head. "It's nothing. Really."

"If it's nothing, then why are you and your entire family staying on this fellow's boat? And if it's nothing, why aren't you in school? What happened to the hundreds of pages you had to read? The Law Review article to write? Finals to study for?"

"You have a trial," she said, dodging his question. "And here you are."

He stroked her cheek. "I'm taking a break to see you."

She rolled her shoulder. "Maybe I'm taking a break, too."

"Lane . . ." He trailed off, a hint of reproach in his voice.

"It, uh, wasn't really a birthday party," she said. She picked up a muffin and started peeling away its paper.

Aaron's eyes narrowed. "What wasn't?" he asked.

"Why we made you leave yesterday," she explained. "What Deena said. It wasn't really a family thing."

"Okay," Aaron said, slowly and patiently. "Then, what is going on?"

"Well," Lane said, "it was a family thing, just not *that kind* of family thing." She edged to the balcony, peering down at Davy and Jason. Her son leaned his head back and waved at her. "Look at me, Mommy! I'm swimming!"

Jason caught the boy under the tummy and swooshed him around in the water, while Davy kicked and splashed and laughed.

"He's okay?" she called down.

Jason laughed. "He's doing great. Aren't you, sport?"

In response, Davy bobbed his head underwater, then came up shaking it, sending water flying like a big, wet dog. Lane laughed, too. "Okay, but—"

"But what? He's fine."

She opened her mouth to argue, then decided against it and just nodded.

"Lane!" Aaron's stern voice drew her back. "What's going on?"

"Oh. Right. Yeah. Well, it's a whole big child-custody thing," she said, blurting out the first thing that came to mind. "Jason's father wants custody of Davy." She took another quick glance at Davy before shifting back to Aaron. "Grandpa is a little nuts."

"Well, then I *can* help," Aaron said. "The firm has a brilliant family law section. Let me hook you up with someone." He moved to the railing and glanced over. "Hey, kiddo," he called. "You look pretty wet."

"Hey, Aaron!" Davy squealed, laughing and splashing some more.

"Hey, yourself," Aaron responded. He squeezed Lane's hand. "So, what do you say? Want me to make some calls?"

"Look at me!" Davy's voice drifted up to the balcony. "I'm a dolphin!"

Somehow, Jason had gotten hold of a ball, and now he held it just above Davy's head. The boy bopped it with his nose, then splashed back under the water.

"You look great, sweetie," Lane called.

The surface of the water became choppy, and Lane looked back, expecting to see the boat's flag flapping in a kicked-up breeze. Instead, it hung limp.

Odd.

"What's that?" Aaron asked, pointing down.

"I don't see anyth—" And then she did. It was just a quick flash of something white and fleshy under the surface of the water. "Jason!" she yelled. "Look out!"

But it was too late. A giant . . . *some*thing . . . burst from the water, one huge tentacle slapping down, taking Davy and Jason under the water with it.

Lane screamed, the world turning black and white like a negative as she clutched the railing and tried to keep from fainting.

Aaron swore, his voice cutting through the fear clouding Lane's mind. Then, "Davy!" he called. In one fluid movement, the lawyer was up on the railing, his shoes left behind on the balcony.

Lane reached for him, but her fingers only brushed the cloth of his khakis. He was gone. Over the edge and into the ocean. One more person she cared for diving right into Hieronymous's clutches.

The Henchman's tentacle smashed over Jason, coming from behind and sucking him and Davy beneath

311

the murky waves. Davy yelped as they went down, then immediately tried to claw his way back to the surface.

But, right at that moment, the surface wasn't the safe place to be. The Henchman—a slimy squidlike creature that lumbered on land but moved with the grace of a jellyfish in the sea—was likely still up there, floundering about, trying to figure out where the man and his boy had disappeared to.

With a tug on his ankles, Jason pulled his son back down. Davy struggled, but Jason kicked them under the houseboat, then gripped Davy's shoulders and looked in his son's eyes. The contact seemed to calm the boy, and Jason's heart beat a little slower.

He was already kicking himself for not expecting the attack. Now all he wanted to do was get Davy back to the safety of his boat's deck—then he'd beat the crap out of one particular Henchman.

First things first. With an eye on the surface to make sure they weren't about to be attacked again, Jason brushed his hand through the water, clearing a space about the size of a basketball—just enough to make an air helmet for a small boy who couldn't hold his breath long enough to suit Jason's purposes.

Davy's eyes widened as they watched the bubble form, then managed to get even bigger as Jason pushed the bubble through the water until it was right next to Davy's head.

Go ahead, Jason said, mouthing the words clearly and distinctly.

His brilliant son knew exactly what he meant—

and in one quick move, Davy popped his head into the bubble and took a long, deep breath.

"Wow," he said, his voice echoing. "Just like an astronaut."

Jason smiled. More points in his column.

Above, the tentacled creature flailed on the surface, its splashing drawing Jason's attention. At first, Jason thought the dumb creature was simply waiting for him and Davy. But then he saw a flash of brown material, and his stomach lurched.

Lane's voice vibrated through the water at the same instant Jason realized—"Aaron!"

Damn. He cursed the mortal, and then immediately took it back. As much as it pained him to admit it, the lawyer had been looking out for Davy. Now Jason had to look out for him.

One silvery tentacle grasped the mortal around the neck, pulling him under the water. Aaron struggled, but the Henchman's grip was too much.

Swearing, Jason pressed his hand against Davy's shoulder, then took the boy's hand and closed it tight around a barnacled wooden mooring. *Stay here,* he mouthed.

Davy had barely nodded his agreement when Jason was up, nearing the surface. Another tentacle reached out for him, but Jason evaded, diving deeper, then flipping around. He kicked the Henchman in the gut—or what he assumed was the gut—and then grasped the tentacle holding Aaron.

The lawyer, thank Zeus, cooperated, twisting sideways as Jason tugged, until he was completely free of the vile Henchman. The mortal clamored to the sur-

face, gulped air, and then dove back down toward
Davy. Jason tensed, wondering how the man would
react to seeing the boy's bubble helmet. But he
didn't have long to worry, because the Henchman
attacked again, this time managing to catch Jason
between two of its wildly flailing tentacles.

Jason struggled, but the suction cups that lined
the tentacles held fast to him. Below, he could see
Aaron leading a helmet-less Davy toward the surface—and looking back at Jason with fear and de-
termination. *Damn.* He needed to get free before the
idiot decided to save him and managed to get caught
all over again.

His son kicked, and in the split second in which
Aaron returned his attention to the boy, Jason
changed. Suddenly he was a dolphin, and the tentacles' suckers no longer adhered to his slick skin.
He slid free, then flipped and aimed back toward
the Henchman, ramming it in the center with his
snout.

Tentacles flailed, but Jason rammed again. And
again. And then once more for good measure. The
creature emitted a low howl—part pain, part frustration. One more time it lashed out, but Jason evaded,
dodging the path of its tentacle and then smashing
it one more time in the midsection.

The ploy worked. The creature gave up, just as
Jason had hoped. As a rule, Henchmen weren't very
bright, and they tended to be easily discouraged.
This one flipped over, diving deep and then, with
tentacles streaming behind it, headed away toward
the open sea.

Jason watched it go, itching to follow. One quick glance over his shoulder and up confirmed that Davy was safe. Aaron was lifting the boy out of the water and into Lane's arms, with Boreas and Zoë standing right nearby to wrap him in a towel.

There wasn't a decision to make. He turned and sped toward the deep black of the ocean. He'd catch the Henchman and destroy it. In doing so, he'd send Hieronymous one damn clear message: Mess with Jason or his family, you'll live to regret it.

Chapter Fourteen

Aaron sat on the deck, bundled in a robe and shivering—and not just from the ocean's chill. Of that, Lane was certain.

"What the hell was that thing?" he asked.

Lane had to smile as she pulled Davy closer, rubbing her son down with a thick terry-cloth towel. Aaron had dived in without hesitation, all because he thought Davy was being attacked by some overeager sea monster.

"A giant squid?" Aaron continued. "Have you notified the marine preserve? They should get someone out here to capture it."

"Already taken care of," Zoë said. She looked at Lane. "They, uh . . . they're sending divers."

"And that other guy?" Aaron continued. "Has he come back? One second he was under the water with

Davy; the next, I only saw that dolphin."

"I'm sure he's fine," Lane said. "He's an excellent swimmer." The truth, of course, was that Jason was long gone. She'd seen him—or rather, she'd seen the dolphin she assumed was him—follow the beast out to sea.

"Even so," Aaron said. "He should be back by now."

"Come on, Aaron," Taylor called from the door. It was a rather transparent attempt to distract the mortal. "Let's find you some dry clothes."

His eyes met Lane's, and she nodded. "Go ahead. I'm not worried. Really."

"Lane . . ."

"Go on." She squeezed his hand. "If you stay in those wet clothes, you'll catch cold."

"Me, too, Mommy?" Davy asked from beneath the bundle of towels in her arms.

"You, too, baby."

Zoë held out a hand. "Come on, kiddo. How about a hot bath? The Pacific's awfully cold."

"A *bath?*" Davy asked.

"Consider it decompression." Lane kissed the top of her son's head. "All Argonauts have to decompress."

"Oh. Okay. Cool." That did the trick, and Davy followed Zoë inside.

Aaron went more reluctantly, with a promise to be right back. Lane barely even heard him. She was already at the rail, her gaze scouring the water, looking for any sign of Jason. Bubbles, fish scales, a dorsal fin, *anything*.

Nothing. The water was perfectly calm, as if making up for the tumultuous moments that had just passed.

Sighing, Lane willed herself to stay calm. Surely Jason was all right. Years ago, she'd been amazed by how comfortable he was in the water. Now that she knew he was practically a fish, she understood why.

He was okay. He had to be. She couldn't bear the thought of losing him twice.

She shook her head, clearing her thoughts. She wouldn't lose him twice, because he wasn't hers. Not this time. And for exactly this reason. She wasn't willing to risk the strain on her heart. Or on Davy's. Not when he went racing off like this after danger.

As she blinked back an errant tear, Aaron reappeared behind her. He was decked out in a pair of gray sweatpants and a Shamu T-shirt that Zoë must have found in Jason's closet. He put his arm around her shoulder and she leaned against him.

Hooking a finger under her chin, he tilted her head up and leaned forward to press his lips lightly against hers. Automatically, she pulled back, then immediately kicked herself for doing it.

"I'm sorry," she said. "I didn't mean—"

He winced, a flash of hurt in his eyes. "You're still in love with him," he said.

"No. No, no." She moved back, out of his embrace, wrapping her own arms around her chest and hugging herself. "Maybe a long time ago," she said. "Not anymore."

"Are you trying to convince me, or yourself?"

She drew in a breath, needing to get oxygen to

her brain. "It doesn't matter. He's not staying. Not for good."

Aaron quirked a brow. "No? He looks pretty attached to you. And he looks just about glued to Davy."

She clenched her jaw. "Yes, well, looks can be deceiving."

Aaron frowned, then glanced once more over the rail. "Look, I know he's a good swimmer, but I really think we should—"

"Should what?" The voice came from below them, and Lane and Aaron both peered over.

Jason! He was safe. Lane closed her eyes and allowed herself one silent prayer of thanks.

Jason pulled himself halfway up the boat's ladder and out of the water, his chest slick, droplets clinging to his arms and face. He clung there, then grabbed a towel from the deck before finally climbing all the way up to join them. "It got away," he said, his face harsh and angry.

"You shouldn't have gone after it in the first place," Lane snapped.

"Are you nuts?" Jason asked, snapping right back at her. "Hieronymous sent it. Do you think I'm going to let him get away with attacking my son?"

"Wait," Aaron said, holding up a hand. "The grandfather sent that creature?"

Lane crossed her arms and raised an eyebrow. Jason had opened the door, he could damn well find a way to close it.

"Jason's dad trains marine life," Taylor said, appearing suddenly on the patio. Lane turned to look at him, one eyebrow quirked. Taylor shrugged, just slightly, the gesture meant only for her. "We think he trained the squid to take Davy."

"That's nuts," Aaron said.

"Dad's a little nuts," Jason agreed.

"So, what does she mean you went after him?" Aaron asked. "I jumped in to help, and for a while you were there . . . then all of a sudden you were just gone."

"I didn't need your help," Jason grunted. "Because of you, I had to watch out for two people."

"Jason!" Lane protested. "He jumped in to save Davy."

"And I'm the one who got the boy out of the water when *you* disappeared," Aaron added, indignant.

Jason took a deep breath. "Look," he began. "I appreciate you getting him back on the boat, but I went after that creature because I was trying to keep my boy safe *permanently*. Not just for the moment."

"Well, it was the moment that mattered," Aaron muttered.

"Stop it!" Lane held up her hands. "Both of you, just stop it." She turned to Jason. "I'm sorry you didn't catch him," she said; then she turned to Aaron. "And thank you for diving in to save Davy. It was very brave." She shot Jason a sideways glance, then leaned over and kissed the corner of Aaron's mouth. "And that's what makes it so much harder—"

"To ask me to leave," he finished for her.

She nodded. "I'm sorry. It's just—"

He pressed a finger to her lips. "No explanation necessary." His glance darted toward Jason. "At least for right now. I know you've got things on your mind."

She breathed a sigh of relief, then walked with him to the door. He kissed the tip of his finger, then pressed it to her nose. Slipping over the threshold, he headed down the pier toward the parking lot.

With a sigh, Lane closed the door behind him. The man was perfect. Brave and charming and wonderful. She didn't love him—she had to at least be honest with herself about that—but she liked him a lot. And she respected the hell out of him.

She was pretty sure he loved her, though. And she knew without hesitation that he adored Davy.

And then there was Jason. He was all those things . . . and even more, she loved him. So help her, she did. But she didn't trust him with her heart, much less with Davy's. He'd run off again, looking for vengeance. Wouldn't he always? Could she live with that?

She drew in a breath, steeling herself. Right now, that didn't matter. The one thing she *was* certain of was that she needed to focus all her attention on keeping her son safe until Friday.

For that, at least, she had a plan.

About the rest of her life, however, she was clueless.

Davy splashed in the tub, delighting in the way Aunt Zoë giggled whenever the water caught her nose.

"You're a mess," the woman said. "You know that?"

"And a handful," Davy agreed. "That's what Mommy always says."

Uncle Taylor passed Zoë the shampoo, and Davy sank down under the water, the new breathing pen he'd created in his mouth. He hated getting shampooed. It always got in his eyes.

"Your mom's right," Uncle Taylor said, his voice sounding all fuzzy and far away from under the water. He reached down and grabbed Davy under the arms, pulling him back up until Davy was sitting, bubbles from his Scooby-Doo Bubble Bath all over his face. Davy blew out a breath, and the bubbles flew through the air. One of them landed on Zoë's nose, and Uncle Taylor laughed.

Zoë quirked an eyebrow, just like Mr. Spock. "Too much of a handful for you?" she asked.

Her husband shook his head. "No way. One six-year-old, I can handle."

"I'm almost seven," Davy said.

"You sure are," Taylor said, coming at him with a washcloth. Davy squealed and tried to dive back under the water, but Taylor had him tight. He ended up giggling and kicking and getting both his bathers and the bathroom floor soaked.

"I'm glad you're up for the challenge," Aunt Zoë said, putting her hand on Uncle Taylor's arm. "Because there's something I've been meaning to tell you." She pressed her lips together, waiting for Davy and Taylor to both quit splashing at each other. "You see," she said, "I'm—"

"Hey, kiddo. You getting all clean?" The door opened, and Jason came in.

Davy bobbed his head. "Uh-huh," he said, still

wondering what Aunt Zoë had been going to say. She sighed and sat back on her heels.

Jason looked at the floor, and then at Aunt Zoë and Uncle Taylor's soaked clothes. "I guess you're getting everything else clean, too, huh?"

"It's more fun that way," Davy said. Then he bit on his lower lip, remembering that this was Mr. Jason's bathroom, and maybe Mr. Jason didn't like when little boys played and made a mess. "I'm sorry. I'll clean it up. I promise."

But Jason just laughed. "Don't worry about it, kiddo. I've been known to do some serious splashing myself."

"Really?"

Jason nodded. "Really." He put a hand on Davy's head, then looked at Taylor. "There's a phone call for you. I think it's Hoop."

Taylor nodded, then climbed to his feet and headed for the door. He stopped long enough to wave 'bye to Davy; then he looked at Zoë. "Did you want to tell me something, sweetheart?"

Zoë just sighed again and climbed to her feet. Davy thought she looked a little green. "No." She shook her head. "It can wait. I'm going to go take a nap."

As Davy's aunt and uncle left, Jason moved over and knelt by the tub. He scooped his hand through the water and gathered a pile of foam, then blew it, sending bubbles flying though the air.

Davy laughed and reached up to pop the bubbles. "Do more, Mr. Jason."

"You know, you *can* call me Daddy."

"I know," Davy mumbled. He kind of wanted to. Really he did. But he just couldn't quite do it. Instead, he slid under the water, then popped back up, sending more bubbles flying.

Jason laughed.

"That was really cool," Davy said. "What you did, I mean. The underwater helmet and then fighting that monster. Are those the kinds of things you're gonna teach me?"

"Sort of," Jason said. "The Council wants you to learn how to use your powers. So, we'll work on all the basic ones. Levitation and speed and agility. And I'll show you how to work a Propulsion Cloak. I'm going to teach you everything I can, and hopefully that'll make the Council happy."

"Really? Cool."

"That means I'll be around for a while," he added. "Is that okay?"

"Sure," Davy said. "I like you. And you like my mom."

Jason smiled, but Davy thought he still seemed a little sad—probably because Davy still hadn't called him *daddy*.

He held out his breathing pen. "Here. This is for you."

"A ballpoint pen?"

"No, silly." Davy rolled his eyes. "You breathe with it." He remembered Jason's fight with the Henchman monster. "But I guess you don't really need something like this."

"Nonsense," Jason said. "I love it." He took a couple of quick breaths from the pen. "It's fabulous."

Davy grinned. "I can make you more stuff, too."

"I'd like that," his dad said; then he held up a towel. "Come on. Your mother's going to think you turned into a fish. And I bet your breakfast is getting cold."

Davy got up and let his father wrap the towel around him. "Mr. Jason?" he said, still thinking about the daddy word. "I'm sorry."

For just a second, Jason looked surprised. Then he smiled, shook his head, and pulled Davy into a hug. When he pushed Davy back again and looked into his face, Jason didn't seem nearly as sad. "No, Davy," he said. "I'm the one who's sorry."

And before Davy could ask what he meant, Jason was standing up and handing him his robe. "Come on, kiddo," he said. "Let's go have some breakfast."

"Professor Plum, in the Conservatory, with the rope," Jason said. He leaned forward over the game board, meeting Davy's very serious eyes. "How about it, sport? Can you prove me wrong?"

Davy shook his head. "Nope."

"Hmmm." Jason tapped his cards. He wasn't *entirely* sure he knew who did it, but he was reasonably certain. Plus, he knew Lane was getting close, too.

And Jason did want to win.

"Okay," he said. "I'm going for it." He reached to the center of the game board, took the little envelope, and popped out the cards—Professor Plum, the kitchen, and the rope. *Hopping Hera.* He'd lost.

Beside him, Boreas shook his head.

Jason glared at him. "You have something you want to say?"

"Nope," Boreas said. He took a bite of the mac and cheese Jason had thrown together for dinner. "Except . . ."

Lane and Taylor laughed, but Jason just scowled.

"Except what?" he asked.

"Except that you're going about it all wrong. Didn't you pay attention during Protector training?"

"Will I get training, too?" Davy asked, distracting everyone.

"Absolutely," Jason said. He met Lane's eyes. "First me, here. And when you're older, you get to go to training camp."

Davy looked at Boreas. "Did *you* go to camp?"

"Yup." The cadet sat up straighter, his chest sticking out. "First in my class."

"Wow," Davy said, and Jason hid a sneer. "What about Aunt Zoë?" Davy added.

"I think she did," Taylor said. He glanced at Lane. "I'm a little worried about her. It's not like her to go to bed this early."

"Oh, please," Lane said. "She's been going non-stop since Sunday. Let the woman rest."

Taylor looked like he had more to say, but Davy piped up again. "So, what didn't you learn, Mr. Jason?"

A muscle in Jason's cheek twitched as he turned to face Boreas. "Beats me," he said. "Ask the director of the oversight committee here."

"Patience," Boreas said. "You rushed in so fast, wanting to win, that you lost."

Lane pressed a hand over her mouth, clearly smothering a burst of laughter.

"The point is to win," Jason said. "And that means you have to be the first to name the cards."

"Exactly," Boring said. "But you didn't win. And Directive nine-four-four-C very specifically states that a Protector shouldn't act until all the facts are in order and the outcome is potentially predictable."

"Potentially predictable?" Taylor echoed.

"You're supposed to be pretty sure you know what's going to happen," Jason said. "That doesn't apply in an emergency, though. Does it, Officer Wise As—"

"Ah-ah," Lane said, casting her gaze toward Davy.

"Uh," Boreas said.

Jason nodded, finally vindicated. "Exactly," he said. "In an emergency, the directives make clear that the goal is containment and protection of any mortals present."

"But we're just playing Clue," Boreas argued.

This time, Lane didn't make any effort to hide her laugh. "He's got you," she said.

Jason couldn't think of any decent response, so he turned his attention to Davy. The boy was yawning. "Bedtime, little man?"

"I am sleepy," Davy admitted.

"I'll tuck him in," Taylor offered. "I wanted to go up and check on my wife, anyway." Lane had offered Zoë the big bed, and her sister-in-law had gratefully accepted, on the condition that she wasn't kicking Davy out of his room.

"Thanks," Lane said. She kissed Davy's cheek. "Just think, tomorrow's your birthday eve."

"Cool," Davy said, snuggling up against his Uncle Taylor's chest.

Jason stood, fighting the urge to take Davy in his arms and tuck him in himself. But the boy looked happy and cozy, and Jason didn't want to push.

"Mr. Jason?" Davy held out his hand, and Jason took it, his heart just about to melt. "Can't I stay up just a little longer? I want to play Mousetrap."

Jason glanced toward Lane for guidance, but no help was forthcoming. "I think it's your bedtime," he finally said. "And besides, we didn't bring that game. Only Clue."

"I don't need the game," Davy said, his voice sleepy. "I can make a mousetrap out of stuff off your boat."

Jason didn't doubt that for an instant. "Sorry, kiddo. It's still bedtime. Maybe tomorrow."

"Okay," Davy yawned. "Thanks for teaching me stuff today."

"You're welcome," Jason said. "I had fun." They'd spent the entire day practicing levitation, and Davy had actually managed to lift Elmer about an inch off the ground. Not bad, considering the boy's powers weren't even really supposed to come into their own until his birthday on Friday.

Of course, if the expression on Elmer's face was any indication, the ferret would just as soon Davy *never* fully grasped levitation. Jason recalled his own antics as a child and figured the ferret had a point.

"I had fun, too," Davy said.

And then, before he could talk himself out of it, Jason leaned over and kissed the boy on the cheek. " 'Night-'night," he said.

" 'Night," Davy repeated. And, to Jason's delight, he didn't try and rub the kiss off.

Taylor said good night, too, then turned and headed out of the room, the bundle of boy flung over his shoulder.

"I guess I'm off to my post," Boreas said. He nodded toward all the dirty dishes scattered across the floor. "Unless you want help with these?"

Lane shook her head. "We've got them. You go ahead."

The cadet nodded, then headed out the door. With Davy's birthday fast approaching, they'd decided Boreas and Jason would trade off on lookout duty. Hopefully, Hieronymous wouldn't show; but if he did, they'd be ready for him.

As soon as the door clicked shut behind Boreas, Lane started gathering dishes. Jason helped, following her into the kitchen with a handful of plates and both of their wineglasses. Before, the boat's kitchen had always seemed too small to him. Now, though, it felt just right. He stood close behind Lane, watching as she filled the sink. He breathed deep, the soft floral scent of her shampoo mixing with the lemony smell of his dishwashing soap.

There was something so *right* about being beside her, passing her dishes, their movements timed nearly to perfection. She reached for the plate he held out, then paused, her head cocked slightly as she regarded him. "What?" she asked, the hint of a smile touching her mouth.

He reached out to stroke her cheek, rejoicing in the way she smiled at him, full of hope and promise. "This was a good day," he said.

She leaned against him, holding a soapy dish in one hand. "The best," she said. She let the dish slip back into the soapy water, then turned to smile at him. "Davy had a great time."

Simple words, but they meant everything. "I hope so," he said. "He's a great kid." His kid. Lane's kid. "You've done a wonderful job with him."

"Thank you." She turned back to the dishes, and he wondered if he'd said the wrong thing, somehow reminded her of his long absence. But no, that would be like reminding her of an elephant in the living room.

He moved behind her, his hands pressing against her arms. "Lane?"

She turned, shifting under his touch until her back pressed against the counter. She was trapped in the circle of his arms. Her cheeks flushed, and he traced the curve of her ear with his fingertip, wondering what was on her mind—hoping it was the same thing that was on his.

She licked her lips, looking down at the floor through her lashes. "It, uh, wasn't just Davy who had a great time." She looked up at him, her eyes wide and full of promise . . . and unspoken questions. "I had a good time, too."

"Lane," he whispered, and his heart lurched. He

pulled her close and stroked her hair. "We'll make it right. We can be a family again."

She stiffened then, and he stifled a cringe, fearful of what she would say.

"I *want* to," she said, her words opening the door to hope. "I want to be with you. I want Davy to have his daddy. Today has made that seem possible, somehow." She clutched his hands, the intensity of her gaze startling him. "But I need to know that Davy and I are your priority."

"You are," he said. "You always have been."

She leaned back against the counter, shaking her head. "Is that why you left me so many years ago—because we were your priority?"

He didn't hesitate. "Yes."

She laughed, the sound harsh, and he hated himself for the mistakes he'd made. Too, he hated his father for . . . well, everything. "Dammit, Lane, I'd just found out who my father was. All those years of the elders looking at me askance, of never getting a prime assignment, of always feeling watched and never completely trusted." He gripped her shoulders. "Don't you see? I had to make everything right. Had to prove myself. I didn't want my child growing up under the same stigma. Not if I could help it."

Her eyes brimmed with tears. "Stigma?" she said, her voice rising. "Davy can live with a stigma a hell of a lot easier than he can live without a father. But I guess that never occurred to you."

Her words hit him like a slap, and he recoiled. "I just wanted to make it right for him," he said.

"For him?" she asked. "Or for yourself?"

He couldn't answer, could only take her hand and hold her close.

"Don't you see?" she continued. "It was a nice thought, but I needed you." A tear trickled down her cheek. "I needed you and you weren't there."

"I'm here now," he said. "And I'm not going away. You two are everything to me. We need to get past this, Lane. I want us to be a family." He stroked her cheek. "I love you, Lane. And whether you'll admit it out loud or not, I know you love me."

"It's not about you anymore, and it's not about me. It's about Davy."

"And that guy Aaron is better for Davy than his own father?"

"Better than a father who won't be there? Yes."

Jason stifled the urge to throw his hands in the air. "I'm *here*," he said. "I'm here, and I'm not going anywhere."

Lane's lips pressed together in a thin line. "I wish I could believe that."

"Dammit, Lane, give me a chance." He stroked her face, twisting a strand of hair around his finger. "I want to make this work," he said. "I want you. I want *us.*"

She exhaled, her breath unsteady, but she didn't argue.

Her silence encouraged him, and he pulled her near, his hands stroked her back, his lips kissed away her fears. "Lane," he murmured. "I'm sorry."

"I know," she whispered. She looked up at him, a small smile on her lips.

Those lips. He couldn't resist, although he knew

he should, and he bent to brush a kiss over them. She sighed—a surprised, dreamy sound—but she didn't pull away. And that was all he needed.

His fingers sank deep into her hair to cup her head, and he held her steady, his mouth seeking the sweet taste of hers. Her lips parted, and his tongue sought entrance. She kissed him with a passion equal to his own, and he moaned, pulling her closer, wanting to consume and be consumed.

"Jason," she murmured, pulling away.

He wasn't about to give her any time to reconsider. With definite purpose, he trailed kisses down her neck, his fingers forging the path. He paused at the buttons on her shirt, managing to work them free, then slipped his hand inside.

She'd been sunbathing earlier, reading law books, and he cupped her breast through the thin material of her bikini. Her nipple peaked, pushing against the cloth, and he closed his mouth over it, bikini and all.

She sighed, the sound of her pleasure working an erotic magic on his body. His blood boiled and his entire body tightened with desire.

"Jason." Lane's voice, a breathy plea, tickled his ear. Her fingers caressed his neck, sliding up to glide through his hair as she moaned.

He pulled away, bestowing kisses up her body, pausing when he reached the indentation at her collarbone. She gripped his shoulders, tight, as if fighting a storm that was building inside.

"I've always loved you," he whispered, as his fingers caressed her back.

Her hands tightened on his shoulders. "I know," she said, her voice barely audible. "And I do love you."

Jason's heart skipped a beat. He loved her. He loved Davy. And she loved him. It was the perfect recipe for a family—except it had already failed once before.

Once again he cursed his father, a wave of regret for everything Hieronymous had stolen from him washing over him. But then he let it go. He slipped his hand down, his fingers tracing under the waistband of Lane's shorts. Her breath hitched, but he didn't slow his assault.

The tips of his fingers stroked the soft skin of her lower belly, brushing lower and lower under her swimsuit bottom until he found the coarse hair there and damp curls. Lane gasped, her head thrown back and her pulse beating wildly in her neck. Jason kissed her throat even as his fingers stroked her, seeking the heat at her core.

She moaned, the erotic noise making him as hard as he'd ever been.

His fingers found her soft folds, and he teased her, rolling the hard nub of her sex between his thumb and forefinger, delighting in the way she writhed against his touch. She murmured his name, and his body pulsed with the need to satisfy her completely, to make Lane his once again.

He could never get the lost years back, but, right now, Lane was his. And, dammit, he didn't intend to lose her again.

* * *

Lane squirmed, needing Jason's touch, wanting to feel him inside her, wanting him to hold her close and murmur soft words.

She wanted everything to be back the way it once was, so very long ago.

His fingers slid over her, and she moved shamelessly, trying to make him touch her just *so*. She wanted to lose herself—to both passion and to Jason. Her body was afire with lust and desperate need, and she'd beg if she had to.

"Jason," she whispered. *"Please."*

He met her eyes. "Tell me what you want."

"You," she said.

"For now, or for always?"

Her heart twisted. "For always," she admitted. "I've always wanted you for always. But—"

He pressed a finger to her lips. "No. Don't say anything. Right now, I just want the good stuff."

She laughed, then caught him around the neck and pulled him close. "Well, then, how's this for good stuff? Make love to me. Make love to me now, or I swear I'll scream."

He hooked his arms under her legs and lifted her, then carried her to the patio.

He moved closer to the railing and she frowned, fearful that she knew what was coming. "Jason?" she asked.

"Trust me," he whispered, putting her on her feet before him.

She opened her mouth to protest, then closed it again. Drawing in a deep breath, she nodded. She *would* trust him. She *did* trust him.

With slow, methodical movements, he peeled off his clothes, revealing a tiny black bathing suit that left nothing to the imagination. Certainly not how much he wanted her.

She licked her lips, reluctantly dragging her gaze upward to meet his.

He flashed a knowing grin. "Your turn," he said.

"I . . . I can't swim."

He took a step closer, his fingers plucking at the elastic waistband of her shorts. "I'm not asking you to."

With a firm tug, he slid the shorts over her hips and down her legs, dropping them to pool around her ankles. Without a word, he took her hand, urging her to step out of them, then led her to the ladder that descended to the water.

He went first, one step at a time down, with her two steps above him. She could feel his breath at the small of her back, the sensation making her body tingle.

At the last step, water splashed her midthigh. With a gentle hand around her waist, Jason plucked her from the ladder, turning her to face him as he treaded water. They bobbed together, legs intertwined, the cool ocean sweet relief from the burning in her blood.

Together, they moved to a buoy, and he gently placed her hands upon it. "I'll be back," he said, disappearing below the surface before she could ask what he meant.

Despite the lights from the boat, she couldn't see into the night-black water. But she could feel. And as the water gently lapped against her shoulders, Jason's mouth caressed her stomach, his lips hot against her skin. A warm, delicious sensation filled her, and she leaned back, half-floating in the water as Jason worked his magic under the surface.

He slipped his fingers under her bikini bottom, urging it off, and Lane shivered from the sudden rush of cool water against her naked skin. Jason's hand skimmed down to cup her sex, his fingers teasing. Every caress offered the promise of something more, but never quite delivered, and Lane's body trembled with anticipation.

Under the water, Jason's tongue skimmed over her belly, lower and lower, as if he were tasting her and couldn't quite get enough. His hands grasped the insides of her thighs; the tips of his thumbs teased flesh more intimate. She squirmed, silently urging him to slide inside her and quench the fire that the water all around couldn't touch.

His hands moved away, and Lane groaned, then moaned in surprised satisfaction when his mouth closed over her, kissing her intimately, his tongue laving her in deep, rhythmic strokes. They built and built inside her until she was certain her body couldn't withstand the force.

With one hand still holding on to the buoy, she slid her other into the water. She buried her fingers in Jason's hair and arched her back, pressing closer. She was on the edge, desperate to tumble headlong into passion, and she writhed shamelessly against him, seeking release.

He pulled away, leaving her hot and tingly. She

moaned in protest, urging him up from under the water, a plea on her lips. "Jason, please, don't stop."

Water cascaded off him, the droplets glistening in the marina lights. "I don't intend to stop," he said. He slipped her bathing suit over the buoy; then he put his own over it as well. He kissed her, catching her in a tight embrace, his erection pressed hard between her thighs.

"Do you still trust me?" he asked.

She nodded, unable to think about anything except having him inside her.

"Let go of the buoy . . ."

She barely had time to comply before he held tight to her hips and pulled her down, impaling her. She gasped, her sex enveloping him, drawing him in.

The water supported them as they moved together. She held tight, wanting him to never stop, wanting to never lose this closeness.

"Lane," he whispered her name, murmuring it over and over as he cupped her behind, pushing against her as he sank deep inside her. Her body burned against his, alive and on fire. She wanted to forget their past and her fears and lose herself in the power of his touch. . . .

Over and over, she thrust against him, as if by joining their bodies, they could somehow rejoin their lives. A slow, delicious pressure built in Lane's muscles, a physical anticipation, a craving, pleasurable in and of itself, but holding the promise of so much more.

She held her breath and closed her eyes, her body meeting his as she struggled to find release. And, just as the stars exploded in her veins, she felt his body tense and quake—and she knew he'd found release, too.

She pressed her legs tight around his waist, rocking with him as wave after wave of pleasure rippled through her. As the last tremors of passion took their course, Lane clutched Jason's shoulders, her fingers pressing into his skin.

"You know I love you," he whispered again. His body slid on hers, warm and possessive.

"I know you do," she said.

Snuggling close, she sighed, feeling sad and happy all at the same time. He loved her, yes.

Once upon a time, that hadn't been enough. But this time he'd promised he'd stay. Her heart twisted a little and she said a silent plea that, this time, he meant it. She wasn't making another huge mistake. This time, love really would win.

Hieronymous whipped the black cloth off, revealing a rather unpleasant-looking contraption with a metallic helmet strapped to dozens of copper-colored wires. The wires led to a perfectly formed glass sphere filled with some sort of glowing gas.

"Here," he said, pointing to the sphere. "This is where I shall collect it." He tapped the helmet with the tip of one long finger, then traced along the wiring. "From the boy, to the wires, and, ultimately, to me."

His smile caused Mordi's blood to run cold. "Perfect," he said. His lips curved into a frown. "Or it would be."

"The boy," Clyde said. "Allow *me* to retrieve him, sire."

"No." Hieronymous moved to his desk, then sat behind it, his fingers drumming on its solid surface. "You are still wanted by the Council. Should you be caught, the consequences would be dire." Hieronymous paused, glancing casually at the monitors lining the wall. "And I still have need of you, so it would be most inconvenient if you were captured."

Mordi shifted, having a feeling he knew what was coming.

"Mordichai," his father said, with a nod toward him. "The child must be acquired and brought here before midnight. You understand the consequences should you fail?"

Mordi swallowed and stepped forward. "Yes, Father." And he did. He understood what would happen if he failed . . . and he knew what would happen if he succeeded.

Part of him wanted to leave this island, head to Olympus, and never look back. Another part of him wanted to please his father. To take up the reins of an empire.

He knew what he *should* do. What he *would* do, however, remained a question.

Lane laughed as Davy poked and prodded at the insides of the television. Behind him, Elmer chattered peevishly.

"You better hurry," Lane said, "or Elmer won't be speaking to you anymore."

Davy just rolled his eyes. "Oh, Mo-om," he said,

drawing out the word. "I'll get it back together." A few more twists of wire and a bit more clanking, and he did exactly that. With a flourish, her show-off son put the casing back on. "See?" he said. "All done."

Lane tried to keep her face serious. "And just what does it do?"

"Shows tomorrow's television," Davy said. "So you won't miss your program."

At that, Lane laughed outright, even as Elmer chittered louder and started bouncing up and down.

"But sweetie," she said, "Elmer's show is coming on *tonight*."

"Mrs. Doolittle" was set to begin in five minutes.

"Oh." Davy picked up his screwdriver. "I'll just take it apart again."

"No, no, no." Lane plucked the screwdriver from his hand. "Elmer can watch the television in Jason's room." She turned to Zoë. "Would you mind taking him up?"

Zoë's head appeared. She was on the couch, holding hands with her husband.

"Oh," Lane said. "I didn't mean to interrupt."

"What were you going to tell me?" Taylor said.

Zoë kissed his cheek. "Later," she said. She stood up. "Come on, Elmer. Let's go see what I'm sure will be your Emmy award-winning performance."

Elmer skittered toward the stairs and Zoë followed. Taylor got up, shook his head, and excused himself to the kitchen.

Lane scowled, feeling like she was missing something. For a second she thought about going after Zoë, but a knock at the door changed her mind.

When Davy got up to answer, she put a hand on his shoulder, halting him. "You can get the door after your birthday, sweetie. Until then, stay behind me."

She peered through the peephole. *Aaron.* She drew in a breath. She needed to talk to him, but that didn't mean she wanted to. She let him in, and he immediately bent down and gave Davy a hug.

"Hey, big guy. How you doing?"

"I'm good," Davy said. "I made a future TV."

"Vivid imagination," Lane said.

Davy tilted his head up. "Can I go play with Jason?"

She looked at Aaron, noting the man's flash of disappointment. But after a second she nodded. "Sure, sweetie. Go ahead."

"I guess I don't rank anymore," Aaron said after Davy had disappeared.

"I'm sorry," she said. "I just—"

"Want him to get to know his father. Of course you do." A sad smile touched Aaron's lips. "It seems like he really likes the guy."

Lane nodded. "Yeah. I think he really does."

Aaron's features hardened. "I take it he's not the only one."

"I . . ." Lane started to protest, but she couldn't find the words. He was right. She drew in a deep breath, searching for courage. "I never wanted to hurt you."

Aaron opened his mouth, and for a second she thought he was going to lash out. But then he took a deep breath and nodded, his eyes infinitely sad. "Believe me, I know that." He shook his head. "And

I never wanted to be second best. We both deserve better than that." He reached into his briefcase and handed her a large envelope.

"What's this?"

"Class notes," he said. "I swung by UCLA and tracked down your study group." He brushed her cheek with his thumb. "If you ever decide the district attorney's office isn't the place for you, give me a call."

"Thank you," she whispered, hoping he understood that she meant for more than just the notes. "I hope . . ."

"What?"

"Everything," she finally said. "I hope you get everything you want. And I hope you find who you want."

"Have you?" he asked, giving her one last look.

"Yes," she answered. The word came to her lips without hesitation. Jason was everything she'd ever desired, everything she'd wanted in a man, a husband, and a father to her child. She'd told herself otherwise, but it had all been just self-protection. Now, she had to believe in him. She had to pray he wouldn't disappoint her again.

"I'm glad," Aaron said, pausing at the door. He squeezed her hand. "Good-bye, Lane."

She watched him go until he stepped from the dock to the parking lot and disappeared into his car. She clutched the knob of the door, hoping she was doing the right thing. But as much as doubt gnawed at her, she knew that, in the end, this was best. She didn't love Aaron, and she did love Jason. She loved him with all her heart, and she needed to trust him. It was scary, yes, but he'd promised to put Davy and her first, and she believed him.

So help her, she did.

They were going to put their family back together and push the past behind them. And they were going to live happily ever after. Everything she wanted, Jason could give her. At some point, she'd had to let go and just trust her heart.

She turned back into the houseboat, going straight for the glass door at the rear, to watch Jason and her son. Jason wasn't there, but Davy was, sitting next to Boreas at a small metal table, clearly waiting for his dad to return.

And then Jason stepped into view, and Davy's face lit up. Lane smiled, seeing how easily her boy went to Jason now. But then Jason kicked the table, knocking Boreas backward. At the same time, he grabbed his son around the waist, then ran to the edge of the boat, pulling a Propulsion Cloak out from under his jacket.

Mordichai.

As Davy screamed, Lane did, too. But it was too late. Mordi was long gone, flying toward the horizon and into the sunset.

And once again, he had her baby.

Chapter Fifteen

Lane's scream still hung in the air when Zoë saw Jason—the real one—dive from the top of his boat into the water, hot on Mordichai's trail.

The clatter of feet rang out on the stairs, and Lane barreled down them, Taylor and Elmer right behind. They followed Zoë onto the patio, racing to Boreas's side.

"Mordichai," Zoë said.

Boreas groaned, pushing the table off him. "I didn't recognize him as a shapeshifter until it was too late."

Lane brushed tears from her cheeks with the back of her hand. "We have to go after them. We have to find Davy."

Boreas shook his head. "Jason shouldn't have gone," he said. "Directive eight-two-seven-b is clear.

It was proven back at the island when Jason almost got himself killed. And you're Davy's mother, so you're even more involved. Plus you're not a Protector. We have to get backup. The outcome of this isn't predictable, so Directive nine-four-four-c prevents us from rushing in. It's too dangerous."

Lane stared at the cadet, her fists clenched at her sides. "This is my *son*, Boreas. And we're going after him."

"But regulations . . ."

"Boreas!" Zoë snapped, her heart wrenching. She clutched her stomach, thinking about her unborn child.

"But the rules . . ."

"Oh, please! I'm sorry Prigg yelled at you, but screw the rules," Zoë said. "Call in backup, but take Lane and get to that island."

Boreas's gaze dropped to the ground, and to his smashed holo-pager. "I think it got busted by the table."

"Okay. I'll take care of getting backup," Zoë said. "You two just go."

Lane took the young Protector's hands. "Please," she said.

Boreas swallowed.

Lane dropped his hands and turned to Zoë. "Fine. If you won't, Zoë will take me."

Zoë shook her head, wishing she could. "I ca—"

"I'll *do* it," Boreas said. "I will." He nodded, as if convincing himself. "I mean, it may not be regulations, but it's the right thing to do."

"It is," Lane said.

Boreas pointed a finger at her. "But no running off on your own. You stick with me."

"Yes, sir."

"It's dangerous," he added.

"I know," Lane agreed with a nod.

"Willingly taking a mortal into peril . . ." he muttered. "They're going to kick me off Olympus for this."

Lane leaned forward and kissed his cheek.

He scowled, then shot Zoë a glare. "At least you'll be going down with me. We're *both* taking her into peril."

Zoë licked her lips. "Uh, I'm afraid you're on your own there."

Taylor frowned. He'd been silent, but now he spoke up. "What are you talking about? We have to go help, too."

"I can't. I'm—"

"Are you kidding?" Taylor asked. "Of course we have to go."

Again, Zoë shook her head. "We're too slow by boat—at least with any boats *I* know how to use." She turned to Boreas. "You'll have to travel by Propulsion Cloak, and you can't carry all three of us."

"We'll take your cloak," Taylor said.

Zoë bit her lip. This wasn't how she'd planned to tell him. "I can't," she said, dodging the issue. "My powers are acting up. I can't trust myself to keep a Propulsion Cloak in the air. It's just Lane and Boreas, I'm afraid."

Taylor pressed his hand to her forehead.

Lane frowned. "Are you okay?" she asked.

"What's wrong?" Taylor said at the same time.

"I'm fine," Zoë said. "Great, in fact." She took Taylor's hand. "I was looking for a better way to tell you, but—"

"Zoë?" Taylor interrupted, the concern clear in his voice. *"What?"*

She shot an apologetic glance Lane's way, then tugged Taylor back toward the door, out of earshot.

Concern flashed in his eyes. "Sweetheart, you have to tell me what's up."

She couldn't help the smile that touched her lips. "I've been *trying* to tell you," she said. "These aren't exactly the circumstances I'd wanted, but . . ." She paused, drawing in a breath. "I'm pregnant."

The worry in Taylor's eyes faded in an instant, replaced by joy and love. His hand immediately went to her stomach. "Oh, babe, that's . . . oh, wow." He blinked, and a huge grin spread across his face. All at once, he threw his hands around her waist and picked her up, swinging her in a circle and laughing. "That's wonderful!"

She laughed. "Yes, it is. But it's messing up my powers."

Taylor looked back toward Lane. "So, you meant it when you said—"

"I really *can't* go. I physically can't get there. We might be halfway over the ocean, and then *plonk,* we'd fall in."

He gnawed on his lower lip, looking at his sister. "I don't want Lane to go either. Boreas can go alone. Lane hasn't got any powers. She'll just be—"

Zoë pressed a finger to his lips. "I know. You think

she'll just be in the way." Her husband's hand was still on her belly, and she covered it with her own. "But, believe me, she's going if she has to swim there. Personally, I'd rather she go with Boreas."

Lane fidgeted on the deck as she watched Taylor and Zoë. They all needed to go—needed to hurry up and retrieve Davy—and she shifted her weight from side to side, trying to stay calm and fight the hysteria fast building in her chest.

After a few minutes, her brother and his wife came back, hand in hand and positively glowing. She had a feeling she knew what they'd been talking about, and Taylor's expression confirmed her suspicions. Pushing down her misery about Davy, she ran to Taylor and spared a moment to share his joy. She gave her brother a quick kiss on the cheek. "Congratulations," she whispered.

"You knew?"

She shook her head. "I guessed."

Zoë laughed. "I've been trying to tell him for days."

Lane threw her arms around her sister-in-law. "Oh, Zo! This is fabulous," she said, and Boreas seconded the comment. "But—"

"Go," Zoë agreed, pointing toward the water. "We'll talk later."

Lane glanced at Taylor, who looked a little shell-shocked, but in an ecstatic he-man-look-what-I-did kind of way. She gave him another quick kiss on the cheek, and he squeezed her hand and swung an arm around Zoë's shoulder. "Go on," he said. "My baby needs his cousin back."

"Right," Lane said. She looked at Boreas. "Let's go kick some Outcast butt."

Boreas shifted his weight from one foot to another. "I want to," he said. "But I don't know where we're going. Not exactly."

Taylor cocked his head. "But you were there."

Boreas nodded. "Yeah, but Jason programmed the boat's autopilot. I never saw the coordinates. I can get us to the general vicinity, I guess . . ."

A fresh wave of fear twisted Lane's stomach. "That won't do us any good. The island's invisible, remember? Without the exact location, we're screwed." She kicked at one of Jason's deck chairs, then collapsed to the deck, a fresh flood of emotion bursting forth. "We have to find him. We have to do something."

"How did Jason find it last time?"

Lane frowned. "The Lite-Brite map. But—"

She clamped her mouth shut. *Elmer.* She needed Elmer.

"Lane?" Zoë prompted. But Lane was already rushing through the boat toward Jason's bedroom, the ferret and the map.

It might not be a GPS, but it was better than nothing.

What had he done? Oh, what had he done?

Mordi paced, skirting the edge of one of the little rivers of water that ran through the main cavern. A few feet away, his father tested the straps that bound Davy's arms, legs, and chest. A helmet kept the terrified boy's head firmly in place. The machine nearby beeped and hummed with life.

Hieronymous was taking no chances. There was one of the little orbs Mordi had seen him pitch at Jason centered on the contraption's flat control panel—just in case. Everything else was set, already turned on, so that at the stroke of midnight the machine did its thing.

All Mordi had to do was get through the night without throwing up.

From his chair, Davy stared up at Mordi with pleading eyes, his mouth taped shut to keep him silent. Mordi looked away, unable to meet the child's glance.

"Your performance today pleases me, Mordichai," Hieronymous said.

"Thank you, Father." The words came out as a croak, and Mordi cleared his throat.

"Come." Hieronymous gestured for his son to approach.

Mordi swallowed but went, even as Clyde glowered at him from the corner.

Hieronymous pressed his hand to Mordi's back. "You will stand at my side as this great moment occurs," he said. He glanced at the clock mounted on the wall. "Only one more hour. Sixty short minutes, and I shall be more brilliant than anyone can imagine." He sighed, thrusting his hands in front of him and flexing his fingers. "It is a great day. Is it not, my son?"

"Yes, sir," Mordi said. "A great day."

He stepped back a pace so he could lean against

his father's machine, afraid that his legs would give out otherwise. He felt queasy and faint and generally nauseous, and right then he wanted more than anything to turn back the clock. But he couldn't. Which meant that he didn't know what the hell he *could* do except go along with his father.

He just hoped like hell that Jason returned in time and somehow managed to save his son.

Jason approached from the water, moving with the stealth of a shark. Since Davy's escape on Tuesday, Hieronymous had beefed up his security, and it had taken Jason over an hour to get past the new and improved booby traps—not to mention the time it had taken to get from the marina to the island.

But he'd made it, and now he was in the middle of the island stronghold's main chamber, floating just under the surface of the water, waiting and watching.

From his peculiar angle he could see Davy, strapped into an ominous machine and looking terrified. Clyde wasn't in his field of vision, but Jason assumed he was up there. Hieronymous stood at the machine's controls, Jason's lapdog of a half brother right beside him. *Damn Mordichai.* From what Jason had picked up, the guy had been on the verge of going straight. So, what the hell had happened?

Hieronymous strode forward, his arms out, his cloak fluttering. He tilted his head back and laughed, a joyous sound that made Jason ill. But at the same time understanding dawned. Looking at his father, Jason sensed the man's power, the personal presence that only a rare few possessed. Mordi had gotten sucked in by it.

Not that his father's charisma mattered, of course. All that mattered was freeing Davy.

A digital clock hung from the ceiling, counting down the time. Thirty minutes and forty-eight seconds. He had just half an hour to rescue his son.

Careful not to make a sound, Jason emerged from the water only far enough to peer around. He needed to locate Clyde, get the lay of the room, and plan his attack.

He'd rushed after Mordi the second he'd seen the creep take off with Davy. Without a Propulsion Cloak, he hadn't been able to catch his brother, but he'd kept up with the pair from below the water— at least until they'd arrived at Hieronymous's island. Mordi and Davy had entered from the air, going through the appropriate entrance. Jason had had to fight his way in from the sea.

Which all meant he was sadly lacking in tools. When Mordi had absconded with Davy, Jason had been reading the paper on the upstairs deck, wearing shorts and a T-shirt. Fortunately, he'd seen a lost diver's knife on the ocean floor, otherwise he'd be entirely without weapons. As it was, he didn't have much of an arsenal. Soggy clothes, a rusty knife, and Davy's ballpoint pen.

Oh yeah. The odds definitely favored the house.

A ear-piercing electronic wail filled the room, like 10,000 car alarms on steroids. Jason's heart picked up its tempo, and he slipped back under the water, afraid Hieronymous's surveillance technology had somehow detected him.

Clyde stepped forward into Jason's line of sight. "An intruder, sir."

"Thank you, Clyde. I believe I discerned that on my own," Hieronymous hissed. "What I have *not* yet figured out is how an intruder has penetrated the complex again. Are your sentries not in place? Did you not increase our defenses? Did I not make myself clear that anything less than perfection tonight would be *severely* punished?"

Clyde nodded, backing away. "Yes, sir. Of course, sir. I'm sure the intruder has been captured already, sir. I'll just go—"

"Do that," Hieronymous said.

As Clyde backed away, a scuffle erupted in the corridor: a flurry of activity, followed by five guards with angry faces. The guards parted, pushing someone forward. *Lane!* And following right behind, Boreas was bound with his own cuffs and lariat.

"Ms. Kent," Hieronymous said, walking over to stand in front of her. "How good of you to join us. It was remiss of me not to send an invitation. Foolishly, perhaps, I didn't think you would accept."

"Please," she said, "let me have my son." A tear trickled down her cheek, but she looked the Outcast straight in the eye without flinching. Jason silently gave her points for that, even as his mind sorted through what the heck to do now.

Part of him was furious that she and Boreas had come, but it was a weak anger. Of course she'd come. Hell, if she'd had to, she would have swum to

the island alone. The bigger part of him was terrified. He'd only just gotten her back, she and his son.
He couldn't—*he wouldn't*—lose them.

Hieronymous cocked his head, as if considering
her question. "Ah, my dear, I'm afraid I'm going to
have to deny your request for the moment. Though
I do commend you for having the courage to ask."
He made a shooing motion, and the guards pulled
her roughly back. They threw her in a limp heap at
Boreas's feet. He immediately knelt down beside
her.

The guards surrounded them, but they didn't in-
terfere. With the lariat around him, Boreas was no
threat.

For that matter, Jason himself was no help.

The clock was ticking, and Hieronymous was looking more and more eager. Jason didn't have a
choice; he had to make a move. Once again his gaze
skimmed the room, and that was when he saw it—
his chance. His clever Lane was slowly inching the
lariat up Boreas's body. When she finally got the
rope over his head, the Protector's powers would return—his rubbery hands could squeeze through the
cuffs, and the guards would be more than occupied.

Perfect.

"Well, well. Look what I found." A smug voice
sounded behind Jason even as the water around him
trembled. All of a sudden he was rising up, trapped
in a net that must have been hidden on the bottom
of the stream.

Damn!

"Another intruder," Clyde crowed. "A little fish in

355

a big net." He gave the net a shove, sending Jason swinging. "Shall we fry him?"

"This is turning into quite the family affair," Hieronymous said. "Had I known, I would have had it catered." He waved a hand. "No matter. There's plenty of fun to be had without food."

"Let my son go," Jason snarled, "or I swear, I'll kill you."

The slow grind of a crankshaft echoed through the chamber, and the net closed tighter about Jason as he was drawn farther up.

Hieronymous tapped his chin. "Let Davy go? Hmmm. Is that what I'm going to do? No, I'm afraid not. But thank you for playing. And if any other answers pop to mind, feel free to give a shout. Who knows? Maybe you'll win a prize."

Time was ticking away, and there wasn't a damn thing Jason could do. He struggled against the ropes, but uselessly. Below him, Lane's eyes met his, dark and determined. She was still inching the lariat up, but there was no guarantee she'd get Boreas released in time—or that the neophyte would be able to save Davy once he was free.

Reaching back, Jason found the knife he'd tucked into the waistband of his shorts. Dull and rusty, the thing barely even qualified as a weapon. But it was all he had. It was he and a rusty bit of metal against Hieronymous, Mordichai, Clyde, and a whole battalion of Outcast minions. Plus, he was trapped in a net.

Not ideal circumstances.

Trying to move surreptitiously but with speed, he

sawed at the ropes binding him. Before his machine, Hieronymous had already forgotten he existed, apparently assuming that his dangling son was no threat at all.

Jason intended to teach his father never to assume anything.

Hieronymous loomed in front of Davy, the expression on his face almost gleeful. "Do you see that clock?" he asked, pointing to the numbers *tick-tocking* their way to midnight. "When it gets to twelve, it will be your birthday." His smile was full of menace. "First, a present for me—then perhaps some cake for you."

"You bastard," Lane screamed. "He's your grandson. He's just a little boy. How can you do this?"

Hieronymous turned slowly to face her. "Why, my dear, I think you overreact. The boy won't be harmed. Not physically, anyway. And he will be making a donation to history. What mother wouldn't want that for her son?"

"*This* mother," Lane snarled. She lunged forward, but two guards restrained her.

Jason held his breath, hoping she wouldn't attack again. She was certainly no match for Hieronymous. But if she would go back to loosening Boreas's lariat, the pair might be a match for those guards.

It didn't matter what she did. The clock was ticking, and as soon as Jason sawed through the ropes, he was going for broke—with or without anyone's help.

His eyes met Davy's, and he saw the hopes reflected there. His chest tightened, and he prayed he didn't disappoint his son.

He *wouldn't* disappoint his son.

Faster and faster, the ragged teeth of his knife clawed at the ropes. The netting creaked, its fraying rope unable to support his weight.

Jason sawed faster, his gaze glued on Hieronymous. The Outcast looked positively giddy. Beside him, Mordi didn't seem to share their father's enthusiasm. The guy picked up the silver orb—Jason recognized it as the type that had knocked him out of commission earlier—and started rolling it between his flattened palms. At first, Jason thought Mordi intended to fire the energy beam. But then he realized his half brother was simply toying with the device—a nervous habit of some sort. Not that Mordi had anything to be nervous about. It was the top of the ninth and his team was winning.

Not for long, though. Jason intended to hit a homer. One final thrust of the knife and the net frayed completely, sending him tumbling to the ground. In that same moment, Lane—bless her—yanked the lariat over Boreas's head.

In a split second, Jason threw his knife, aiming it at Hieronymous's chest. At the same time, Boreas's arm shot across the room, landing with a *sproing* against Clyde. The guard captain, who'd been rushing Jason, tumbled backward, landing next to the stream even as Hieronymous tried to evade Jason's throw. The blade sank into his flesh, though, and Hieronymous collapsed to the ground.

Lane and Boreas raced for Davy, and Jason rushed

toward Hieronymous, needing to be certain his knife had done its job.

It hadn't.

He was barely two steps away when his Outcast father rolled to his side, a low groan escaping his throat. The knife protruded from his upper arm; blood oozed from the wound.

Near the machine, one of the guards had caught Lane. A burly one had her by the elbows, and Boreas was battling several others, letting them spring and bounce off him as he tried to fight his way to Davy.

Mordi ran forward, his expression unreadable, the silver orb still in his hand.

"Throw it," Hieronymous called, his voice thin but loud. "Don't let them get to the boy."

And before Jason could react, Mordi threw. But instead of smashing into the ground, the orb seemed to arc up, right in front of Jason.

Startled, Jason grabbed it, clutched it tight to his chest.

"You fool!" Hieronymous hissed. "You bloody, incompetent fool!"

"I'm sorry," Mordi said. "My aim . . . it went wild." But the apology was hollow, and triumph, not fear, shone in the man's eyes.

Hell, if Jason didn't know better, he'd say that Mordi had intended for Jason to catch it. And his half brother didn't seem to have armed the thing. It didn't make any sense. . . .

Well, whatever the reason, he had the orb now. In one fluid motion, he smashed it into the ground, then popped Davy's breathing pen into his mouth.

The chamber filled with gas, and everyone was breathing it. *Everyone.*

Except Hieronymous remained unaffected, just like he had been the first time.

"Fool," the Outcast hissed. "You can't defeat me. Not if you want to save your son."

Instinctively, Jason took a step toward his father, then paused, the import of what he was doing hitting him. *It was 11:58.* If Davy was still in that machine when the clock struck midnight . . .

Ignoring Hieronymous, he rushed toward Davy, his fingers clawing at the straps and buckles and locks. Behind him, he heard Hieronymous scuffle away. It didn't matter. Nothing mattered except Davy.

11:59.

Behind him, Lane lay motionless on the floor. Davy was their son and, dammit, he was *not* going to fail.

Just one more buckle.

The damn thing stuck. Until it was loose, the helmet was still on Davy's head. With every ounce of strength in his body, Jason tugged. *Thank Hera!* The buckle finally snapped.

Davy slid down, out of the chair and—more importantly—out of the helmet. "Daddy," the boy whispered, the word barely audible over the slur of his drug-induced stupor. But it was enough; Jason's heart soared.

Midnight.

The machine buzzed and sputtered, but Davy was safe. Jason had rescued his son.

A motion on the far side of the room caught Jason's eye: Clyde slithering into one of the three streams that exited the island. And Hieronymous was already gone.

"Jason," Lane called. "*Go.* You can still catch him!"

Jason swallowed. This was his chance, what he'd been waiting for. And Lane was urging him on. Yet Jason stayed put, his arms tight around his frightened son as Lane crawled over.

"It's okay," she said. "I know now it doesn't mean you love us less. Sometimes you just have to fight the bad guys." She took his hand and squeezed. "Really. Go."

But Jason didn't. Instead, he just swung an arm around Lane and held both her and Davy close. Backup would arrive soon, and *they* could go after the Outcast boss. Not Jason. Not now.

He pulled Lane tighter into his embrace and kissed Davy's hair. After seven long years, he was out of the revenge business.

With a sigh, he looked at the two people in his arms—his family.

Oh, yeah. Life was good.

Backup burst into the room through each of the corridors, not exactly in the nick of time, but at least arriving. Behind the force of cloaked Protectors strode Zephron, a golden walking stick clasped in his hand.

Lane barely even blinked at all the activity. She simply sat on the floor with Davy wrapped in her arms, and Jason's arms tight around her.

My guys. With a satisfied sigh, Lane snuggled into them.

"Mommy, you're squishing me."

Jason chuckled, and Lane released her hold. "Sorry," she said. "I'm just glad you're safe, sweetie."

Davy wriggled free. "Can I go check on Mr. Boreas? I want to see his arm do that rubbery thing again."

Lane licked her lips, not really wanting the boy out of her sight. Apparently, Davy had recovered much faster than she.

A hand closed over her shoulder. "Let the child go to his friend," Zephron said. "There's nothing here to hurt him. Not anymore."

After a second's hesitation, Lane gave Davy a quick nod, and he rushed off. She climbed to her feet, Jason's hand tight in hers. She'd never met this High Elder in person and, frankly, she was a little awed.

"So Davy's safe now?" she asked. "It's really okay?"

Zephron inclined his head, just slightly. "I don't know if anyone is truly safe from Hieronymous forever," the High Elder said. "But this complex has been secured by Council forces. The boy is safe in this room."

Lane licked her lips. "And once we leave here?"

"He'll be safe in the world, as well. At least as much as anyone is. Davy's powers are locked in now. Hieronymous is no longer a threat to his intellect."

Lane's entire body relaxed, as if the High Elder had just removed two tons of bricks from her shoulders. "Will you catch him?" she asked.

"Eventually," Zephron answered. "He is cunning, but I like to think we are more so." He smiled at Jason, a warm, grandfatherly expression. "But you, young man, will not be on the team assigned to locate and retrieve him."

"I know," Jason said. He gave Lane's hand a squeeze. "I don't want to be."

"Will Boreas?" Lane asked. She'd grown fond of the cadet, and wanted to see him do well.

A pleased look swept the High Elder's face. "I think Boreas will be happy with his new assignment, as well as with his performance review." He met Lane's eyes. "Even though he did bring a mortal into peril."

"Oh." She wrinkled her nose. "I kind of made him."

"Of that, my dear, I have no doubt."

"What about Mordichai?" Jason asked.

"Ah, yes. Your half brother." Zephron turned from side to side, his gaze taking in most of the chamber. "It appears that he has managed to escape."

Lane cocked her head, surprised that Zephron didn't seem more upset. "He was on probation, wasn't he? What's going to happen?"

"Don't worry," Zephron said. "I assure you that Mordichai will get what's coming to him."

Lane frowned again, wondering at the nonanswer. She was about to ask Zephron to explain when Davy trotted back up and tugged at the High Elder's robes.

Mortified, Lane pulled him back.

Zephron merely smiled, the corners of his eyes

crinkling. "Yes, young man?" he prompted.

"I want to go home," Davy said. He slipped his hand into Jason's. "Daddy? Can you and Mommy take me home now, please?"

"I think that's a great idea," Jason said.

Lane agreed. And as the High Elder left them alone, she hooked her arms around Jason's waist and tilted her head up to look into his eyes. "Before we go," she said, "I don't think I've properly thanked you."

"No?"

She shook her head. "No. But I'm going to remedy that right now." Lifting up on tiptoe, she closed her mouth over his, trying to convey a world of emotion in a single kiss: hope and love and a thank-you. And, most of all, she wanted him to sense the promise of a future.

He broke away, pulling back to look deep into her eyes. Her love shone there, she knew. Deep and crystal clear. She sighed and snuggled close. Davy clung to her legs.

After a few minutes Jason shook his head and laughed happily. Taking her hand in one of his, and Davy's in the other, he said, "Come on, sweetheart, let's go home."

She swallowed. "Our home?"

"Absolutely," he said, and Lane's pulse sped up.

"Are we going to live on Jason's boat, Mommy?" Davy asked.

Lane cocked her head. "I think maybe we are."

Jason knelt in front of his son. "Would you like that, sport? Living on a houseboat?"

Davy nodded. "Can Dorothy have a bigger bowl?"

"Absolutely," Jason said.

"And can I have a puppy?"

Lane stifled a giggle, and Jason shot her a frown. "We'll see," he said. "After all, there's no yard."

"Oh." Davy considered for a while. "Well, then, how about a baby brother?"

At that, Jason tugged Lane close. He kissed her gently on the lips. "Now *that*," he said, "is something I'll be happy to discuss with your mother."

Davy seemed excited. "Can I, Mommy? Can I have one?"

Lane laughed. "What about a baby sister?"

Her son made a face. "Yuck. Girls."

Lane just laughed and squeezed Jason's hand. "I don't know," she said. "Spit-up, poopy diapers . . ."

"I missed out on those the first time around," Jason said. "I think you owe me."

She laughed at his teasing. "*I* owe *you*? Hmmm." She stopped walking long enough to give him an appraising stare. "Maybe," she finally agreed. "But only because I love you."

And she did. Loved him with all her heart and soul.

He kissed her, the kiss telling her what she already knew: that he loved her, too. And Davy. And all of Davy's unborn siblings. Hopefully, there would be a brother *and* a sister. "I love you, too," he said.

"I know." She smiled and squeezed his hand. "So, tell me," she said, then paused to nibble on her lower lip. "Are there any *more* surprises? Or do I know all your secrets now? You're a Protector. Your

365

father's not a very nice guy. Does that about cover it?"

He laughed, then swung Davy up onto his shoulder. "That's it," he said. "Except . . ."

Her eyes widened. "Except?"

"Have I told you about the full moon . . . ?"

Epilogue

"Where is he, Mommy?" Davy asked. "I don't see Daddy anywhere."

"Right there, sweetie." Lane pointed to the far side of the holding pool. "See? He's behind Shamu."

As if he could hear her, Jason burst forth from the water, a shining, gleaming dolphin. He leaped over Shamu, his body glimmering in the fading moonlight.

It had taken Lane a few months to get used to her husband's monthly after-hours excursion to Sea World, but now she cherished the wee morning hours alone with Davy as they waited for Jason to come back to them.

Lane rubbed her rounded belly, wondering if their little daughter was going to inherit her father's aquatic powers. Lane almost hoped she would. Certainly they couldn't be more of a handful than Davy reprogramming, rewiring, and re-everythinging each and every electronic device on their houseboat.

Still, she had to laugh. After Davy's rescue, the Inner Circle had promoted Jason to Protector First Class. With that vote of confidence, suddenly boarding school was no longer a necessity. Instead, Jason was charged with training his son.

He did fine with the instruction on the basics like levitation, but Davy's technological skills were a little out of Jason's league. And it amused Lane to no end to watch her husband and son sit on the floor together, with Davy patiently explaining why the electrical current needed to flow in a certain direction. For his part, Jason was doing well to find the on/off switch on his coffeemaker.

He tried, though, to help his son. And Lane loved him all the more for it.

The first rays of sunlight streaked across the sky, and Lane held her breath, her eyes searching the calm surface of the water, looking for her human husband.

Shamu cruised by, one fin raised in greeting, and Davy waved back. Lane did, too, but her salutation was halfhearted, because she'd seen a more important sign: the telltale ripple in the water.

She watched as Jason emerged, stepping out of the water like one of the gods from whom he'd descended. His body glistened and gleamed, and when he saw her, he smiled, the gesture full of promise and desire.

Water cascaded from his chest. Lane sighed, enjoying the magnificent view as he moved forward, then grabbed a towel from the concrete and wrapped it around his waist.

"Daddy!" Davy raced over and threw his arms around Jason's legs, managing to get fully soaked in the process.

"Hey, sport," his father said. "How's my guy?"

"I'm good, Daddy," Davy announced. "I made an electronic lifeform that has retracting Ninja blades, but Mommy won't let me play with it in the house."

Jason laughed. "Don't look at me, kid." He pulled Lane close when she approached, and she snuggled up, not caring at all that she was going to end up just as wet as he.

"And how are my girls?" he asked, putting his hand on her belly.

"Missing you," she said.

He kissed her nose. "Do you have it?"

Lane nodded, then reached into her pocket, pulling out his wedding ring. She held it out for him. "Still love me?" she asked, in what had become their monthly ritual.

He slipped his finger through the ring. "I do," he said, his eyes showing he told the truth.

Lane's heart beat faster, those words filling her soul with joy as they always did. "I know you do," she said, pressing a light kiss to his cheek. "And I do, too."

Aphrodite's Passion

JULIE KENNER

Aphrodite's Girdle is missing, and Hale knows the artifact will take all his superpowers to retrieve. The mortal who's found and donned it—one Tracy Tannin, the descendent of a goddess of the silver screen—wasn't exactly popular before the belt. Now everyone wants her. But the golden girdle can only be recovered through honest means, which means there is no chance for Hale to simply become invisible and whisk it away. (Although, watching Tracy, he finds himself imagining other garments he'd like to remove.) Maybe he should convince her she is as desirable as he sees her. Only then will she realize she is worth loving no matter what she is wearing—or what she isn't.

___52474-0 $6.99 US/$8.99 CAN

Aphrodite's Kiss
Julie Kenner

Crazy as it sounds, on her twenty-fifth birthday Zoe has the chance to become a superhero. But x-ray vision and the ability to fly are only two things to consider. There is also her newfound heightened sensitivity. If she can hardly eat a chocolate bar without convulsing in ecstasy, how is she to give herself the birthday gift she's really set her heart on—George Taylor? The handsome P.I.'s dark exterior hides a truly sweet center, and Zoe feels certain that his mere touch will send her spiraling into oblivion. But the man is looking for an average Jane no matter what he claims. He can never love a superhero-to-be—can he? Zoe has to know. With her super powers, she can only see through his clothing; to strip bare the workings of his heart, she'll have to rely on something a little more potent.

___52438-4 $6.99 US/$8.99 CAN

CRAZY FOR YOU

KATE ANGELL

From the moment she spots his hamburger-and-French-fry emblazoned boxers with the word *supersized* on them, Bree knows Sexton St. Croix is trouble. Here is a man with just one thing on his mind, but Sex has hired her to do a job, and she'll let nothing get in her way.

Sexton St. Croix's luxury ocean liner is haunted—by the ghost of an unflappable flapper named Daisy. Now, in an effort to persuade Daisy to "cheese it," he's opened the ship to a veritable psychic circus. He is counting on Bree's "clairsentience" to save his bacon. Her exquisitely sensitive fingers can detect the emotional vibrations of an 80-year-old love triangle, while her tender touch unlocks secrets in his own heart.

JENNIE KLASSEL

IT HAPPENED IN SOUTH BEACH

If she's a beauteous, bodacious babe, gettin' down, gettin' it on, gettin' her man, she's definitely *not* good old Tilly Snapp. So what's the safe, sensible twenty-six-year-old Bostonian doing in Miami's ultra-hip, super-chic South Beach?

She's on the trail of the fabled Pillow Box of Win Win Poo—the most valuable collection of antique erotic "accessories" in the world. And she's after the fiend who murdered her eccentric Aunt Ginger. And while Tilly might not know the difference between a velvet tickle pickle and a kosher dill, with the assistance of the sexy yet unhelpful Special Agent Will Maitland, she's about to get a crash course in sex-ed.

Meet the new Tilly Snapp, Sex Detective.

South Beach ain't seen nothin' yet.